"There they are!" An outrider pointed due east.

To Hamnet Thyssen, those wiggles on the horizon might have been anything. His eyes weren't particularly bad, but they weren't particularly good, either. Before long, he made out mammoths, mammoths with men atop them. Those could only be Rulers. The Bizogots herded mammoths and used them, but didn't ride them. Till they saw the Rulers in action, riding mammoths had never occurred to them. Now they were wild to learn the art. If they survived and stayed free, maybe they would.

If.

Before long, the Rulers spied the Bizogots, too. They stopped heading south and swung toward the west. They used their common battle formation: mammoths anchoring the center of their line, with warriors on riding deer out to either wing. Horses were better riding animals than deer, even if they lacked antlers. But fighting against mammoths was like fighting the Glacier.

The Glacier is melting, Hamnet reminded himself. The Bizogots could beat mammoths. They could, yes, but it wouldn't be easy.

The Golden Shrine

Harry Turtledove

A TOM DOHERTY ASSOCIATES BOOK
NEW YORK

This is a work of fiction. All of the characters, organizations, and events portrayed in this novel are either products of the author's imagination or are used fictitiously.

THE GOLDEN SHRINE

Copyright © 2009 by Harry Turtledove

Edited by Teresa Nielsen Hayden

A Tor Book
Published by Tom Doherty Associates, LLC
175 Fifth Avenue
New York, NY 10010

www.tor-forge.com

Tor® is a registered trademark of Tom Doherty Associates, LLC.

ISBN 978-0-7653-5640-6

First Edition: October 2009
First Mass Market Edition: November 2010

Printed in the United States of America

0 9 8 7 6 5 4 3 2 1

The
Golden
Shrine

1

Spring on the Bizogot steppe came late, and grudgingly. The Breath of God blew down from the Glacier and over the frozen plain long after southern breezes began melting snow and bringing green back to the Raumsdalian Empire. At last, though, as the sun stayed longer in the sky day by day, the weather north of the tree line began to change, too.

Even down in the Empire, Count Hamnet Thyssen reckoned spring a minor miracle. Up on the Bizogot steppe, the miracle seemed not so minor; spring was harder won here. All the same, Hamnet had a bigger miracle to celebrate on this bright, mild, blue-skied, sunny day. He and his friends had lived through the winter.

"And I tell you," he remarked to Ulric Skakki, "I wouldn't have given a counterfeit copper for our chances when we set out last fall."

"Why not, Your Grace?" With his auburn hair and foxy features, Ulric could don the mask of innocence more readily than Count Hamnet, who was large and dark and somewhere between stolid and dour. "Just because it was a toss-up whether our side wanted us dead more than the enemy did?"

"That will do for a start," Hamnet answered, which made Ulric laugh as merrily as if he were joking.

"What do you say?" Marcovefa asked. The shaman from the cannibal tribe that lived atop the Glacier looked like a Bizogot: she was large and blond and robust. The language her folk used sprang from the Bizogot speech, but from a strange, distant dialect. And her people had been isolated for centuries from the clans who roamed the steppe. She was learning their speech as she was learning Raumsdalian—learning them both as foreign tongues.

Hamnet Thyssen explained in slow, simple words, partly in Raumsdalian and partly in the Bizogot language. He wished the Empire were doing more to fight the Rulers, the mammoth-riding invaders who'd swarmed through the Gap after the Glacier melted in two. The stocky, swarthy, curly-bearded invaders made ferocious fighting men and even more fearsome wizards.

Everyone thought so except Marcovefa. Her own powers equaled or exceeded those of the Rulers' sorcerers. Hamnet often wondered why that should be so. His best guess was that the scattered folk who dwelt up on the Glacier did without so many material things. They had no crops. They knew nothing of wood. They knew no animals larger than foxes. They couldn't work metal—even stone was sometimes hard for them to come by.

No wonder, then, that their magical skills were strong. They had to have *something* going for them up there in the perpetual cold and the perpetually thin air. Thus wizardry flourished alongside desperate poverty. So it seemed to him, anyhow. Marcovefa didn't think of herself or the folk among whom she'd grown up as poor. But then, she'd had no standard of comparison till she came down to the Bizogot steppe with Hamnet and his comrades the summer before.

She laughed at his worries now. "It will be as it is, that's all," she said. "All we can do is try to make it turn out the way we want it to."

"Well, yes," Hamnet said. "I don't think of that as *all*."

Marcovefa laughed again, louder this time. "But it is. Soon enough, nothing will matter anymore, because we will be dead."

She made Ulric Skakki laugh, too, on a different note. "Later, I hope—not sooner," he said. "I don't plan on dying for quite a while yet."

"No, eh?" Hamnet said. "Why did you come up to the steppe again, in that case?"

"Maybe I'm a fool," Ulric said. He was a great many things: scout, raider, thief, assassin. Hamnet Thyssen had never made the mistake of reckoning him a fool. Other mistakes, certainly. That one? No—he wasn't such a big fool, or that particular kind of fool, himself. Then Ulric aimed a wry smile at him. "Or maybe you have such pretty eyes, I couldn't resist."

Count Hamnet snorted. He took his pleasure—and, too often, his pain—from women. So did Ulric Skakki. Hamnet had never thought pretending otherwise was funny. Ulric did.

"What are you going on about?" Trasamund rumbled. He was the very image of a Bizogot jarl, a clan chief. He was a big man, bigger than Hamnet. He had a hero's muscles, a hero's appetite for strong drink and willing women, a hero's courage. Strong sun and chill winds had carved harsh lines that gave dignity to his bluffly handsome features.

He was, these days, a jarl almost without a clan. The Three Tusk Bizogots lived close by the Glacier. Trasamund was one of the first men through it, one of the first to begin exploring lands cut off by ice for thousands of years.

And the Rulers had fallen on his clan first when they swarmed into the lands on this side of the Glacier. Trasamund had been down in the Empire then. The only thing he could have done had he been among his clansmen was die with them. He knew that, but blamed himself anyhow.

"I was just telling Count Hamnet how beautiful he was, and he was getting all embarrassed about it," Ulric said archly.

"If I didn't know the two of you . . ." Trasamund let his voice trail away. Hamnet knew what he wasn't saying. The Bizogots scorned men who lay with other men, which was putting it mildly. Trasamund didn't know what to make of men who lay with women but affected not to. No Bizogot seemed to have thought of that particular vice before. Hamnet sent Ulric a not particularly warm glance. He didn't want Trasamund thinking of him like that.

Grinning, Ulric blew him a kiss. So much for the not very warm glance. "If you were half as funny as you think you are, you'd be twice as funny as you really are," Hamnet said.

"And I'd still be funnier than you," Ulric said. Hamnet shook his head like a man bedeviled by bees. He was unlikely to need to worry about bees this far north. Soon enough, though, midges and flies and mosquitoes would spring to life in every pond and rill and puddle left by melting snow and ice. Everything on the Bizogot steppe burst with life in the springtime—including the pests. Ulric Skakki seemed to be trying his best to get himself included in their number.

More Bizogots rode up from the southwest to take over the watch. Hamnet Thyssen was glad enough to head back to camp. He made a point of talking with Marcovefa and Trasamund, and of ignoring Ulric. The adventurer noticed. He laughed at Hamnet, who ignored him harder than ever. Ulric Skakki kept right on laughing. Hamnet kept right on fuming.

"If you let him bother you, he wins, you know," Marcovefa said.

"I suppose," Hamnet answered. "But if I don't let him bother me, that says I shouldn't have been bothered to begin with, and he wins anyhow. So what am I supposed to do?"

"You could kill him." Marcovefa wasn't joking. The Bizogots brawled at any excuse or none. Her own clan, like the others scattered over the top of the Glacier, had grown more ruthless than the folk from whom they were descended. They'd had to; life up there gave them even less margin for error than the ordinary Bizogots had. To Marcovefa, the frozen steppe was a land of riches and abundance. If that didn't say how desperately impoverished her folk were, nothing could.

All the same, Hamnet shook his head. "We need him. And—" He broke off, one word too late.

"And what?" Marcovefa asked. Of course she noticed. She wasn't just a shaman. She was an uncommonly observant woman.

Hamnet's cheeks heated. When he answered, he spoke in a low voice, because he didn't want Ulric to hear. But, however reluctantly, he spoke the truth: "And he'd be more likely to kill me, curse it." He was a formidable warrior. He was sure he could beat Trasamund, even if the Bizogot was bigger and stronger than he was—Trasamund had more courage than he knew what to do with, but less technique than he needed. Ulric Skakki was no braver than he had to be, but he coupled a wildcat's speed and grace with more skill in fighting with weapons or without them than anyone else Hamnet had ever known.

"If you quarrel, I could magic him." Marcovefa paused. "I think I could. He's a strange one, no doubt about it."

Had she ever seemed doubtful about her own spells before? If she had, Hamnet Thyssen couldn't remember when. She mocked the sorcery she found down here below the Glacier, both that of Bizogot shamans and that of Raumsdalian wizards. She even mocked the Rulers' sorcery, which far outdid anything either Bizogots or Raumsdalians could manage. If she wasn't sure her spells would bite Ulric . . .

"How is he different from the rest of us?" Hamnet asked.

Marcovefa shrugged. "He's slipperier than anyone else I've ever seen. He might find a way to slide out from under any charm I set on him."

"Ah." Hamnet thought it over, then nodded. "I can see that. Sounds like Ulric, all right . . ."

TENTS MADE FROM the tanned hides of woolly mammoths straggled across the plain. Bizogot camps were disorderly affairs—this one, put together by survivors from several shattered clans, more so than most. Dogs not far removed from wolves ran at Hamnet and the other newcomers. They barked and snarled and growled, but didn't quite attack.

"Miserable beasts." Marcovefa didn't like dogs. There were none up on the Glacier. Her folk tamed voles and hares so they could have a more reliable food supply, but that was as far as they went along those lines. She asked, "Why keep them around, anyway?"

"They work. They guard," Hamnet said. Two dogs

tripped over each other's feet. They both went sprawling. He added, "They give us something to laugh at."

"I suppose so." But Marcovefa didn't seem convinced. She pointed to the running pack of boys and girls who followed the dogs. "Isn't that why people have children?"

"One reason, I suppose." Hamnet Thyssen had no children he knew of. A lot of things might have been different if he had.

"Have you got anything for us?" one of the boys yelled. He held out a grimy hand for whatever he could scrounge. Bizogots scrounged without shame, wherever and whenever they could. Where they couldn't scrounge, they often stole.

"Don't give *him* anything." The girl who spoke used a dialect different from the boy's. They came from separate clans, and never would have joined together if the Rulers hadn't spread disaster across the Bizogot steppe. She added, "He's nothing but a miserable nosepicker anyway."

"Liar!" the boy shouted, and pitched into her. They were at an age where size mattered more than gender, and she had half a head on him. He might have been bold, but he was soon down on the ground and snuffling. By the way his nose ran, he hadn't picked it any time lately.

"Serves him right for being stupid," Marcovefa said.

"Yes, but . . ." Hamnet raised his voice: "Enough! *Enough*, by God!" He yelled loud enough to make the girl stop. She eyed him in surprise. "Enough," he said once more. "We're all one clan here, or we might as well be. You made him sorry for jumping you—fair enough. But don't humiliate him. Save that for our real enemies—the Rulers."

"Who are you, to talk about all of us being one clan?" the girl demanded. "You aren't even a Bizogot." *You aren't even a human being*—she didn't say it, but it was what she really meant.

"So what?" Hamnet Thyssen returned. "The way it looks to me, there are only two clans left: the Rulers, and everyone who hates them. Which side are you on?"

She thought about that. Then, roughly, she pushed the boy away from her. "If I get the chance to kill the Rulers, I will. If anyone says anything different, I'll kill him." She couldn't have been more than eleven, but she plainly meant every word.

"Good enough." Hamnet pulled a chunk of smoked musk-ox meat from his pocket and tossed it to her. She caught it, stuck it in her mouth, and began to chew. Bizogots needed strong teeth; the dried meat was almost as tough as wood.

Liv and Audun Gilli and a captive from the Rulers came out of a nearby tent. Liv nodded to Hamnet. "By the racket the dogs made, I thought it might be you," she said.

"If it's not me, it's an attack, and that would be worse," Hamnet answered.

Liv nodded. She was a striking woman, with proud cheekbones, blue, blue eyes, and golden hair unfortunately hacked off short. It was also dirty and greasy, as Bizogot hair commonly was. (So was Hamnet's. Washing during the winter on the frozen steppe was asking for chest fever.) She'd been the shaman of the Three Tusk clan till the Rulers smashed it.

She'd also been Hamnet Thyssen's woman till she decided she liked Audun better. Maybe like called to like; Audun was a wizard, even if one with an unfortunate fondness for guzzling everything he could find. Or maybe that had nothing to do with it. Couples came together. Too often, they also came apart.

Hamnet could look at her and deal with her without

wanting to kill her or to kill himself. He could even deal with Audun Gilli without wanting to kill him . . . most of the time. All that struck him as very strange, if not downright marvelous. When Gudrid played him false and left him, he'd lingered—wallowed—in a trough of misery for years.

But Liv hadn't played him false. She'd only shifted her affections. Amazing, the difference that made. Liv didn't torment him with bygone days that could never come again, either. Hamnet wondered how it was that she came from the barbarous Bizogots while Gudrid was an allegedly civilized Raumsdalian.

Of course, civilization had its sophisticated pleasures, elaborate revenge among them. Why Gudrid thought she needed elaborate revenge on Hamnet . . . one would have to ask her. Since she was hundreds of miles to the south, all comfortable in Nidaros, he couldn't very well do that—and he didn't want to, anyhow.

Marcovefa pointed to the captive. "I see you, Dashru," she said.

Dashru nodded. "I am seen," he answered unhappily. He spoke the Bizogots' language with a thick accent and bad grammar. He was shorter than most Bizogots, but wider through the shoulders. His hair and beard were black and curly, his eyes polished jet, his nose a proud scimitar.

That was the only pride he had left. Rulers who had the bad luck or lack of fortitude to fall into enemy hands were dead to their own folk forever after. They were dead in spirit, too, after suffering such a disgrace. Some slew themselves when they found the chance. Others, like Dashru, lived on, but not happily. Never happily.

"Teach us more of your language," Hamnet said.

Dashru sighed and nodded again. "I do that. You not learn well, though."

"We try," Hamnet said. "You don't learn the Bizogots' tongue easily, either."

"Grunting of deer. Squawking of geese," Dashru said disdainfully.

"We think the same of your speech," Hamnet told him. Dashru made a horrible face, as if he'd smelled something nasty.

The trouble was, the Bizogot language and Raumsdalian on the one hand and the Rulers' tongue on the other were as different as chalk and tobacco. Bizogots and Raumsdalians spoke related languages. The vocabulary wasn't the same, but here and there words in the one tongue sounded something like those in the other. The Bizogots had more complicated noun declensions than people in the Empire used, while Raumsdalian had a battery of verb tenses the mammoth-herders lacked. But the basic principles underlying both languages were similar.

All the words in the Rulers' language were different. That was bad enough, but not unexpected: why believe a language that had grown up beyond the Glacier *would* have familiar vocabulary? The grammar, though . . . Whoever put together the grammar in the Rulers' language had to be twisted. So Hamnet Thyssen thought, anyhow. He knew Dashru felt the same way about the Bizogot speech, but he didn't care.

When the Rulers talked to one another, they used a word order Hamnet found perverse. They slapped pieces of words together to make bigger, more complicated ones. They used particles to show how the pieces fit together. Why anyone would want to talk like that, Hamnet had no idea. But the invaders found it as natural as he found Raumsdalian.

Dashru worked his way through a lesson on numbers. That was one more thing that drove Hamnet crazy. For one of something, the number and the thing it described were singular, and in the subjective case. For two, three, or four of something, the number and what it described were singular—why?—and in the possessive case. For five and above, they were plural and in the possessive case.

"This makes no sense," Hamnet said.

"He is right," Marcovefa said. That made Hamnet feel better; he'd wondered if he was missing something he should see.

Dashru only shrugged. "We talk like this. What do you want me to do? Tell you we talk some other way?"

Yes, Hamnet thought. He wouldn't have been sorry to hear a lie just then, if it made the Rulers' language easier to pick up. "But *why* do you do it this way?" he asked.

"Because we do," the captive answered. "Why do you talk like you do? That is *really* stupid."

He meant it. Count Hamnet could hear as much. The Raumsdalian turned to Marcovefa. "Can you cast a spell to make the language easier to learn?" he asked her. "Is there a spell for translating from one language to another?"

"Up on the Glacier, we all used the same tongue. We needed no spell like that," she answered. She eyed Dashru. "Do your shamans use translating spells?"

"Yes, but I don't know how they work," he said. "I am herder, fighter. I know nothing of magic."

Hamnet Thyssen believed him. The Bizogots hadn't captured any of the Rulers' wizards. Those wizards were stronger than any shaman except Marcovefa. They were also fierce warriors in their own right—and perhaps even more determined not to be taken alive than the ordinary fighting men of their folk.

Marcovefa looked thoughtful. "A spell like that shouldn't be too hard to shape," she said. "The law of similarity would apply. One word for a thing or an idea is bound to be similar to another for the same thing or idea. They both point toward the same original, which makes them point toward each other, too."

That probably made perfect sense to her. It made more sense to Hamnet than the way the Rulers counted, but not much more. He would never make any kind of wizard, and he knew it. The aptitude wasn't there.

"Do you want to go on, or do you want to make a magic?" Dashru asked in the Bizogot language.

"We go on," Hamnet replied in the Rulers' speech. That seemed a simple enough answer, but Dashru's wince told him he'd made a hash of it somehow. Resignedly, he asked, "What did I say wrong?"

First, Dashru told him what he did wrong asking what he did wrong. Then the prisoner told him what he did wrong saying they would go on. He could hear the mistakes, too. He doubted he would ever speak without making them fairly often. If he could get the Rulers to understand him and could understand some of what they said, that would do.

"I don't aim to be a poet in their tongue," he told Marcovefa.

"It is an ugly language," she agreed. "It is even uglier than Raumsdalian." *So there*, Hamnet thought.

Dashru was offended. "The Rulers' tongue is not ugly!" he said. "It is full of strength, full of power. It is fit for . . . well, for rulers. No wonder you folk do not care for it. You are part of the herd, for us to milk and shear and slaughter as we please."

"If you think that way, if you act that way, you will make everyone on this side of the Glacier fight you to the death," Hamnet said.

"So what?" Dashru returned. "After we kill you all, we settle the land ourselves. We do what we want with it." For a moment, he sounded like a proud warrior, part of a proud folk. But only for a moment. As he remembered where he was, he deflated like a pricked bladder. "I will not see that, I who am nothing."

"I can tell you what you will see," Hamnet Thyssen said. "You will see the Rulers whipped back through the Gap, back beyond the Glacier, like the dogs and sons of dogs they are."

Dashru laughed in his face. "A bison may bellow before it goes over the cliff, but it goes over all the same. And even the bison here have small horns. They are weak, as the folk here are weak."

"Do not laugh too soon," Marcovefa warned him.

The prisoner laughed again. "You are another who pretends to be stronger than she is."

Marcovefa looked at him. She muttered something in her own dialect of the Bizogot language. It really was almost a separate tongue in its own right; Hamnet couldn't recognize more than a couple of words. Her hands shaped quick passes, all of them aimed at Dashru.

He stared defiantly back at her. After a moment, defiance changed to alarm. He shouted something in his own language. Hamnet Thyssen made out "Away with you!" in the midst of guttural gibberish. Dashru's fingers twisted in a sign much like the one the Bizogots used to turn aside evil.

That seemed to buy him a few heartbeats of relief, but no more. Marcovefa went on muttering. Dashru started to have trouble breathing. His face went a mottled purple above the edge of his beard.

"Will you kill him?" Hamnet asked.

"Unless he admits I am stronger, I will. And I will roast his heart afterward and eat it, too." Marcovefa would have sounded more excited talking about an unexpected shower. And when she spoke of roasting Dashru's heart, she meant it. Up atop the Glacier, captives from another clan were meat, nothing more.

The Rulers were a proud folk. Many of them would have died before yielding in a trail of strength, especially against someone from outside their own folk. But Dashru had already yielded once. Maybe that prompted him to drop to his knees. Or maybe getting sorcerously asphyxiated would have weakened almost anyone.

Whatever the reason, he choked out, "Mercy!" with what had to be close to his last breath.

By the look in Marcovefa's eye, she would sooner have butchered and cooked him than given him what he wanted. But he'd done what she said he had to—or most of it, anyway. "I am stronger, yes?" she demanded in the Rulers' language.

"Mercy!" Dashru said again, and then, reluctantly, "Yes."

A moment later, he was sucking in great gulps of air. He got back his usual swarthy coloring. "You insult me again?" Marcovefa asked.

Dashru shook his head. "No," he said. "No, wizard lady."

"Better not." Marcovefa made as if to spit in his face, but contemptuously turned her back instead.

"Enough lesson of speech?" Dashru asked Hamnet Thyssen. He wasn't going to have anything more to do with Marcovefa, not if he could help it. Count Hamnet had no trouble understanding that.

"Enough language lessons, yes," he answered. Dashru got out of there as fast as he could. Again, Hamnet would have done the same thing.

"You are too soft on him," Marcovefa said. "He is a captive, a rabbit on the fire. He should remember."

"He isn't likely to forget, not now," Hamnet said.

"If he hadn't got out of line, he wouldn't have needed the lesson," Marcovefa said, adding, "Did you see how useless his countercharm was?"

"Yes." Count Hamnet wondered whether the countercharm would have been useless against Liv's sorcery, or Audun Gilli's. He didn't think so, though he wasn't sure.

"Now I know more of what the Rulers do. I know more of how they think. I want to fight them. I want to beat them," Marcovefa said.

"You'd better want to. And you'd better do it, too," Hamnet said. "Without you, we haven't got much chance."

"Foosh!" Marcovefa said—a dismissive noise. "Their magic is not so much. You shouldn't have such trouble with it." She paused. "Of course, the magic you people down here know isn't so much, either."

"That's why we need you," Count Hamnet said. "If anything happens to you . . ." He shook his head. He didn't want to think about that. He would lose his woman. In the ordinary run of things, with the sorrows he'd known in his love life, that would have been disaster enough and then some. Since the Bizogots and the Empire would likely go under the Rulers' yoke in short order, his love life, for once, wasn't his biggest worry.

The lewd glint in Marcovefa's eye said she thought he was thinking about it. "You find some other woman to give you what you want," she teased.

"Where will I find another woman who can give me the Rulers driven back beyond the Gap?" he asked.

She pointed north. "Same place you found me—up on top of the Glacier."

"I didn't want to make that trip once. We wouldn't have tried to climb the ice then if the Rulers weren't going to kill us if we stayed on flat ground." Hamnet shuddered at the memory of that fearsome ascent. "We wouldn't have had a chance if that big avalanche hadn't made the slope less impossible than it usually is."

"It is not easy," Marcovefa admitted. "If it were, my folk would have come down from the Glacier long ago. Our enemies drove us up there, too—so our songs say. I believe them. No one would have gone up there unless he had to."

"All right, then," Hamnet Thyssen said. "Don't talk foolishness. Everyone on this side of the Gap needs you." He slipped his arm around her waist. "I need you in a way the rest of the people don't, though."

"You think so, do you?" She gave him a sidelong glance and a mocking smile. "So no other men on this side of the Gap would want me?"

That wasn't true. She was pretty enough that any man might want her. Hamnet answered with guile of his own: "You'd scare most of them off once they found out you might carve them into steaks if they made you unhappy."

"Foosh!" Marcovefa said again. "I don't butcher anyone from my own clan—and a lover is about the same as a clansman."

"Well, *that's* a relief." Hamnet was kidding, but kidding on the square. He and Marcovefa both started to laugh. The world might be coming to pieces around them. Might be? It was. If the Glacier hadn't come to pieces, none of what happened since would have been possible. But you couldn't keep looking at anything so large for very long, not without your mind snapping. If something funny came along close by, you'd laugh.

Which didn't mean the bigger troubles went away. Not looking at them for a little while helped them seem more tolerable, though. Whether they really were . . . was a question Hamnet ignored for the time being.

* * *

A SCOUT RODE into the Bizogots' camp. He pointed north and east. "There's a band of those musk-ox turds riding south," he said. "They won't pass too far from us."

"How big a band?" Trasamund asked. That was the right question, sure enough. If it was too large, these remnants of half a dozen shattered Bizogot clans would have to fight shy of it for fear even a hard-won victory would leave them too weak to fight again.

The scout considered. "Maybe half a dozen war mammoths," he said. "More of the miserable mushrooms on their riding deer, of course, but not too many. I think we can take them."

"I bet he's right," Ulric Skakki said to Hamnet. "Scouts always see bigger forces than the ones that are really there."

"Most of the time, anyhow," Hamnet said. He raised his voice to question the Bizogot: "Did they look like men who intended to settle down when they found good grazing, or did they seem on their way to somewhere else?"

"Hard to know for sure," the scout said, and Hamnet Thyssen nodded impatiently. After more thought, the man went on, "If they wanted to stop, the grazing was good where they were. They were moving pretty steady."

"Heading for the Empire," Ulric murmured.

Count Hamnet nodded again. The Rulers already had an army down there fighting against Sigvat II's soldiers. Hamnet wondered whether Sigvat wished he'd taken all the warnings he'd got more seriously. Too late to worry about that now, for Sigvat and for everybody else.

Trasamund made a fist and slammed it into his thigh. "Let's hit them!"

Hamnet Thyssen and Ulric Skakki looked at each other. "What do you think?" Ulric asked.

"We might as well," Hamnet said. "If we can break the links between the Rulers' big army down in the south and the Gap, we've done something useful. They'd better have a tough time reinforcing their men down in the Empire."

"I suppose so." Ulric didn't sound thrilled. After a moment, he explained why: "Any time you say something that starts with 'If we can . . . ,' I start worrying about it."

"Me in particular, or anybody?" Hamnet inquired.

"Anybody," the adventurer replied.

"Well, good. I wouldn't want to be singled out," Count Hamnet murmured.

Trasamund went on shouting, trying to fire up the Bizogots and get them moving that very moment. A crack squadron of imperial cavalry would have had trouble riding off to war as fast as he wanted the mammoth-herders to move. When the Bizogots didn't get cracking fast enough to suit him, he yelled louder than ever.

A Bizogot who wasn't from the Three Tusk clan complained, loudly and profanely. Trasamund knocked him down and kicked him. The man came up with a knife in his hand. Trasamund kicked him again, right where it did the most good. The other Bizogot crumpled, clutching at himself.

"*He* isn't going to ride to war," Hamnet said.

"I don't think so," Ulric agreed in shrill falsetto. He lowered his voice in two different ways to continue, "Trasamund's going to get killed if he keeps doing that. One of these days, the other fellow will stick him before he can kick."

"Well, you don't see Bizogots living to get old very often, do you?" Hamnet said. "It's a rough life up here, and they don't make it any easier on themselves."

"They never make anything easy on anyone, including themselves." Ulric shrugged. "It makes them tough—if the Empire had to take the beating the nomads have, it would have gone belly-up to the Rulers a long time ago. But you're right—they pay the price for it."

They rode east as if they never once thought about the price. Hamnet and Ulric rode with them. If Ulric worried, he didn't show it. Hamnet Thyssen looked worried even when he wasn't. He was now. He rode close to Marcovefa, to protect her if he could. He understood she was more likely to protect him than the other way around, but he would do what he could.

Audun Gilli and Liv also rode together. Which one of them would protect the other was anyone's guess. A couple of other Bizogot shamans, dressed like Liv in clothes all fringed and decorated with little bells, rode with the fighters, too. Maybe they could help, maybe not. Hamnet didn't think they could do any harm.

The land was as flat as if a heavy weight had lain on it not long before. And so one had: the Glacier had lingered far longer here than down in the Empire. Every so often, Hamnet rode past a boulder left behind by the retreating ice.

If the Rulers had a scout up on top of a frost heave—a pingo, the Bizogots called such a thing—he could spot the oncoming horsemen from a long, long way. Count Hamnet didn't think they would. That was a ploy for an army staying in one spot, not for men moving south as fast as they could.

"Here's hoping they're just warriors, with no wizard along," he said to Ulric Skakki.

"Yes, here's hoping," Ulric replied. "We could use an easy fight for a change."

Snowshoe hares bounded away from the Bizogots. Ptarmigans flew off, wings whirring. The hunting up here was marvelous, especially in the brief burgeoning season of the year. Hamnet thought it was a shame he was hunting a quarry that could hunt him, too.

"There they are!" An outrider pointed due east.

To Hamnet Thyssen, those wiggles on the horizon might have been anything. His eyes weren't particularly bad, but they weren't particularly good, either. Before long, he made out mammoths, mammoths with men atop them. Those could only be Rulers. The Bizogots herded mammoths and used them, but didn't ride them. Till they saw the Rulers in action, riding mammoths had never occurred to them. Now they were wild to learn the art. If they survived and stayed free, maybe they would.

If.

Before long, the Rulers spied the Bizogots, too. They stopped heading south and swung toward the west. They used their common battle formation: mammoths anchoring the center of their line, with warriors on riding deer out to either wing. Horses were better riding animals than deer, even if they lacked antlers. But fighting against mammoths was like fighting the Glacier.

The Glacier is melting, Hamnet reminded himself. The Bizogots could beat mammoths. They could, yes, but it wouldn't be easy.

As the two little armies closed with each other, Trasamund harangued the Bizogots: "This is our chance for revenge! We can hurt them! We can kill them! It doesn't matter that they beat us before! We are the Bizogots, the lords of this land! Time to offer up some blood to God!"

The blond barbarians cheered. They wanted to believe they could beat the Rulers. They wanted to forget their clans were shattered and they were pounded together into a makeshift fighting force the way bits of meat got stuffed into a sausage casing. At least till the arrows—and the spells—started flying, they could.

But Ulric Skakki caught Count Hamnet's eye. "How often have we heard that speech?" he asked.

Hamnet shrugged. "What's he supposed to say? 'We might as well give up, because they're going to wallop the snot out of us'? I don't think so."

"Well, when you put it that way, maybe not," Ulric allowed. "But I've listened to the same bluster too often before a losing battle."

"We won't lose. We'll win." That wasn't Hamnet Thyssen. It was Marcovefa, who sounded even more sublimely confident than Trasamund did.

"With you working magic for us, we have a chance, anyhow," Hamnet said. She made a face at him. He wasn't a confident man. He didn't shrink from a fight against the Rulers, but he'd seen too many of them go wrong.

Marcovefa only laughed. "Now they try a spell to throw insects at us. They think we cannot beat the likes of *that*?" She laughed again.

She might have thought it was funny, but alarm trickled through Hamnet. The Rulers had used that spell in a battle the year before, and the swarms of bugs they threw at the Bizogots and their animals drove them mad and paved the way for the invaders' victory. Liv and Audun Gilli had had to abandon their own magic to weaken the enemy sorcery even a little. Would Marcovefa be able to do anything else while she fought it?

Even if she couldn't, Liv and Audun rode with the Bizogots today. If Marcovefa could keep the Rulers' wizards busy, the two of them might work magic on the enemy. That Liv had once worked a different kind of magic on Hamnet . . . he shoved down in his mind. He didn't have time to fret about Liv now, any more than he had time to fret about Gudrid.

A gnat flew into his left eye. He rubbed his face and sent Marcovefa a reproachful look. Maybe it was a natural gnat, not one the Rulers had inspired. Maybe Marcovefa was just weakening the spell, not blocking it altogether. He supposed he could forgive her a gnat or two. But why did this one have to find *his* eye?

Trasamund drew his blade and brandished it over his head. It was a two-handed sword, which meant he needed a well-trained horse to use it. He couldn't hang on to the reins and swing it at the same time. While he used it, he had to guide his mount with knees alone.

Arrows started flying. Hamnet shot again and again, emptying his quiver as fast as he could. The Rulers had used spells to break bowstrings, too. Not this time, or, if they were trying that magic, Marcovefa wasn't letting it get anywhere.

Here and there, invaders and riding deer crashed to the ground. Some lay still, others writhed and thrashed in pain. Bizogots also went down. Whatever Marcovefa was doing, she wasn't interfering with the Rulers' archery. Therein lay her greatest danger: one of those flying shafts might find her.

No sooner had that thought crossed Hamnet's mind than Marcovefa caught an arrow out of the air. She kissed the tip and threw it back at the Rulers—maybe at the man who'd shot it. Hamnet was able to watch, because it glowed as it flew . . . and it flew faster than any shaft ever launched from a horn-backed bow. It caught an enemy warrior square in the chest, and he didn't move after he slid off over his riding deer's tail.

"How did you do that?" Hamnet shouted.

She winked at him. "Magic," she answered, as if he didn't know.

"Could you hit a war mammoth with an arrow like that?" he asked. In any fight between Rulers and Bizogots, the invaders had the edge because they could ride mammoths and fight from them.

Marcovefa thought about it. "Maybe," she said at last. "Those long-nosed marmots have a lot of protection, though." Did she mean the thick leather armor the mammoths wore or the Rulers' ward spells? Hamnet didn't know.

He didn't have much time to wonder, either. The rival forces came to close quarters. Trasamund worked fearsome execution with that two-handed blade. Hamnet drew his own sword and traded cuts with an enemy warrior till their mounts carried them past each other.

Trasamund guided his horse toward a mammoth. Hamnet wondered if battle fury had driven the Three Tusk jarl out of his wits, but there was method to his madness. He sprang down from the horse and hewed at the mammoth's left hind leg. The huge beast let out a horrid bleat of pain and toppled, hamstrung.

The warriors atop the mammoth shrieked as it crashed to the ground. One tried to leap clear, only to be crushed by that mountain of falling flesh. Another did jump free, but it did him no good. Trasamund cut him down before he could even get to his feet. Then the jarl remounted and rode toward another mammoth.

"He can't do that twice!" Ulric Skakki exclaimed.

"I didn't think he could do it once," Count Hamnet answered.

Now the Rulers knew what Trasamund had in mind. They shot at him again and again. An arrow in its throat, his horse sank like a ship that had hit a rock. But it had got him close to the woolly mammoth. Careless of his own safety, he dashed forward. His huge sword swung in an arc of mayhem and struck home. The mammoth bugled distress. Like the other great beast, it went down.

And that was as much as the Rulers wanted. Their war mammoths had given them the edge in every fight with the Bizogots. Against a berserk madman who would maim them without caring whether he lived or died, they had no sure defense. They turned and fled north as fast as their riding deer and the mammoths still hale would carry them.

Hamnet Thyssen would have called for a pursuit had the Rulers tried to keep going south. If they were heading away from their army down in the Empire, he was content to let them go. They'd hurt the Bizogots, too. This little band couldn't stand too much hard use, or it would fall to pieces.

For now, the Bizogots made the most of victory. They dismounted and methodically finished off any wounded Rulers they found. No one went near the thrashing, crippled war mammoths. "I hate to waste all that meat," a Bizogot said. "It could feed us for quite a while. But . . ."

"If we come back tomorrow, we can fight the lions and the bears and the dire wolves and the foxes and the teratorns for the scraps," Ulric Skakki said. He was bound to be right. The beasts wouldn't leave so much flesh lying around for long. But right now those mammoths could still kill.

"We can butcher the deer that went down. They won't give us any trouble," Hamnet said.

"And the horses," Liv added.

"And the horses," Hamnet agreed without enthusiasm. He wasn't fond of horsemeat, and nothing would ever make him like it. But nothing went to waste on the Bizogot steppe. With meat to be had, the nomads would take it.

Marcovefa looked at the Rulers' swarthy, curly-bearded corpses. "They would be tasty," she said. "Plenty of flesh on them—they didn't go hungry."

Well, almost *nothing goes to waste on the Bizogot steppe*, Hamnet thought. Marcovefa's clan, up atop the Glacier, thought nothing of eating dead enemies. Life there was even harsher than it was here.

He shook his head. "People down here don't do that." Or if they did do it, they never talked about it. Who could say what went on in poor clans in harsh winters? Even the folk who might have talked wouldn't; the strongest taboo possible lay on admitting one had tasted man's flesh.

"Seems a shame to let them lie there for your birds and

big foxes." Marcovefa used the name she'd made up for dire wolves.

They'd gone round that pingo before. Instead of doing it again, Hamnet asked: "How strong was the magic the Rulers threw at you?"

"Nothing special," she answered. "If my folk could ever come down from the top of the Glacier, they would show the Rulers and everyone else what real rulers are."

She was probably right. It might happen one day, as the ice continued to melt and avalanches offered easier paths down. Hamnet Thyssen refused to worry about it. His great-great-grandchildren could do that, if he ever had descendants of his own. Marcovefa had just been talking about dining on his main worry.

She wouldn't get away from it, either. "You know," she said, "with the enemy inside you, you can work real magic against him. You know him in a way you never would without eating him."

"No," Hamnet said again. "Not unless you think you can beat the Rulers all by yourself. No one down here wants anything to do with a cannibal. It may be all right for you, but we have strong bans against eating people."

The alarming thing was, Marcovefa thought about it. Only after that consideration did she reluctantly shake her head. "Maybe not by myself," she said. "Too much might go wrong. But it is a foolish ban."

"All customs look foolish to people who don't follow them." That wasn't Hamnet—it was Ulric. "But if you laugh at them, that's one of the easiest ways I know to make everybody hate you."

"When we were up on the Glacier, we stayed polite to your clan," Hamnet added. "We gave them the meat we carried with us—"

"So they wouldn't eat you instead," Marcovefa broke in.

"Well, yes," Hamnet said. "But we didn't try to stop them from butchering their enemies after a fight we helped them win. And we didn't say anything when they ate men's flesh. We just didn't eat any ourselves."

"Our customs are right," Marcovefa maintained.

"For you," Ulric said. "Not for everybody. Same with ours."

If he hadn't added the last three words, the shaman from atop the Glacier would have got angry at him. Hamnet Thyssen could see the warning signs on her face. He wouldn't have wanted to anger any wizard, let alone one as powerful as Marcovefa. But Ulric managed to disarm her. She gave him a grudging nod. "Maybe," she said.

The butchery went on. Even if the Bizogots left the hamstrung mammoths alone, they had plenty of meat. Once they saw that, they stopped caring so much about leaving some behind.

"Not elegant, maybe, but it's a victory," Ulric said.

"We need victories. We don't see them often enough," Hamnet replied. "Now we've given the Rulers a poke, and we'll see what they do next."

"You have a knack for making everything sound so delightful. You always did." Ulric Skakki batted his eyes. Count Hamnet picked up a pebble and threw it at him. Ulric's hand dropped to the hilt of his sword, but he was laughing. So was Hamnet Thyssen. You could do that after you won a battle.

Somewhere to the north, the Rulers wouldn't think anything was funny right now.

DAYS STRETCHED AS spring advanced. Nights shrank. The air was murmurous with birds and with bugs. Down at Sudertorp Lake, the reed-choked waters by the shore would be full of nesting ducks and geese and swans.

For years, the Leaping Lynx Bizogots had lived well off the waterfowl: so well that they built stone houses to live in during the spring and summer, though they had to follow the herds the rest of the year. But the Rulers had shattered the Leaping Lynxes the year before.

"Who's holding Sudertorp Lake now?" Hamnet asked Trasamund. "Anyone? Have the Rulers garrisoned it?"

"I don't think so," the jarl answered. "By the time they got down there, most of the birds would have flown. They're strangers here. They might not even know how rich it gets come spring."

"Then we ought to go there," Hamnet said. "If they are taking the waterfowl, we should drive them off if we can. If they aren't, we ought to take the birds ourselves. The hunting is easy—the Leaping Lynxes show that. We could spend less time tending the herds and more time rousing the Bizogots against the Rulers."

Trasamund plucked at his beard. "It could be. I hate to walk in on a clan's territory when I'm not at war with it, but—"

"You know the Leaping Lynxes are shattered," Count Hamnet said. "We've got some of them with us. Put it to them, if you want. Ask if they'd rather see the Rulers eating their waterfowl, or if the birds should go to their own kind."

The Bizogot chieftain rumbled laughter. "You're sneakier than you look, Thyssen. If I ask them like that, by God, I know what they'll say."

"That's the idea," Hamnet said. "If you ask the question the right way, you'll get the answer you want."

"Unless I don't," Trasamund said. "With Bizogots, you never can tell. We are a free people, we are." He sounded proud of his folk's freedom.

Hamnet Thyssen nodded somberly. "Yes. That's so.

And I can't think of anything that's done you more harm in your fight against the Rulers. If you made war as a unit instead of by clans that didn't want to stand with other clans, wouldn't you have had more luck?"

He strode off, leaving Trasamund staring after him. As he walked, he wondered, too late, if he'd just sunk his own scheme. If the Three Tusk jarl got angry at him, wouldn't he be less likely to want to follow a suggestion no matter how sensible it was? *Why didn't that occur to me sooner?* he wondered unhappily.

But he knew the answer. If something came to him, he was likely to say it. He'd helped ruin things with Liv by blurting out questions he should have swallowed. That might have gone wrong anyway, but he'd sure given it a push.

He must have still been scowling when he came up to Ulric Skakki, because the adventurer said, "What's gnawing at you now? You look like somebody just told you you'd have rocks for supper."

"No, the rocks are in my head. I've been stupid." Hamnet explained how he'd botched things with Trasamund.

Ulric raised a quizzical eyebrow. "At least you know you messed up. Most people never figure that out."

"But how do I keep from making the same mistakes over and over?" Hamnet asked.

Ulric looked at him. "If I knew the answer to that, don't you think I'd do it myself? If you find out, let me know."

Count Hamnet must not have offended Trasamund too badly. The jarl shouted the rest of the Bizogots into moving toward Sudertorp Lake. On they went, driving their herds before them. They crashed into what had been the grazing grounds of several tribes, but no one complained.

"Can you imagine the wars we would have started if we tried this journey before the Rulers came?" Trasamund asked, and he let out a gusty sigh.

"You don't need to sound so disappointed," Ulric Skakki said.

"Scoff all you please," the jarl said. "The glory of the Bizogot folk is shattered forever."

"Not if we can beat the Rulers," Hamnet said. "Then you can get back a lot of what you lost. . . . Well, some of it, anyhow."

"Some, maybe. But so many clans have broken up. So many fine grazing grounds are up for grabs now. The steppe will never be the same." Trasamund sighed again. "Nothing can ever be the same. When the world crashes down, you don't lift it up onto your shoulders again."

Hamnet winced. His own world had crashed down twice, first when Gudrid left him for whomever she pleased, then when Liv chose Audun Gilli instead of him. His body was seamed with scars from swordstrokes and arrows that had got home. Scars seamed his soul, too. None of the wounds his body bore disabled him. He wasn't so sure about the ones inside.

Dire wolves began tracking the musk oxen with the Bizogots. The big wolves knew enough to stay out of bowshot. That meant they weren't desperately hungry; if they had been, they would have gone for the kill and worried about everything else later. Sometimes there wasn't much difference between a wolf and a man.

The dire wolves' scent was enough to spook the musk oxen. They formed a defensive circle on the plain, the bulls and big cows facing out and protecting the smaller females and calves with their horns. As long as they stayed in the circle, the Bizogots who herded them couldn't go anywhere, either. That meant the whole band of Bizogots either had to halt or to split and leave the herdsmen behind with the balky beasts.

Trasamund solved that with direct action, the way a

Bizogot jarl might be expected to solve a problem. At his bawled commands, some of the Bizogots attacked the dire wolves. Hungrier wolves might have gone after the horsemen who galloped down on them. This pack turned and ran. Only a couple of them got shot, and one of those didn't seem badly wounded. It certainly ran off at a good clip.

The other dire wolf made more more than a few paces before it went down. Blood ran from its mouth. The arrow had pierced a lung, and maybe its heart as well. It writhed and twisted and quickly died.

"Are they going to leave the carcass there?" Marcovefa sounded shocked.

"They'll skin it, I suppose," Hamnet answered. Sure enough, a Bizogot bent down to do just that.

"What about the meat?"

"We have enough," he said. "The only time we eat dire wolf is when we're very hungry and can't get anything better. And some of the Bizogots here are from the Red Dire Wolf clan. They may not eat of their own fetish animal."

"That, at least, I understand," said the shaman from atop the Glacier. "The other . . ." She shook her head. "You have so much down here. You can afford to waste things. We ate little foxes when we could catch them. You can just leave these big foxes out to rot. So strange."

"If you had herds of mammoths and musk oxen, or herds of riding deer like the Rulers, would you still eat fox meat?" Count Hamnet asked.

"I don't know. I hope so," Marcovefa answered.

With the wolves driven off, the Bizogots shouted and waved and got the musk oxen moving again. It took longer than Trasamund wished it would have. "Miserable, stubborn creatures," the jarl grumbled.

"And they're different from Bizogots because . . . ?"

Ulric Skakki asked politely. Trasamund rewarded him with a glare.

"Their heads are harder," Count Hamnet suggested.

"Are you sure?" Ulric didn't sound as if he believed it.

"Funny men. Funny as a funeral," Trasamund said. "Keep joking, funny men, and maybe it will be your funeral."

"If the Rulers haven't killed me yet, I'm not going to lose any sleep about you." Ulric blew him a kiss.

Trasamund set a hand on the hilt of his sword. "Maybe you should."

"Maybe I should do lots of things I'm not very likely to do," Ulric replied with a yawn.

"Maybe one of them is know when to keep your mouth shut," Hamnet suggested.

The adventurer looked comically astonished. "There are such times?" Count Hamnet gave up.

They rode on. Every so often, a small band of Bizogots would join them. Hardly ever did one man come in alone, as might have happened in the Empire. Up here, winters were so hard and long that one man was unlikely to survive them on his own, as he might have in Raumsdalia. The Bizogots had to cooperate to live.

But the land was too niggardly to support anything more than clans. The only way Hamnet Thyssen saw for the mammoth-herders to go from folk to nation was by conquering richer country farther south—by invading the Raumsdalian Empire, in other words. In days gone by, he'd brooded about such things. Now he needed to brood about a folk that had invaded the Empire, not about one that might.

When the Bizogots came to Sudertorp Lake, they came to its western edge, where a natural dam of rock and permanently frozen earth contained the waters that had flowed into its basin as the Glacier retreated across the Bizogot steppe. "All this water!" Marcovefa exclaimed. "Not frozen water!"

"Not now, no," Hamnet agreed. "It freezes every winter, though." Winter before last, he'd ridden across the ice covering Sudertorp Lake. He'd almost died, too, when the Rulers' magic split the ice and nearly spilled his comrades and him into the freezing waters below.

"And this is supposed to be a great thing?" Marcovefa laughed at him. "Where I come from, the Glacier never thaws."

"Really. I didn't notice when I was there." Count Hamnet didn't do light sarcasm as well as Ulric Skakki, but he did manage to squeeze a chuckle from the shaman from atop the Glacier.

Swifts and swallows skimmed low above the water, snatching insects out of the air. Ducks and geese and swans and coots and grebes and loons nested amidst the reeds and rushes. Tall herons stabbed fish out of the water with swordlike beaks.

Hamnet wondered what the fish ate during the winter. One another, probably. He imagined Sudertorp Lake holding one very large, very ferocious fish at the start of each new spring. Obviously, the picture was impossible. That didn't stop it from forming.

A lion drinking at the edge of the lake looked up when it heard or smelled or saw the Bizogots bearing down on it. Its snarl showed formidable fangs—not fangs to match those of the sabertooths farther south, but formidable all the same. When the snarl didn't intimidate the Bizogots, the lion trotted away, dark-tufted tail tip held proud and high.

On the other side of the Glacier, big hunting cats had stripes instead of a mane. The Rulers called them tigers. Hamnet Thyssen wondered whether any of them had come down through the Gap. *Just our luck if they have*, he thought. But the Rulers were worse predators than tigers or lions or dire wolves or bears.

"I'm surprised we don't see more eagles up here, getting fat off all the waterbirds," Ulric Skakki remarked.

"They make their nests out of twigs. They build them in trees or on cliffsides," Count Hamnet said. "No twigs. No trees." He waved. "No cliffs, either."

"A point. Three points, in fact," Ulric said. "All right. Fine. Have it your way. I'm not surprised. It makes perfect sense."

"Nothing makes perfect sense." Hamnet eyed the adventurer. "Including you."

Ulric clutched his heart. "I am wounded to the slow— which has a harder time getting out of the way than the quick."

"What *are* you going on about?" Trasamund asked, and then answered his own question: "More Raumsdalian foolishness, I doubt not."

"Well, you wouldn't expect us to spout Bizogot foolishness, would you, Your Ferocity?" Ulric replied in calm, reasonable tones. "We leave that to you."

The jarl muttered under his breath. "The day will come when you've joked once too often."

"I shouldn't wonder," Ulric said. "All the more reason to enjoy myself before it does, don't you think?" He studied Trasamund the way a natural philosopher might study a nondescript beetle. "Or do you think?"

Hamnet Thyssen studied Trasamund, too, and studied the tide of red rising from his neck to his cheeks. "*I* think that's enough of that," he said. "Do recall, we are supposed to be on the same side."

"Oh, I recall. My insults to my enemies are more pointed." Ulric mimed drawing and loosing a bow. "In the next engagement, in fact, I'll use the points you made about eagles' nests, or the absence thereof."

"You are quite mad," Trasamund said.

Ulric Skakki inclined his head like a nobleman receiving a coveted compliment. "Your most humble and sometimes obedient servant, Your Ferocity. In point of fact, though, when the wind blows from the south I do know a hawk from a heron. The herons are the ones that nest in the reeds."

"Mad," Trasamund repeated. Hamnet Thyssen was inclined to agree with him.

They saw a few of the Rulers' riding deer as they traveled east along the northern shore of Sudertorp Lake. The deer weren't in large herds, though, and the Bizogots and Raumsdalians didn't come across any of the squat, ferocious invaders from beyond the Gap. Count Hamnet supposed the deer were stragglers that wanted to wander the Bizogot plains on their own without caring about what the Rulers wanted.

He sympathized with them. The Bizogots wanted to do exactly the same thing. Unfortunately, the Rulers had other plans.

"Such strange beasts." Marcovefa set the thumbs of both hands on her forehead above her eyes and spread her fingers wide, miming antlers. None of the animals that lived atop the Glacier, Hamnet recalled, had antlers or horns. They had to seem odd to Marcovefa: odder even than the horns of musk oxen or cattle, because the antlers had so many tines.

"They fend off enemies with them. They dig with them. The males fight with them," Hamnet said. "Down in the Empire and nearby lands, only stags have antlers—the does do without. But with these riding deer, both sexes carry them, though the males' are larger."

"Why don't we kill them?" the shaman asked.

"The Bizogots like waterfowl better, when they can get them," he answered. "Don't you?"

She shrugged. "I ate birds up on the Glacier. Mostly small ones, yes, but sometimes ones like these, too. The deer are new. They don't taste like musk ox or anything else. New tastes are more interesting to me."

Venison *was* different from musk ox. But it wasn't as different as duck or goose. "If you want to shoot one, you can do that," Count Hamnet said. "I'll help you eat it if you do."

"Do you want me to?" Marcovefa asked.

"I'd just as soon eat fat goose," he answered. "If you'd rather have venison, though, I won't complain. I'll help you put it away, the way I said I would."

"That would be good. I don't want to waste it," Marcovefa said seriously. Even more than the regular Bizogots, the folk who lived atop the Glacier had a horror of waste. Count Hamnet supposed that was why they were cannibals. Understanding it didn't make him want to imitate it.

When the riders spotted a deer wandering along, Marcovefa strung her bow. She sang to the arrow she nocked. The chant was in her own dialect, which meant Hamnet could make out only a few words. He guessed the charm was to make the arrow fly straight and true, but he would have guessed the same thing if he couldn't have understood any of it.

Marcovefa drew the bow to her ear and let fly. The arrow, charmed or not, struck the deer just behind the left shoulder. The animal started to run, but its legs went out from under it after a few strides. It fell to the steppe, thrashing feebly.

"Good shot," Hamnet Thyssen said. "Can you charm them against men the same way?"

"Sometimes. Not always. Men are harder," Marcovefa answered.

"Countercharms?" Hamnet wondered.

"Those, too. But men don't want to be shot. Their will opposes the spell," she said. "Animals don't know anything about it till it happens. To an animal, everything is a surprise."

"I hadn't thought of that," Hamnet said. "I never imagined it would matter in magic."

"Everything matters. Finding out where, finding out how—that's what a shaman does." Marcovefa dismounted and went over to the riding deer. Hamnet would have waited till it stopped kicking, but it didn't try to savage her. She swiped a knife across its throat. With a human-sounding sigh, it died as its blood rivered out.

Up atop the Glacier, they would have saved that blood for puddings and sausages. They might have down on the Bizogot steppe, too, if they weren't traveling. Marcovefa gutted the deer. They would have used more of the offal up atop the Glacier, too. She looked not so much unhappy as resigned when she pushed the rest of the carcass away from the steaming pile of guts.

"Too much left for the big foxes again," she said.

"Nothing to worry about," Hamnet said. Venison steak was just about as good as waterfowl. When it came to a choice between venison chitterlings and, say, roast duck, he would have plumped for roast duck.

As usual, people carrying big slabs of raw, bloody meat made the horses snort and flare their nostrils and sidestep. Count Hamnet fed his mount a few early-ripening berries. Bribery worked almost as well as it would have with people.

THEY ROUNDED THE easternmost corner of Sudertorp Lake. Hamnet rode bareheaded. The sun was warm enough to make him sweat. He wasn't the only one, either; he watched Audun Gilli undo his jacket and swipe a sleeve across his forehead. "By God!" Hamnet exclaimed as inspiration stuck. "We could bathe here. We really could."

Everybody stared at him. He didn't blame the Bizogots and Audun and Ulric for gaping. Chances to bathe didn't come often on the frozen steppe. But it wasn't frozen now, which was exactly the point. It was a pleasant day, they had plenty of water, and even the lake wouldn't be too cold.

"Why not?" Trasamund said. "Why not, by God? The women here with us know what men look like, and the men know what women look like. Anyone who lets his hands get gay, I hope he drowns."

Dying was easy among the Bizogots. Drowning wasn't. Hamnet Thyssen wasn't sure he'd ever heard the word in their language before. The literal meaning was *smothers in water*, so he couldn't doubt what Trasamund meant.

The jarl told off a few men to hold horses while the rest washed. They would take their turn later. The rest of the Bizogots and the three Raumsdalians stripped off their clothes and splashed at the edge of the lake. Everyone had a tan face and hands and was pale everywhere else.

"Not all *that* bloody warm," Ulric Skakki muttered, trying to rub dirt off his arms.

"We won't get chest fever from it," Hamnet said. "Up here, that will have to do." He was filthy. He couldn't remember the last time he'd bathed. Nobody else was any cleaner, though. If you were no dirtier than anyone around you, how dirty you were could stop mattering for a while.

"Not as good as a tub, but better than anything I knew before I came down off the Glacier," Marcovefa said. "No lakes like this there. Even the springs freeze in the wintertime."

Hamnet did and didn't want to stare at her lean, athletic body. Seeing it in the sunshine pleased him, yes. Despite chilly water, though, he didn't want to show everyone else how much it pleased him, and he feared he would.

When he got a glimpse of Liv, he deliberately turned away. Seeing her naked only reminded him of what had been and wasn't any more. He splashed himself and scrubbed hard.

"I hate the idea of getting back into my grimy clothes," Audun Gilli said.

"If you want to stay naked, you can do that—for a few weeks, anyhow." Count Hamnet didn't want to put on the smelly furs again, either. He knew too well he had no choice.

Somebody splashed somebody else. In a heartbeat, everybody was splashing everybody else. Pretty soon, the men started ducking one another. It was a good thing they'd all left their weapons behind on the shore. A hulking Bizogot tried to shove Ulric underwater. The mammoth-herder flew over the adventurer's shoulder and splashed into the lake on his back.

He came up coughing and puffing and blowing, water dripping from his beard and the end of his nose. But his blue eyes glowed. "How did you do that? Teach me!"

"Another time, maybe," Ulric said. "When we've got our clothes on again."

A woman let out an irate squawk. Then she did her best to smother with water the Bizogot who hadn't listened to the jarl. The man tried to apologize, but he was spluttering too hard—and laughing too hard, too. Then she hauled off and hit him. Bizogot women were solid and strong. She packed a mean punch. The man stopped laughing and howled instead.

"Enough!" Trasamund shouted. He could sound author-itative even naked—no mean feat. "You gave him what he deserved. He still needs to be able to fight."

When Hamnet came out of Sudertorp Lake, he let the sun and the southerly breeze dry him. Then he climbed back into his clothes. They seemed even nastier now than he'd thought they would. And, of course, they were crawl-ing with lice. Before long, he would be once more, too. And, before long, he wouldn't notice the sour stink that clung to them any more.

As Ulric dressed, he made a face and said, "*Some* peo-ple weren't very good at keeping clean." No one would ever have imagined he might be one of those people.

The Leaping Lynxes' stone huts weren't far from the east-ern end of Sudertorp Lake. They'd built them by the marshes where the waterfowl nested most thickly. Some of the refu-gee Leaping Lynxes sighed to be coming home under such sorry circumstances. Other Bizogots seemed surprised and impressed that their countrymen had built any kind of per-manent housing.

Then a man came out of one of the stone huts. He wasn't especially tall, but thick in the chest and wide through the shoulders. He had black hair and a long, thick, elaborately curled beard. In short, he belonged to the Rulers. He car-ried a bone staff in his right hand. Fire leaped from it as he pointed it at the Bizogots.

Flame engulfed a mammoth-herder and his horse. The man screamed. So did the animal, and galloped across the steppe. Fire still clung to it; and to its rider. The horse ran on long after it should have dropped. Hamnet wondered whether the sorcerous conflagration burned and preserved at the same time, to make torment last and last.

Laughing, the wizard raised the bone staff and pointed it at another Bizogot. The man ducked, not that that would have done him any good. Flame sprang forth from the staff once more.

Marcovefa raised a hand and spoke sharply in her own dialect. The flame stopped before it reached the Bizogot. The wizard from the Rulers stared as if he couldn't believe his eyes. Then the streak of fire started to slide back toward him, faster and faster. He stared again, this time plainly in horror, and shouted something in his guttural language.

More Rulers came out of other huts. Some of them must have been wizards, too, for they carried staves like the first man's. When they added their strength to his, they stopped the fire just before it recoiled on him.

Marcovefa bit her lip as the flame ever so slowly began to move out again, this time toward her. Audun Gilli and Liv began incanting, too, to give her what aid they could. All together, though, they were not quite a match for the sorcerous power the Rulers had gathered here.

But there were ways around that. Hamnet Thyssen needed a few heartbeats longer than he might have to realize as much. When he did, he wasted no more time. He strung his bow, aimed at the closest enemy wizard, and let fly. The Rulers' sorcerers normally brushed arrows aside with some small spell or another. Putting forth all their strength against Marcovefa, they had no time or energy for such minor wizardries.

The arrow caught the sorcerer square in the chest. He looked absurdly surprised as he clutched at himself. His knees buckled; he slumped to the ground. Ulric Skakki and the Bizogots started shooting right after Hamnet did. Two or three other sorcerers fell, wounded or killed. That meant the lot of them couldn't concentrate on Marcovefa any more. And she proved more than equal to anything but the lot of them.

They might have paid less attention to the fire one of them had first unleashed. She didn't. When they shielded themselves against arrows, they left themselves vulnerable to the flames. They screamed when their bone staves caught fire, and screamed again when they did.

They dashed this way and that, trying to quell the flames. Some of them had the presence of mind to plunge into Sudertorp Lake. But not even water quenched the fire. Like sulfurous oil, they went right on burning. Steam rose from the lake.

The fire didn't touch the Rulers who weren't wizards. They tried to flee. The Bizogots rode after them. Slaying enemies who ran from them made ever so much better sport than fleeing themselves.

"I thank you," Marcovefa said, riding up alongside Hamnet. She leaned toward him and brushed her lips across his. "Even for me, a few too many there at first." Something kindled in her eyes. "Later on, I thank you properly. We have to make do with words right now."

"Best thing I've heard today," Hamnet answered, deadpan. Marcovefa laughed. He went on, "Why had so many of their wizards gathered here?"

"Better to ask them than me—except I don't think any of them are left alive." Her nostrils flared. "And most are too cooked—too charred, that is the word you use—to be worth eating."

"Yes." Count Hamnet left it right there. That stink had invaded his nose, too. At least he didn't confuse it with the smell of roasting pork, the way he had up atop the Glacier. Remembering how he'd hungered for man's flesh before realizing what it was still raised his hackles.

"Well, these huts are ours now, by God—ours by right of conquest," Trasamund said proudly. "The Rulers ran off the Leaping Lynxes, and now we've run off the Rulers. We may not be a neat, tidy clan of the old-fashioned kind, but we'll have to make do. Times aren't what they were before the Rulers came, either."

Ulric Skakki stared at him in artfully simulated disbelief. "A Bizogot jarl admits the times are changing? What is this sorry old world coming to?"

"I don't know. By the past couple of years, nothing good," Trasamund said. "But I'm not dead yet, and some more of those maggoty musk-ox turds are. That, I like. And I know the world is changing. Was I not the first man through the Gap?" He struck a pose, there on horseback.

Ulric didn't tell him no. But the adventurer had gone through the Gap the winter before him. None of the Three Tusk Bizogots knew Ulric had crossed their grazing grounds, and he didn't want it known.

Trasamund pointed to the wizards' blackened corpses. "A good thing these burning bastards didn't start grass fires. That could have been a nuisance."

"I hadn't thought about it, but you're not wrong," Count Hamnet said.

"Grass fires can be very bad," Trasamund said. "Not now, but later in the year—at the end of summer and the start of fall, before the first snows. We don't get much summer rain here, and things dry out. When fires start, they can spread and spread. They can ruin grazing grounds. When that happens, wars follow. You have to have somewhere to take your herds. Or, if the fires catch the animals, you have to grab someone else's. When it's that or die, you do what needs doing."

"I suppose so," Hamnet said. He'd fought in plenty of wars with less behind them than life and death.

Trasamund pointed to the stone huts. "Let's make sure we haven't got any more vermin skulking in there." A Raumsdalian would have spoken of serpents or scorpions. The frozen steppe lacked a few unpleasant things, anyhow. The jarl of the Three Tusk clan went on, "We can live off the fat—by God, the goose grease—of the land . . . for a while, anyhow. Then things get hard again. They always do, curse them."

No more Rulers remained. Hamnet Thyssen did wonder why so many wizards had come together. When he wondered out loud once more, Ulric said, "To plot mischief against us. Why else?"

"I can't think of any other reason, either," Hamnet replied. "I wish I could."

"Maybe your lady friends and Audun will figure out what they were up to from the stuff they left behind," Ulric said.

Hamnet gave him a stony look. "Liv is not my lady friend these days. You may perhaps have noticed."

"Perhaps." Nothing bothered Ulric Skakki—or if it did, he didn't let it show, which served about as well. Still in that blithe vein, he went on, "You don't *have* to hate a lover after she leaves you, you know. You can, yes, but it's not a requirement. Liv's a lady—no doubt about that— and she makes a good friend whether you're sleeping with her or not."

"Do I tell you how to run your life?" Hamnet growled.

"As a matter of fact—yes."

That caught Hamnet with his mouth open. He closed it before a bug flew in—at this season of the year, a real worry on the Bizogot steppe, not just a way for mothers to scold their children. He feared Ulric was telling the truth. He *did* like to run other people's lives, not just his own. Feebly, he said, "Well, I'll try not to do it any more."

"No, no. Try to do it less," Ulric said, which only made his confusion worse.

COMPARED TO PROPER houses, Raumsdalian houses, the huts the Leaping Lynxes had run up were sorry. Their roofs were thatch over a framework of bones held together with sinew. No one had tended to them since the Rulers ran the Bizogots away from Sudertorp Lake. That left the huts draftier than they might have been. During springtime, though, it wasn't such a great hardship.

Hamnet and Marcovefa took one of the huts for their own. He threw out the bones and other trash that had accumulated in there. Marcovefa gave him a quizzical look. "Why bother?" she said. "It doesn't stink or anything."

"You don't care much about housekeeping, do you?" he said.

"I don't care any about housekeeping," Marcovefa answered. "Why bother? I save caring for things that matter."

He supposed that made sense. Lots of people he knew had made sense lately: Marcovefa, Ulric Skakki, even Trasamund. To quote Ulric, what was this old world coming to?

But . . . to stay friends with a woman who'd left you? To stay friends with a woman who'd left you for a weed of a man like Audun Gilli? Hamnet could believe Ulric was friends with a swarm of women in the Empire and on the frozen steppe and likely elsewhere as well. Ulric didn't take anything or anybody seriously. If he ran into a woman he'd slept with once upon a time—well, so what? He wouldn't fret about it.

When Hamnet met a woman, though, he always thought she was *the* woman. And he hated admitting even to himself that he might have made a mistake. If things didn't work out, then, of course he blamed the woman for the failure. How could you stay friends with someone you blamed?

He glanced over at Marcovefa. If things went wrong between them, would he wind up shunning her, too? He suspected he would. He seemed to work that way, whether Ulric Skakki approved or not.

She was looking at him, too. She beckoned. "Now that we have this clean floor thanks to you, we ought to use it. I said I would thank you for that arrow before. Now I will." She shrugged out of her jacket.

It was still light outside. Bizogots cared much less about privacy than Raumsdalians. Living the way they did, that was no surprise. It also held true for their cousins from atop the Glacier. Hamnet preferred privacy, but he'd spent enough time among the Bizogots to do without it at need.

Had she thanked him any more thoroughly, he thought he would have fallen over dead. He couldn't imagine a more enjoyable way to go. After his heart stopped thudding quite so hard, he said, "I should save you more often."

"Why not?" Marcovefa agreed lazily.

She seemed in no hurry to put her clothes back on. When Hamnet was younger, he would have tried for a second round in a little while. Now that he was the age he was, he knew he would have to wait longer. Most of the time, he took that for granted. Sprawling naked beside an inviting woman who was also a powerful shaman, he realized he might not have to.

"Can you do anything magical to get him back into shape again in a hurry?" he asked.

She looked at him sidelong. "What do you want me to do?"

"I don't know. You're the wizard," he said.

"How about this?" She leaned over and did something. It should have raised the dead. Raising the middle-aged proved a bigger challenge. She muttered to herself, then murmured to herself, then began a chant in her own dialect. The tune she chose almost made Hamnet start to laugh. Down to the southwest of the Raumsdalian Empire, the Manche barbarians had wizards who could charm snakes with music. Marcovefa had never seen a snake—well, she'd never seen a two-eyed snake, anyhow—but her tune was a lot like theirs.

And it worked. Like a charmed snake, he rose to the occasion. She nodded to herself. "There it is," she said. "Now what do you want to do with it?"

He did laugh then, so much that he lost what she'd given him. She didn't seem too annoyed about repeating the spell. Hamnet found something to do with it after all. Marcovefa seemed contented afterward, too.

"Again?" she asked then.

Count Hamnet remembered that. He remembered thinking about the answer. He didn't remember giving it, which was fair enough, because he fell asleep before he could. When he woke up, he found Marcovefa had pulled a blanket cut from a mammoth hide over the two of them. He was still bare under the hide. A moment later, he discovered she was, too.

It was still light outside. No: it was light again. The brief northern night had come and gone, and the sun was shining from a different direction now. Marcovefa stirred only a couple of minutes after Hamnet did. "Happy now?" she asked him. Her voice said she was smugly certain of the answer.

And he nodded. "With you? Yes, I should hope so." But he went on, "I'd be happier if we could drive the Rulers back beyond the Gap."

Marcovefa grunted. She got out from under the blanket and, in a marked manner, got into her clothes. She paused only once, to say, "No wonder you lose women."

"No wonder at all," Hamnet agreed mournfully, wondering if he'd lost her, too. All he did was answer the question she asked him. He didn't even forget to say something nice about her. But then he went on to the rest of what was in his mind. Too late—as usual—he realized that was his mistake. When would he ever learn? No. *Would* he ever learn, late or otherwise?

"You are what you are, that's all." Marcovefa seemed to be reminding herself. She shrugged. "Well, who isn't?"

Since she seemed willing to leave it there, Hamnet Thyssen didn't push it, either. As he also dressed, he decided not pushing it was a good idea, and progress of a sort. That also would have been too late to do him any good had he decided the other way.

The Bizogots had a fire of dried dung going. They were roasting meat above it. Hamnet's stomach rumbled. There were appetites, and then there were appetites. Filling your belly wasn't so much as making love, but you wouldn't go on making love very long, even with sorcerous assistance, if you were empty.

Hamnet got a musk-ox rib. Instead of gnawing on it, he gave it to Marcovefa. Then he grabbed another one for himself. Maybe she would recognize the peace offering, maybe not.

She certainly ate with good appetite. Bizogots always did, and their close kin from atop the Glacier even more so. And the only way she could have got more off the bone was with a rough tongue like a lion's. Her tongue wasn't the least bit rough. Hamnet knew that as well as a man could.

She took another rib, and denuded that one, too. "You people are so lucky to have such big meat-beasts," she said. "Do you know how lucky you are? Voles, pikas, hares . . . That's all we knew. Well, that and the beasts that go on two legs."

"I was up there. I saw how you lived," Hamnet said. "You did what you could with what you had. People everywhere do the same." He thought of the Manches again, and of how they scraped a living from their desert. That wasn't the same as what the Bizogots did, but it wasn't necessarily easier, either.

"There is so much more to have down here," Marcovefa said. "The animals . . . The trees . . . The—what do you call them down in the Empire? The crops! That's it. Plants that aren't berries, but you can eat them anyhow. And the big berry things that grow on trees—"

"Fruit," Hamnet said. Apples and pears and plums surprised the Bizogots, too. They had nothing like them.

Marcovefa wasn't done. "And the head-spinning stuff,

the smetyn and the beer and the wine . . . Once in a while, we find mushrooms to send shamans into the spirit world. You go whenever you want. You are so lucky! I am so jealous!"

Count Hamnet wouldn't have called getting drunk going into the spirit world. When he did it, he mostly did it to forget whatever was troubling his spirit. But it was new and wonderful to the shaman from atop the Glacier. Everything was new and wonderful to Marcovefa. She was like a child in a fairyland. If it sometimes looked like a nightmare to Hamnet, maybe he was the jaded one.

And maybe he'd seen enough of the world down here on the ground to have a better notion of what was what than she did. He suspected that was so, but didn't make the claim out loud. He didn't feel like arguing. Besides, he might have been wrong. He rather hoped he was.

Ulric Skakki also snagged a second rib. He took a bite, then nodded to Hamnet. "Cozy little place we've got, isn't it?"

"Till the Rulers find out we're here," Hamnet replied. "How long do you think that will take?"

"Depends on whether any of them got away yesterday," the adventurer said. "I don't *think* so, but I'm not sure. Or maybe one of the wizards got word out magically, and they already know. Won't be long any which way. When the wizards don't show up wherever they're supposed to, the Rulers will come see why not."

That was less palatable than juicy musk-ox meat. "I wish you didn't make so much sense," Hamnet said.

Ulric only shrugged. "If you don't like the answers, don't ask the questions."

Hamnet Thyssen sighed. "I don't like the answers. Who would? But I needed to hear them."

"Well, there you are, then," Ulric said. "Now you've

heard them. I don't think the Rulers will get here before we finish breakfast—at least if we hurry." He bit another chunk of meat off the rib. Ears burning, Hamnet ate some more, too.

"We need to send out patrols," Trasamund said in his usual tone of brooking no arguments. "If the Rulers are moving to the north and south, we need to know about it."

"Suppose they're going around the west end of Suder-torp Lake." Ulric Skakki liked arguments, brooked or not. "What do we do then?"

Trasamund scowled. "Why would their wizards meet here if their main route runs around the other end of the lake?" he demanded.

"Well, you've got something there," Ulric said. "How much, I don't know, but something."

The jarl gave him a sardonic bow. "More than I ex-pected from you, by God. You never admit you're wrong, do you?"

Hamnet could have told him that was the wrong thing to say to Ulric. He didn't need to; Ulric proved quite ca-pable of demonstrating it on his own: "When I am wrong, I don't have any trouble admitting I am—unlike some people I could name. The difference is, I'm not wrong very often, so naturally you wouldn't have heard me talk about it much."

"You are a funny man," Trasamund rumbled. "Funny as my nightmares."

"Really? Let me take a look." Ulric Skakki ambled over and peered into the Bizogot's left ear. He started to laugh. "You're right. That is a funny one in there."

Cursing, Trasamund cuffed him—or tried. Ulric caught his arm before the blow landed, caught it and twisted. Trasamund let out a startled grunt of pain. When he tried to get away, Ulric twisted harder. "You'll break it if you do much more," Trasamund said. Hamnet admired how calmly he brought out the words.

"That's the idea," Ulric answered. "When you go hitting people who didn't hit you, you can't look for them to like it. Well, maybe you can, but you'll be disappointed."

"Let go of me, and I'll cut you in half," Trasamund snarled.

Ulric gave back a merry laugh. "You really know how to get a man to do what you want, don't you, Your Ferocity?"

"What do you expect me to say?" the Bizogot asked.

"How about, 'Sorry, Skakki. Now I know better than to talk to people with my fist'? That ought to do it." Ulric jerked on Trasamund's arm a little more. Something in there creaked. Count Hamnet heard it plainly.

Despite Trasamund's courage, his face went gray. He choked out the words Ulric Skakki wanted to hear. The adventurer let him go and jumped back in case he still showed fight. Trasamund didn't, not right away. He worked his wrist to make sure it wasn't broken after all. Once satisfied of that, he managed a glare. "I'll pay you back for that one day, Skakki," he growled.

"You're welcome to try," Ulric said politely. "But would you give any man leave to hit you for a joke?"

"No man has leave to hit me, no matter why," Trasamund said.

"Then why did you think you had leave to hit me?" Ulric asked.

"Because he was doing the hitting, not taking the blow," Hamnet Thyssen said when the Bizogot didn't answer right away.

That won *him* a glower. "When I want you putting words in my mouth, Thyssen, I'll stick out my tongue for you," Trasamund said.

"Better that than sticking your foot in your face," Hamnet observed.

Trasamund looked blank for a moment. Hamnet realized he'd translated a Raumsdalian phrase into the Bizogot's language. Then the jarl got it. His hand went over his shoulder so he could draw his great blade. But he winced when his fingers closed on the leather-wrapped hilt. The wrist still pained him. Maybe it even made him thoughtful. He let his hand drop, contenting himself with saying, "Your time will come, too."

"I don't doubt it. Everyone's does," Hamnet agreed. "But I hope it doesn't come at your hands. That would mean we're fighting each other, not the Rulers."

Trasamund chewed on that. By his expression, he didn't care for the taste. "Well, you're right," he said at last: an astonishing admission from any Bizogot, and doubly astonishing from him. Then he added, "But once they're whipped, don't think I've forgotten about you."

Count Hamnet bowed. "Once the Rulers are whipped, Your Ferocity, I will meet you wherever you please. I will meet you here. I will meet you down in Nidaros. I will meet you in the doorway to the Golden Shrine, if that tickles your fancy."

"The doorway to the Golden Shrine, is it?" Trasamund threw back his head and laughed. "By God, your Grace, you're on! Once we beat the Rulers, I'll cut your heart out in the doorway to the Golden Shrine." He held out his hand. "Bargain?"

"I'll meet you there, surely." Hamnet Thyssen clasped with him. "As Ulric says, you're welcome to try. You may get a surprise, though—and if you do, it may be your last one."

"I'm not afraid of you. I'm not afraid of Skakki, either,"

Trasamund said. "You can go on about surprises as much as you want. Death is always the last surprise."

Ulric threw his hands in the air. "When a Bizogot jarl gets philosophical on you, it's time to go do something else." He mooched off.

"That one." Trasamund shook his head in mingled exasperation and affection. So Hamnet judged, anyhow—those two emotions always warred in him when he thought of the adventurer. Trasamund went on, "What are we going to do about him?"

"Turn him loose against the Rulers," Count Hamnet said. "If that's not the most important thing we're doing, we're doing something wrong."

"We've done plenty of things wrong," the jarl said, which was only too true. "Not that one, though—not lately, anyhow. They taught us their lessons the hard way."

"So they did." Hamnet left it there. The hard way was the only way the Bizogots understood—when they understood any way at all.

HAMNET GNAWED ON a roasted goose leg as he rode across the Bizogot steppe. Ulric Skakki was working on a swan's drumstick. That would have been an expensive delicacy down in the Empire. At Sudertorp Lake, the swans bred in as much exuberant profusion as the smaller waterfowl.

And Sudertorp Lake was merely the largest of the many lakes and ponds and puddles dotting the flat ground that was still frozen a few feet down. Count Hamnet looked toward the northern horizon, but he couldn't see the Glacier. See it or not, he knew it was there.

Ulric understood what his glance meant. "Do you really think that whole mountain of ice is going to melt away?"

"Before I went through the Gap, I would have told you

no," Hamnet said. "Now? I suppose it will, one of these days. The world will be a different place then. I won't be here to see it, though, and neither will you."

"I suppose not," Ulric said. "Seeing what—and who—was on the other side's been interesting enough, and then some."

"Yes. And then some." Hamnet Thyssen's gaze focused more sharply on ground much closer. First glances could—and often did—deceive. The steppe had little dips and rises that had a way of hiding trouble till it was right on top of you . . . or, sometimes, right in back of you.

Every time something moved, Count Hamnet's hand started to go to his sword or his bow. And things did move, again and again. Small birds nested among the small bushes. Voles and lemmings scurried. Weasels chased them. Hares hopped. Short-eared foxes loped after them and noisy-winged ptarmigans.

A snowy owl swooped down. It rose again with a lemming in its claws. Prey still writhing feebly, it flew past Hamnet and Ulric just out of bowshot. Hamnet felt the bird's golden eyes on him till at last it turned its head in a different direction.

"God-cursed thing," he muttered.

"If it's only an owl, I don't mind it," Ulric Skakki said. "But if it's one of the Rulers' wizards in owl shape, come to look us over the way they do . . ."

"If it is, it just got an eyeful," Hamnet said. "Two eyes full, in fact."

"I doubt it was a wizard this time," Ulric said.

"Oh? Why's that?" Count Hamnet asked.

The adventurer spread his hands in wry amusement. "Well, it looked us over. It looked us over good. And it didn't fall out of the sky laughing. That makes me think it must be an ordinary owl."

"Heh," Hamnet Thyssen said. "I wish that were the kind of joke that made me laugh."

"So do I," Ulric replied. "I don't like wasting them. We're in a mess, you know. The Rulers can whip the Bizogots. They can whip the Empire. The only thing they haven't shown they can whip is Marcovefa, and there's only one of her. A little bad luck, and we're all in a lot of trouble."

"Yes." Hamnet left it right there. If anything happened to Marcovefa, the Bizogots and Raumsdalia would suffer, true. But so would he. The last woman in the world who thought he was anything out of the ordinary . . . He shook his head. That wasn't quite right. She was the last woman in the world who made *him* think he was anything out of the ordinary. That made her a rarer bird yet.

Rare as a wizard from the Rulers magicked into owl's shape? Hamnet didn't know. He couldn't tell. Marcovefa could have if she'd been along. She was busy back at the Leaping Lynxes' huts: busy with something sorcerous, though Hamnet couldn't have said what it was.

She didn't mind working with Liv and Audun Gilli. Sometimes Hamnet could accept that. Sometimes it bothered him. It didn't bother Marcovefa, though, and she paid no attention to Hamnet's occasional grumbles.

He supposed he could see the logic behind that. Working against the Rulers counted for more than personal squabbles. It made perfectly good sense. He'd even pointed out as much to Trasamund. Understanding it and liking it were two very different things.

"What's going on inside your head?" Ulric Skakki asked. "You look like you want to murder somebody."

"The owl." Count Hamnet lied without hesitation. Ulric was too good at divining what went on inside him. Hamnet didn't want the adventurer to know he was worrying about his latest woman. Ulric would only laugh at him and tell him things he didn't want to hear. Even if they were true—or maybe especially if they were true—he didn't want to hear them.

Ulric Skakki eyed him now. Hamnet wondered if the adventurer would start telling him things even after he'd lied. That would be humiliating. And if Hamnet lost his temper and turned away, Ulric would laugh at him, and laugh and laugh. That would be more humiliating yet.

But Ulric didn't twit Hamnet. Instead, he pointed to the northwest. "Something over there," he said. "Don't know what, but something."

"I didn't see it," Hamnet Thyssen confessed.

"Well, it's there," Ulric told him. "We'd better find out what the demon it is, too, because it's liable to be dangerous." He rode off to see what he'd spotted.

"A dire wolf, maybe, or a lion." Count Hamnet followed. He made sure his sword was loose in the scabbard. He strung his bow and reached over his shoulder to check on the position of his quiver. He adjusted it a little, then nodded to himself.

Ulric laughed harshly, watching him. "You don't believe that yourself."

"It may not be likely, but it's possible," Hamnet said.

"All kinds of things are possible. It's possible the Rulers really are nice people who want the best for us," Ulric said. "It's possible, sure, but it's not bloody likely."

Count Hamnet shut up.

His eyes narrowed as he scanned the ground ahead. Lots of little dips where a man on foot might hide—and the flowers and grasses and little bushes here grew as thick as they ever did on the Bizogot steppe. Hamnet thought of snakes. No real vipers up here—the mammoth-herders thought Raumsdalians were lying when they talked about them. But a man from the Rulers could prove more dangerous than any rattlesnake ever hatched.

"There!" Ulric Skakki pointed. Hamnet was a good hunter, but Ulric was better. He could follow a trail that baffled the noble, and he spotted motion Count Hamnet missed. Hamnet missed it till it was pointed out to him, anyhow. Then he too saw the shifting shrubs up ahead.

"Not a wizard, anyway," he said as he rode toward them with Ulric.

"No, eh? How come you're so sure?" the adventurer asked.

"Don't be stupid." Hamnet was pleased to get a little of his own back. "If the bastard were a wizard, he wouldn't be running from the likes of us, would he?"

Ulric grunted. "Not unless he was a cursed stupid wizard, I suppose."

"The Rulers don't seem to have many of those," Hamnet Thyssen answered. "I wish to God they did."

"Would make life easier, wouldn't it?" Ulric agreed. "Now, if you were a Ruler stuck on foot, where would you hide from a couple of savage fellows from the wrong side of the Glacier who're trying to do you in?"

"Right about there—that birch thicket." Now Hamnet Thyssen pointed. He and Ulric both laughed, even if it wasn't really funny. None of the birches grew much higher than his knees. They were shrubs, bushes, not the trees they would have been south of the line where the ground stayed frozen all the time. But at this season of the year their leaves gave good cover.

Good, yes, but not quite good enough. The birch bushes stirred; someone was trying to crawl deeper into the thicket. Two bowstrings twanged. Hamnet wasn't sure whether he or Ulric let fly first. A grunt of dismay, bitten off short, said at least one arrow struck home.

"Give up!" Count Hamnet shouted—one of the fragments of the Rulers' language he'd acquired. He added another one: "We no kill captives!" To the Rulers, any kind of yielding looked like shameful weakness. Many of them preferred death to surrender. Many—but not all. The fights across the frozen plain and inside the Empire had taught Hamnet as much. He might despise and distrust the invaders, but he'd found that some of them were ordinary enough to go on breathing if they saw the chance.

All Hamnet got this time was more wiggling among the leaves. He and Ulric Skakki looked at each other. They didn't bother nodding, but both shot at about the same time again. Another involuntary grunt of pain told of a wound—or of someone desperate who was cunningly bluffing.

But Hamnet didn't think so. He slid down from his horse and drew his sword. "Let's find out what the"—he added an obscenity—"knows."

Ulric also dismounted. "Let's make sure one of those things isn't that you're a real idiot."

Count Hamnet gave the adventurer a mocking bow. "I never need to worry about the different nasty things that might happen to me, not when you're around. You come up with more of them than I ever could."

"Always at your service, Your Grace." Ulric sounded more like a trusted retainer than a comrade-in-arms.

They plunged into the low thicket together. They both made plenty of noise, hoping to panic their quarry into moving and showing them where to go. And it worked. The leaves not far from where they'd shot the Ruler started thrashing. The Raumsdalians hurried that way.

"Embarrassing if four or five of the buggers are hiding under there," Ulric remarked.

"*Embarrassing* is hardly the word," Hamnet Thyssen

said. Ulric laughed, for all the world as if they were trading quips at an elegant salon—say, Earl Eyvind Torfinn's—
down in Nidaros, goblets of wine in their hands instead of
sword hilts.

But only one Ruler hid in the birch bushes. When Hamnet and and Ulric split up to attack from two directions at
once, the invader from beyond the Gap called out, "Don't
kill me! I yield!" in the Bizogot language.

"Good God!" Count Hamnet burst out. Ulric Skakki
didn't say anything, but he looked as astonished as Hamnet felt. That harsh, guttural accent was familiar, but not
in a woman's contralto.

"I bleed," she said. "You said you would spare me. Will
you help me, and not—?" She broke off. *Not rape me and
then cut my throat or knock me over the head* was what
she had to mean.

Bleed she did. She had an arrow through her right hand
and another in her left calf. Raping a wounded woman
wasn't Hamnet Thyssen's idea of sport. He wondered
whether it was Ulric's. If it was, the adventurer gave no sign
of it. "I will draw the arrow in your leg," he said, and drew
out a spoonlike device. He'd left one of those with a Bizogot shaman, but must have got another down in the Empire. As he got to work, he added, "By the way, what's your
name?"

"Tahpenes," she said through clenched teeth.

IV

Well, well. Isn't this intriguing?" Ulric Skakki said as he extracted the arrow from Tahpenes' leg. She kept her teeth clenched and didn't let out a peep all through the unpleasant process. Hamnet had seen that the Rulers' warriors were made of stern stuff. The same appeared to hold for their women.

"Intriguing? Not the word I'd use," he said, using Raumsdalian like Ulric. They wanted Tahpenes worried, or he supposed they did; not being able to understand them would push her down that road.

He eyed her with more than a little curiosity of his own. She was the first woman of the Rulers he'd seen close up. Liv had spoken slightingly of their looks. They weren't tall and blond. They weren't even tall *or* blond. Tahpenes had hair so black it was almost blue, dark brown eyes, and a formidable blade of a nose. She also had broad shoulders and formidable arms. If she weren't multiply wounded, she might have been dangerous.

She might be dangerous anyhow.

Ulric bandaged her with matter-of-fact competence.

"What will you do to me? Uh, with me?" she asked in the Bizogots' tongue.

"Whatever we want," Ulric said before Count Hamnet could answer. Had the adventurer done some raping and knocking over the head in his time? Hamnet Thyssen wouldn't have been surprised. He didn't want to ask, even in Raumsdalian.

"Right now," he said, "we'll take you back for questioning."

Tahpenes winced. Count Hamnet had no trouble figuring out why. When the Rulers questioned people, they put them to the question. By all accounts, they were good at that kind of thing, and they seemed to enjoy it, too.

"We don't intend to torture you right now," Hamnet said, trying to reassure the new captive.

"Not unless you show us we need to, anyhow," Ulric Skakki added, trying to do anything but. Hamnet sent him an aggrieved look. If that bothered Ulric, he concealed it very well. In Raumsdalian, he said, "We may have to do some nasty things to her. You never can tell. And even if we don't, she'd better think we're ready to. Otherwise, she'll just decide we're soft."

"Mmh," Hamnet Thyssen said unhappily. He didn't like the idea of torturing women. He didn't like the idea of torturing men, either, which didn't mean he'd never done it. And Ulric had a point. The Rulers were much too likely to judge the Bizogots and Raumsdalians as soft. Keeping Tahpenes healthily on edge wasn't the worst idea in the world.

"Can you stand?" Ulric asked her, returning to the Bizogots' tongue.

"I think so," she said, and showed she could.

"Wait," Hamnet said as Ulric started to lead her back toward the horses. The adventurer raised a gingery eyebrow. "Search her," Count Hamnet told him. "Otherwise, you're liable to sprout steel in some uncomfortable spot."

"My, my. And here I took you for a dewy-souled innocent," Ulric Skakki said. Hamnet answered that with the rude noise it deserved. Ulric laughed, then shook his head. "The worst of it is, you're right. I may not find everything even with a good frisking, but I sure won't if I don't check her at all." Ulric gave Tahpenes a bow of sorts. "This isn't personal, you understand. Just something I'd better do to keep you from sticking me while I'm not looking."

She didn't say anything. If Ulric hadn't told her the search wasn't personal, it wouldn't have been hard for her to think it was. He patted her through her clothes and then reached under them. Chances were she would have slapped his face if she didn't figure that was a fast way to get herself killed.

He came up with several small, slim holdout blades, too. "Think I missed anything, Thyssen?" he asked when he thought he was done.

"Her hair," Hamnet said at once. After a moment, he added, "And women have a hiding place men don't."

"So they do," Ulric said, and then, "You have anything shoved up your twat, Tahpenes?"

"No," she said.

"If you do, I'll kill you," Ulric told her. "But the Bizogot women can find out about that when we get back to our camp. As for your hair . . ." He didn't ask her about that. He patted and prodded at it, and was rewarded with a couple of long, stout pins. "Wouldn't want one of these poking out of me."

"Neither would I." Hamnet nodded to Tahpenes. "Have any more? Give them up now and no blame to you. If you say no and we find them . . . well, you won't like that, I promise."

"One more, is all." The woman pulled it out and gave it to Ulric Skakki. He accepted it with a sour smile; he liked missing things he should have found no more than anyone else would have.

"All the same, you can bloody well ride in front of me," Ulric said. "That way, Hamnet and I will both have a shot at you if you decide to get smart."

"That way, you can put your hands all over me," Tahpenes replied, distaste in her voice.

"If I feel like it," Ulric said. "What makes you think you've got anything I'd want to grope? And as long as you're alive and we don't peel you out of your trousers here and now, what makes you think you've got any business complaining?"

Tahpenes answered the first question with a dirty look, the second with what was probably intended for a dignified silence. Ulric helped her climb up onto his horse. That did interest her. "These are strange animals, your riding deer with no antlers," she said as he got up behind her.

"We like 'em," Ulric answered. He nodded to Hamnet. "Keep an eye on her. Just because she doesn't know what a horse is, that doesn't mean she wouldn't do her damnedest to steal one."

"Really? I never would have guessed." Like the adventurer, Hamnet Thyssen used the Bizogots' tongue. They wanted Tahpenes to know they were alert.

She didn't try anything as they rode back to the stone huts the Leaping Lynxes had built. When she realized where they were going, one of her strong, dark eyebrows rose. "What are you doing here?" she said. "This is where our wizards were meeting."

"*Were* is right," Hamnet told her. "I don't think any of them got away."

"Sure hope not, anyhow," Ulric Skakki put in.

Tahpenes turned around to stare at him. She looked away in a hurry when he blew her a kiss from close range. "This is not possible. You are not of the Rulers. You are of the herd, to be ruled as we think best. How could you beat our wizards?"

"Wasn't too hard," Count Hamnet answered. "And here's a lesson for you: if something happens, it isn't impossible. You should remember that."

"How dare you mock me?" Tahpenes demanded.

"We enjoy mocking silly ideas. It makes us laugh," Ulric answered.

"You are not afraid." By the way Tahpenes said it, she might have accused them of cheating at dice. She was at least as arrogant as the men of her people. *Why am I not surprised?* Hamnet thought wryly. Tahpenes went on, "Folk of the herd should be afraid. Something is wrong, something is perverse, if you are not."

"Get used to it, sweetheart," Ulric Skakki said cheerfully. "You've beaten us more than we've beaten you, sure, but we've won often enough so we know we can. Ask your wizards if you don't believe me—if you can find any of them alive *to* ask, I mean."

"But you cannot beat our wizards." Tahpenes might have been stating a law of nature. She doubtless thought she was. Well, too bad for her.

She suddenly let out an indignant squeak. Hamnet Thyssen didn't see exactly what Ulric had done to her, but it was something that damaged her dignity. The adventurer said, "That's to remind you not to talk nonsense. You see we did, so why do you say we can't?"

Tahpenes didn't answer. She was one sadly confused Ruler. Count Hamnet almost didn't blame her. If not for

Marcovefa, the wizardry from her folk would have dominated anything the shamans and sorcerers from south of the Gap could do against it.

A Bizogot spotted the two horses coming back to the stone huts. He rode toward them. "Who've you got there?" he called.

"A captive." Hamnet stated the obvious.

"It's a woman!" The Bizogot was full of clever observations. "Did you bring her in for the sport of it?"

"No, for questioning," Ulric answered. "If she lies to us, then we can have fun with her. But if she tells the truth, she's worth more for that."

"Says you," the mammoth-herder exclaimed. "I sure don't think so."

"Well, if you want to fight me, we can do that," Ulric said easily. "Just let me know what you want me to do with your body once you're dead."

That took longer to sink in than Hamnet thought it should have. This Bizogot plainly wasn't overburdened with brains. And if he had as much pride as a lot of his comrades, he would fight Ulric on general principles. For a moment, Count Hamnet thought he would do just that—in which case, he would have died, and in short order, too.

Instead of charging, though, he jerked his horse's head around and rode away. Hamnet didn't reckon him a coward; few Bizogots were. But he must have heard the anticipation in Ulric Skakki's voice. Ulric didn't just know he could kill; he looked forward to it. And that was plenty to put the Bizogot's wind up.

It made Tahpenes thoughtful, too. "You act more like a man of the Rulers than one from the herd," she remarked.

A moment later, she let out another shrill, irate squeal. "Tell you what—you don't insult me, and I won't feel you up," Ulric said. "Deal?"

Tahpenes was silent for some little while. At last, she said, "I did not think I was insulting you. I meant it for praise."

"I know," the adventurer said. "That's part of what's wrong with you. You need to understand that your new neighbors don't love you. We don't admire you. We don't want to be like you. And we're strong enough to make what we want matter. If we weren't, would we have caught you?"

She looked unhappy—no, unhappier. "I thought I could spy on you without drawing notice. It seems I was wrong."

"It does, doesn't it?" Ulric Skakki's tone of voice suggested she was an idiot for thinking any such thing.

"It's all of a piece," Hamnet said, more to Ulric than to their captive. "The Rulers think they can do whatever they want, get away with whatever they want. Sooner or later, they'll find out they're wrong." *They'd better, or they'll end up winning this fight after all.*

"They all think like that, don't they?" Ulric had a knack for embellishing other people's thoughts. "Maybe they should have called themselves the Herd, not the Rulers. They all act the same, like so many, uh, riding deer."

"How dare you speak of us like that? How *dare* you?" Tahpenes snarled. "You don't know what you're talking about."

"Doesn't stop you from talking about us," Hamnet said. "Why should it stop us from talking about you?"

The answer blazed in her black eyes. Hamnet Thyssen read it there. The Rulers had the right to do as they pleased, because they were the Rulers. Lesser folk existed only on sufferance. When those "lesser" folk had captured you, though, bragging about how wonderful and mighty you were could prove inexpedient. For a medium-sized wonder, Tahpenes was smart enough to see that.

Hamnet pointed ahead. "There are the houses the

Leaping Lynx Bizogots built. Yes, those are the houses where your precious wizards met. They died right in front of them."

Were he speaking Raumsdalian, he would have called the stone structures huts. He always thought of them that way when he used his own language. Here, though, he wanted to make them seem impressive to Tahpenes. She was a nomad herself; any permanent buildings were bound to be large and imposing in her eyes.

"Here comes Trasamund." Ulric pointed to the burly jarl.

Tahpenes knew the name. "We beat his clan when we first came here," she said.

"So you did," Count Hamnet agreed. "Why don't you tell him all about it? Don't you think he'd want to know just how you embarrassed the Bizogots he led?"

Tahpenes didn't answer. She didn't boast to Trasamund, either. Pretty plainly, she was clever enough to see the obvious. Just as plainly, that put her several lengths ahead of most of the Rulers.

MARCOVEFA HAD TROUBLE with the idea of prisoners. "This woman doesn't know very much," she complained to Hamnet Thyssen. "We've got most of what she does know. Keeping her alive is nothing but a waste of food."

"We can spare it," Hamnet said. "Are you hungry?"

"Hungry? No, by God!" Marcovefa laughed. "So much food right now—all these waterfowl—I'm getting fat. No one up on top of the Glacier gets fat. No one, not unless you have something wrong with you and you die soon."

Only the rich got fat down in the Empire. That was one way you could tell they were rich: they always had plenty to eat. Hardly any Bizogots grew fat. In the springtime, the Leaping Lynxes had been the exception. So many

ducks and geese and swans and other birds bred at Sudertorp Lake, what the Bizogots took barely dented the abundance.

Now Trasamund's band was reaping the same benefits.
Hamnet could smell duck grease on his own mustache. He
said, "You aren't fat. You're just right." He hoped Marcovefa believed him, because he meant it.

"How do I know that?" she asked.

"Well, if I haven't shown you, I must be older and feebler
than I thought I was," he said. He knew exactly what he
could do. For a man his age, it wasn't bad at all. Of course,
he did get magical help every now and then, too.

"You are only a man. Men will say anything so they can
do that." Marcovefa dismissed half the human race with a
wave of the hand.

Instead of arguing with her, Hamnet changed the subject: "Have you learned anything worthwhile from Tahpenes?"

"Maybe a little," Marcovefa said grudgingly. "Not
much, but a little."

"Like what?" Hamnet asked.

"I have learned I would not want to be a woman among
the Rulers," Marcovefa answered. "They are for screwing,
for birthing warriors, for doing what men tell them to do.
And that is all, poor fools."

To Hamnet Thyssen, that sounded a lot like women's
life among the Bizogots—or, for that matter, down in the
Empire. Women took their revenge with adultery and other
betrayal. He knew more about that than he'd ever wanted to
find out. If he said something along those lines, he would
only make Marcovefa angry. So he asked, "How are things
different up on the Glacier?"

"My folk don't think a woman with a working brain is
poison," Marcovefa answered. "They like clever women,

in fact. If women are shamans, then more men can hunt
and fight. It is so here, too, I have seen."

Slowly, Hamnet nodded. That was true enough. Liv
filled the bill. His mouth tightened, as it often did when he
thought of her. He knew he'd tried too hard to hold on.
Knowing didn't tell him how to stop doing things like
that. He wished it would have.

He couldn't even blame Liv too much, the way he did
with Gudrid. Liv hadn't sneaked around behind his back.
She'd warned him what she was going to do, and then
she'd done it. And if Audun Gilli made her unhappy—or,
more likely, when Audun Gilli made her unhappy—she'd
leave him the same way.

As for Gudrid . . . No, he didn't want to think about her
at all. And so he asked Marcovefa, "It's different with the
Rulers?"

"I should say it is!" Indignation snapped in her eyes.
"To them, a woman is nothing but a twat with legs. That is
how you say it, yes?"

"If that's what you want to say, that's how you say it, all
right," Count Hamnet agreed gravely.

"As long as a woman has the brains to lie down and
open up"—Marcovefa demonstrated lewdly—"that is all
the Rulers want."

That was all quite a few men from this side of the Glacier wanted in a woman, too. "No woman shamans among
them, though?" Hamnet said.

"None," Marcovefa answered. "This Tahpenes chit, she
didn't think it was possible. Even when Liv worked magic
in front of her stupid pointed nose, she still didn't think
it was possible. Some people are so stupid, you wonder
how they stay alive. Some people are so stupid, you wonder
why they stay alive."

Count Hamnet wanted whatever weapons he could find against the Rulers. "Do you think we could stir up trouble between their men and women?" he asked. "Once the women find out we let women do more things here, will they squabble with their menfolk? Will that turn into anything we can use?"

Marcovefa kissed him. "You have a sneaky, wicked way of looking at the world—do you know that?"

"It all depends," Hamnet said. Ulric Skakki thought he was a natural-born innocent. Hamnet feared the adventurer was right. Otherwise, how could he have stayed blind to so many things for so long? But even an innocent by imperial standards might look like a sophisticate to someone who'd come down from the Glacier not long before. "Do you think that might work?"

"It might—no way to know till we try," Marcovefa said. "But how do we even begin?"

"Not hard." Sure enough, Hamnet did feel like a sly sophisticate. He cherished the feeling, knowing it might not come again anytime soon. "Let Tahpenes see how things are here. Maybe even play things up while she's watching. Then let her get away. She takes trouble for the Rulers with her, stuck inside her own head."

"Let her get away?" Marcovefa's eyes widened. "I would never think of that, not in ten thousand years. When you have a captive, you keep a captive. Maybe you fatten up a little, if you can spare the food, but you keep."

Once it formed, the picture of Tahpenes' butchered carcass turning on a spit didn't want to leave Hamnet Thyssen's mind. He remembered the smell of roasting man's flesh. He'd been hungry for it till he realized what it was. To the folk who lived up on the Glacier, people from other clans were, quite literally, fair game.

He scowled at Marcovefa, partly joking, partly not. "You did that on purpose, to make me imagine things I don't want to think about."

"As long as you don't imagine eating Tahpenes while she is still alive." Marcovefa shrugged. "Not much worry there. Not a pretty woman."

"No. Not," Hamnet said, and then, "You make me sound like a man of the Rulers." He did think the invaders' strong, harsh features suited their men better than their women.

"I am sorry," Marcovefa said. "I meant to insult you, but I did not mean to insult you that much."

"Er—right," Count Hamnet said. His more-or-less beloved from atop the Glacier could be—and usually was—devastatingly frank. To keep any more arrows from flying his way, he asked, "How can we let Tahpenes escape without her knowing she isn't doing it all on her own?"

"That is a hard question," Marcovefa answered. "The Rulers are such fools. They think everything is over if you are a captive. The men don't try to get away because they know their own folk won't want them back. Maybe it is different for a woman. We can hope so."

"Yes." Hamnet nodded. "Otherwise, it would be like a dog you couldn't chase away even if you wanted to."

"Dogs." Marcovefa made a face. "What good are they? They help with the herding, but is that enough to be worth the food they eat? You people down here don't eat them unless you are starving. They are nothing but a waste of time."

There were no dogs up on the Glacier. There wasn't enough food up there to support them. There was barely enough to support people. Hamnet Thyssen wondered what Marcovefa thought of pampered lap dogs—dogs that didn't even pretend to earn their keep—down in the Raumsdalian Empire. He also wondered what she made of cats.

But back to dogs . . . "People like them," Hamnet said. "And they like people. Knowing somebody or something likes you—that's worth a lot to a lot of people."

"Maybe. If you can't find people to like you, though, you have to be pretty hard up to care about a stupid dog," Marcovefa said.

"A lot of people *are* pretty hard up," Count Hamnet said. He didn't add that he'd been that way himself. Sometimes dogs were easier to deal with than people. Dogs expected so much less from you. Again, he didn't say anything about cats. Cats didn't particularly like people. They just exploited them. *Parasites with purrs*, he thought.

"Dogs are slaves. They're bred to like people. They have no choice," Marcovefa said, which was true enough. Then she surprised Hamnet by adding, "Cats, now, cats are free. I liked cats when I saw them in your Empire. Cats do what they want, not what you want. I would make a good cat."

Count Hamnet needed no more than a moment to nod. "Yes," he said. "I think you would."

NOT QUITE ARTFULLY enough, Tahpenes contrived to meet Hamnet away from everybody else. "Will you answer some questions?" she asked.

"Maybe," he answered. "It depends on what they are."

"This Bizogot folk, it truly has shamans who are women?" she asked.

"You've seen that. Why do you even need to ask?" he said.

"But I can't believe it's real," Tahpenes said. "The Rulers say only men can work magic."

He shrugged. "What do you expect me to do about that? People can say anything they please. Sometimes it's true. Sometimes it's nonsense."

"We are the Rulers. We do not speak nonsense," Tahpenes said stiffly.

He laughed in her face. "Everybody talks nonsense. Not all the time, but sometimes. Your folk are people, like anybody else. You're full of nonsense, too."

"We are not like anybody else. We are the Rulers. You have seen our might." Tahpenes was full of herself, and full of pride for her folk.

"I've seen that you're a prisoner. I've seen that you have found some things here you didn't know about before. If you don't want to believe them, what does that make you? Besides a fool, I mean."

She glared at him. Then she wiped the glare off her face and gave him a smile instead. That made him sure what game she was playing. "I don't want to be a prisoner any more," she said, softening and sweetening her voice as much as she could.

"Your other choice was getting killed, probably after some unpleasant preliminaries," Hamnet reminded her. "Don't you think this is better?"

"Going back to my own folk—that would be better," Tahpenes said. "I would do almost anything for help to get back to my own folk." She looked at him from under lowered eyelids.

She was about as seductive as a dire wolf. She would only have got angry if he told her so; realizing as much persuaded him not to bother. "I have a woman I'm happy with," he said, and let it go at that.

"One of those yellow-haired sluts," she said scornfully. "They aren't much—skinny, whey-faced . . ."

"Don't let Marcovefa hear you say that. She'll turn you into a vole," Hamnet said.

"She is strong," Tahpenes admitted. "Wizards from the

herd are not supposed to be strong. How does she get that way?"

By living on top of the Glacier with nothing, Hamnet thought. He didn't intend to explain to Tahpenes.

"Will you help me get away?" Tahpenes persisted. "All I have to give you is myself. I will do that, and gladly."

Count Hamnet found himself in a strange position. He wanted Tahpenes to escape, but he didn't want her. And he had—and had earned—a horror of infidelity. He also had a suspicion he thought well-founded that telling a woman he didn't want her was an insult that would have called for seconds had its like passed between two men. And so, as sternly as he could, he said, "I didn't capture you just to let you get away again."

She bit her lip. "I thought you were a kind man. You could have killed me. The way we look at things, you should have killed me."

"Taking prisoners when we can is our custom," Hamnet said.

"A foolish custom," Tahpenes said. Count Hamnet wondered what she would have thought if she knew Marcovefa felt the same way. Or maybe she did know. Marcovefa wouldn't hold back about something like that. She would use it for a weapon, to make a captive afraid and to make her talk.

"Foolish or not, it's what we do," Hamnet said. "And I'm afraid you picked the wrong man."

"Well, I wasn't going to ask that Ulric Skakki," the woman from the Rulers said tartly. "I could suck him till the inside of my cheeks turned to leather, and he'd still break every promise he made me. If you made one, I think you would keep it."

"Maybe I would, but I'm not making any." Hamnet

Thyssen couldn't resist asking, "Does Ulric know what you think of him?"

"If he doesn't, it's not because I haven't told him," Tahpenes answered.

"What did he do?"

"He laughed and said, 'You say the sweetest things, darling.' He's a rogue. He's proud he's a rogue." Tahpenes sighed. "And the honest man is too honest. And the Bizogots . . . They *would* screw me and then cut my throat so I couldn't tell any stories about them." She shuddered.

"Then you might as well get used to being a captive," Hamnet said.

"It is a disgrace. Even for a woman, it is a disgrace," Tahpenes said. "Lying down with a man from the herd is as nothing beside it."

"Nice to know what you think of me," Hamnet remarked.

"Not just you. Any of your folk. Any of these blond Bizogots, too," she replied.

Nothing personal, he thought. *Oh, good. Does that make it better or worse?* He couldn't decide. The truth was, the only thing she wanted was to get away from here, and she'd do anything she needed to do—anything at all—to get what she wanted.

She eyed him. "Will you tell the others now? Tell them I want to go back to my own folk?"

"Do you think I need to? Do you think they don't already know?" Easier to parry questions with more questions.

"Who can guess what folk of the herd know or don't know?" Tahpenes said. "Maybe they think I am docile, the way they are."

Hamnet Thyssen burst out laughing. He couldn't help himself. He didn't remember the last time he'd been so surprised or heard anything so funny. "Bizogots docile?" he said. "Tell that to Trasamund, by God! You'll leave here, all right, but you won't be able to tell your people what you found out."

Tahpenes frowned. "I don't understand. What are you talking about?"

"He'll kill you for the insult, that's what," Hamnet answered. "And I will tell you how docile Trasamund is. He beat one of your men, a fellow named Parsh, at Bizogot stand-down on the other side of the Glacier a couple of years ago."

"What kind of stupid sport is that?" Tahpenes asked.

"Two men stand face-to-face. They take turns hitting each other till one of them can't stand up and swing any more. He knocked Parsh cold. When Parsh woke up—it took a while—he cut his own throat." Count Hamnet grimaced. He didn't like that memory.

"He would. The disgrace of losing to someone not of the Rulers . . ." Tahpenes nodded to herself. What Parsh did made sense to her, even if it didn't to Hamnet. The woman from Parsh's folk went on in thoughtful tones: "Bizogot stand-down, you say? No, that does not seem docile."

"Trasamund uses his hands to tell the weather these days. He broke both of them punching Parsh, and they pain him when a storm is coming," Hamnet said.

"My brother broke his arm when he was a boy. He can do that," Tahpenes said.

"You have a brother?" Hamnet didn't know why he hadn't thought of her as coming from a family. Maybe because the Rulers seemed too perfectly military for such mundane things as families. They might have been stamped from molds.

They might have been, but they weren't. Tahpenes nodded. "I have two brothers, and also a sister," she said. "They will wonder what has happened to me."

"Plenty of Bizogots and Raumsdalians wonder what's happened to their kin, too," Hamnet Thyssen said.

Tahpenes only gaped at him. He'd looked for sympathy from her—he'd looked, but he hadn't found it. She didn't care. The Rulers didn't care. To them, other people weren't human beings. It was as simple as that. Count Hamnet didn't know what anybody could do about it. The only thing that occurred to him was getting rid of all the Rulers.

Which sounded easy enough, till you set about doing it.

Dejectedly, Tahpenes turned away from him. "I will go back to the encampment now," she said.

"I'd better come with you," Hamnet said. "Just in case you might happen to wander in some other direction instead. By accident, of course."

"Of course," she said, as demurely as she could. She recognized a joke, even if a man from the herd made it.

She limped only a little. "Your wounds are healing well," Hamnet said.

"Well enough," Tahpenes agreed. "The worst wound now is in my spirit because I am a captive."

Count Hamnet almost told her about the wounds the Rulers had given the Bizogots and the Empire. Then he decided he might as well save his breath. She wouldn't understand what he was talking about. As far as she was concerned, the folk on this side of the Glacier deserved what happened to them because they presumed to stand against the Rulers.

Audun Gilli took charge of Tahpenes when she got back to the almost-town the Leaping Lynxes had built. The Raumsdalian wizard spoke much less of the Bizogots' tongue than he should have; Tahpenes was probably more fluent. But Hamnet didn't think she could get away from him . . . unless he let her, that is.

"Did you have fun with the little charmer we caught?" Ulric asked.

"She isn't little, and she isn't charming. Other than that, well, no." Hamnet paused, then added, "She has a low opinion of you."

"Only proves she's a keen judge of character," Ulric said blithely, which left Hamnet nowhere to go. Then the adventurer gave him somewhere, because he asked, "And how did she express her distaste?"

Hamnet told him.

Ulric Skakki threw back his head and laughed. "Yes, I've heard that from her. She'd be right, too, if my taste in women were bad enough to include her. By God, Thyssen, even *your* taste in women isn't that bad."

"Leave my taste in women out of this," Hamnet growled.

"Oh, I see." Ulric favored him with a mocking bow. "You get to insult me however you choose, but I don't have the right to return the disfavor. Yes, that's a fair bargain all the way around."

"You asked me what Tahpenes told me about you," Hamnet said. "I only repeated it. If I want to know what you think about me, I promise I'll ask. Till then, I'm not interested."

"You only repeated it." Ulric Skakki did some repeating himself. He also did some more laughing. "You didn't *enjoy* repeating it or anything? Oh, no. Not you. You're too good and pure and righteous for that."

Count Hamnet's ears heated. "You make a sport of twisting other people's words, don't you?"

"Why not? It's the most fun you can have with your clothes on," Ulric answered. "But I don't need to do any twisting here. Don't worry, though—I love you, too." He gave Hamnet a noisy, smacking kiss on the cheek.

Hamnet shoved him away. "You've done that before. I didn't like it then, and I cursed well still don't."

"I see. And you think I did enjoy it when you twitted me. You have an odd way of looking at the world sometimes, Your Grace." Ulric Skakki followed up the mocking title with a mocking bow.

"I ought to—" Count Hamnet cocked his fist, but he didn't swing. Unfortunate, surprising, and painful things happened to people who swung at Ulric. And, still more unfortunately, surprisingly, and painfully, the outlander had a point. The fist opened. "I ought to apologize, I suppose. And so I do: your pardon, I beg." Hamnet bowed stiffly.

Ulric stared. "Be careful, Your Grace. If you don't watch yourself, you'll take all the fun out of life."

V

Hamnet Thyssen had begun to wonder if he would ever see another Raumsdalian besides Ulric Skakki. The man who rode into the Leaping Lynxes' village looked hungry and weary and scared almost to death. The Bizogots gave him a roast duck and a skin of smetyn, after which he perked up remarkably.

He nodded to Hamnet. "You're Thyssen?"

"I am Count Hamnet Thyssen, yes," Hamnet said. Ulric snickered off to one side. Hamnet didn't care. In dealing with the Empire, his dignity was about all he had to fall back on.

"Sorry . . . Your Grace," the Raumsdalian said. "I am Gunnlaug Kvaran, a messenger from His Majesty, Sigvat II. I am the fourth man he sent out. Did any of the others reach you?"

"Not a one," Count Hamnet replied. Gunnlaug muttered something his beard muffled. Hamnet asked the question he was no doubt intended to: "And how are things in the Empire these days? They must be pretty bad if Sigvat wants to talk to the likes of me."

Gunnlaug Kvaran nodded grimly. "Things couldn't be much worse. Those cursed Rulers are demons in human shape. They—" Instead of snickering, Ulric Skakki burst into loud, raucous laughter. Gunnlaug sent him a reproachful look. "You scorn our troubles? You must be Skakki."

"I not only must be, I am," Ulric answered. "And I don't scorn your troubles. I scorn God-cursed Sigvat, and I scorn Count Hamnet and me, too. We tried to tell you what kind of trouble was heading your way, and the thanks he got was . . . an inside view of the dungeons under the imperial palace. Hamnet loves Raumsdalia in spite of everything, but Hamnet owns a castle and he's a sentimental fool besides. Me, I was just glad to get away."

A sentimental fool? Hamnet Thyssen had thought of himself as a lot of different things, but that was a new one. Gunnlaug said, "Well, you were right, if it makes you feel any better."

"Not much," Ulric said. Hamnet nodded—he felt the same way. Ulric went on, "If Sigvat told us the same thing—"

"It still wouldn't make much difference, not any more," Count Hamnet broke in. Ulric looked surprised, but now he nodded.

"Then what are you people doing up here?" Gunnlaug Kvaran asked.

"Fighting the Rulers, by God!" Trasamund boomed. "What else is there that's even half as much worth doing?"

"I don't understand," Gunnlaug said.

"You're Sigvat's man, all right," Ulric said. "He doesn't understand, either."

"We're fighting them because *we* want to," Count Hamnet added, "not because the Raumsdalian Emperor wants us to."

Ulric shook his head. "No. That's not strong enough. We're fighting them *even though* Sigvat wants us to."

"True," Hamnet said, which made Gunnlaug Kvaran looked unhappier yet. Count Hamnet hadn't thought he could.

Trasamund didn't loathe Sigvat quite so much as Hamnet and Ulric did—but then, the Bizogot jarl hadn't passed any time in the Emperor's dungeons. Rough sympathy in his voice, he said, "Well, you managed to get here, Kvaran, where none of the other poor sorry southern bastards did. So tell us what's going on down there."

"Nothing good," Gunnlaug answered. "We still hold Nidaros, or we did when I set out, anyway. But the Rulers are plundering just about everything north of there. Their soldiers fight as if they don't fear death—"

"They mostly don't," Hamnet said. "They fear losing more. Death happens. Losing is a disgrace."

"If you say so," Sigvat's messenger said bleakly. "I wasn't finished, though. They have wizards the likes of which we've never seen the likes of."

Ulric snickered again. Hamnet Thyssen forgave Gunnlaug his fractured syntax. "We tried to tell you," he said once more.

"Well, you were right. There. I said it again. Does it make you happy? His Majesty *does* say the same thing. Does *that* make you happy?"

"Kicking Sigvat in his iron arse might make me happy—or not so unhappy, anyway," Count Hamnet replied.

"You'd only give him a concussion of the brain." Ulric Skakki sounded bright and pleasant, eager to be useful.

"Will you help us? Can you help us? I'm supposed to take your answer back to Nidaros," Gunnlaug said.

"So you get to run the gauntlet twice? God help you,"

Hamnet said. "And I might have known Sigvat would want us to help him. He doesn't care a fart's worth what happens up here."

"It's not Raumsdalia," Ulric said. "Why should he?"

"You still haven't answered my question," said the messenger from the Empire. "Can you help us? Will you? What word do I take back to His Majesty?"

"He has the whole Empire," Hamnet Thyssen said. "We have one wizard from Raumsdalia, a few shamans, and some Bizogots." One of the shamans was Marcovefa, but he didn't mention that. He went on, "What are we supposed to be able to do that Sigvat can't? Why are we supposed to be able to do it?"

"You are supposed to be able to beat the Rulers, Your Grace," Gunnlaug told him. "I don't know why, and His Majesty doesn't know why, either. But for whatever reason, you worry them. They want you. They want you enough to put a fat price on your head, alive or not."

Count Hamnet had heard that before. He'd heard it often enough by now that he had to believe it—which was not to say it made any sense to him. "Even the Rulers can be stupid sometimes," he growled.

"And so can Sigvat, God knows," Ulric Skakki added. "We have our worries, and he has his. Some of them are the same—some, yes, but not all."

"You want to beat the Rulers, too, don't you?" Gunnlaug Kvaran sounded anxious. And well he might, for he continued, "You wouldn't . . . go in with them . . . would you?"

Trasamund answered that before either Hamnet or Ulric could: "No! We aim to boot them off the Bizogot plain! We aim to beat them back beyond the Gap! We aim to kill them all, if we can! You can tell your precious Sigvat that. You can tell him he cursed well should have listened to Count Hamnet here, too. In fact, you'd better tell him that—you hear me, Kvaran?"

"I hear you, Your Ferocity," Gunnlaug said, without promising he would take the jarl's words back to the Raumsdalian Emperor. Hamnet wondered how much it would matter. Even if Sigvat still held Nidaros, could his messenger get through the Rulers again? What were the odds? Bad, Hamnet was sure.

"Sigvat has heard me, too, by God," Trasamund said. "If not for me, Count Hamnet and Ulric never would have fared north. They never would have gone beyond the Gap. They never would have seen the marvels on the far side."

"We never would have bumped into the Rulers, either," Ulric said. "We have a lot to blame you for, Trasamund."

Trasamund bared his teeth in what might have been a friendly smile or might have been something else altogether. Gunnlaug Kvaran wore the expression of an outsider at a family squabble. Hamnet suspected Ulric Skakki was shading the truth. Even had Sigvat sent other Raumsdalians beyond the Gap, the Rulers would still have broken in. In that case, the noble and the adventurer would have been fighting them down in the Empire instead of up here. Would that have been better, worse, or just different? No way to know.

Gunnlaug Kvaran bowed to him and to Trasamund. "I go to take your reply to His Majesty," he said.

"Not right this minute, you bloody idiot!" Ulric burst out. "Stay a while. Rest. Eat some more. Let your horse rest, too. You still have to make it back across the plains before you even try sneaking through to Nidaros."

That was such obvious good sense, not even Gunnlaug argued against it very hard. Plainly a duteous man, the messenger had to see that duty also involved keeping himself and his horse fit. A couple of Bizogots carrying fat geese back from the marshes at the edge of Sudertorp Lake didn't hurt in changing his mind, either.

He was gnawing on a roasted duck leg when he saw Tahpenes and recognized her for what she was. He almost dropped the leg in his lap. "What's she doing here?" he demanded.

"The laundry, a little cooking . . . she sweeps the floors of our huts, too," Ulric answered. "If you want your horse curried, I daresay she could attend to that."

Gunnlaug scowled. "You are not a serious man, Skakki. His Majesty warned me about you, and I see he was right."

"Thank you," Ulric replied, which left the messenger without much of a reply. The adventurer often had that effect on people, as Count Hamnet had found to his own discomfiture.

Tahpenes also eyed Gunnlaug with a certain amount of surprise. What was going through her mind? How much did she care that one set of her folk's enemies had managed to link up with the other? Did she wonder if the Raumsdalian newcomer was an avenue to escape?

One thing she didn't seem to realize was that her captors wanted her to get away. They couldn't make that obvious without making her wonder why. One day soon, though, she probably would contrive to escape. Count Hamnet hoped so, anyhow. Then everyone here could relax.

Hamnet spoke to Trasamund about that. The jarl heard him out, then grinned and laid a finger by the side of his nose. "It might work," he said. "Has a halfway decent chance, anyhow, which is more than I can say for some other notions that have come up."

They feted Gunnlaug Kvaran. They gave him a fresh horse. Hamnet and Ulric and Trasamund and even Audun Gilli gave him encouraging messages to take back to Sigvat II. *Why not?* Count Hamnet thought cynically. *Talk is cheap.*

Gunnlaug proved less eager to leave after tasting Bizogot hospitality. Hamnet Thyssen didn't know if one of the big blond women with the band took him into a hut and gave him something to remember her by, but he wouldn't have been surprised. The mammoth-herders were an earthy folk, and took—and gave—their pleasures as they saw the chance.

Almost all of them turned out to say farewell to Gunnlaug when he finally did ride off to the south once more. Men clasped his hand and clapped him on the back. Women hugged him and kissed him and wished him well. A little wistfully, Ulric Skakki said, "The only times I ever got fancy sendoffs were when lots of nasty people were chasing me. Gunnlaug doesn't know how lucky he is."

"He's getting a fancy sendoff for a reason, too," Hamnet replied. "If we're all here telling him what a fine fellow he is—"

"Yes, I know," Ulric broke in. "If we're all making much of Kvaran, we've got an excuse for not paying attention to Tahpenes. Now we see if she's smart enough to figure that out, too."

Gunnlaug Kvaran rode away. Some of the Bizogots trotted after him for as far as half a mile. As far as Count Hamnet was concerned, if they wanted to work that hard, it was up to them. He just watched the Raumsdalian messenger get smaller and smaller in the distance.

When he went to look for Tahpenes after the farewells, she was nowhere to be found. He went and told Trasamund. The jarl told the Bizogots. The mammoth-herders made a great show of beating the bushes for their escaped captive. Everyone was *so* disappointed when they didn't catch her.

"MAY I TALK to you, Your Grace?" Audun Gilli asked.

"You're doing it," Count Hamnet answered gruffly. "Go ahead."

"Er—right." The wizard was hangdog and slapdash at the best of times. Since Liv had gone to him from Hamnet Thyssen, this wasn't the best of times. But he forged ahead: "I don't want you to be my enemy."

"I'm not," Hamnet said, which was . . . partly true, anyhow. He went on, "If you expect me to be your friend, you ask for too much, though."

"I suppose so," Audun said. "But I would like to be able to put my head together with yours without worry about its getting bitten off."

"Would you?" Hamnet Thyssen said. Audun Gilli gave back an eager nod. Hamnet shrugged. "People want all kinds of things they aren't likely to get."

"Do you, uh, still want Liv back?" the Raumsdalian wizard asked.

That question was more interesting than Hamnet wished it were. He was contented enough with Marcovefa. She had her quirks, but she was bound to think he had quirks of his own. And even if he was contented with her, that didn't mean he didn't want Liv back. It didn't mean he didn't want Gudrid back, either, and she was hundreds of miles away, married to Eyvind Torfinn, and despised him to boot. Losing a woman meant something was wrong with you. So it seemed to Count Hamnet, at any rate.

He knew his answer was evasive: "If she doesn't want me back—and she doesn't—what difference does it make?"

"It makes a difference." Audun spoke with doleful conviction. "I didn't expect this to happen, you know."

"I'm willing to believe you." Count Hamnet wished he'd turned his back and walked away when the wizard started talking to him.

Then the hilt of his sword and the hilt of the dagger next to it on his belt started chattering to each other. "He says he believes us." The dagger hilt's voice was a high, squeaky version of Audun Gilli's.

"He says all kinds of things. What do I care?" The sword hilt sounded a little like the way Hamnet had before his voice broke.

He didn't think he was losing his mind. Audun Gilli had a gift for endowing inanimate objects with sarcastic personalities. It was a small magic, but one that sometimes had its uses. "Well, if he says he believes us, why doesn't he sound like he believes us?" the dagger hilt asked peevishly.

If Hamnet looked down, he suspected he would see his face on the sword hilt, Audun's on the dagger. He didn't look down. The shrill voice that sounded like his said, "He's not that good a liar, I guess."

Hamnet Thyssen snorted. He tried to hold it in, but he couldn't. Then he tried not to laugh out loud, and found he couldn't do that, either. "Tell my cutlery to shut up, will you, please?" he said to Audun Gilli.

"He wants us to shut up!" The voice that sounded like Audun's sounded properly indignant.

"He's got his nerve, he does!" said the voice that sounded like Hamnet himself. "If he thinks *I'm* going to shut up, he's—" It cut off.

"Right," Audun Gilli finished for it.

"You have an interesting way of making your points sometimes," Count Hamnet said.

The wizard's narrow shoulders went up and down in a shrug. "People who wouldn't pay attention to me on a bet start listening when their tools do the talking. I'm not your enemy, Your Grace. I don't want to be your enemy. We already have the same enemy. All this other business was getting in the way of that."

After a considerable pause, Hamnet said, "You shame me."

"I don't want to do that, either," Audun answered. "You don't have to love me—you're not going to love me, and who could blame you? But for God's sake will you stop treating me like I'm not there?" Hamnet hit him, not quite hard enough to knock him down. "What was that for?" the wizard squawked.

"Well, you can't say I was treating you like you weren't there," Hamnet answered stolidly.

"No, I can't—and I bloody well wish I could," Audun said.

"Hrmp." Now Count Hamnet seemed affronted. "First you want it one way, then you want it the other."

"I wanted you to talk to me, not punch me!"

"What should I say to you after you took my woman away? A lot of people talk with their fists after something like that."

Audun Gilli sighed. "Your Grace, I didn't take Liv away from you. Nobody can do anything like that with her. If you don't know I'm telling the truth, you never knew her at all. She decided she didn't want to stay with you. After that"—he kicked at the dirt—"she took me, not the other way round."

He hadn't tried not to get taken—Hamnet Thyssen was sure of that. What man in his right mind *would* try not to get taken if a woman like Liv decided she wanted him? The wizard wasn't wrong. The wizard was much too poignantly right.

"You aren't talking again," Audun pointed out.

"Afraid not," Count Hamnet agreed. "Trying to count all the different ways I'm a jackass. There are a lot of them."

"Welcome to humanity, Your Grace," Audun said. "I often wonder why God bothered with us in the first place."

"Maybe we'll know if we ever find the Golden Shrine." Hamnet looked out across Sudertorp Lake, as if he expected the legendary temple to rise from its waters. Whether he expected it or not, he didn't get it.

"You don't ask for much, do you?" the wizard exclaimed. "We went to the ends of the earth—by God, we went past the ends of the earth—and we never saw a trace or heard a rumor. The Rulers don't seem to know anything about it."

"Maybe that means it's on this side of the Glacier after all." Count Hamnet shrugged. "Or maybe it means the Shrine was never anything but a pipe dream. I don't know. I don't think anyone else does, either—if I had to guess, I'd say nobody ever will."

"If I had to guess, I'd say you were right," Audun replied. "We'll find out—or, more likely, we won't."

Hamnet Thyssen nodded. "I imagine men a thousand years from now will still go chasing the Golden Shrine. By then, this will all be forest, and only fragments will be left of the Glacier." He glanced over to Audun Gilli. "There. I'm talking to you, by God. Are you happier?"

"Yes, Your Grace. Are you?"

"Mm—maybe. Yes, I suppose I am." Hamnet gnawed at the inside of his lower lip. "If you like, you can tell Liv I'm sorry."

"You can do that yourself, too," Audun said.

"I'd rather you did. I might . . . say some other things

besides, and chances are that wouldn't help. Besides, something like that, it won't matter if it comes from me or from you. Not now it won't."

"No, not now," Audun said. "Earlier . . . Well, no wizard's ever found a spell to let you fix now what you made a hash of back then. Probably just as well. Things would get knotted up worse than a musk-ox-wool cape knitted by somebody who never learned to knit."

"Can't quarrel with you there. And people would make mistakes 'fixing' mistakes. . . . What a mess!" Hamnet said.

"Life is complicated enough. Too complicated, sometimes," Audun Gilli said.

"Can't quarrel with you there, either." Count Hamnet turned away. He supposed he could deal with the Raumsdalian wizard. He even thought he might be able to talk to Liv again one of these days, though he didn't want to do it any time soon. Showing enthusiasm for either prospect was more than he had in him.

"You know what you look like?" Ulric Skakki asked as he and Hamnet rode across the steppe with a band of Bizogots out searching for the Rulers.

"No. What?" Hamnet asked, as he was surely meant to do.

"You look like somebody who wants to kill something."

"Oh." Count Hamnet looked around. His eye carefully didn't light on Audun Gilli, who was along to help if the Rulers they ran into had a wizard along. "Is that all?"

"Isn't that enough?" Ulric didn't look Audun's way, either. Maybe he was too polite—anything was possible—or maybe he really didn't know what was making Hamnet's stomach hurt. Either way, he went on, "If you go out there looking to slaughter the first thing you see, sometimes you don't worry about staying alive while you're bashing and smashing."

"Don't worry about me," Hamnet said. "I'll be fine."

"Right." Ulric plainly didn't believe him. Since Hamnet knew he was lying, he didn't try to insist.

One of the Bizogots pointed east. "Look at the teratorns circling over there. Lots of them—something big is dead," he said. "Maybe we should find out what."

No one said no. If something big was dead, or if more smaller somethings were, very likely it or they had got killed. And if things had got killed, there was a good chance the Rulers had killed them.

Hamnet Thyssen steered his horse with knees and reins. He did watch Audun Gilli as they all rode toward the carrion birds. The wizard seemed rather birdlike himself, the way he flapped his arms every time the horse strode. Audun would never make a picture rider; any equestrian trainer down at Nidaros would have screamed his head off at such bad form. But nobody on the frozen steppe cared about style. Audun got the job done, and that was all that mattered.

They took longer to get to the teratorns' feast than Count Hamnet had thought they would. Teratorns were so big— big enough to dwarf even condors, let along lesser vultures— that they tricked the eye into thinking they flew closer than they really did.

When they did see why the teratorns were spiraling down out of the sky, they discovered it had nothing—nothing obvious, at least—to do with the Rulers. A mammoth had fallen over and died. Teratorns and smaller scavengers stalked around that mountain of meat. Even on the ground, the teratorns stood out, and not only for their size: their bare-skinned heads were wattled and hideously gaudy.

They let out loud, indignant croaks now, because they

couldn't get at the food they craved. Lions and dire wolves were stuffing themselves with mammoth meat. Whenever a teratorn tried to rush up and steal some, the beasts that could also kill snarled threats. The great birds retreated.

Every so often, one of them would leap into the air. Foxes prowled around the dead mammoth, too. They also wanted their share of the scraps—or a vulture would do, if they couldn't get anything else.

"Well, this was a waste of time," Hamnet Thyssen said.

"How right you are," Ulric agreed readily. "We could have written epic poetry or gone to a fine eatery or played a couple of games of draughts while we rode across the steppe if it weren't for those miserable teratorns."

Hamnet's ears heated. "You know what I mean. We didn't accomplish anything coming here."

"Right again!" Ulric Skakki sounded more enthusiastic than ever, always a bad sign. "If not for this dead mammoth, we could've chased the Rulers back beyond the Gap by now."

"You're making yourself annoying on purpose," Hamnet said.

"That's better than doing it by accident, wouldn't you say?" the adventurer returned. "At least I know what I'm up to."

Audun Gilli pointed north across the frozen steppe. "Someone else is heading this way. Maybe we weren't the only ones to wonder what was dead here and how it got that way."

"This way, that way, any way at all," Ulric Skakki said. "When somebody writes the history of this war nobody will ever write, he can call this fight the Battle of the Dead Mammoth."

"Somebody writes the history nobody will . . ." Count Hamnet gave it up as a bad job. He looked to his weapons instead. With them, he had a better notion of what he was doing.

"Have they got a wizard with them?" Trasamund asked Audun, reaching over his shoulder to draw his two-handed sword.

That, Hamnet realized, was an important question— maybe *the* important question. If the Rulers had no wizard along, then Audun Gilli gave the Bizogots the edge. But if the Rulers did . . . If they did, Audun was liable to be in over his head. Marcovefa might scoff at the sorcery the men from beyond the Gap used, but it was stronger than Bizogot shamans or Raumsdalian wizards could match.

Count Hamnet imagined himself riding back to the Leaping Lynxes' huts and telling Liv Audun had died valiantly fighting the Rulers. He wouldn't sound as if he was gloating. He'd give Audun all the credit he deserved, and more besides. And Liv would dissolve in tears, and he would hold her and try to console her. . . .

He laughed sourly, realizing what an idiot he was. For one thing, Liv would be furious if Audun died while he survived. For another, if the Rulers slew Audun they were much too likely to slay him, too.

"Well, we found them," Ulric Skakki said, methodically examining his arrows. "Not quite the way we expect to, but we found them. And now we get to see how sorry we end up that we did."

"I thank you." Hamnet bowed in the saddle. "Whenever I think things are bad, you always remind me they're really worse."

Courteous as a cat, Ulric returned the bow. "Nice to know I'm of some use to you anyhow, Your Grace."

"Let's ride!" Trasamund bellowed. Hamnet Thyssen wasn't sorry to follow him. He wasn't just riding away from the dead mammoth and the scavengers clustered around it. He was riding away from his own imagination . . . and getting away from it might be the best thing he could do.

The Rulers might have been drawn by the teratorns gliding down to try to steal mammoth flesh, but they didn't need long to realize they weren't the only ones who had been. They shook themselves out into a battle line. Some of them were on their riding deer, others on horses they must have seized since coming into the Bizogot country. They didn't have any live war mammoths with them. That by itself raised Hamnet's spirits, and probably those of everyone else in the war band.

Audun Gilli gasped. "They—have a wizard!" he choked out.

"Hold him off," Hamnet said urgently. "We'll see if we can kill him."

He glanced over to Ulric, who nodded. They'd done this before, or tried to. Killing enemy wizards was the best way to make sure they couldn't use their spells against you. The best way if you could do it, that is.

Surveying the Rulers' line, he had no trouble picking out the wizard. As usual, he was the one who hung back behind his comrades. Maybe that was cowardice. It was bound to be good sense. Killing the wizard hurt the enemy much more than killing one of their warriors would have.

As archers on both sides started to shoot, Ulric asked, "Are you game?"

"Not especially, but I don't think we've got much choice. Do you?" Hamnet said.

"No. I only wish I did. Well . . ."

The adventurer spurred his horse forward at a gallop, spurting out ahead of the Bizogots' line. Hamnet Thyssen went with him. As his horse thundered toward the Rulers, he tried not to think about what a tempting target he made.

"Three Tusks! The Three Tusk clan!" Trasamund roared, and he joined the charge, too. Hamnet had no idea whether the jarl intended to go after the wizard, too, or whether he just wanted to close with the hated Rulers as fast as he could.

Wherever the truth lay, Trasamund distracted the foe from Hamnet and Ulric. Trasamund could distract anybody from anything. Count Hamnet had thought the Bizogot was larger than life ever since he first met him two years earlier in Sigvat's palace down in Nidaros. Two years! Was that all? Hamnet Thyssen had to think about it, but he nodded a moment later. It seemed much longer.

An arrow thrummed past his head. A moment later, so did another one, even closer. He stopped worrying about how long it had been since he met Trasamund. Worrying about how long he'd keep breathing was more urgent.

A Ruler on horseback swung to try to block his path. Hamnet cut at the swarthy, curly-bearded man. Their swords belled off each other. Sparks flew as iron grated against iron. Then Count Hamnet was past. His foe looked comically surprised. The Ruler must have thought Hamnet was after him in particular.

Well, fellow, you're not as important as you think you are, Hamnet thought. *That probably hurts worse than a sword cut would have.*

There was the wizard, astride a riding deer—no newfangled mounts for him. For the moment, he seemed to have no idea Hamnet was closing in on him. His attention was aimed at the Bizogots' line, and likely at Audun Gilli.

Then Ulric Skakki shot an arrow into the riding deer's flank. No doubt he'd aimed for the wizard. But archery from horseback was a tricky business. The riding deer didn't shriek the way a wounded horse might have. But it did jerk and jump and buck like a wounded horse. And the wizard, who'd expected no such thing, went off the deer and onto the dirt with a thump.

The deer bounded away. The wizard scrambled to his feet—which might have been a mistake, because it made him an easier target for Hamnet Thyssen's sword. The sharp edge glittered in the sun as Hamnet swung the blade. It bit into the wizard's neck with a noise straight from a butcher's shop. The impact almost tore the sword from his hand.

Blood sprayed, then fountained. The wizard let out a bubbling scream. Hamnet urged his horse into as tight a turn as it could make, in case he needed to strike again. He saw at once that he didn't. He had no idea how the wizard stayed on his feet with blood gushing from him that way.

Stand the wizard did. The Rulers, say what you would of them, seemed as hard to kill as serpents. The man's eyes speared Hamnet. His lips shaped a word. Hamnet had learned only tiny fragments of the Rulers' language, but he thought he knew what that word was.

You.

To his horror and dismay, the wizard's hands came up. He started to shape a pass. Then Ulric Skakki galloped past and struck with the sword from behind. The wizard's head leaped from his shoulders. Body convulsing, he toppled and finally died.

"Tough bugger," Ulric remarked. "I thought the one you landed would be plenty to do for him."

"So did I," Count Hamnet answered. "Well, he's gone now."

"He looked like he was still trying to cast a spell on you, even with his head already half gone," Ulric said.

"He did, didn't he?" Hamnet said uneasily. *You.* He'd heard that and things like it too often from the Rulers. For some reason, they worried about him. He wished he knew

why. There were plenty of days when he felt more dangerous to himself than to the invaders from beyond the Gap.

"Must be nice to have them love you like that," Ulric
said.

"I could live without it." Count Hamnet's voice was dry.

The adventurer chuckled. "Probably quite a bit longer
than with it. Which reminds me—how long are we going
to live if the bastards turn on us?"

Not long, was the first thing that occurred to Hamnet.
But the Rulers had no chance to do it. They were fighting
for their lives, outnumbered by the hard-pressing Bizogots,
and suddenly without sorcerous support. And Audun Gilli
took advantage of that. The Rulers suddenly started staring at their swords and bows. The weapons must have
started talking to them—the same spell Audun had used
again and again, but never before, so far as Hamnet knew,
on the battlefield.

Audun didn't speak the Rulers' language. He still had
trouble with the Bizogots' tongue. But a sword that suddenly started spouting Raumsdalian might have proved
even more alarming. For all the Rulers knew, their blades
were cursing them. If Audun Gilli had any sense—never a
sure bet—the swords were doing exactly that.

Hamnet looked for Trasamund. The jarl of the Three
Tusk clan was trading lusty sword strokes with an enemy
warrior. Trasamund fought for the fun of it, as a lot of
Bizogots did: a taste that had always struck Hamnet as
perverse.

He roared in triumph when one of his great strokes got
home. Maybe the Ruler's boiled-leather corselet kept the
edge from his vitals. Whether it did or not, though, that blow
had to break ribs. The invader reeled on his riding deer.
Trasamund's next hack, undefended, sheared away half his
face.

Maybe that broke the Rulers. Maybe they would have decided they'd had enough about then anyhow. They broke off the fight and fled back toward the north. The riding deer had shorter legs than horses, but still fled fast enough to let a good many Rulers on them get away.

"We beat 'em, by God!" Trasamund boomed.

"So we did," Hamnet agreed.

"Yes, so we did. The Battle of the Dead Mammoth—huzzah!" Ulric Skakki said. "And if we win another hundred victories just this big, they may start to notice us."

"Scoffer!" Trasamund said.

Ulric graciously inclined his head. "At your service, Your Ferocity." Hamnet Thyssen wondered if Trasamund would explode. But he didn't, not after a winning fight. He threw back his head and laughed instead.

VI

After the Bizogots returned in triumph to the Leaping Lynxes' village, Hamnet Thyssen took Trasamund aside and said, "This can't go on much longer."

"What? Why not, by God?" The jarl had a skin of smetyn clenched in his big fist instead of a sword hilt, but he hadn't started drinking yet. "We'll drive the stinking buggers mad."

"That's why," Hamnet answered. "They won't let us get away with it much longer. Either they'll bring more men down from beyond the Gap—"

"If they've got 'em—" Trasamund broke in.

"If they have them," Count Hamnet agreed. No one on this side of the Glacier knew how many Rulers there were or how wide a territory they ruled. *Too cursed many* and *too wide* were the only sure answers. But Hamnet went on, "If they don't, they'll bring their army up from the Empire to deal with us—or a good piece of it, anyhow. And don't you think a good piece of that army could do the job?"

Trasamund scowled. "Not if Marcovefa's magic puts the flyblown fornicators to rout, the way it's supposed to."

"There's only one of her," Hamnet reminded him. "I hope she can deal with their wizards. I don't know if she can deal with all of them, but I hope so. If you think she can deal with the wizards and the warriors, you may be asking too much."

"Then *we* deal with them." Trasamund thumped his own chest. "We! The Bizogots! The hero-folk!" He broke into rolling verse.

Hamnet Thyssen wanted to bash him in the head with a rock and let in some sense. Unfortunately, he didn't see any suitable bashers close by. "Stop that!" he said when Trasamund showed no sign of letting up. "We don't have that many Bizogots here—not enough to beat a real army."

Instead of answering, Trasamund pulled the stopper from the skin, raised it to his mouth, and drank a long draught. "Ahh!" he said, smacking his lips, when he finally came up for air. "I needed that."

"Why won't you worry about what's going to happen, curse it?" Count Hamnet demanded.

"I can't make more Bizogots," Trasamund said reasonably. "Well, I can, but no matter how willing the women are, the brats need twenty years before they're worth anything in a brawl, and we don't have that long." Hamnet snorted. Ignoring him, the jarl of the Three Tusk clan went on, "So why are you nattering at me to fix something I can't do anything about?"

"They *are* going to hit us." Hamnet clung to the rags of his temper by main force. "What will you do—what will we do—when that happens? Run away? Where will we go? How will we keep the Rulers off us once we get there?"

"You have more frets than a mammoth has fleas," Trasamund said, and took another swig from the smetyn skin. "Whatever comes will come, and God will see to it that it all turns out all right."

"The way he has so far?" Hamnet inquired, acid in his voice.

"Go away. Bother me later." Trasamund drank deep again. "I want to get drunk. I want to screw my brains out."

"What brains?" Hamnet asked, more sardonically still.

"Go howl," the Bizogot told him. "I'll worry about your worries, but when I feel like worrying about them. Not now!"

"When you were too late coming back to your clan from Raumsdalia, that was just one of those things that happen. It wasn't your fault," Hamnet Thyssen said. "But if you're too late getting ready for trouble any fool can see coming, who's left to blame but you?"

He thought the only way to get Trasamund to listen to him was to be brutal. He turned out to be righter than he'd guessed. The jarl dropped the precious skin of smetyn and charged him, bellowing like a bull woolly mammoth. Hamnet was a big man, Trasamund bigger still. They grappled, cursing and punching. Count Hamnet managed not to get thrown under Trasamund, but pulled the Bizogot down beside him onto the ground. Hamnet did his best to knee Trasamund in the groin, but the jarl twisted and took the blow on the hip.

"Well, this is sweet."

Ulric Skakki's light, ironic tones didn't prove enough to get Hamnet and Trasamund to stop pounding on each other. Then a bowstring thrummed. An arrow stood thrilling in the ground only a few inches from the fighters' faces.

"Enough!" Ulric's voice got sharper. "If I shoot again, my aim may not be so good—or so bad, depending on how you look at things." He reached over his shoulder for another shaft.

Cautiously, Hamnet pushed Trasamund away from him. The Bizogot let him do it. Neither was sure Ulric wouldn't shoot them to make them stop fighting. Such drastic measures were very much his style.

Hamnet tasted blood. When he spat, he spat red, but no teeth seemed broken. He'd blacked one of Trasamund's eyes. Dishonors between them seemed even. That dismayed him; he thought he should have thrashed the Bizogot.

"And what were you gentlemen discussing when you decided words weren't exciting enough to suit you?" Ulric kept an arrow nocked. His words were more piercing, though.

"What to do next," Trasamund answered, gingerly rubbing at the eye that had met Count Hamnet's fist. *Lucky it wasn't my thumb*, the Raumsdalian thought.

"Our hero here doesn't want to do anything much," Hamnet said. "Just sit around and wait for the Rulers to jump on us."

"Probably better schemes than that." Ulric Skakki could also sound judicious when he felt like it.

"If I want to know what you think, Skakki, I'll ask you," Trasamund growled.

"Well, I don't think we want to wait *that* long," the adventurer said. "We might have things to do in the meantime."

"You Raumsdalians can joke and eat fat goose and screw your women and take it easy," Trasamund said. "You already know no true Bizogots will take you seriously. If *I* say something, though, you'd better believe they'll hop to it." He thumped his chest with his fist and struck a pose.

Hamnet Thyssen didn't strike him, but he came close. "Then why the demon don't you say something to them?" he snapped. "If you let things drift, the Rulers will call the tune instead."

"Must be what he has in mind," Ulric said helpfully.

"After we're dead, the lions and teratorns can make the plans."

"Bah!" Trasamund stuck his nose in the air and lumbered off.

After spitting again—still red—Hamnet sighed and said, "He reminds me of a bull musk ox in mating season. All he wants to do is bang heads."

"And screw," Ulric said. "Don't forget screwing."

There had been times when Hamnet wished he could. But that wasn't what worried him now. "What are we going to do about it?"

"Nothing much we can do that won't make things worse," Ulric replied. "If dear Trasamund comes down with a sudden case of loss of life, who takes over for him? Won't be us. He's right about that—the Bizogots won't follow us. And the rest of the men are worse muttonheads—musk-ox heads, if you'd rather—than he is."

"We're stuck with him, I'm afraid," Count Hamnet said mournfully. "And I'm afraid because we're stuck with him, too."

A RAVEN FLUTTERED down out of the sky and landed on Marcovefa's left shoulder. She reached out and scratched its head as if it were a cat. It brought its formidable beak alarmingly close to her eye before it croaked something in her ear. She croaked back. They might have been conversing. For all Hamnet Thyssen knew, they were.

Several Bizogots stared at the spectacle of woman communing with bird. Hamnet didn't, but only because he'd seen it before up on the Glacier and during the harrowing descent to the Bizogot steppe. At last, one of the mammoth-herders worked up the nerve to ask, "Is that your fetish animal, wise woman?"

"Not the way you mean it." Marcovefa caressed the raven some more. It croaked again, with obvious pleasure. She went on, "But it still tells me things."

"Like what?" Hamnet asked.

"Where the carrion is. I don't have to watch teratorns. And where the carrion is, most of the time the Rulers are, too."

"Ah." The Raumsdalian noble nodded. "That is worth knowing, yes. But why hasn't one come to you for a while?"

She shrugged. "Ravens do what they want, not what you want. If they were only a little worse, they would make fair people."

A little worse how? Hamnet wondered. Then he wondered if he wanted to know. He ended up not asking. What he did ask was, "Where is the carrion these days? Where are the Rulers?"

Marcovefa croaked at the raven. The big black bird with the shaggy feathers answered. It swung its head to look northwest. Then it swung it again to look almost due south, toward the Raumsdalian Empire. "You see," Marcovefa said.

"Well, so I do," Hamnet agreed. "But have the Rulers come out of the woods, then? Have they left the Empire?" If they had, he thought they were stupid. They would have a much easier time feeding themselves inside the Empire than up here. He wondered if they realized the territory they roamed on the far side of the Glacier was more like the Bizogot steppe than the Empire.

Marcovefa and the raven croaked back and forth some more. But all Hamnet got from her was another shrug. "The bird doesn't know," she reported. "Why should it care about people who aren't dead?"

"They'll make us dead if they get the chance," the Raumsdalian noble said. "But I don't suppose the raven cares about us while we're alive, either. Well, maybe about you—a little, anyhow."

"A little," Marcovefa agreed. "It thinks I'm interesting because we understand each other some. If we didn't, it would only want to peck out my eyeballs after I'm gone."

"You say the most cheerful things," Hamnet Thyssen told her. The Bizogots were more fatalistic than most Raumsdalians. And Marcovefa was more fatalistic than most Bizogots. Part of that might have been her own character. Part was surely growing to womanhood atop the Glacier. Just as the Bizogots had a harsher life than denizens of the Empire, so Marcovefa's clan lived in a way that would horrify—had horrified—any Bizogots who saw it.

"Do I tell lies?" Marcovefa asked.

"Not here," Hamnet said. She grinned, unoffended. He went on, "Do you know any way to make ravens interested in live people? If we had flying eyes, that would help us a lot." He told her about the Rulers' wizard who'd turned himself into an owl to spy on the Bizogots and Raumsdalians.

"A raven is a smart bird, but only a bird," Marcovefa said. "Why should it care?"

Plainly, she didn't think Hamnet would have an answer for her. But he did: "If we can find the Rulers, we can fight them. If we fight them, the ravens will get plenty of fresh food." *Maybe including us*, he thought. He'd run that risk whenever he went into battle. Sometimes, though, it seemed bigger than others.

Marcovefa grinned again, this time in delight. She blew him a kiss. "Yes, that may work . . . if the bird can see so far ahead. Have to find out." She started croaking at the raven. It made strange, throaty noises back at her. She croaked again and again.

The raven tilted its head to one side. If it wasn't thinking things over, Count Hamnet had never seen anything, man or beast, that was. What went on behind those bright jet eyes? How much *could* a bird anticipate? Hamnet was no bird, so he didn't know. From everything he'd seen, ravens were more clever than most other flying feathered creatures. But could this one understand the promise of more meat down the line if it did something rather than something else?

It said something to Marcovefa. Ravens could learn to speak human words, but this one wasn't doing that. It had its own way of getting ideas across, one only vaguely connected to human language. Had Marcovefa needed magic to learn it, or had study sufficed?

He couldn't ask her now; whatever she was using, she needed to concentrate hard to get meaning from the sounds the raven was making. When it finally finished, she said, "It will try. Maybe it will forget. Maybe the other ravens won't understand what it needs. But it will try."

"As much as we can expect, I suppose." Hamnet expected nothing from the raven. That way, he couldn't possibly be disappointed. Anything he did hear from the bird or its fellows would come as a pleasant surprise.

He looked at life the same way. The view had advantages and disadvantages, as everything did. When things went wrong, he had little trouble accepting it—most of the time—because he'd looked for nothing better. (Where he did look for something better, as with Gudrid and Liv, disillusionment proved doubly bitter.) When things went well, he tried not to show the surprise too much.

"This is right on the edge of what a raven can do," Marcovefa said. "Maybe over the edge. The bird here is smart, even for a raven. I don't know if all of them can do what it can."

She croaked some more at the big black bird. Count

Hamnet knew nothing of the language of ravens, and knew he never would. If he had to guess from tone, though, he would have said she was telling this one how bright it was. It preened—literally. Did that mean it understood the praise and accepted it? You would have to be a raven—or Marcovefa—to know.

The bird sprang into the air. Wind whistled out between its wing feathers as it flapped. It wasn't an arrow with a beak, the way a falcon was. But it could outsoar and out-maneuver a falcon. Ravens harried hawks for the sport of it, then tumbled out of the way in the air to keep the birds of prey from turning on them.

Ravens harried hawks, jays harried ravens, mocking-birds harried jays, kingbirds harried mockingbirds, hum-mingbirds harried kingbirds . . . and dragonflies probably harried hummingbirds. Hamnet Thyssen looked for a les-son there, but couldn't find one he liked. Everything large and fearsome had something small and feisty that an-noyed it. No, not much of a lesson.

Which didn't mean it wasn't true, on land as well as in the air. Right now, the Bizogots seemed small and feisty, the Rulers large and fearsome. That was how things looked if you were a Bizogot or a Raumsdalian up here beyond the tree line, anyhow. The Rulers probably had a different view of it.

The only view of the Rulers Hamnet wanted was one of their backs as they rode off beyond the Gap once more. He wondered if he would ever get a view like that. He feared he wouldn't, even if the Bizogots and the Empire somehow beat the invaders. The Rulers would be part of the political landscape from now on. The Gap would be open from now on, too. More Rulers—or even other invaders—could sweep down out of the north. The world had got bigger and more complicated.

When he said as much to Marcovefa, she gave him a wry smile. "This happened to me when I came down off the Glacier," she said. "Everything new, everything strange, everything—" She threw her arms wide to show how much her world had expanded.

"You've done well," Hamnet told her.

She shrugged. "People are still people. That's the biggest thing. The world is strange. The animals are strange. But people? No."

"People are always strange," Count Hamnet said. *Especially women*, he added, but only to himself.

Marcovefa smiled again and nodded. "But they're strange the same way here as they are in my clan up on the nunatak."

"On the what?" Hamnet said.

"Nunatak," Marcovefa repeated. "That's our word for a mountaintop that sticks out above the Glacier."

"Oh." Hamnet Thyssen had probably heard the term while he was atop the Glacier himself, and while he was on that mountaintop—that nunatak. If he had, though, it had gone clean out of his mind. He wasn't surprised. He hadn't been at his best up there. None of the Bizogots or Raumsdalians had. He thought for a moment longer. "It doesn't sound like a Bizogot word at all."

"Maybe it isn't. Our songs say other folk were up there when our forefathers came," Marcovefa answered.

"What happened to them?" Hamnet asked.

"We ate them," she answered calmly.

He didn't splutter and make disgusted noises, because she so obviously wanted him to do just that. All he said was, "Seems as though you ate some of their words, too."

"It could be." Marcovefa's expression was comically disappointed. Yes, she'd aimed to get more of a rise out of him.

One corner of his own mouth quirked upward. People didn't get everything they wanted—not even a powerful shaman like Marcovefa. Nobody got everything. Maybe that meant the Rulers wouldn't.

Or maybe it meant the Bizogots and the Empire wouldn't. Who from each side got how much . . . would tell the tale till the Glacier melted, and maybe even after that.

TALL, DARK, ANVIL-TOPPED clouds floated ponderously across the sky. The air was hot and muggy, still and sullen. Wiping his forehead with the back of his wrist, Ulric Skakki said, "Whew! This is the kind of weather you'd expect a thousand miles south of here."

"Yes, and you'd complain about it down there, too." Hamnet Thyssen had taken off his tunic. His hands and face were tanned dark, but his arms and torso were pale as a Bizogot's, though the mat of hair on his chest was dark, not golden. Right now, his skin was slick with sweat.

Ulric gave the clouds a dirty look. "If we're going to have a thunderstorm, I wish we'd *have* it. It would wash the air clean of this garbage." He shed his tunic, too.

"That would be good," Hamnet agreed.

But the thunderheads rolled by, one after another. Count Hamnet did hear thunder once, far off in the distance. No rain fell anywhere nearby. The air remained close and stuffy.

Marcovefa walked by with *her* tunic off. Hamnet's jaw dropped. Ulric's eyes widened. Unless they were bathing, Bizogot women didn't go bare-breasted in public (neither did Raumsdalians). "What are you doing?" Hamnet managed after a couple of false starts.

"Trying to stay cool, same as you." Marcovefa mimed a panting fox. "I never knew weather like this up on the Glacier. I feel like I am wading in hot soup."

"Don't sunburn your, uh, self," Ulric said, gallantly not looking at what he was really talking about.

"I be careful," Marcovefa said, and walked on. Anyone who wanted to tell her to cover up would need to be a braver man than either Raumsdalian.

After she was gone, Hamnet and Ulric eyed each other. They both shrugged at the same time. "Look on the bright side," Ulric said. "Maybe she'll start a new trend."

"Right," Hamnet said tightly. He wondered what he would have done had Gudrid or Liv acted so scandalously. Odds were he would have pitched a fit, and maybe had a stroke. He wondered why he wasn't pitching a fit now. Partly because Marcovefa was a law unto herself, no doubt. And, perhaps, partly because he'd already pitched enough—or too many—fits about women.

Have I learned something? he wondered. *Or am I just too bloody tired to get upset about things right now?*

Ulric Skakki looked around: not in Marcovefa's direction. The adventurer's nostrils flared, as if he were a dire wolf seeking a scent. "The air is nasty," he said.

"Hot and muggy enough and then some, that's for sure," Count Hamnet agreed.

But Ulric shook his head. "Not what I meant. It's bad that way, too. But I don't like the way it *feels*. Do you have any notion of what I'm talking about?"

"No." Hamnet was nothing if not direct.

"Didn't think so." Ulric gave him a bow that should have been mocking but somehow wasn't. "It feels like something horrible is going to happen to us any minute."

Hamnet Thyssen raised an eyebrow. "Foretelling? I didn't know you'd gone into the wizard business. Have you talked with Audun Gilli or Liv about this?" He didn't think he wanted Ulric talking with Marcovefa, not while she was running around without her tunic.

The adventurer's chuckle said he knew what was going through Hamnet's mind. But his mirth quickly faded. "I will talk with them, by God. I don't know if they'll tell me I'm daft. If they don't, I don't know whether they can do anything about it. Better to find out, though." Lithe as a tumbler, he got to his feet.

With a grunt and a creak, Count Hamnet rose, too, and followed him. Hamnet also tried to feel the air. To him, it felt like . . . air. Hot, sticky air, but air and nothing else but. He thought Ulric was letting his imagination run wild. That wasn't like the adventurer, but neither was his turning wizard.

Audun Gilli sat in the shade of the hut he shared with Liv. He hadn't shed his tunic, but looked suddenly thoughtful as Ulric and Hamnet came up to him. Maybe he would before long.

"What's up?" Audun asked. The look he gave Hamnet was slightly apprehensive. He might have cleared the air, but he knew Hamnet would never love him.

But Ulric did the talking, finishing, "Have I just got the fidgets on account of this beastly weather, or am I feeling something real?"

"Well, I haven't sensed anything like that," Audun Gilli answered. Count Hamnet started to give Ulric an I-told-you-so look, but the wizard went on, "Which doesn't have to prove anything. Have you talked to Marcovefa yet? I'd bet she's more sensitive than I am."

"I thought I'd wait till she puts on more clothes," Ulric said blandly. "She might not be distracted, but I would be."

"She's not wearing any less than the two of you," Audun pointed out—he'd seen her, too, then. He'd seen quite a bit of her, in fact.

"That's what she told us," Ulric Skakki said. "It looks better on her, though. And I know better than to argue with a shaman, I do." His saucy grin dared Hamnet to make something of that. Hamnet ignored him. With a small sigh, Ulric went on, "If you say I ought to talk to her, I guess I'll go do it." This time, he wasn't grinning when he spoke to Hamnet: "You're welcome to tag along again, Your Grace. I'm not going to talk about anything I don't want you to hear."

Not while I'm there, you're not, Hamnet thought. All he said was, "I want to get to the bottom of this, too."

The Leaping Lynxes' village wasn't very big. Finding Marcovefa didn't take long. She raised an eyebrow when Ulric and Hamnet came up to her. "Are you two going to try to tell me what to do again?" she asked, an ominous note in her voice.

Hamnet shook his head. "No. This is something else." He gestured to Ulric Skakki.

Ulric told the story one more time. He looked Marcovefa in the eye while he was doing it. If his gaze slipped farther south, it wasn't in any obvious way. "So," he said, "have I got the vapors, or is this something we need to worry about?"

Marcovefa looked as thoughtful as if she were fully clothed. "I don't know," she said. "I don't feel this, but I haven't looked for it, either."

"Maybe you should," Hamnet said.

"Yes." She nodded, which made her jiggle. Hamnet couldn't pretend not to notice, but he didn't dwell on it, either. There was a time and a place for everything. Ulric's face might have been carved from stone. Marcovefa swung around in a circle, as if she too were casting about for a scent. When she came to the northwest, she stopped, looking startled.

"Something?" Hamnet and Ulric asked together.

"Something," she agreed. "Something not good. Something very not good."

Her grammar was shaky, but Hamnet understood what she meant. "What are those bastards trying to do to us?" he growled. Suddenly even the damp heat of the day seemed suspicious and unnatural. Maybe he was starting at shadows—but maybe he wasn't. With the Rulers, he couldn't be sure.

Before Marcovefa could answer, a Bizogot woman named Faileuba came up to the shaman from atop the Ice and said, "I don't feel good." She didn't sound good; her voice was a sickly whine. She didn't look good, either. Her face had a hectic flush, and she swayed on her feet.

Marcovefa set the palm of her hand on Faileuba's forehead, then jerked it away again. "Fever," she said. "Very much fever."

A big blond man called Eberulf lurched toward Marcovefa, too. "Something's wrong with me," he muttered. Before Marcovefa could touch him, he keeled over. He looked the way Faileuba did, only worse.

"Disease?" Hamnet Thyssen said. "Or sending?"

"Sending," Ulric answered without the least hesitation. "Has to be. Everything fits together too well. And . . . Do you remember the Rock Ptarmigans?"

"Yes." Hamnet wished he didn't. The Rulers had destroyed the whole western clan with a sorcerous pestilence the year before. What their dead encampment looked like when Trasamund's band found it was the stuff of nightmares.

Marcovefa said, "Yes," too. She nodded to Count Hamnet. "Go get Liv and Audun. I don't care if they're screwing—go get them. I need their help. This is as very bad a magic as I have seen from the Rulers."

"Right," Hamnet muttered. He didn't know why Marcovefa had picked him to run her errand—to rub salt in his
wounds? But whatever he felt would have to wait . . . unless he wanted to start feeling the way Faileuba and Eberulf did. He hurried back to the hut his former lover and the
Raumsdalian wizard shared.

They were both outside it now, looking worried as they
tried to tend to a couple of sick Bizogots. "I don't care
what Marcovefa wants—we can't come right now." Liv
sounded harried. "I don't know what these poor people
have. Whatever it is, it's nasty."

"It's worse than nasty. It's sorcery from the Rulers,"
Hamnet said. "Ulric thinks it's the same sorcery that wiped
out the Rock Ptarmigans. So does Marcovefa. She says
she needs your help."

"Good God!" Audun Gilli exclaimed. Was he shocked
by remembering what had happened to the Rock Ptarmigans or by the idea that Marcovefa might need anybody's
help? Count Hamnet wasn't sure which was more star-
tling, either.

"Well . . ." Liv seemed to think that was a complete sentence. She nodded to Audun. "What are you waiting for?"

"Nothing," he answered. The Bizogots they were trying
to treat protested feebly. Audun spoke to Hamnet in Raumsdalian, which they were unlikely to understand: "Best thing
we can do for these poor buggers is block that sorcery . . . if
we're able to. Marcovefa needs help? God!" So that was
what was on his mind. Hamnet Thyssen couldn't pretend he
was surprised.

Several Bizogots called out to Liv and Audun as they hurried along. The pangs seemed to be hitting more mammoth-
herders. Seeing people around him suffering, Count Hamnet
examined himself for symptoms. How could you help doing

something like that? He felt fine. A heartbeat later, he felt guilty for feeling fine.

Liv blinked when she saw Marcovefa. Hamnet had forgotten she wore no tunic—and if that didn't prove the Rulers' magic had him worried, what the demon would? Ulric Skakki was still on his feet, and seemed fine. Maybe the Rulers were aiming at Bizogots alone. Maybe it was nothing but coincidence.

"What do you need from us?" Liv asked Marcovefa.

"Do you know the yellow stone called lynxpiss?" Marcovefa answered.

"Yes," Liv said, at the same time as Audun answered, "It isn't really lynx piss, you know. It's a stone like any other."

Marcovefa's nostrils flared. "I asked of it by its name, not by its nature. Use that lynxpiss stone against the fever. And if you have a lodestone, it will also help ward against perils of death. Quick, now—no time to waste."

"What will you be doing?" Liv asked.

"I will punish those who send this wicked shamanry," Marcovefa replied. Then, for one of the rare times since Hamnet had known her, she hesitated. "If I can," she added. "Here, for once, the Rulers are almost as strong as they think they are. This is shamanry different from anything I ever saw up above the Glacier."

Liv and Audun started arguing about where they might have stowed the lynxpiss stone. Audun dashed off. He returned in triumph with a transparent yellow crystal. Liv kissed him. Hamnet Thyssen did a slow burn. Didn't she have more self-respect than that? His own current lover stood there bare-breasted, but that was different. Hamnet might not have thought so till Liv kissed Audun, but he did from then on.

"A lodestone," Liv said. "Does anyone have a lodestone?"

"I have a little one," Ulric Skakki said. "Here." He pulled a small, rusty-looking stone from a pouch on his belt and tossed it to Liv. The shaman deftly caught it.

"*Why* have you got a lodestone?" Hamnet asked.

Ulric only shrugged. "Well, they're fun to play with. And they're interesting. And you never can tell when something will come in handy. It's like a holdout knife, you know? You can go for years and years without ever needing a holdout knife. But when you need one, you'll need it bad."

Liv and Audun were using the lodestone and the yellow crystal—what was it really? tourmaline?—on a sick Bizogot. The Rock Ptarmigans' shamans must have tried something like that when their people fell ill. Much good it had done them. Count Hamnet wished that last handful of words hadn't crossed his mind.

But he couldn't pay attention to Liv and Audun, or even to his own worries, for long, because Marcovefa said, "Hamnet—I need your help."

He started. "Whatever I can give you," he said.

"Your strength. Come stand by me. Set your hand on my bare skin. . . ." Marcovefa suddenly laughed. "*There?* Well, if you want. It will do. I can draw from you. I try not to take too much."

What happens if you do? Hamnet wondered. Maybe he didn't want to know. Maybe, if she took too much, he would just quietly fall over dead. He shrugged. So what? It was an easier end than most of the ones he could imagine.

He could, or thought he could, feel strength flowing out of him and into her. No—out of him and through her. Her right arm speared out toward the northwest. She might have been aiming at an enemy warrior. She might have been, but the range here was far longer and the effort required far more.

Because she was drawing on Hamnet's strength, he

could sense some of what she was doing with it. The link between them was stranger but in a way more intimate than when their bodies joined in the usual fashion. He felt her long-range grapple with the Rulers' wizards. They were trying to down her with the same sickness that had felled so many Bizogots. In his mind's eye, he saw the sickness as a greenish miasma. Whether that had anything to do with reality, he couldn't have said.

Marcovefa herself might have been the sun: not the sun of the Bizogot steppe, not even the sun of Nidaros, but the hot, fierce sun of the southwestern desert where the Manche bandits skulked. If she could burn through that ugly, roiling miasma . . . It would be like a fresh breeze blowing away the nasty, humid air that oppressed the encampment.

He wondered if the vile weather and the vile sickness were connected. One more thing that wouldn't have surprised him.

But the roiling green stuff he imagined he saw didn't want to burn away. Indeed, it clung ever tighter to Marcovefa. If it could seize her before she could dispel it . . . He didn't know what would happen then. He did know it wouldn't be good.

Without being asked, Ulric Skakki took his left hand. The adventurer's strength flowed through Hamnet and into Marcovefa. No, the shaman from atop the Glacier wasn't mocking the Rulers and their wizardry any more. Maybe this wasn't the fight of her life, but it was the toughest one she'd had since descending to the plains the Bizogots roamed.

Maybe Ulric's strength tilted the balance. Before, Marcovefa had struggled to hold her own against the Rulers' sorcery. Now she blazed brighter and brighter in Hamnet's imagination—if that was what it was. The choking fog surrounding her, clutching at her . . . Did it start to fade, or did it draw back as if in fear of the spiritual glow that came from her? Hamnet had trouble putting it into words, but both amounted to the same thing.

"Ha!" she cried aloud. Across however many miles it was, Hamnet Thyssen felt the Rulers' wizards flinch away from her. That cry might have been Trasamund's fearsome two-handed sword, swung with all the furious power the Bizogot jarl had in him. "Ha!" Marcovefa said again. The enemy wizards broke and fled her strength—those who could. In much more mundane tones, Marcovefa told Hamnet, "You can let go of my tit now, thank you very much."

He did. "You broke them," he said.

"Yes. I did." But she didn't take it for granted, the way she once had. "You gave me good help—both of you did. And I thank you for it." Her eyes rolled up in her head, and she crumpled to the ground.

VII

Only two Bizogots died of the sorcerous plague. Audun Gilli and Liv did all they could; Count Hamnet thought they succeeded better than anyone could have expected. They weren't satisfied. Wizards seldom were satisfied with anything short of perfection.

Marcovefa was not only dissatisfied, she was also furious—and more than a little frightened. "They could have killed me," she told Hamnet that evening in the hut the two of them shared. "They should have killed me. If they made their plague strike me first, maybe they kill us all, the way they killed the Rock Ptarmigans."

He nodded. "That's what enemies try to do, you know. I'm glad they didn't think to make you sick first—or maybe they couldn't at long range."

"Maybe." She sounded dubious, and still very angry. "They aren't supposed to be able to do that to me!"

Hamnet Thyssen sighed. "Everybody except you has been saying, 'The Rulers are dangerous,' all along. You're the one who's been going, 'No, no, they're easy. I can beat them with one hand tied behind my back.'"

"And I've done it, too!" Marcovefa's pride flared. "Except when I got hit in the head, I've done it every time."

"A good thing, too. We'd be ruined if you hadn't," Count Hamnet said. "But even if you have beaten them every time, it won't always be easy. There are lots of them, and only one of you. And even if you think they're bad wizards, they're better than anyone else down here below the Glacier except you. You need to be careful, the same way you would have up on the Ice. The shamans from those other clans up there were as strong as you were, right?"

"Oh, yes. Some of them were stronger," Marcovefa said at once. "But they were—are—of my own folk. Not these Rulers. Do you like to think your horse is smarter than you are?"

"Hold on!" Hamnet held up a hand. "The Rulers are the ones who call everybody else 'the herd.' They think they can do whatever they want with other people because they think other people are just beasts. I don't want us to think that way. If we do, how are we any better than they are?"

Marcovefa gave him a sharp-toothed grin. "They are much uglier."

Stubbornly, Count Hamnet shook his head. "That's not good enough. Curse it, I'm serious about this."

"Yes, I see you are. But I wonder why," Marcovefa said. "Is it that important?"

"I think so," Hamnet said. "Up on the Glacier, suppose another clan made a great magic by eating some of its own people. Would you use that same kind of sorcery yourself?"

"Eat its own people to make magic?" Marcovefa looked revolted, which made Hamnet sure he'd picked a good example. "No, we would never do that. That would be wickedness itself. It—" She broke off and sent Hamnet a sour stare. "All right. I see what you are saying."

"Good. I'm glad." Hamnet Thyssen hoped he didn't

show just how glad he was. If Marcovefa hadn't seen his point, he would have worried about her almost as much as he worried about the Rulers. She wasn't quite so alien to the Bizogots and Raumsdalians as they were, but she wasn't far removed from it, either.

He must not have kept his face as still as he hoped, because Marcovefa laughed at him. "After we beat the Rulers, then you can bash me over the head," she said.

His ears heated. "The Rulers are a menace because they don't care anything about our ways and don't want to learn. You do want to learn—and you follow our customs now that you're down here with us. You haven't eaten man's flesh since you came down from the Glacier."

Marcovefa mimed picking her teeth. "How do you know?"

"Stop that!" Count Hamnet said. "You're just sticking thorns in me to make me jump."

"And why not?" Marcovefa replied. "I did some jumping of my own today. That was more of a magic than I thought the Rulers had in them."

A warrior with a sword and a helmet and a byrnie could easily beat armorless foes who carried only daggers. If he faced a lot of foes like that, who could blame him for getting careless? But if he stayed careless against an enemy with gear like his own, odds were he'd end up bleeding on the ground. Count Hamnet didn't know magic worked the same way, but he couldn't see any reason why it shouldn't.

He wondered if he ought to point that out to Marcovefa. Reluctantly, he decided not to. If she couldn't see it for herself, she wouldn't want the lecture. She might need it, but she wouldn't want it.

"What did you do to the wizards who were sending the sickness?" he asked instead. That seemed safe enough—and he wanted to know.

"I made them stop," Marcovefa answered. "Past that, I don't know. I don't care very much, either."

"All right." Hamnet wasn't sure it was. Up till now, Marcovefa had thrashed the Rulers' wizards with monotonous regularity. Well, it would have been monotonous, anyhow, if it hadn't been so essential. If it got to the point where she couldn't thrash them like that . . .

If it got to that point, the Bizogots and the Raumsdalian Empire were in a lot of trouble. As far as Count Hamnet knew, Marcovefa was the one effective weapon they had against the Rulers. If she wasn't so effective—what did they have then? As far as he could see, they had nothing.

"I think I need a slug of smetyn," he said. "It's been a hard day."

"Harder for me, so bring me some, too," Marcovefa said. She drank cautiously most of the time, being new to smetyn and ale and beer and wine. She'd hurt herself the first couple of times she tried drinking. She hadn't had any idea what a hangover was. She did now, and respected the morning after . . . again, most of the time.

The way she poured the fermented milk down today said she wasn't worrying about the next morning. Hamnet didn't suppose he could blame her. She'd just had a brush with a very nasty death. So had he, come to that. He drank more than a slug himself.

Marcovefa sent him an owlish stare. "What are you sitting there for?" She didn't slur her words, but spoke with exaggerated precision. "Aren't you going to screw me?"

"Well . . ." That question had only one possible answer, unless he wanted an unholy row. "Yes." Some time later, he asked, "Is that better?" He rubbed his left shoulder, then sneaked a look at the palm of his hand. She hadn't bitten him *quite* hard enough to draw blood.

She stretched like a lion after a kill. "What do you think?"

"If it got any better than that, I don't know if I'd live through it." Hamnet was stretching things, but not by much. Never a dull moment with Marcovefa.

Her smile said she liked the answer. She drank more smetyn. Then she said, "In a little while, we do it again."

"I'll try," he said. "I may need some magic to hold up my end of the bargain."

"I can do that," Marcovefa said, and he'd seen that she could. She went on, "Or we could do other things besides just screwing."

"Whatever you please," Hamnet Thyssen said. They weren't prudes, up there on top of the Glacier. They didn't have much in the way of entertainment, so they made the most of what they did have—lovemaking included.

And he ended up doing more than he'd thought he could. There were advantages to having a shaman for a lover. There were also disadvantages. Liv had left him, but she hadn't hated him. He hoped Marcovefa wouldn't hate him, either, if she ever decided to leave. If she did hate him, he'd need to look for a place to hide—and he'd need to hope he could find a place like that with a shaman after him.

"What do you suppose the Rulers think about us right now?" Ulric Skakki came up with interesting questions to make time go by while riding on patrol.

"Nothing good, I hope," Count Hamnet said.

Ulric dropped the reins in his lap for a moment so he could sarcastically clap his hands. "Brilliant, Your Grace! Bloody fornicating brilliant! A lesser mind would be incapable of such analysis."

"Oh, bugger off," Hamnet said, which made the adventurer laugh out loud.

But Ulric didn't give up: "If you were the Rulers, how would you try to get rid of us?"

"Annoy us to death?" Hamnet suggested, and Ulric laughed again. But the question got Hamnet thinking. Slowly, he said, "Magic didn't work—came close, but it didn't work. Little raids haven't worked, either. What's left? Using an anvil to swat a fly—coming down on us with everything they've got. Or do you have some different kind of scheme in mind?"

"No, not me." Ulric shook his head. "To tell you the truth, I hoped you did."

"Afraid not," Hamnet Thyssen said.

"Pity." Ulric didn't let the chatter stop him from looking around every few heartbeats. "What do we do if they decide to land on us with both feet like that?"

"Probably can't fight if they come at us with everybody and his favorite mammoth," Hamnet said. Ulric Skakki nodded, which disappointed him; he'd wanted the adventurer to tell him he was wrong. Sighing, Hamnet went on, "If we can't hold them off, we'd better run."

"Seems logical," Ulric agreed. "Next question is, where? Sort of all over the landscape, or some place in particular?"

Count Hamnet smiled in spite of himself. "Chances are, going somewhere in particular would be smart."

"Oh, good! I knew you were a clever fellow." Ulric made as if to clap his hands again. Hamnet made as if to punch him; sarcasm could wear thin. As if ignorant of that, the adventurer went on, "Now let's see how clever you really are. If you have to run somewhere, where do you want to run?"

That required some thought. Hamnet Thyssen didn't

like the first answer he came up with, so he tried to see if he could find a better one. To his dismay, he couldn't. Reluctantly, he gave the first one: "The Empire. Better my own people should jail me than the Rulers should kill me . . . I suppose."

"Yes, I suppose so, too," Ulric Skakki said. "And no, I don't like it any better than you do. But what choice have we got? The Bizogots are shattered, all up and down the plain, and as far across it to east and west as we can reach. The Empire isn't doing all that well, but it isn't shattered, either."

"Well, it wasn't when that last messenger made it up here, anyhow," Hamnet said.

"You're right. It wasn't then." Ulric nodded. "He said Nidaros hadn't fallen. If it has by now, Sigvat II's bound to be dead, and—"

"And that's bound to help what's left of Raumsdalia," Count Hamnet broke in.

Ulric showed his teeth in what looked like a grin but wasn't. "How right you are! It's no wonder His Majesty has brown eyes, is it?"

"Eh?" Hamnet was a beat slow getting the joke. Then he did. "Oh. No, no wonder at all, by God. Whatever they find to take his place—even if it's the old drunk who sweeps out the stables—is bound to be better."

"You don't *like* Sigvat, do you?"

"He stuck his head up his arse when we found the Rulers. He stuck me in a dungeon when I kept reminding him about that. And he stuck us with Gudrid when we went up through the Gap. Why the demon should I like him?"

"Interesting which one you put last," Ulric murmured.

"Oh, shut up. So I'm not over Gudrid yet. So chances are I never will be. So what are you going to do about it?" Hamnet said.

"Mm, when you put it that way, probably nothing," the adventurer replied. "All right—back to the Empire . . . if we can get there. Good-sized army of Rulers already down there, remember. If they move up against us—"

"Why would they do that?" Hamnet said. "It'd be like a sabertooth walking away from a buffalo carcass to chase after a yappy little fox."

"A sabertooth wouldn't be that stupid," Ulric admitted. "I'm not so sure about people. And we haven't just yapped at the Rulers. We've nipped them a few times—and nobody else on this side of the Glacier seems able to do even that much. They have their reasons for coming after us. Besides, they're afraid of you, remember."

Hamnet Thyssen laughed bitterly. "If they are, they're every bit as stupid as you make them out to be. Too much to hope for, though, I fear."

"They're smarter than you are, because they've got some notion of what's dangerous to them," Ulric said.

"Oh, I know what's dangerous to me, all right," Hamnet said. "I ought to, after all the mistakes I've made with them."

"You may be dangerous to women. That doesn't mean they're dangerous to you," Ulric told him.

"If they're not, God save me from running into anything that is," Count Hamnet said.

"You take things too seriously," the adventurer said.

"I've had things happen to me that need to be taken seriously," Hamnet retorted. "Not everybody slides through life with a greased hide the way you do."

"Just goes to show you don't know me as well as you think." Ulric shrugged. "Doesn't matter, not really. We decided what we needed to decide. Only thing left now is convincing Trasamund."

That sent Hamnet laughing again. "You don't ask for much!"

"Oh, he'll come around. He'll yell and fuss and bellow till he works all the indigestion out of his system, and then he'll be fine. He doesn't sit around brooding like some people I could name." Ulric sent Hamnet a pointed glance.

When Hamnet suggested a few things Ulric could do if he didn't like it, the adventurer only laughed. That made Hamnet offer more suggestions. Ulric laughed harder. Hamnet knew Ulric was trying to get his goat. The adventurer was good at getting what he wanted, too. Instead of swearing any more, Hamnet subsided into quiet fury.

That wasn't what Ulric Skakki wanted. "Come on, Thyssen—swear some more," he said. "You need to get it out of your system, too, and I don't care if you call me names. You wouldn't be the first one, God knows."

"If you don't care, what's the point?" Hamnet said.

Ulric started to laugh some more, but broke off. "All right. Fine. I give up. Do what you want to do, no matter how idiotic it looks. Never mind that the Rulers worry about you. They're nothing but a pack of fools. We're all a pack of fools. Everybody in the whole stupid world's a fool—except you."

That set Hamnet swearing again. Ulric Skakki bowed in the saddle, which only irked Hamnet more. "If the Rulers are so stinking afraid of me, *why*? What have I done?" he demanded. "They've trounced the Bizogots while I was up here. They've trounced the Empire while I was down there. I'm useless, is what I am."

"Are they better wizards than the ones we've got, or are they worse?" Ulric asked. "I mean Raumsdalian wizards and Bizogot shamans—leave Marcovefa out of it."

"They're better, and you know it as well as I do," Hamnet Thyssen snapped. "Why talk about what's obvious?"

Ulric bowed again. "Why? Because it's so obvious, you don't want to look at it. If they've got better wizards than we do—and they've got 'em, all right—then they can see things we can't. And one of the things they see is that Count Hamnet Thyssen means trouble to them."

"Only goes to show they're not smart all the time," Hamnet said stubbornly.

"You don't want to believe me. You wouldn't believe me if I told you it got cold up here in the wintertime," Ulric Skakki said. "Fine. Don't believe me. But ask your lady love. If she says it, you'd better believe it."

"She's not my lady love," Hamnet muttered. That was part of his problem, too. He slept with Marcovefa. He kept company with her. He liked her—when she didn't scare the piss out of him. Love her the way he'd loved Gudrid and Liv? No matter how much he wanted to, he couldn't come close. She was too strange . . . and she didn't seem to want him to love her, either.

He didn't try explaining that to Ulric. He would have had trouble explaining it to himself. But it was there, and it ate at him at the same time as the troubles against the invaders did.

By the way Ulric eyed him, he didn't need to explain it. The adventurer was alarmingly good at understanding how people worked. To Hamnet, that came close to being magic—dark magic. "Lady love or not, ask her anyway. She'll give you a straight answer. Maybe she'll even figure out why the Rulers get all weak in the knees when they think about you."

"Oh, go howl!" Hamnet said. But the seed, once planted, wouldn't go away.

MARCOVEFA LOOKED AT him. For all Count Hamnet could tell, she looked into him, looked through him. "Why do the Rulers fear you?" she said. "Why do you care so much about why? Isn't it enough to know that they do?"

"No, curse it," Hamnet said. "As far as I can see, it's nothing but stupidity. They have no reason to do it. Trasamund is more dangerous to them than I'll ever be. The Bizogots listen to him. Nobody listens to me here. Nobody listens to me down in the Empire, either. God knows *that's* true."

"You worry too much about things," Marcovefa said.

Hamnet Thyssen laughed harshly. "Now tell me something I didn't know. But I think the Rulers worry too much about me."

"If you want me to"—by the way Marcovefa said it, she meant, *If you're daft enough to want me to*—"I can try a divination to see why. I don't know what it will show. I don't know if it will show anything."

"Try," Hamnet said. "If it doesn't do anything else, maybe it'll make Ulric Skakki shut up. That'd be worth a lot to me all by itself."

She raised an eyebrow. "All right," she said. "We see." She smiled to herself as she picked up a small earthenware bowl. She admired pottery. So did the Bizogots, who got it in trade from the Empire. Their nomadic way of life didn't let them build the kilns they would have needed to make their own bowls and pots and jugs. "I will be back," she told him. "I need water for this divination. I will look into the water in the bowl and see what it shows."

"All right. We have scryers who work like that," Hamnet said.

She nodded. "I am not surprised. Anyone who does magic would think of this. Easier to keep water in a bowl than to weave a basket that holds it."

"Yes." Count Hamnet nodded, too. The Bizogots also had that art. Raumsdalians didn't. No need for it in a land where potters worked in every village.

Marcovefa ducked out of their hut. It wasn't far from

the edge of Sudertorp Lake; she soon returned, carrying the bowl carefully so she wouldn't spill the lake water. "Come outside," she told Hamnet. "The sun will help show what there is to see."

"If you say so." Hamnet expected the perpetually curious—perpetually nosy—Bizogots to crowd around and watch her work magic. But they didn't. Maybe keeping them away was another magic. Hamnet couldn't think of anything else likely to do it.

The shaman from atop the Glacier began to chant in her own dialect. Hamnet Thyssen had learned bits and pieces of it, but not enough to follow her song. Follow or not, he knew about what she had to be saying. She was asking for calm water, in which she could see what would happen in days to come.

She bent low over the bowl, still chanting. The water inside lay utterly still. To Hamnet, it was only water. To Marcovefa, it would show what lay ahead more clearly than a mirror of polished silver down in Nidaros showed a fair lady's reflection.

Then, without warning, the bowl broke. Marcovefa exclaimed in surprise. The water spilled out and carved a couple of tiny gullies in the dirt in front of the hut.

"I didn't know it was cracked," Hamnet said.

"It wasn't," Marcovefa answered.

"But it must have been. It wouldn't have done that if it weren't," Hamnet insisted.

She shook her head. "No. That was part of the scrying. Look." She picked up the pieces of the bowl, then dug something out of the dirt with her fingernail. She held it under Hamnet's nose.

His eyes crossed as he tried to focus. "A little scrap of crystal. So what?"

"It's more than that," she said.

"Well, what is it, then?"

"Something to do with the divination."

"How could it be? It wasn't even in the water."

"It was under the water. That's what matters."

"You aren't making any sense," Hamnet said impatiently.

Marcovefa looked annoyed—not at him, but at herself. "I can't make sense about this—not as much as I want to, anyhow. The scrying broke apart when the bowl did."

"You mean you don't know what's ahead?" Hamnet felt like kicking something. "We just wasted the time and the bowl?"

"No." She shook her head again. "I learned . . . something, anyhow. You will face the Rulers here, in the land of the Bizogots."

"Not down in Raumsdalia?" Hamnet said in some surprise.

"Maybe there, too. But when it matters most, it will be here."

"And what happens then?"

"Then . . . the bowl breaks." Marcovefa gave him a crooked grin he would have thought he'd be more likely to see on Ulric Skakki's face. "You don't always find out everything you want to know."

"Of course not," Hamnet said. "That would make things too easy."

Marcovefa nodded, even if he'd meant it for a sour joke. "Yes. It would. But if I do not know what happens after the bowl breaks, neither do the Rulers. I saw that much, anyhow."

"Can you get another bowl and try again?" Count Hamnet asked.

"I am not brave enough," the shaman answered. "When the bowl broke and the water spilled, that told me I was not supposed to know any more. But the Rulers know what they are about. Whatever happens here, it happens on account of you."

"I'm going to go out and punch Ulric in the chops," Hamnet said.

"Why?"

"For being right."

"Ah." Marcovefa nodded once more. "Yes, that makes sense. Not many worse things a man can do."

Now he thought she was joking—but if she was, she hid it very well. "I still can't believe it," Hamnet said. "I'm nobody in particular. Why does this have to land on me?"

"Why *not* you? It has to land on someone. Or else it lands on no one, and the Rulers win without a real fight," Marcovefa said. "But you aren't 'nobody in particular.' Who has been beyond the Glacier? Who has been to the top of the Glacier, too?"

"Ulric. Trasamund." Hamnet Thyssen hesitated, then produced two more names: "Audun Gilli. Liv. So why me?"

"One in five is not 'nobody in particular,'" Marcovefa said. "Who has loved a woman from your folk, from the Bizogots, and from my folk? Only you."

"Is that why?" Hamnet was more appalled than anything else. He started to blurt, *Much good it's done me*, but swallowed the words. He didn't want to anger Marcovefa.

Swallowing words around a shaman didn't always help. By Marcovefa's expression, she knew what he was about to say even if he didn't say it. "I do not know if that is why or not," she said. "Maybe. Maybe not. But there is more to you than you want to see."

"More to land me in trouble," he said.

"That, too," she agreed, which didn't make him any happier. "Maybe also more to get you out, though."

He laughed. "When was the last time I wasn't in trouble?" He knew the answer to that, whether Marcovefa did or not: "The day before Sigvat's courier got to my castle to tell me I had to come to Nidaros, that's when. One thing after the other."

"Am I one thing—or the other?" she asked sharply.

"Of course you are," Hamnet said. "You know it as well as I do, too. You wouldn't be able to stand yourself if you didn't make trouble. Go ahead—tell me I'm wrong."

Marcovefa preened. She tried to pretend she hadn't, but she couldn't do it. Then she said, "Well, maybe I am. But not just trouble to you. Trouble to your enemies, too. You have lots of enemies."

"Who?" Count Hamnet said. "Me?" He was convincing enough to make Marcovefa poke him in the ribs. She didn't kick him in the ribs: he supposed to show him she wasn't his enemy . . . yet.

THREE DAYS LATER, another rider from the Empire came into what had been the Leaping Lynxes' summer village. Per Anders looked relieved to find Hamnet Thyssen there. "God be praised!" he said. "I bring you a letter from His Majesty." He took a fancy, beribboned, multiply sealed rolled parchment from his saddlebag and presented it to Count Hamnet with the best flourish a weary man could manage.

"Oh, joy," Hamnet said as he took it.

"Happy day," Ulric Skakki agreed.

The courier glanced from one of them to the other. "Does the honor of hearing from the Emperor—of having a letter in his own bright hand—not please you?"

"No," Hamnet said shortly.

"Sorry, Anders—not your fault," Ulric added. "But either he's going to lie to us or he's going to beg from us or he's going to do both at once." His voice elaborately casual, he went on, "So tell me—does the Empire still hold Nidaros?"

Per Anders flinched. "How the demon did you know it was lost?"

"Well, it wasn't the last time a rider made it up here, but we sent that poor bugger off with a flea in his ear," the adventurer answered. "It's the logical place for the Rulers to aim at, and they've got wizards we mostly can't match. So . . . Sigvat got away, did he? Where's he holed up now?"

"Aarhus," Anders said unwillingly. Count Hamnet whistled under his breath. Aarhus lay a long way south of Nidaros: four or five days' travel. The small sound drew the courier's attention back to him. "Aren't you going to read that?"

"I don't know. Am I?" Hamnet asked, not at all in jest. Per Anders winced. But Ulric was right—it wasn't the horseman's fault. He'd risked his life to obey Sigvat II, a man who, to Hamnet's way of thinking, had long since proved he wasn't worth obeying. Hamnet took a certain grim pleasure in tearing the ribbon and cracking the blobby red and green seals.

"Well? What sort of horse manure have we got here?" Ulric asked as Hamnet unrolled the parchment.

Hamnet didn't answer, not right away. Anders was right: the letter was in the Emperor's own hand, which made it much harder to read than if one of his secretaries had written it. Where were they now? Dead? Fled? How many poor bastards had the Rulers found in the dungeons under Sigvat's palace? What did they do with them? Turn them loose? Broil them for supper? Hamnet didn't think the Rulers were cannibals, but how could you be sure?

Sigvat II swore he'd lost Nidaros by treachery. Maybe it was even true. Count Hamnet couldn't see that it mattered now one way or the other. The Emperor also swore he would get the capital back by himself, which Hamnet didn't believe for a minute. Then he wrote, *We all need to work together against these savage, barbarous foes.* Hamnet Thyssen swore under his breath. Of all the things he hated, agreeing with his much-unloved sovereign stood close to the top of the list.

He wordlessly passed the letter to Ulric. "About what you'd expect," the adventurer said after going through it faster than Hamnet had. "His toes are scorched, and he wants us to come pull him off the fire."

"We're already doing more than he knows about," Hamnet said. "Not a lot of Rulers getting down to the Empire."

"The ones already down there are bad enough," Per Anders said. "More than bad enough. If you and the mammoth-herders here can come south to help us, Sigvat will be grateful."

Both Hamnet Thyssen and Ulric Skakki burst out laughing. "Do you think we were whelped yesterday?" Ulric asked. "No Emperor's ever grateful for longer than it takes him to pull up his pants again, and Sigvat's worse than most."

"Then you won't come?" Anders sounded tragic. "God help Raumsdalia."

"If God would help Raumsdalia, Sigvat wouldn't need us," Count Hamnet said. "We didn't tell you we wouldn't come. But if we do, we'll do it for our reasons, not Sigvat's."

"What reasons have we got?" Ulric seemed genuinely curious.

"What we've got to decide is, do we hate Sigvat worse than the Rulers?" Hamnet replied. "I know what Trasamund and Marcovefa will say. So do you."

Ulric Skakki grimaced. "Well, yes. They will say that. But they don't know Sigvat the way we do."

"No. They're lucky," Count Hamnet said.

That got a laugh from the adventurer and another wince from Per Anders. The poor courier seemed to do nothing but flinch, listening to the way Hamnet and Ulric roasted his sovereign—and theirs. "If you won't do it for Sigvat's sake, do it for the Empire's," he said. "Please. I beg you." He actually dropped to his knees and held out his hands palms up, as if pleading for mercy from foes who'd beaten him.

"Get up, you donkey," Hamnet said gruffly.

"Yes, do. This is embarrassing," Ulric agreed.

"I have no pride. I have no shame," Per said, staying on his knees. "Why should I be embarrassed? I am trying to serve Raumsdalia."

"With stewed parsnips on the side, I have no doubt," Ulric Skakki said. The courier looked blank for a moment, then sent him a reproachful stare. Ulric went on, "His Grace is right. Get up. You won't just have one barbarian invasion on your hands—you'll have two."

"We can deal with Bizogots. We've always dealt with Bizogots," Per Anders said.

"Don't let Trasamund hear you talk like that, or you'll be talking out of a new mouth in your neck," Hamnet Thyssen warned. But Anders was right. The Bizogots were a nuisance to the Empire. The Rulers were a deadly danger to it—and to the Bizogots as well.

"You'll come south, then?" Now Per did rise, and brushed mud from the knees of his trousers.

"I'm afraid we will." Count Hamnet spoke without enthusiasm. "As you say, not for Sigvat—be damned to Sigvat—but for Raumsdalia."

"Reasons don't matter when you're doing the right thing," Anders said.

"Reasons always matter." Hamnet sounded—and was—

very sure of himself. Ulric Skakki looked as if he wanted to argue, but held his tongue.

Marcovefa proved willing to go down into the Empire again. Trasamund proved eager. Neither reaction surprised Hamnet Thyssen. "We'll go! We'll clean them out in the south, and then we'll come back and clean them out here in the north, too," Trasamund boomed. He drew his big sword and flourished it above his head. "By God, we'll run them back beyond the Glacier!"

"No, we won't," Ulric said. "Don't be a bigger idiot than you can help. Maybe, if we're lucky enough, we can beat them down in the Empire. Don't ask God for what he's not about to give you."

"Who are you, to say what God can and can't do?" the jarl retorted. "Has he been talking to you?"

"He has," Ulric said solemnly, and Trasamund's eyes widened. The adventurer went on, "He told me, 'Don't listen to the big Bizogot with the bad temper, because he doesn't know what the demon he's talking about.'"

Trasamund snorted and made as if to cuff him. Hamnet had seen that Ulric could flip anybody who came at him, even if the attacker was much the bigger man. He didn't bother now. He just ducked away.

Per Anders wanted everyone to jump on a horse and ride off on the instant. That didn't happen; the courier must have known it wouldn't. The Bizogots rode out the next day. Hamnet thought that was pretty good.

Ulric didn't seem to. When Hamnet asked him why, he answered, "How much decent weather have we got left?"

Hamnet grunted. When would the Breath of God start blowing down from the north? Summer up here—summer in Nidaros, for that matter—got cut cruelly short by the frigid wind off the Glacier. Some years, it got cut shorter than others. "Nothing we can do about it any which way except go on as long as we can," Hamnet said.

"No doubt. No doubt." By the way Ulric said it, he would have bundled up the Breath of God in a leather sack and stolen off with it if only he could. But some things were beyond even his formidable talents.

"I don't know how much good we'll do." Hamnet looked at the small, makeshift army. Bizogots from half the clans on the steppe rode with Trasamund. Maybe they would follow the jarl's orders, maybe not—which was true of any force of Bizogots ever put together. They might have counted for something in terms of surprise. In pure fighting terms, they weren't worth much . . . save only Marcovefa.

She could do things no one else could even hope for against the Rulers. She could, yes—but would she? No way to know, not till she did or she didn't. And if she didn't, they were all ruined.

"We'll find out," Ulric said, which echoed Hamnet Thyssen's thoughts much too closely for comfort.

VIII

"Trees! Thank God!" Per Anders pointed toward the southern horizon. Sure enough, a dark smudge of evergreen forest showed up there. The Raumsdalian courier went on, "Up here in the Bizogot country, I keep thinking everything is too big, too wide. I might as well not be there at all—nobody would notice if I disappeared."

"Well, I know what you mean," Hamnet Thyssen said. "Too much landscape, no edges anywhere. And the sky is even bigger."

"No edges anywhere," Per repeated. "Yes, that's about right. It was better when I got to those shabby little huts by the lake. Then, at least, I could tell where things started and stopped."

"What do you mean, Anders? 'Shabby little huts'?" Trasamund said ominously. "I tell you, there is nothing else like them in all the Bizogot country." He'd complained that the Leaping Lynxes' permanent dwellings made them seem like Raumsdalians. But, to a man from the Empire he didn't know well, he naturally seemed proud of what his own folk had done.

"You've seen Nidaros, Your Ferocity." Per Anders tried to stay polite without backing down. "Next to the palaces and mansions there, these, uh, houses aren't impressive."

"Yes, I've seen Nidaros," Trasamund agreed. "So what? All those fancy palaces and mansions . . . the Rulers hold 'em now."

Per bit his lip. That shot went home. And it moved Count Hamnet's thoughts in a direction they hadn't found before. "Tell me," he said, as casually as he could, "do you happen to know whether Earl Eyvind Torfinn got out of Nidaros before the Rulers took the place?"

"I couldn't say, Your Grace," Anders answered. "I don't think he was one of the band who broke free with the Emperor, though."

"All right. Thanks," Hamnet said. So maybe Eyvind got away and maybe he didn't. But that wasn't really what Hamnet was thinking. So maybe Gudrid got away and maybe she didn't—that was more like it. Most of the time, you could count on Gudrid to land on her feet . . . or on her back, if that was what she needed to do. But in the chaos of a sack, who could say?

What if she was dead, knocked over the head or forced to serve a gang of men till they got tired of swiving her and cut her throat for one last thrill? *I ought to laugh. It would serve her right*, Hamnet thought. And part of him did feel like laughing—but not all, not all.

Looking around, he found Ulric Skakki gazing at him with ironic speculation. Did the adventurer know what was going through his mind? He wouldn't have been surprised. Ulric knew more than was good for him about all kinds of things. Deliberately, Hamnet looked away. Ulric chuckled. No, he wasn't easy to evade.

As they neared the firs and spruces, some of the Bizogots muttered among themselves. The forest was as strange and unwelcoming to them as the frozen steppe was to Raumsdalians. The mammoth-herders complained that they felt all closed in when trees surrounded them. Some Raumsdalians felt the same way, but not so many.

"Well, Thyssen? Shall we look for a border post or just plunge into the woods?" Trasamund asked.

"Better to look for a post, I think," Hamnet said. "They have roads leading south from them."

The jarl grunted. "All right. Makes sense."

They found what was left of a border station, though it had been burned. White bones in the ruins said the guardsmen hadn't got away. A road—or at least a track—did lead south from it. As the Bizogots rode in amongst the trees, they did more muttering. Dark, aromatic branches hid the sun and most of the sky. "It's like riding inside a tent," one of the big blond men said.

"Like riding inside mammoth guts," another put in.

"Smells a good deal better," Ulric said. That didn't seem to encourage them.

"Watch out for short-faced bears," Hamnet said. "They like to hide behind tree trunks and then jump out at whatever they think they can kill. Chances are they won't bother a big band like ours, but you never can tell." The Bizogots didn't like hearing that. Up on the steppe, most of the time you could see danger coming from a long way off. That didn't always mean you could get away from it, but you could see it. The mammoth-herders didn't care for the idea that it might lurk behind trees.

Neither did Hamnet Thyssen. Short-faced bears weren't the only danger, or the worst one. If the Rulers wanted to lay an ambush here, they could. Marcovefa likely had the best chance of sniffing one out. But she looked no more comfortable in the forest than most of the Bizogots did. She'd come down into the Empire once before, which didn't mean she liked it here.

"What's the first town down this road?" Hamnet asked Ulric. The adventurer might not have been everywhere, but he came close.

"It's Lonsdal, isn't it?" Ulric sounded uncertain, but only, Hamnet was sure, for politeness' sake.

"Lonsdal. That's right," Hamnet said. "I've heard the name, but I don't think I ever went through the place."

"You didn't miss much," Ulric Skakki said. "It's about what you'd expect up here: a hole in the ground with a stockade around it. If the Rulers have come through, I don't suppose it's the better for that."

"Not many places are." Count Hamnet thought of the Rulers plundering Earl Eyvind's mansion down in Nidaros. He thought of them laughing drunkenly as they threw ancient codices into the fire one after another. He thought of them leering as they pulled Gudrid's provocative gowns out of her closet. Would they throw those away? Would they put them on women of their own, or on Raumsdalian women staying alive by doing what they could for the new conquerors?

Or would Gudrid, wearing one of those gowns, somehow charm the invaders into leaving Eyvind Torfinn's home intact? She wouldn't do it for Eyvind's sake; Hamnet was sure of that. But for her own? A different story altogether.

Could she bring it off? Hamnet only shrugged. He had no way to know. But it was possible, maybe just as possible as the mental picture of her corpse naked in a gutter, raped to death.

When they got to Lonsdal, they found the Rulers *had* been here before them. The stockade was down: not undermined, but blasted by some sorcery. Much of the town seemed to have burned. The stench of death lingered in the air, though the carrion birds had taken what they could.

Some people still lived here. They peered from the doorways of buildings that survived. "Good God! More barbarians!" somebody shouted in what sounded like despair.

"We'll fight!" someone else yelled. An arrow arced through the air. It landed well short of the Raumsdalians and Bizogots, but served as a warning even so.

"You idiots! We're not invading you! We're here to fight the God-cursed Rulers," Hamnet Thyssen bellowed.

"You always did know how to make friends," Ulric Skakki said, much more quietly. Hamnet waved him to silence.

The locals went back and forth with one another. At last, warily, one of them came out into the open and approached the newcomers. "You don't *talk* like a damned foreigner," the fellow said.

"I'm not," Hamnet answered. "We're at war with the people who did this to you. Have you got any food at all you can spare us?"

"Maybe a little," the man said dubiously.

"Or maybe more than a little," Trasamund rumbled. "Do you want to see what damned foreigners can do if you make them angry?"

"No," the local said. "But we already had one set of robbers go through here. How much do you think they left us?"

And you're another set of robbers. He didn't say that. Trasamund didn't catch it in his voice. Count Hamnet did. By the way one corner of Ulric's mouth quirked up, so did he. And, by the way Marcovefa raised an eyebrow, so did she.

"Do what you can," Hamnet said. "We came south off

the Bizogot steppe to fight the Rulers. We can't do it on empty bellies, though."

"Oh, joy," the local told him. "Well, if you whip 'em, don't chase 'em back this way. Don't reckon we could live through it if they came through Lonsdal one more time—or if you were right behind 'em again."

The locals coughed up some bread and some flat rounds made from rye and oat flour and some smoked meat. Even more reluctantly, they produced a little beer. Hamnet would have bet they had more than they were showing. He couldn't blame them too much for holding back, though. They had to go on living, too.

They didn't invite any newcomers to use their houses or their beds. In fact, they made it plain the Bizogots and the Raumsdalians with them had better keep clear unless they wanted a fight. Hamnet worked hard to keep the mammoth-herders from losing their tempers. More often than not, Bizogots responded to a challenge with a fist in the teeth.

"We'll post guards tonight around our own camp," Trasamund declared, "the same as we would anywhere in enemy country." He glared at Hamnet as if daring him to say they were anywhere else.

Hamnet didn't. All he said was, "Sounds like a good idea to me."

"If the people we're trying to help are liable to jump on us in the dark, what's the point of helping them?" the jarl asked.

"They've already had a lot of trouble. They think we're more of the same," Hamnet answered.

"If they do jump us, they'll find out how right they are." Trasamund made a fist.

"That doesn't do us much good. It doesn't do them much, either," Hamnet said.

"Beats the demon out of getting ambushed by a bunch of skulking murderers in the night," Trasamund retorted.

"Set some obvious sentries," Hamnet said. "And set some who aren't so obvious. The locals won't have the nerve to try anything."

"We'll make them sorry if they do," the Bizogot said.

The folk of Lonsdal didn't. Even more reluctantly than they had the evening before, they came up with some food in the evening. They didn't cheer out loud when the Bizogots rode south, but they weren't far from it. Hamnet could see that in their faces. If you lived in a place like this, you had to want the outside world to leave you alone most of the time. The folk of Lonsdal hadn't got enough of what they wanted.

RIDING SOUTH, HAMNET wondered what the Rulers would do to thwart him. The short-faced bear that had attacked his comrades; that, on dying, had proved not to be a natural bear at all but a shaman or wizard in sorcerous disguise . . . He asked Marcovefa if the enemy had anything like that in mind this time around.

Her nostrils flared, as a lion's might when it sought a scent. After a moment, she shook her head, saying, "I feel nothing."

"Can they be fooling you?" he persisted.

Marcovefa's nostrils flared again, this time in scorn. "Not likely!" she said. But then she hesitated. "Maybe not impossible," she admitted, and Hamnet admired her for that. "Since the sickness spell, I think their shamans are not stupid and hopeless all the time."

Hamnet reminded himself that the magicians she mocked were far stronger than the best Bizogot shamans and Raumsdalian wizards. "Well, if you do sense anything, don't keep it a secret," he said.

"I will not do that," she said. It didn't have the *Don't worry, little boy* flavor it might have before she learned the Rulers could be dangerous to her. Or maybe she was just getting better at not hurting his feelings.

They hadn't gone much farther before they discovered the Rulers *were* doing their best to stay annoying. The road suddenly ended. Actually, no: it didn't end, but it stopped being usable. Trees had fallen across it in wild disorder, tangled together worse than jackstraws. Going forward—going straight forward, anyhow—was impossible.

"Magic?" Hamnet asked Marcovefa.

"Magic," she agreed. "But not new magic. They did this a while ago."

"I'm surprised the folk from Lonsdal didn't know," Ulric Skakki said.

"How do you know they didn't?" Hamnet said. "Maybe they did, but they weren't about to tell the likes of us." Ulric grunted and gave back a reluctant nod.

"What do we do about it?" Trasamund asked. "I don't know much about trees." He proved he didn't—he was speaking the Bizogots' language, but he used the Raumsdalian word for trees. He had to; his own tongue lacked a name for them. "Can we clear them out of the way with magic and go on?"

"Likely easier to slip into the forest and go around the jam," Ulric said.

Marcovefa nodded. "Yes. This is so. Often magic can make a mess better than it can clear a mess."

"Well, all right." By the way Trasamund said it, it wasn't. "Trees all around? Not even a path through them?" He muttered something under his breath.

"There, there." Ulric clicked his tongue between his teeth in mock—and mocking—sympathy. "You can hold my hand if it bothers you."

The jarl suggested several other things he could do with his hand. None of them had much to do with holding someone else's . . . or with trees, come to that. Ulric Skakki only grinned. Still swearing, Trasamund plunged into the forest. Where one Bizogot would go, others would follow. They might not like it much, but they would do almost anything to keep from seeming cowards.

To Hamnet Thyssen, it was only a forest. The one down by his castle in southeastern Raumsdalia had more broad-leafed trees than evergreens, while this one was almost all conifers. As far as he was concerned, though, the difference was one of degree, not of kind. He didn't mind having trees all around him. He took it for granted. Roads were fine when you were traveling, but not when you were hunting.

Although the day was cool, sweat poured off Marcovefa. She liked trees, and being among trees, even less than Trasamund did. "We'll get back to the road soon," Hamnet assured her.

"Not soon enough!" she said.

"You know, the Rulers come from treeless country, too," Ulric remarked. "Maybe they don't like being closed in, so they have a pretty good notion our Bizogots won't like it, either."

"Do they wonder about how herd animals think?" Hamnet used the Rulers' name for other people.

"As little as they can get away with, I suspect, or likely something less than that," Ulric said, which struck Hamnet as cynical and probable at the same time.

Whatever the reason, the Rulers didn't harass their foes in the forest except for the fallen trees. The Bizogots breathed loud sighs of relief when they came out into open country once more. Pointing to an apple orchard ahead, Trasamund said, "A few trees every now and then are all right. We can go around them—we don't have to get stuck amongst 'em."

Another Bizogot added, "It won't be like they're trying to eat us up."

Count Hamnet and Ulric and even Audun Gilli exchanged amused glances. Only someone who didn't know trees was likely to imagine them as predators. Hamnet thought of the plums near his castle. He tried to imagine one of them waylaying passersby. The picture didn't want to form.

"Remember," Trasamund said, "if you see anybody riding a deer, he's the enemy. Kill the bastard before he kills you."

"Always a good idea with enemies," Ulric agreed. "They hardly ever give you a hard time once they're dead."

"Hardly ever?" Hamnet Thyssen said. "What do you do with the ones who haunt you?"

"Exorcise 'em," Ulric answered at once. "Everybody needs a little exorcise now and then." Hamnet gave him a reproachful stare, which he ignored.

Most of the time, travelers coming down from the south would have seen horses and cattle and sheep in the fields. Not now. Count Hamnet was saddened but not surprised. The Rulers would have stolen or killed as many animals as they could get their hands on. And the local farmers would have fled with the rest: off to the west or east or south, any direction but the one from which the invaders were coming.

Even without livestock, the land seemed rich to the Bizogots. Something else about it surprised them, too. "You use some of the land for one thing and some for another," a mammoth-herder said. He might have been talking about a clever piece of sorcery. "I can tell by what grows and the way you have fences." Up on the broad, trackless steppe, fences were only a waste of time and work.

"We have the notion that land belongs to the person who works it," Hamnet said. Things were more complicated than that, but it would do for a start.

And it was plenty to shock the Bizogot. "Land belongs to the clan," he declared. He might have been stating a law of nature. He probably thought he was.

"Different peoples have different customs," Count Hamnet said. "Not always right. Not always wrong. Just different."

"Land belongs to the clan," the Bizogot repeated. His folk, for instance, rejoiced in stubbornness—mulishness, a Raumsdalian would have called it.

"Never argue with a blockhead," Ulric Skakki said in Raumsdalian. "You won't convince him, and it only irks you."

"Who are you calling a blockhead?" the Bizogot demanded, also in Raumsdalian.

"You," Ulric answered calmly. "Just because you can be a blockhead in more than one language doesn't mean you're not a blockhead."

"By God, I ought to cut your liver out for that," the mammoth-herder said.

"We need Skakki." Trasamund's voice went hard and flat. "Anyone who wants to fight him has to fight me first."

"I don't have to hide behind your skirts. If this unwashed ruffian thinks he can take me—" Ulric began.

Trasamund cut him off with a sharp chopping gesture while the offended Bizogot shouted angrily. "I know you don't need to hide," the jarl said. "I know you can cut Ottar here into dogmeat, too." The Bizogot—Ottar—shouted again. Trasamund took no more notice of him than Ulric had of Hamnet not long before. He went on, "We need you, too, Ottar, only not so much. If I have to choose between the two of you, I choose Skakki."

"He's not even of our blood," Ottar said. "Since when do you choose people who sit around all the time over proper nomads?"

Before Trasamund could say anything to that, Ulric laughed in Ottar's face. "You go back and forth over the same range all the bloody time, and you call yourself a nomad? Have you traveled beyond the Gap? Have you gone up onto the Glacier? Have you ever seen the deserts in the far southwest? Have you been through the jungles beyond the desert? Nomad? Ha!" He laughed again.

Count Hamnet eyed Ottar, wondering what he'd do next. When Ulric went after a man, he flayed him with his tongue. Would Ottar try to wipe out the insult with blood? Or would he go off somewhere and lick his wounds?

He did neither. He tried to fight back with words, jeering, "Talk is cheap. Just because you say you've been to those places doesn't mean you have."

"I've been through the Gap with him. I've been up on the Glacier with him, too," Trasamund said. "The hot places I don't know, but they wouldn't surprise me."

"I've been in the desert," Hamnet Thyssen added. "It is the way Ulric says it is. I haven't been in the jungle myself—I haven't fared that far south. But what I've heard about it from other people makes me believe Ulric's been there, too."

Ottar looked at him. He looked at Trasamund. And he looked at Ulric Skakki. Then, shaking his head, he rode away from the adventurer. Hamnet thought that was one of the smarter things he could have done.

A SQUAD OR SO of Raumsdalian soldiers sat around a fire, roasting a sheep they'd probably lifted. They looked up in alarm when the Bizogots rode down on them. A couple of men stared to run, but they really had nowhere to run to. "Hold it right there!" Trasamund bawled, and hold it they did.

"You aren't the new barbarians. You're the other barbarians." The Raumsdalian who spoke sounded almost indignant, to say nothing of confused.

"Yes—that's us, the other barbarians," Count Hamnet said. Hearing perfect Raumsdalian come from his lips, seeing a swarthy man among the blond mammoth-herders, only confused the soldiers more.

"Who the demon are you?" one of them asked.

"Count Hamnet Thyssen," Hamnet answered, and waited to see what would happen next.

The name meant nothing to some of them. Others, though, jerked as if stung by wasps. "Hamnet Thyssen!" exclaimed the soldier who'd asked his name. "There's a fat price on your head. Did you know that?"

"No, but I'm not surprised," Hamnet said. "Since the Emperor sent a man"—he waved toward Per Anders—"to bring me back to Raumsdalia, I don't think you could collect that price right now."

"Of course, you could be wrong," Ulric Skakki said silkily.

"I suppose so," Count Hamnet said. With Sigvat II, being wrong was easy. His ingratitude towered higher than the Glacier and sank deeper than the bottom of Sudertorp Lake. If you trusted him, you had only yourself to blame.

"What do we do with them?" Trasamund asked—a good, practical question.

"What are they doing here?" Ulric added—another good question. Hamnet suspected the soldiers were there because they'd been part of an army the Rulers shattered. A few questions proved he was right. Ulric asked the stragglers, "Are you ready for another go at the bastards who beat you before?"

Some of the Raumsdalians nodded without hesitation. Others just sat there looking unhappy. They didn't want another go at the Rulers. All they wanted was to stay where they were, run away from danger, and scavenge as they got the chance. *They might as well be coyotes*, Hamnet thought scornfully.

"Come on," he told them. "If Raumsdalia loses, none of this will do you any good. You'll just be part of the Rulers' herd, and they'll cull you whenever they feel like it. Is that any way for a man to live?"

"Beats getting an arrow through your brisket or some nasty magic coming down on your head," a soldier said.

"That will happen anyhow," Hamnet said. "It won't happen today, maybe, because the Rulers are busy farther south. But if they win down there, they'll clean you out up here, too. Or do you think I'm wrong, too?"

By the miserable, hangdog expression on the soldier's face, he didn't think Count Hamnet was wrong, however much he wished he did. "I don't ever want to fight those buggers again," he mumbled.

"Would you rather they came hunting you after they cleaned out everybody else?" Hamnet asked. The Raumsdalian trooper looked unhappier yet.

Trasamund lost patience with him, as the jarl was apt to do: "Or would you rather we rolled over you and then went on and fought the Rulers ourselves? We'll use you people if we can, but we won't waste time on account of you."

That persuaded the Raumsdalians. Hamnet Thyssen might have known it would. They couldn't hope to fight the host in front of them. How well they'd fight against the Rulers . . . Hamnet and Trasamund would just have to wait and see. But if they were going to build their fighting tail, they would have to use odds and sods like these. How many bands, some only four or five men, some perhaps a couple of dozen, wandered through the northern part of the Empire these days? Dozens? Scores? Hundreds? Hamnet couldn't know, but he thought his guesses were pretty good.

"You can persuade people to do nearly anything," Ulric Skakki remarked, "as long as all their other choices seem worse."

"If that's not philosophy, it ought to be," Hamnet said.

"Ha!" the adventurer said. "Save that kind of nonsense for Earl Eyvind. There are tricks to riding a horse, and there are tricks to driving people. That's one of them—or it sure looks like one to me."

"To me, too," Count Hamnet agreed. "Why else are we here?"

Trasamund answered that before Ulric Skakki could: "We're here to beat the Rulers. If we don't do that, we're just pissing into the wind."

A Raumsdalian would have talked about spitting into the wind. That made the jarl crude by imperial standards. It didn't make him wrong, however much Count Hamnet wished it would have.

He glanced over to Marcovefa. Without her, this motley band of Bizogots and Raumsdalians had little chance against the invaders beyond the Glacier. Hamnet Thyssen shook his head. He laughed at his own foolishness. Without Marcovefa, this ragtag band had *no* chance against the Rulers, none whatsoever. Were it possible to have less than no chance, the band without Marcovefa would have.

Yet she herself was almost as alien to her comrades as the Rulers were. In some ways, she was more alien. Yes,

Rulers who failed at anything important or who found themselves about to be captured often killed themselves to escape what they saw as disgrace. But they didn't devour the corpses of their defeated foes. Hamnet knew why Marcovefa's folk had become cannibals. Up atop the Glacier, meat of any sort was too scarce, too precious, to let any of it go to waste. It made her no less strange, no less appalling, to those who didn't share her customs.

One of the Bizogots pointed southeast. "There's one of the God-cursed riding deer the God-cursed Rulers use!" he shouted.

Men looked to their weapons. Marcovefa, Audun Gilli, and Liv were warriors only in emergencies. That didn't mean they weren't about to fight. And their fight might prove harder and more dangerous than anything swordsmen and archers and lancers faced. Without Marcovefa, it surely would have been. With her, the odds improved.

Before Hamnet could wonder how much they improved—the sorcery-spread sickness had jolted Marcovefa's confidence—a Raumsdalian who'd just joined them asked, "What did the fellow with the yellow whiskers say?"

Hamnet swore under his breath. He and Ulric were both fluent in the Bizogots' tongue. Audun Gilli, Per Anders, and Marcovefa could get along in it. Most of the mammoth-herders knew at least some Raumsdalian. But these imperial troopers had never had any reason to learn the northerners' speech.

He translated for them. Then he spoke to Ulric: "We've got a new complication, or an old complication back again."

"Oldest cursed complication in the world—except for men and women diddling where they aren't supposed to," Ulric agreed. He paused. Seemingly of its own accord, his left eyebrow quirked upward. "Nothing personal, Your Grace."

"Right. Nothing personal," Count Hamnet said tightly. Was it his fault two of his women had diddled where they weren't supposed to? (If you listened to them, the answer was yes. If you listened to Ulric Skakki, it was also yes. Hamnet didn't want to listen to any of them, either in person or inside his own mind. With the enemy out there in front of him, he didn't have to, either.)

That Ruler wasn't alone. He was an outrider from a small troop of men. Seeing so many foes bearing down on them, they found no disgrace in fleeing. Their warrior's code was stern, but not always senselessly so.

Riding deer were admirable beasts in many ways. They showed great endurance. Their antlers, even if bluntertined than those of the deer near Hamnet's castle, made useful weapons. All that said, they remained slower than horses. The mounted Bizogots and Raumsdalians soon gained on them.

The Rulers had found out about horses since coming down through the Gap into the world Hamnet knew—the world he'd long believed to be all the world there was. They kept looking back over their shoulders to gauge how much trouble they were in.

Before long, they started reaching for arrows. Their formidable bows outranged the ones Raumsdalians and Bizogots carried. That wasn't the worry uppermost in Hamnet's thoughts, though. "Have they got a wizard with them?" he called to Marcovefa.

"What?" she shouted back.

"Have—they—got—a—wizard—with—them?"

"Oh," Marcovefa said, and then, "I don't think so."

Hamnet had to be content—or rather, discontented—with that. He strung his own bow and nocked an arrow. The Rulers began to shoot first. Even loosing arrows backward, they could hit from a distance their foes found impossible to match. A Bizogot swore when a shaft pierced the palm of his hand.

But, because horses were faster than riding deer, the Bizogots and Raumsdalians soon started shooting back with some hope of success. A wounded deer bounded away from the rest of the troop, its rider unable to control it. Another deer crashed to the ground. With luck, the Ruler it carried wouldn't come through that unscathed. And an invader, hit in the neck as he turned back to shoot, slid off his mount and lay motionless.

Marcovefa began to sing in the saddle. Not so very long before, she wouldn't have tried that. She was a better, more confident rider than she had been. And no wonder— till she came down from the top of the Glacier, she'd never imagined animals like horses and riding deer, let alone mounted ones.

The shaman pointed in the Rulers' direction. She might not have known anything about riding deer till she came down onto the Bizogot steppe, but her magic now was plenty to send them mad. They started bucking and bounding over the dreary landscape, regardless of what the men on them wanted. The Rulers couldn't get away, and they couldn't fight back—the worst of both worlds.

But they wouldn't give up. Several of the men who'd been bucked off their deer drew swords and stood back-to-back, ready to make the best fight they could. A couple of warriors who'd managed to hang on to their bows went on shooting at the Bizogots and Raumsdalians as if nothing were wrong.

"They're tough buggers," Ulric Skakki said, not without admiration, as he shot an enemy bowman from behind. He was not a sporting fighter, but he was a very effective one. "Almost makes you wish they were on our side."

"No, it doesn't," Hamnet Thyssen growled. "It only makes me wish they were all back on the far side of the Gap where they belong."

"Don't hold your breath. Even if we somehow beat them down here, don't hold your breath," Ulric said. "They're part of the mix now, I'm afraid. And the Gap won't be what it is now for very much longer, either."

"Huh?" Hamnet didn't get an answer right away. He urged his horse up into a gallop so he could cut down an embattled warrior of the Rulers. But Ulric's odd comment stayed in his mind. He asked the adventurer about it again after the fighting ended.

"What? D'you think I'm wrong?" Ulric said.

"How can I tell? I don't know what you're talking about," Hamnet replied.

"No, eh? You're dense today, aren't you?" As usual, Ulric had charm.

"I must be," Hamnet said. "Otherwise, I wouldn't waste time on you."

That won him a grin. "You say the sweetest things," Ulric Skakki told him. "Well, think about it a little. The Glacier is melting. That's why we've got the Gap at all. What happens when the Glacier melts some more? The Gap won't be this little thing where you can pee from one side to the other." He exaggerated, but not enormously. "Pretty soon, it'll be ten miles wide. Before too long, it'll be a hundred miles wide. And when it is, we might as well call it the Highway instead of the Gap, because we won't have a God-cursed chance of keeping anything from the other side out."

"Oh," Hamnet said. He plunged his sword into the soft loam to get more blood off the blade. That made much too much sense. He'd had the same thought himself, but he hadn't followed it to see where it might lead. "Maybe the

Golden Shrine is under the Glacier somewhere, and it'll come out once the ice melts some more."

"Maybe you're an idiot, but I hadn't thought so till now," Ulric said cheerfully. "Don't hold your breath waiting for the Golden Shrine to show up. There. That's the best advice you ever got, unless somebody was smart enough to tell you to keep away from Gudrid before it was too late."

"Leave Gudrid out of this." As always, anger filled Count Hamnet's voice when he talked about his former wife.

This time, Ulric gave the anger nothing to light on. "All right," he said. He didn't even add that, if this ragtag army with the strange sorceress beat the Rulers, it would prop up not only Gudrid but also Sigvat II. Why mention it, when Hamnet could figure it out for himself? Hamnet not only could, he dutifully did. Ulric sent him a benign smile, watching him do it. The adventurer could be dangerous all kinds of ways.

Trasamund walked by, carrying the head of a dead Ruler by the curly beard. None of the invaders had surrendered. They had the courage of their convictions—and much good it had done them. Trasamund seemed happy enough. He wasn't dangerous in so many ways as Ulric Skakki was, which didn't mean he wasn't a dangerous man.

"Well, we whipped this bunch of them, anyway," he said, pausing for a moment.

"So we did," Ulric agreed. "Now—how many more bunches do we have to whip before we're done?"

"How am I supposed to know?" Trasamund asked suspiciously.

"Somebody should, don't you think?" Ulric asked.

"Don't bait him," Hamnet Thyssen said.

"Who, me?" The adventurer was the picture of innocence. That had to mean he was most likely to be guilty. Hamnet didn't know how he knew that, but know it he did.

IX

The Bizogots and Raumsdalians rode through the fertile farmland that had been the bed of Hevring Lake till its ice dam melted through and spilled its waters over the scabrous badlands farther west. Hamnet Thyssen sighed. "I don't know if I want to see sacked Nidaros or not," he said.

"Sigvat's the one who ought to see it," Ulric Skakki said. "We ought to rub his nose in it, so he gets some idea of how many mistakes he made and how big they were."

Count Hamnet laughed at him. "Sigvat's more likely to get pregnant than to get an idea."

"That hurts too much to be funny," Ulric said, but he laughed anyhow.

"Things don't look so bad here," Trasamund remarked.

A few houses and barns had been burned. Hamnet supposed those were places where the locals showed fight against the Rulers. He didn't see much in the way of livestock. Either Raumsdalians had escaped with their horses and cattle and sheep or the invaders had stolen or slaughtered them. But grain still ripened in the fields. Hardly any fruit trees had been cut down. Trasamund might not be the best judge of what the Raumsdalian countryside was supposed to look like, but he didn't sound like a crazy man, either.

Local farmers, the ones who still survived, had learned their lesson. As soon as they saw armed men in the distance, they fled. They didn't wait around to find out whose side the warriors were on. As far as they were concerned, no warriors were on their side. Hamnet would have had a demon of a time persuading them they were wrong.

"You got rich. You got fat. You got lazy." Marcovefa sounded like a judge passing sentence. "You Bizogots, you Raumsdalians. Fat and lazy."

"Us, rich?" Trasamund said. "Honh! Not likely!"

But his bluster lacked its usual passionate conviction. He'd seen what things were like up on top of the Glacier and in the mountain refuges that stuck up above the ice. By Marcovefa's standards, even the poorest Bizogots on the frozen steppe were rich beyond the dreams of avarice.

"How much of Nidaros is left, do you think?" Audun Gilli said. "Can we go around the place, or do we need to go through?"

Some small part of Hamnet did want to see the capital in ruins. Nidaros was Sigvat's city, and Gudrid's, not his. Back when he was living in his own castle down in the southeast, he wouldn't have minded if something horrible happened to the place. So he'd told himself then, anyhow. As he'd found before in other ways, getting what you thought you wanted didn't always make you happy.

Hamnet wondered if anything would ever make him happy. His former wife and the Emperor groveling at his feet? A slow, sour smile crossed his face, like sunshine briefly breaking through on a drizzly day. He might not win lasting happiness from that, but it would do for a little while.

"Well?" Audun persisted. "Do we have to go through Nidaros?"

"We'll decide when we get closer," Hamnet said. "We'll see how things are around the place—that'll tell us whether we need to go in."

The wizard nodded. "All right. Good enough. It's not as if I've got family there to worry about." His mouth twisted. Hamnet remembered that he himself wasn't the only one to know hard times. Audun had lost house and wife and children in a fire, and spent years after that drinking so he didn't have to think about it.

Per Anders pointed ahead. "Is that serai still open, or did the Rulers sack it?"

"No smoke from the chimney," Ulric Skakki said. "That's never a good sign."

Sure enough, the serai was deserted. The stench of death lingered in the taproom. A corpse, mostly skeletal, lay behind the bar. "Looks like we're on our own for supper and drinks," Hamnet observed.

"Does kind of, doesn't it?" Ulric said. "Unless this poor bugger died of old age waiting to get served. I've known a few serais like that."

"So have I—but this isn't one of them." Hamnet Thyssen pointed to the skull. It bore a dreadful wound, most likely from an axe but perhaps from a sword. The fellow who'd owned it—the tapman?—didn't die of starvation.

"Yes, that's a splitting headache, all right," Ulric agreed. Then he stooped and lifted a couple of stoppered jars the man's corpse had partly covered. "And the Rulers really are a pack of barbarians from the back of beyond. They don't even know how to do a proper job of plundering."

He scraped away at the pitch sealing one stopper with the tip of his dagger. Once he could wiggle the stopper, he worked it free with the dagger and his thumb and forefinger. "What have you got?" Audun Gilli sounded more than a little interested.

Ulric sniffed, then swigged. "Yes, that's mead, all right. Pretty good mead, too." He swigged again, as if to make certain. Audun also looked more than a little interested. He looked thirsty, as a matter of fact. Ulric passed him the jar.

He drank, then drank some more, then drank some more after that, and finally delivered his verdict: "You're right. That is pretty good mead." He took another swig, just to make sure . . . or just because he wanted to.

"Save some for the rest of us," Ulric said, snatching the jar back.

"You might want to be able to walk when you're done, too," Hamnet said.

"Mm—I might." By the way Audun Gilli said it, he wasn't even close to sure he'd care about walking.

"Let me try some of that," Trasamund said. Looking resigned, Ulric Skakki gave him the jar. The Bizogot raised it to his lips. His larynx worked. He made at least as big a dent in the mead as Audun had. When he finally lowered the jar, he nodded. "Not bad at all."

"Do I get to try it, too?" Hamnet Thyssen asked pointedly.

"If there's any left." Trasamund shook the jar and listened to the slosh inside. "Still some, anyhow." He held it out to Hamnet.

The Raumsdalian noble shook it, too, and hefted it. "Not bloody much. You're a pig, Your Ferocity—and so are you, Gilli." He drank. The mead was as advertised—and there *wasn't* bloody much of it. He drained the jar.

"You've called me plenty worse than that," Audun said.

Count Hamnet threw the jar down on the floor, not quite at the wizard's feet. It smashed, even though the floor was only rammed earth. Audun Gilli sidestepped smartly to dodge one flying sherd. "You deserved what I called you, and more besides," Hamnet said in the flat voice of formal hostility.

"We've been round this barn before—too often." Ulric Skakki worked at the stopper on the other jar. "We don't need to hear it all again." He sniffed. "Besides, this one's wine." He thrust it at Count Hamnet. "Here—you go first."

"Bribing me, are you?" Hamnet said. The adventurer gave back a bland smile and a nod. Instead of making something of it, Hamnet drank. Sweet and strong, the wine ran down his throat. He took his fair share or a little more, then lowered the jar. "Pretty good wine," he reported, deadpan.

"You—! Give me that!" Trasamund started to snatch the jar out of his hands. So did Ulric. They glared at each other. They didn't quite square off, but they left the feeling that they would if somebody didn't do something in the next few heartbeats. Hamnet did something: he gave Audun Gilli the jar.

Trasamund and Ulric both glared at *him*. Audun looked astonished. Count Hamnet *was* astonished, at himself. This was the first time he'd done anything for Audun since the wizard took Liv away from him. He hadn't meant to; all he'd meant to do was annoy Ulric and Trasamund. Well, he'd managed that.

Audun wasted no time before sampling the wine. As Trasamund's had not long before, his larynx bobbed up and down. "Not bad at all," he allowed after reluctantly lowering the jar.

Ulric grabbed faster than Trasamund. He drank, and

made as if to go on drinking. Trasamund growled deep in his throat, like a lion warning a dire wolf it had better clear off from a carcass. Ulric was not a man to be intimidated like that, but he was a man who would share . . . when he felt like it.

He passed Trasamund the wine jar a bare instant before the jarl would have stolen it from him and perhaps started a real fight. "Ahh!" Trasamund said after his first gulp. "Those grapes died happy, by God!"

"They probably died when pretty girls squashed them with bare feet," Ulric Skakki said. He raised a more or less leering eyebrow. "Worse ways to go, I daresay. Ugly girls squashing you with bare feet, for instance."

Trasamund was drinking again, and almost choked. When he stopped spluttering, he said, "Is that really how they smash grapes? Women stepping on them? Or are you making it up to fool a Bizogot who doesn't know anything about wine except that it tastes good?"

"By God, Your Ferocity, in the fall there are women with purple toes down in the south where the grapes grow," Ulric said gravely, holding up his hand as if taking an oath. "They have big wooden vats full of grapes, and the women get in there and hike up their skirts and—"

"Trample out the vintage," Audun Gilli finished for him. "Sometimes the men will do it, too, but it's mostly women."

He pointed at the wine jar Trasamund was holding and murmured a charm. The jar grew a face: a pretty, spoiled-looking face. In a squeaky voice, it said, "And you can just quit thinking about looking up my skirt, too, you—you *man*, you. There I am, working my feet as purple as your nose, and you've got your mind in a cesspit!" Animating such things was Audun's favorite magical sport.

"My nose isn't purple!" Trasamund might have been answering a woman, not an enchanted jug.

Ulric Skakki looked artfully astonished. "You mean that isn't a plum stuck on to the front of your face?"

Like a lot of Bizogots, Trasamund had been down in Raumsdalia often enough to know what a plum was. His whole face turned red, if not purple. "One day you *will* talk too bloody much, Skakki. You'll be sorry for it when you are—you'd best believe you will."

"People keep telling me so," the adventurer said. "It hasn't happened yet, though. One day I'm going to get tired of waiting."

Trasamund muttered into his beard. Whatever he said, he didn't say it loud enough to get through the facial shrubbery. Trading insults with Ulric was a losing game; he gave worse than he got. As Count Hamnet had seen—and discovered, painfully, for himself—fighting Ulric was also a losing game. Which left . . . what? Loving him, maybe? Hamnet Thyssen scowled. That also struck him as an unappetizing choice.

HAMNET FOUND HIMSELF looking east as he rode across what had been Hevring Lake's bottomland. He saw Per Anders doing the same thing. Catching Sigvat's courier at it made him realize he was doing it, too. A little sheepishly, he said, "If the Rulers sacked Nidaros, not much point looking for the city smoke rising from it, is there?"

Per blinked. "No, I guess not," he answered, also sounding sheepish. "Force of habit."

"I know. I was doing the same thing," Hamnet said. "And I'll probably start doing it six or eight more times, till I get it through my thick head that that smoke cursed well won't be there."

He did, too. Late the next afternoon, they came close enough to Nidaros to get a good look at what the Rulers had done to the Raumsdalian capital. Hamnet could have done without it. It was almost as hard on him as seeing Gudrid's naked corpse would have been. And Nidaros itself hadn't betrayed him, even if important people inside the city had.

Nidaros' gray granite walls could have held out every Bizogot ever born for a thousand years. So Raumsdalians said, anyhow, and Hamnet Thyssen wasn't inclined to argue with the conventional wisdom there. Those stout walls had held out the Rulers . . . for a little while. Not for long enough.

The granite blocks didn't seem to have been overthrown. No: what happened to them was worse. It looked as if they'd been melted back into the lava from which they'd formed. Stone had flowed and run like hot fat, if not quite like water. What had happened to the men up on those walls when the granite melted? Nothing good— Count Hamnet was sure of that.

"Do we want to go in there?" Trasamund wondered aloud.

"Depends," Ulric answered. "If only a few people lived through the sack, if only a few people are back, then we can scrounge as much as we need. There'll be plenty of food and the like. But if a lot of the vultures that walk on two legs are prowling around in there, we're just wasting our time. Your choice, Your Ferocity."

"Let's go up, get a closer look," the jarl said. "Then we can figure out whether going in is smart or not."

"That's sensible," Ulric said. "But what the demon? Let's do it anyway." Trasamund sent him a curious look, but didn't try to parse the adventurer's comment. Hamnet did, and felt his head start to whirl. He gave it up as a bad job.

Somewhere not far from the western wall was the house Earl Eyvind and Gudrid had shared, the house that looked out on the Hevring bottomland. Did it still stand? Had the

Rulers plundered it? If they hadn't, was anything about the Golden Shrine still there, or had Eyvind Torfinn managed to pack up all his assembled knowledge when he fled?

Hamnet remarked on that to Ulric. "Should we go there?" he asked. "Or do you think it's a waste of time?"

"Mm . . . You ask interesting questions, and I wish to God you didn't." Ulric plucked at his beard. "Maybe we ought to see, eh? It's not too deep into the city. We can't get into too much trouble heading over there—I hope."

"Oh, we can always get into trouble." Hamnet Thyssen spoke with mournful conviction. "But will we get into worse trouble going in or staying clear?"

"Interesting questions, like I said." Ulric Skakki didn't make it sound like a compliment. By the way he said it, Count Hamnet might have come down with a rare—and socially embarrassing—disease. After a moment's thought, the adventurer looked pleased with himself. "Why don't we ask the wizards? They can tell us what kind of fools we are."

"I already know that. We're big fools, or we wouldn't be here," Hamnet said. "I want to know what we can do about it."

"Amounts to the same thing in the end," Ulric answered cheerfully.

They did talk to the wizards. Marcovefa, Audun Gilli, and Liv put their heads together. Marcovefa looked up at the sun. Liv opened her arms wide and spread her fingers wide, as if to trap a lot of air so she could smell it. Audun Gilli plucked up a pinch of earth and tasted it.

After that, they put their heads together again. Hamnet got the notion they were deciding on their verdict. Was that good? Bad? Indifferent?

Audun spoke for all of them: "You can go in if you want. We don't think it will make things any worse."

"Will it make them any better?" Ulric Skakki inquired, a heartbeat before Count Hamnet could ask the same question.

Audun and Liv and Marcovefa seemed equally surprised. They put their heads together one more time. When they broke apart again, Liv gave the answer for them all: "We don't know. That isn't plain."

"Well?" Hamnet asked Ulric. "What do you want to do?"

"Let's go," Ulric said. "I'm a ghoul at heart. I do want to see what Nidaros is like after a sack. Maybe it'll give us something new to tell Sigvat."

"The only thing I want to tell him is where to head in," Hamnet said grimly.

"When the Rulers chased him out of Nidaros, he found out where he was heading in, by God," Ulric replied. "I won't say it didn't serve him right."

"He'll say that," Hamnet predicted. "Nothing's ever his fault. If you don't believe me, just ask him."

Per Anders also wanted to go into Nidaros, to see what had become of it. They recruited a squad's worth of Bizogots to go with them and help keep them safe from whatever happened to be loose in the city. If the Bizogots did some plundering while they were there, Hamnet was willing to look the other way. Ulric seemed more than willing. He looked ready to do some plundering of his own.

They made the final approach to the fallen capital on foot. "No surly gate guards to persuade that we're worthy to go in," Hamnet remarked.

"I wonder if those whoresons tried asking the Rulers

their snooty questions," Ulric said. "If they did, they deserved whatever happened to them."

Listening to them, Per Anders looked pained. "You men are not proper Raumsdalian patriots," he said stiffly.

Ulric Skakki gave back a raucous laugh. "You just noticed?"

"What are you going to do about it?" Hamnet added.

"I'm going to wonder why His Majesty wants anything to do with the likes of you," the courier replied.

"Simple," Hamnet said. "He needs us. We can do something he wants done. We can give the Rulers a hard time—or he thinks we can."

"And then he'll figure out some fancy way to screw us," Ulric said. "That's the other thing he's good for—putting it to people who ought to be his friends."

"That's not fair," Per said.

"You're right," Hamnet Thyssen agreed. The Emperor's man looked vindicated till Hamnet finished, "Sometimes he's a lot worse than that. I wonder if the Rulers freed everybody they found in his dungeons."

"Not likely," Ulric said. "Nidaros would look a lot more crowded if they were running around loose."

Nidaros didn't look crowded—it looked all but deserted. Like any big city, it depended on constant deliveries of food from outside for survival. When those deliveries stopped, the people in the city could do one of two things: they could leave, or they could starve. If most of them left—or died—what was left and what modest supplies remained might keep a much smaller population going.

When Hamnet and Ulric and their companions strode into the city, somebody took a look at them and then dashed around a corner. "Well, what does that mean?" Ulric wondered. "Are we too tough to mess with? Or is he getting reinforcements? We'll find out—soon, I expect."

"Let them come," a Bizogot said. "Been a while since I killed anything."

"You're a friendly fellow, aren't you?" Hamnet said.

"I am, by God—to my friends," the blond barbarian said seriously.

Along with the magic that melted the walls, Nidaros had seen several fires. The wind must have been quiet: they hadn't spread very far, and they hadn't come together in a firestorm. Still, the sour scent of stale smoke lingered in the air. The Bizogots grumbled—charred rubble offered scant loot.

"What if this happened to Eyvind's house?" Hamnet worried.

"Then we go back," Ulric said. "Then we wasted our time coming in. That's all anybody can say. We didn't know till we tried. If the house is gone, we think about what we ought to do next."

That made sense. And what else *could* anyone say? They would know when they got there. Till they got there, they wouldn't.

If they got there. The Bizogots hadn't gone more than a few steps into Nidaros before they drew their swords and nocked arrows. No one had attacked them. No one but that one fellow had even shown himself. But the air shouted danger.

Hamnet took what he thought was the most direct route. And it would have been—if not for the barricade across it. *Something* moved behind the barricade. "Feel like a fight?" Ulric asked.

"No," Hamnet said.

He waited for the Bizogots to say they wanted nothing more. They didn't, not even the "friendly" warrior. Along with the others, he shook his big blond head. Hamnet didn't think they were afraid of whatever robbers had set up the barricade. Nidaros—all the buildings in Nidaros—was what intimidated them.

Ulric Skakki didn't feel like a fight, either. "Good," he said. "Let's see if we can slide around instead. If I remember how these alleys work . . ."

He soon proved he knew Nidaros far better than Count Hamnet had ever dreamt of doing. "Why were you following me?" Hamnet asked him.

"Why not? You were heading in the right direction. If we could do it the easy way, I didn't mind," the adventurer answered. "Since we can't—"

"You should have been a burglar."

"I have been, a time or three," Ulric said equably. He raised his voice a little: "Keep an eye on the doors, you Bizogots. If we run into trouble, it'll pop out of them." To Hamnet alone, he added, "I wouldn't have to say that to Raumsdalians. They'd know. But most of these boys never *saw* a door before they rode down into the Empire."

Not five minutes after he delivered his warning, three men leaped into the alley in front of his group. Two of them carried swords. The other had an axe. They were skinny and tough—and looked horrified, like a cougar that suddenly discovered it was facing a sabertooth.

Bowstrings thrummed behind Hamnet. Two arrows hit the axeman. One got one of the swordsmen. Another flew past the second swordsman. The Bizogot who'd loosed it cursed—a short shot, but he'd missed it.

The brigand with the axe crumpled. The swordsmen ran back into the building from which they'd emerged. One was swift as a weasel. The other—the wounded man—hobbled through the door. They slammed it behind them.

"That was easy," a Bizogot said. "Even if Kolli can't shoot straight." Kolli let out an indignant yelp.

"It *was* easy," Hamnet agreed. "But it wouldn't have

been if four or five more of those bastards had jumped out behind us, too."

The Bizogot was thoughtfully silent. Ulric went up and prodded the axeman with his boot. The robber groaned, lost in his own wilderness of pain. He wouldn't get up again. Ulric took his weapon. "Anybody want this?" he asked. "You can make a lot of trouble with it."

Two Bizogots played a finger game to see who got it. "Are you going to finish him?" Hamnet asked while the winner brandished his new toy.

"No," Ulric said. "He wouldn't have done it for me, so demons take him. If his friends haven't run away, let them take care of it. Come on."

They all strode past the axeman. A little to Hamnet's surprise, nobody kicked him or did anything else to make him hurt worse. He was dying anyhow, so that was only a small mercy.

Hamnet wondered whether the three robbers had friends who would aim to avenge them. His hand tightened on the leather-wrapped hilt of his sword. But the men seemed to have been on their own.

He and his comrades passed through another block that had burned. The Bizogots muttered among themselves. They'd seen grass fires before, no doubt. Maybe they'd seen a tent or two burn. But, as with doors, big fires, fires that chewed up lots of buildings, were new to them since they'd come to Raumsdalia. They didn't like them. Well, Hamnet didn't, either. And, to his sorrow, he'd seen a lot more of them than they had.

"We'll look foolish if Eyvind's house is nothing but charcoal," he said.

"Yes, we'll have made ashes of ourselves, sure enough," Ulric agreed. Count Hamnet winced.

"Let's go find out." Maybe Per Anders didn't notice the

atrocious pun. Maybe he just didn't care. If he didn't, Hamnet admired his detachment.

Earl Eyvind's house still stood. But the front door hung open. Hamnet didn't think that was a good sign. Ulric said, "Don't worry about it. Can you see some Ruler or local thief staggering out of here with his arms full of *books*?" He laughed the idea to scorn.

Hamnet's hand tightened again on the hilt of his sword. "I keep thinking that, if I go in there, the first thing I'll do is run into Gudrid."

"Well, you bloody well won't," Ulric Skakki said impatiently. "She isn't here, and good riddance to her."

Or did he say *Gudriddance*? Count Hamnet eyed him, but Ulric's cheery smile was proof against his scrutiny. They went inside. The adventurer proved right: Gudrid wasn't there.

Someone had looted the house. Hamnet had no idea whether it was the Rulers or Raumsdalian robbers. Whoever it was seemed to have done a good, thorough job. All the rich ornaments that had adorned the place were gone. So were most of the paintings and woven wall hangings. The rest were slashed, or else thrown on the floor and trampled.

When Hamnet Thyssen saw them, he got a bad feeling about Earl Eyvind's books. And sure enough, the scrolls and codices Eyvind had spent a lifetime accumulating lay torn and despoiled on the floor of his bedchamber. Hamnet sadly shook his head, knowing how much labor a scribe needed to copy a book.

"Sometimes people are no cursed good," he growled.

Ulric raised one eyebrow. "You only noticed just now?"

"As a matter of fact—no," Hamnet answered.

"Is anything here worth salvaging?" Per Anders asked.

"Sure doesn't look like it." Ulric started to turn away and head back toward the entrance.

But Count Hamnet said, "Wait." Ulric Skakki did, this time with both eyebrows high. Hamnet went on, "When I knew Gudrid, she'd always have secret hiding places for . . . things. They'd be clever ones, too, places where most people wouldn't think to look. Somewhere in this house, she'll have more hidey-holes."

"Yes, but will they hold anything we want?" Ulric asked.

"How do we know ahead of time?" Hamnet replied with a shrug.

"How do we know where to look for these, ah, hidey-holes?" Per Anders said. "Do we tear the whole place to pieces?"

"A lot of that's taken care of," Ulric pointed out.

"Look at things out of the corner of your eye," Hamnet said. "I make no promises, but I think it's worth trying. Gudrid's . . . sly. She's not too smart—even if she'd say the same thing about me—but she has her own kind of cleverness."

He looked around the bedchamber. Whoever'd ruined Eyvind Torfinn's books had also slashed the featherbed Eyvind and Gudrid once shared. Feathers floated in the air as Raumsdalians and Bizogots stirred them up. Hamnet didn't think Gudrid would have secreted anything inside the mattress—too easy, too obvious. The bedframe, on the other hand . . .

Which side would she have slept on? The right, if she'd kept the same arrangement she'd had with him. He poked and prodded at the bedposts on that side, and rapped them with his knuckles.

"By God, that's as hollow as Sigvat's head!" Ulric

exclaimed when the sound suddenly changed. Per Anders let out an irate cough.

Both Ulric and Hamnet ignored him. "It is, isn't it?" Hamnet said. Per coughed again. Hamnet went right on ignoring him.

Gudrid doubtless had some tricky spring or catch set into the post. Hamnet felt for it, but couldn't find it. "Here, let me try," Ulric said. "I've had practice getting into places where I don't belong."

His hands were smaller and slimmer than Hamnet Thyssen's. By the way they prodded the bedpost, they were also much more knowledgeable. Well, he'd said he was practiced at the burglar's trade.

Something clicked. "Ha!" Ulric said. He reached for the top of the bedpost again. This time, the top three inches or so came off in his hand. "Ha!" he said again. He reached into the hollow and pulled out a rolled sheet of parchment. "Well, well. What have we here?"

"Open it," Per Anders said.

Ulric did. He read a little of it, then grimaced and shook his head. "Letter from an old lover," he said.

Hamnet only shrugged. "Why am I not surprised?" He went over to the other side of the bed, stirring up more feathers as he did, and started rapping at the bedposts there. One sneeze later, he found another hollow. "Come here, Ulric. Does this one work the same way?"

"If it doesn't, she had to pay extra—you can count on that." Ulric felt the bedpost. He nodded. "Uh-*huh*. Now we do this, and. . . ." A click rewarded him. "There you go."

"What's in it?" Per Anders sounded intrigued in spite of himself.

"Don't know yet." Ulric turned to Hamnet. "Want to do the honors this time?"

Plainly, he expected Hamnet to say no. Because that

was so plain, Hamnet nodded and said, "All right." Ulric had already started to reach into the concealed hollow. He drew back and bowed to Hamnet, as if to say it was all his.

Now that Hamnet had the honor, he wondered if he wanted it. It would be just like Gudrid to put something sharp and perhaps poisoned in a hole like this, to surprise any stranger who chanced on it. But, having asked for the privilege, he couldn't very well change his mind.

He'd already noticed that his hand was bigger than Ulric's. He had to squeeze it painfully tight to reach down into the hollowed-out bedpost. Gudrid wouldn't have had any trouble here—he was sure of that.

Just when he started to think this hollowed-out space was empty, his fingertips grazed something at the bottom. He did some more twisting, and managed to get it between his index and middle fingers. It wasn't a parchment; it felt hard and cool and metallic.

Count Hamnet drew it up. "What have you got?" Ulric asked.

"I don't know yet. . . . It's jewelry." Hamnet could hardly hide his disappointment. He held the thing in the palm of his hand: a small gold replica of a building with a domed roof. "Do you recognize it?"

"Not me," Ulric Skakki replied. "It's not modeled after any place in Nidaros—I'd lay money on that. What about you, Per? Every seen any real building like it?"

"No," the courier said. "If I had to guess, I'd say it came straight out of a jeweler's imagination."

"Seems likely," Hamnet agreed. The piece included a loop through which a chain might go. He imagined it nestling between Gudrid's breasts. He'd never seen it there; he was sure he would have remembered it if he had. But how much did that mean? Anything?

"Shall we look for more of these hiding places?" Per

asked. "Or do we see they have nothing important in
them?"

Ulric looked at Hamnet Thyssen. Hamnet shrugged.
He wanted to throw the little gold model away. Instead, he
dropped it back into the hidey-hole. "Let's get out of here."
He waited till all the Bizogots tramped out of the bedchamber before leaving himself. He made it plain he *was*
waiting, too, so none of them could steal the bauble. That
earned him a few hard looks. Had the piece been bigger,
he might have had a fight on his hands—or he might have
chosen differently.

"You're a dangerous fellow," Ulric remarked as they
left Eyvind Torfinn's house. "Gold doesn't tempt you."

"Gold that had anything to do with Gudrid doesn't,"
Hamnet answered. "Let it go. Let's get out of Nidaros in
one piece. Anything besides that is a bonus."

The adventurer grunted. "Well, you're bound to be right.
We'll have to slide around that barricade again, and we'd
better pick a new way to do it, too, or those lovely fellows
we ran into before will try to make us pay."

"Pick your route," Hamnet said. "I won't quarrel with
you, whatever it is. I want to get away from here—that's
all."

"I know what you mean," Ulric said. "I can feel the
goose's footsteps on my grave, too."

As a matter of fact, that wasn't what Hamnet Thyssen
meant. He kept rubbing the palm of his hand against his
trouser leg as he followed Ulric through the maze of alleys
that zigzagged between the main streets. Ulric never seemed
to have any doubts about where he was going. Hamnet did,
more than once, but Ulric proved right in the end.

No one troubled them while they made their getaway.
"Maybe God watches over us," Per Anders said in glad
surprise as they trotted out through the open gates.

"Maybe," Hamnet and Ulric said together. Neither man sounded as if he believed it.

"Well?" Trasamund asked when they got back to the Bizogots' encampment.

"Wasted trip, I'm afraid," Ulric said. Count Hamnet nodded.

Marcovefa looked sharply at Hamnet. "You had something," she said. It wasn't a question.

"A trinket of Gudrid's," he said. "Nothing important."

"You think not?"

"What do you want me to do?" he asked irritably. "Go back and get it for you?"

For a moment, he thought she would say yes. He thought, in fact, she would insist on coming with him. But then she hesitated, and finally shook her head. "No, no point," she said at last. "The bone comes from the beast, but the bone is not the beast."

"What does that mean?" Hamnet asked. She didn't answer.

X

The Rulers rode along as if they hadn't a care in the world. There were two or three dozen of them—most on the deer that must have come down from beyond the Glacier, a few riding horses. They didn't disdain what they found the Bizogots and Raumsdalians using. A war mammoth led the troop.

"Let's go get 'em," Trasamund said. Nobody told him no. His force far outnumbered the invaders. By the way the Rulers paraded along south of Nidaros, they expected no enemies in this part of the Empire.

As in so much of life, what they expected and what they got were two different things. Their heads twisted toward the oncoming foes in what couldn't be anything but horror. Despite that, none of them made as if to flee. Maybe they knew it would do them no good, since riding deer couldn't outrun horses. Or maybe running never crossed their minds. As Hamnet Thyssen had seen more often than he cared to remember, the Rulers were formidable.

They formed a battle line: riding deer on the wings, horses near the center, and the war mammoth anchoring the whole thing. And then one man on a deer rode out in front of the line. The fringes and animal tails and sparkling crystals adorning his costume declared what he was: a shaman.

"Well, well," Ulric Skakki said. "No wonder they think they can take us."

"No wonder at all," Hamnet said. "But this bastard never ran into Marcovefa."

He glanced over to her. She probably didn't notice him: her eyes were on the enemy sorcerer. A lion doubtless eyed a fat sheep the same way. This fellow in his fancy clothes didn't know he was a fat sheep, but he was about to find out.

With a harsh shout—or maybe it just seemed so to Hamnet's ears, since he knew little of their language—the Rulers rode forward. Their shaman still held the lead. They started to shoot when they were still well out of range. Or so Hamnet would have thought, but their arrows landed among the Bizogots and Raumsdalians. A Raumsdalian soldier who'd joined Trasamund's band clutched at his throat and slid from the saddle.

When Trasamund's men answered the enemy archery, their shafts did fall short. The Rulers' wizard held up his hand as if defying not only arrows but the whole world.

Then a red-shouldered hawk perched on that outstretched hand. Its talons closed on—and in—the wizard's flesh. Somehow, his screech of pain resounded over the battlefield. He beat at the hawk with his free hand. Its hooked beak nipped his fingers. It pecked at his face.

Marcovefa laughed. With the shaman distracted, archery went back to normal. The Bizogots and Raumsdalians were well within range of the Rulers now. Men and beasts on both sides began to fall. The mammoth trumpeted in anger and distress when an arrow pierced its sensitive trunk. The

Rulers on the great beast's back managed to keep it under control, though. It was well trained—and they were experienced.

And their shaman proved not the worst of wizards, either. Even though he was bleeding, he managed to make the red-shouldered hawk fly off. A moment later, lightning crashed down out of a clear blue sky not far from Marcovefa's horse. The beast snorted and reared at the thunderclap. Hamnet hoped she could stay on—she was anything but an experienced rider. She managed—awkwardly, but no equestrian judges stood around doling out style points.

As the horse came down on all fours, Marcovefa laughed again. Count Hamnet wondered why. Then he realized that lightning bolt was intended to blast her black and smoking, and that she'd successfully turned the stroke. Sorcerous judges would have given her as many points as the rules allowed.

The Rulers' shaman realized the same thing at about the same time as Hamnet. He threw up his blood-splashed hands in what had to be despair. He'd done everything he knew how to do—and it didn't work. What could he do now but wait for Marcovefa's revenge?

Hamnet nocked an arrow, drew the bowstring back to his ear, and let fly. The string lashed the leather brace on the inside of his wrist. The shaft caught the shaman in the chest, right between two glittering chunks of crystal. The man threw up his hands once more. He slumped down against the riding deer's neck.

"I would have given him worse than that," Marcovefa called.

"He's dying. What's worse than that?" Hamnet asked. Marcovefa's feral smile suggested that she knew several answers. Count Hamnet was just as glad he didn't know any of them.

He didn't have time to worry about them, either. Without the shaman to protect the Rulers' ordinary fighting men, they didn't last long. Few of them even tried to surrender: they sold their lives as dearly as they could. Hamnet had seen the invaders behave that way more often than not. Say what you would about the Rulers, they didn't lack for courage.

The warriors on mammothback charged again and again, but the Bizogots and Raumsdalians simply rode out of their way and kept shooting arrows at them from the sides and rear. After a while, the last enemy soldier slumped down on the mammoth's back, either dead or too badly hurt to go on fighting. The mammoth itself must have been almost mad from pain; it had nearly as many arrows sticking out of its hide as a porcupine had quills.

"I feel sorry for the poor thing," Ulric Skakki said as the mammoth lumbered off toward the south. "Not its fault the people who trained it are a pack of dire wolves who walk on two legs."

"Maybe not," Hamnet said, "but if my neighbor has a dog that tries to bite me, I'm going to kill it before it can."

"We ought to kill that mammoth—put it out of its misery," Ulric said.

"Go ahead," Count Hamnet told him. The adventurer gave back a reproachful look.

"You want it dead?" Marcovefa said. Before either Ulric or Hamnet could answer, she pointed at the mammoth and chanted something in her peculiar dialect. The huge beast walked along for another couple of strides. Then it fell over. Its sides heaved only once or twice before they stilled. It was, without a doubt, dead.

"Good God!" Hamnet said. "How did you do that?"

"I put—how do you say it?—a clog in its heart," Marcovefa answered. "Nothing can live with that. Not vole, not fox, not man, not mammoth. It is a very easy spell to make. Can be countered, but easy to make."

Hamnet Thyssen looked at her. "You can kill anyone you want, whenever you want?"

She shook her head. "No, no, no. Spell takes some time— you saw that. And I have to see the man—or the animal—to use it. And it can be countered. Even one of your puny amulets will stop it most of the time. I didn't know if the Rulers warded their mammoths that way. They didn't ward this mammoth. Shall we butcher it? Plenty of meat."

Some of the Bizogots were already riding over to do just that. Hamnet wasn't wild about mammoth meat. It was tough and gamy. But it was meat, and it was there. He had a little sausage and some hard bread in his belt pouch. A bellyful of meat—even tough, gamy meat—didn't sound bad at all.

And it didn't turn out bad at all. He ate and ate. "You can stuff yourself like a Bizogot, by God," Trasamund said admiringly.

"I've got used to going without," Hamnet answered. "When there's plenty, I make the most of it."

"Here." A Bizogot used a hatchet to split a bone that had been lying in the fire. "Want some marrow?"

"I won't say no." Hamnet scooped some out with a chunk of meat so he wouldn't burn his fingers. The marrow tasted stronger than any that came from cows or sheep or pigs or horses. But it was good. He suspected even teratorn marrow would be good, though he hoped he never got desperate enough to find out.

"Let me have a bit of that." Ulric Skakki didn't worry about whether the marrow was hot. He reached in, grabbed what he wanted, and stuffed it into his mouth. Maybe his fingers and palm were even more callused than Hamnet's. Maybe he was just hungrier.

Marcovefa sighed and patted her stomach. "Up on the Glacier, we don't have feasts like this. Unless—" She broke off with a sly smile. "Seems a shame to waste the warriors, but when you have game this big, I suppose I can see why you don't bother with them."

"You . . . eat people?" Per Anders didn't know what things were like up on top of the Glacier.

"Not really people—never anybody from my clan, and those are the only true people," the shaman answered. She smacked her lips. "But two-legged meat, once you cook it well, is the best there is. Better than mammoth, better than mutton, better than duck, better than anything."

Per glanced toward Count Hamnet. Was he slightly green, or was it only Hamnet's imagination? "You can tell her to stop teasing me now," he said. "No matter how she goes on, I won't believe her."

"You'd better," Hamnet answered. "She means it."

"Don't *you* start!" Per Anders was determined not to believe.

"By God, Anders, I'm not joking," Hamnet said. Ulric and Trasamund nodded to show Hamnet meant it. Hamnet went on, "They don't waste anything up there, anything at all. They can't afford to. And that includes waste the meat that comes off an enemy's carcass."

Per Anders looked from one of them to the next. He must have decided they weren't joking, because he got up shaking his head and walked away from them. Hamnet Thyssen let out a sour chuckle. "See how we win friends wherever we go?" he said.

"He is a foolish man," Marcovefa said.

"No, he's just a man who's never been up on top of the Glacier," Hamnet said.

"A lucky man, in other words," Ulric Skakki put in.

Marcovefa sent him a dirty look. "I never knew we

were poor. I never knew we were missing so many things. You do not miss what you never had." She licked her lips. "But I do miss man's flesh. I had that up there, but it would turn your stomachs if I ate it here."

"You're right—it would," the adventurer agreed. "I've eaten a lot of nasty things in my time. You can't believe some of the things you'll try if you get hungry enough. I never did turn cannibal, though. I haven't got a lot to be proud of, but that's something, by God."

"Pooh!" Marcovefa said. "You don't know what you're talking about. Man's flesh isn't nasty. Man's flesh is good. Like I say, the best meat there is."

"Well, you're welcome to my body—but only after I'm done using it," Ulric Skakki said.

"You've already got my body, but not for stewing, I hope," Count Hamnet added. Marcovefa thought that was funny. After a moment, so did Hamnet. Winning a skirmish made everything look better.

THEY PUSHED SOUTH, picking up more Raumsdalians who wanted to fight the Rulers. Some of the men from armies the invaders had shattered had gone home. Others had turned bandit. Still others seemed willing to try again as long as they had someone to lead them against the enemy.

"Our own officers ran away," one man angrily told Hamnet. "What the demon good are they if they won't stand and fight?"

"They didn't all run away," a new recruit said. "But most of the ones who did fight got killed." He paused, then admitted, "Watching them get killed set some of the others running."

Count Hamnet made a grinding noise deep in his chest.

"I sometimes wonder whether Raumsdalia deserves to live."

"Who do you suppose appointed the officers?" Ulric answered his own question: "Sigvat did, that's who. And what did Sigvat do when the Rulers got to Nidaros? He ran away, that's what. It's no wonder the officers take after their master."

The new recruits stared at him. "If one of our captains heard you say something like that, he'd horsewhip you," said the soldier who'd complained that the officers had run.

"He might think so," Ulric said lightly.

"Oh, he'd do it, all right. He'd . . ." The soldier seemed to take his first good look at the adventurer. He paused, then changed course: "Well, maybe not. He was mighty fond of his own skin."

"A sensible fellow," Ulric said. "Of course, if we were all that fond of our own skins, nobody would ever hurt anybody else for fear of what would happen to us. But it doesn't work that way, worse luck."

"We've both got the scars to prove it," Hamnet said, and Ulric nodded. Hamnet went on, "Better to dish them out than to wait while they heal up, though." Ulric Skakki nodded again. So did the Raumsdalian soldiers rejoining the fight.

And so did Trasamund. "Always better to give than to receive," he said, and reached over his shoulder to touch the hilt of his two-handed sword.

"I have a question," Hamnet said. Everybody looked at him. He asked it: "How long before the Rulers figure out they've got trouble behind them as well as in front of them? What do they do once they realize it?"

"That's two questions," Ulric pointed out.

"If you've got two answers, I'll listen to them," Count Hamnet said.

Ulric made as if to turn out his pockets and go through his belt pouches. Hamnet Thyssen waited. He knew the adventurer was trying to annoy him, and would win a point if he succeeded. When Hamnet just stood there, Ulric said, "My guess is, it won't be long. And when they do realize it, they'll turn on us. It's not like they've got any reason to be afraid of Sigvat."

"Too right it isn't," Hamnet said. "And that's about what I was thinking, too. We've better be ready for the worst they can do to us."

"Why are you telling me? You need to talk to your lady love," Ulric said. "Without her, the best we can hope for is to hightail it off to some place where the Rulers won't come for a while."

"Not so bad as that." But Trasamund didn't sound as if he believed it himself.

"We usually say things won't be so bad when we bump up against the Rulers," Ulric said. "And they usually aren't. They're usually worse."

Trasamund had brightened till he finished. Then the jarl glowered at him. "Curse it, why can't you leave that part out?"

"Because I'm trying to tell the truth?" Ulric suggested. "I know Bizogots don't always understand the word—"

"What do you mean?" Trasamund said indignantly.

"Oh, you know it's true as well as I do." Ulric sounded impatient, to say nothing of tired. "What gets you people through the winters up there except lies swapped back and forth? Don't tell me any different, either. I know better. Anyone who's passed a winter up on the plains knows better."

"Those are just for the sport of it. Nobody believes

them. Nobody expects to believe them," Trasamund said. "When we need to tell the truth, we can do it as well as anybody else. I've heard plenty of Raumsdalian liars, too." He fixed Ulric with a significant stare.

"Who, me?" the adventurer said. "If you can prove anything I've ever said is a lie, go ahead and do it."

"How am I supposed to? You talk about places nobody else has ever been to. You're the only one who knows if there's any truth in you at all."

"Hamnet's been to some of those places," Ulric said. "He knows whether I'm telling the truth or not."

Thus prodded, Hamnet said, "I've told you before, Trasamund: Ulric hasn't lied about any places where I've been, anyhow. I would have let you—and him—know about it if he had."

"Huh." Trasamund didn't want to believe him, either. "But he talks about places you've never seen, too, Thyssen. As far as anybody knows, he's making all that up as he goes along."

"I don't think so, and I'll tell you why," Count Hamnet said. Trasamund could have looked no more dubious had he practiced in front of a mirror. Ignoring his expression, Hamnet went on, "Here's why. When we went up onto the Glacier, Ulric could talk with the people we met there. How? Because he'd run into Bizogots who spoke a dialect like theirs way over by the western mountains."

"He didn't talk about that before we went up onto the Glacier," Trasamund protested.

"No, but he'd done it. He's done some things you haven't done, Your Ferocity, and seen some things you haven't seen, and you might as well get used to it," Hamnet said.

"Oh, don't tell him that," Ulric said. "Now I'll be able to lie as much as I please, and he'll have to swallow all of it. Where's the challenge in that? Where's the sport?

Making somebody believe a really juicy lie shouldn't be easy. You should have to work at it."

Count Hamnet exhaled through his nose. "You're not helping, you know."

"How about that?" Ulric said cheerfully. "Anybody would think I was trying to be difficult or something."

"Anybody would think you were trying to be Skakki," Trasamund said. Ulric bowed, as if at a compliment. Trasamund threw his hands in the air.

MARCOVEFA KEPT LOOKING back over her left shoulder so often that Hamnet asked, "Did you get a crick in your neck when you slept last night?"

"No." She shook her head. "I keep looking to find the way north."

He pointed out the obvious: "We're riding south."

"Not always," Marcovefa said.

"What does that mean? What do you sense?" Hamnet asked.

"One day, we will ride north again. We will need to know the way." Marcovefa sounded like most of the shamans and wizards Hamnet had known: she obviously knew what she meant, and she just as obviously had trouble telling him. Or maybe she simply didn't want to.

He tried his best to make sense of it. "When will we ride north again? How far north will we ride? Back to Nidaros? Back to the woods? Back to the Bizogot steppe?"

"Back to the Golden Shrine," Marcovefa answered.

That told him both more and less than he wanted to know. "Where is the Golden Shrine? How will we find it?"

"It is where it is. We will find it when we need to find it." Marcovefa shook her head again. "We will find it when it wants to be found." She looked back over her shoulder once more, as if she expected it to spring up from the wheat field they'd just passed, a field that might never be harvested.

"You're not helping," Count Hamnet complained, as he had with Ulric.

"I am giving you the best answer I can," Marcovefa said. "It is true. Do you want me to lie instead?"

"It may be true, but it doesn't tell me anything," Hamnet complained.

Marcovefa shrugged. "Before I came down from the Glacier, if I asked you where Nidaros was, what could you have told me? You would have said, 'It is far to the south.' If you talked about the Bizogot steppe or the forest or the badlands where Hevring Lake spilled out, what would they have meant? Nothing. Less than nothing. I did not know what any of those things were."

Count Hamnet thought about that. Slowly, he asked, "Are you telling me I'm still up on the Glacier as far as the Golden Shrine is concerned?"

"Yes, I tell you that." Marcovefa looked pleased that he'd understood so well. "When you need to know, you will know. Till you need to know, you don't need to worry about it."

She might have been pleased, but Hamnet wasn't. "You make it sound like I'm a little child."

"When it comes to the Golden Shrine, we are all little children." Now Marcovefa spoke with what sounded like exaggerated patience. She paused. "Maybe your Eyvind Torfinn is a big child. He know more about the Golden Shrine than most people. But no one is more than a big child. How could it be otherwise? For now, the Golden Shrine is hidden. Who has seen it, to say what it is like? Have you?"

"You know I haven't," Hamnet Thyssen answered angrily.

"You might be surprised. But all right, then. Neither have I. Neither has anybody. So what is the point of getting all upset?"

"We need the Golden Shrine," Hamnet said. "Won't it help us against the Rulers? Can we beat them without it?"

"We can do whatever we have to do." Marcovefa was nothing if not evasive.

More slowly than he might have, Hamnet realized she was being evasive on purpose. "You're not telling me everything you know."

"You are not a shaman. I am telling you everything you can grasp." Marcovefa opened and closed her hands. "I am telling you everything I can grasp, too. I know more than I understand. Does that make any sense to you?"

"No," Count Hamnet said. A moment later, he amended that: "Maybe." He'd known something was wrong between Gudrid and him before he understood what it was. He didn't like to think of the Golden Shrine in those terms. It was supposed to be good and pure and holy. Gudrid . . . wasn't.

"You worry too much," Marcovefa said seriously.

Hamnet Thyssen burst out laughing. "Now tell me something I didn't know!" he exclaimed.

"You should not do this." The shaman from atop the Glacier made not doing it sound easy as could be.

He bowed to her. "How do you propose that I stop?"

"Wait till we camp tonight," she answered. "I will stop you from worrying—for a while, anyway."

That gave him something to look forward to. He would have looked forward to it even more if Marcovefa hadn't kept on glancing north. She always peered over her left shoulder—never over her right. Maybe that meant something sorcerous. Maybe it was just her habit, and he'd never

noticed it before. Now he shrugged. He was too proud—
and too stubborn—to ask.

And, when they did camp, she kept her promise with an
eager ferocity he did his best to match. Sure enough, making love did stop him from worrying . . . for a while, anyway. You couldn't worry when the world exploded in joy.
Afterward, though? Afterward was a different story.

But Hamnet didn't worry long. Sleep claimed him before
his thoughts could get all knotted up. Even as his eyelids
sagged shut, he sent Marcovefa a suspicious glance. He
wasn't usually one to start snoring right after love. Not usually, maybe—but tonight he was.

He woke before daybreak the next morning. Marcovefa
lay beside him, snoring softly. He smiled—and waited for
all his worries to come flooding back. They didn't, though.
His mind felt washed clean, almost as if he'd got over a
fever that left him out of his head for a while.

Was that magic? Or only a prolonged afterglow? Was
there a difference?

When she woke up, he tried to ask her. She didn't want
to listen to him. "Do what you need to do today, whatever
it turns out to be," she said. "Yesterday is gone. You can't
bring it back. You can't change it. So what difference
does it make? Tell me that."

"I remember it," Hamnet said stubbornly. "If not for
the skirmish yesterday morning, we wouldn't be eating
venison for breakfast today."

"You never know." But Marcovefa smiled.

"I wish you could see this country the way it ought to
be," Hamnet said. "Here south of Nidaros, this is the heart
of the Empire. But nothing is the same because of the
cursed war."

Marcovefa shrugged. "It is what it is, that's all. Every

bit of it, even the worst, is better than the mountaintop where my clan lives." She blinked. "I wonder what will happen when the Glacier melts back and the mountain is part of the rest of the world again. Not in my lifetime, but not so long, either."

"No, not so long," Hamnet agreed. If it wasn't in his lifetime, though, he had trouble worrying about it. He looked south. "I hope your clan doesn't come down into a world the Rulers are running."

"Rulers wouldn't run it once my clan got through with them," Marcovefa said. Count Hamnet feared she was an optimist. But maybe she knew what she was talking about. Her clansfolk were formidable people. They had to be, to survive at all up on the Glacier. In easier circumstances, they and the other small, thinly scattered clans up there might give anybody a run for his money.

"Come on," Trasamund said when they emerged from their tent. "We just beat one bunch of those buggers. Let's ride south and find more of them—lots more."

Nobody told him no.

No, NOBODY TOLD Trasamund no. Still, as the Raumsdalians and Bizogots rode away from their camp, Ulric Skakki brought his horse up alongside Hamnet's and said, "Sometimes God gives you what you ask for—just to show you you're a fool to ask for it. How many more of the Rulers do you really want to run into?"

"Good question," Hamnet admitted. "How do you propose to drive them out of the Empire if we don't run into them, though?"

"Well, that's a good question, too," Ulric said. "We're liable to run into too many of them all at once—that's what bothers me. They really have swarmed down here, haven't they? Raumsdalia's a big, tasty dog, and it draws plenty of fleas."

"The Rulers are worse than fleas," Hamnet Thyssen said. "And of course this country is better than the land farther north. Even the Bizogots like it better here than up on their steppe—well, most of them do, anyway."

"Bread. Beer. Fruit," Ulric said. "Oh, they've got a few berries up there, but that's about it. Smetyn doesn't match beer—to say nothing of wine. And without bread . . ." He shook his head, as if to say civilized life was impossible. He wasn't so far wrong, either.

A large, black plume of smoke rising in the southeast marked some sort of struggle. Pointing toward it, Trasamund said, "We ought to see what that is."

"He's been eating meat again," Ulric Skakki said sadly.

"Mammoth meat and venison," Count Hamnet agreed. "So have you. Why doesn't it turn you all bloodthirsty?"

"Because I've got more sense than that?" Ulric suggested. That was more polite than saying, *Because I'm not a Bizogot barbarian off the frozen steppe*, but it amounted to the same thing.

He didn't have more sense than to keep from following the jarl as Trasamund rode toward the pillar of smoke. Neither did Hamnet Thyssen. The Raumsdalian noble caught Marcovefa's eye. "Are you ready for more trouble?" he asked her.

"As much as these Rulers can give," she answered. By the way she said it, she didn't think that would be much. She'd beaten their wizards again and again. On this side of the Gap, she was the only one who had.

Hamnet thought about the lands on the far side of the Gap. The country the Rulers roamed was nothing special—it reminded him of the Bizogots' territory. Somewhere over there, though, would be better land, land like Raumsdalia and the realms to the south. What kind of people lived on it? And what kind of wizards did they have there, if they could keep the Rulers penned up on those cold and nearly useless plains? That was a worrisome thought.

It was also a thought he didn't have time for. Now he could see what was burning: a village just too small to be a walled town. Most of the black, greasy smoke poured from one building. *An oil storehouse?* Hamnet wondered.

He didn't have time to worry about that, either. The Rulers were still sacking the village. They were killing the men who fought back—and some of the ones who didn't—and amusing themselves with the women. Atrocities didn't seem to change much from one side of the Glacier to the other.

The Rulers might have laughed when they saw the Raumsdalians and Bizogots riding toward them. *More easy enemies to get rid of,* they must have thought. A man came out on a riding deer to face the oncoming foes alone. He was either a wizard or a maniac. Hamnet knew which way he would have bet.

When the wizard pointed at the incoming arrows, they fell out of the sky. Then, all at once, they didn't any more. One of them just missed puncturing the enemy shaman. Every line of his body shouted astonishment. He pointed again, as if to say, *Listen when I tell you something!*

But the arrows, thanks to Marcovefa, didn't listen. One of them grazed the Ruler's riding deer. The animal bucked. Hamnet was sure he would have done the same thing. He was also sure he would have been ready for it. It caught the Ruler by surprise, though. Next thing he knew, he was sitting on the ground with Raumsdalians and Bizogots thundering toward him on horseback.

He pointed at a lancer, and the Raumsdalian's spear-point missed him. The next attacker's sword bit. The wizard let out a shrill shriek that seemed to hold more indignation than pain. How could this be happening to *him*? Weren't such torments reserved for folk of the herd?

Evidently they had been . . . up till now. No longer. Once the first swordstroke went home, the Ruler's magic seemed to melt away like snow in springtime. By the time the army swept past him and into the village, he wasn't good to look at any more.

The Rulers in the village cried out, too, in surprise and dismay. Their wizard hadn't been used to seeing his magic fail. They weren't used to going unprotected against their enemies' magic. But Marcovefa filled them with terror. They couldn't even fight back with their usual dogged courage. They ran pell-mell, throwing aside their swords to flee the faster.

Killing them as they ran didn't seem sporting to Hamnet Thyssen. Then he remembered the battle in the woods the year before. When a glancing blow from a slingstone put Marcovefa out of action, the Rulers had used a spell much like this against the Raumsdalian army Hamnet led. They hadn't been embarrassed to terrify their foes, or to slay them even though they couldn't fight back.

Marcovefa had held that spell at bay till she got knocked cold. Was sending it back at the Rulers now a measure of revenge? If it was, Hamnet hoped she found it sweet.

Not all the Raumsdalians had been panicked by the Rulers' magic. So, now, a few of the enemy fought back in spite of Marcovefa's spell. Hamnet got a stinging cut on the back of his hand from one stubborn warrior. The man lay sprawled in death on the grass—much good his courage did him.

The last thing the villagers had expected was to be delivered from their tormentors. They cheered and capered at the same time as they mourned. Some of the women seemed eager to give their rescuers what the Rulers would have taken by force. Nine months from now, some of the babies would probably have the fair hair and light eyes that marked the Bizogots . . . and their byblows.

"Now this is a welcome," Trasamund said as he disappeared with a buxom brunette. "I'll give her something to remember me by."

Ulric Skakki raised an eyebrow. "And we'll hope she doesn't give him something to remember her by." He mimed scratching furiously at an intimate place.

"You take a chance whenever you lie down with a woman." Count Hamnet paused, considering. "And I suppose she takes a chances whenever she lies down with you."

"Of course she does." Ulric mimed a bulging belly this time.

"Well, yes, that, too, but it isn't what I meant." Hamnet hesitated again, wondering exactly what he did mean. Slowly, he went on, "You can wound a lover in ways you can't wound somebody who isn't. You take a chance that you'll get hurt, or that you'll hurt the other person."

"Life is full of chances. So you bet—and sometimes you lose," Ulric said. "If you don't bet at all, no one notices when you die, because you were hardly alive to begin with."

Hamnet Thyssen grunted. He'd gone years not betting— not betting his heart, anyway. He'd risked his life again and again. With a hole in the center of it, the chance of losing it hardly seemed to matter. At last, he fell in love again . . . and then he fell on his face again.

"Women are strange creatures. You can't live with them, but you can't live without them, either," he said. "Do you suppose they say the same thing about us?"

"Why are you asking me?" Ulric Skakki returned.

"People have called me a lot of different things, but I don't think anybody ever said I had to squat to piss."

"Thank you," Hamnet said. The adventurer raised a questioning eyebrow. Hamnet explained: "If I ever needed a cure for romantic thoughts, you just gave it to me."

"We aim to please," Ulric said loftily. "And you don't need a cure. You just need better aim yourself sometimes." That gave Hamnet something new to chew on.

XI

A Raumsdalian scout galloped back toward Hamnet Thyssen. "Mammoths!" he shouted. "Stacks of mammoths!"

Hamnet tried to imagine mammoths piled one atop another. He felt himself failing, which was bound to be just as well. "How far are they?" he asked. "Do the Rulers know we're here? Are they heading this way?"

The scout pointed south over his shoulder. "Not very far," he said as he reined in his blowing horse. "Not far enough, by God! When you get to the top of the next little swell of ground, you'll see 'em yourself. They didn't spot me—or I hope like anything they didn't, anyhow—but they were coming toward us like they mean business. And I bet they do. How the demon do we stop 'em?"

"Marcovefa!" Count Hamnet called. "Did you hear what he said?"

"I heard," she answered. "What do you want me to do about it?"

"Narfi asked a good question. How the demon *do* we stop them?" Hamnet said. "Will the spell you used against the war mammoth in the last fight work again? Can you use it over and over, till all the Rulers' mammoths fall down dead?"

"If nothing wards them, it will work." Marcovefa seldom lacked for confidence. "I can use it again and again. If they have stacks of mammoths, I cannot kill them all, though. I get too tired. It is like screwing—sometimes all you can do is all you can do."

"Heh," Hamnet said uneasily. Only Marcovefa would have connected lovemaking and murderous magic. It never would have occurred to him, anyway. In his mind, the two amounted to the same thing, regardless of whether or not they really were. "Form line of battle!" he yelled. "The Rulers are heading this way with mammoths! Marcovefa will take care of them for us." *I hope*, he added, but only to himself. "We'll finish off the buggers on riding deer or horses or rabbits."

"Rabbits?" Ulric Skakki said, stringing his bow.

"You never can tell," Hamnet answered. He pointed south himself. "There are the ones on mammoths."

Those war mammoths might not have come in a stack, but they surely came in a swarm. Hamnet Thyssen wasn't sure he'd ever seen so many of them all in a line. Several Rulers sat atop each one: the man who guided it, a lancer with a long spear, and anywhere from one to three archers. They shouted when they spied the Raumsdalians and Bizogots ahead of them.

"Any time you're ready," Count Hamnet told Marcovefa, in lieu of shrieking, *For God's sake do something about them!*

Her crooked grin said she had a good notion of what he wasn't saying. He was embarrassed, but only a little. He couldn't work up a whole lot of shame over fearing war mammoths. Who in their right mind didn't?

Marcovefa didn't. Her grin got wider. "More mammoth meat than we can eat. Plenty for big birds, big foxes," she promised. Hamnet couldn't see dire wolves as big foxes, but she did. She pointed her right forefinger at the closest war mammoth and chanted the little tune in her own dialect. Hamnet Thyssen waited for the war mammoth to drop dead. He waited. And he waited. And he waited some more.

And nothing happened.

Marcovefa stared at her index finger with the indignant reproach a man might give his bow if the string snapped when he needed it most. She aimed again. She chanted again. Hamnet waited again.

Nothing happened again—or, possibly, nothing still happened.

"Um, I don't mean to fuss or anything, but if she's going to do something, she ought to do it pretty soon," Ulric said.

"It doesn't look like the magic's going to work today," Hamnet told him.

"Well, well. Isn't that interesting?" Ulric replied. Between the two of them, they'd given themselves perhaps the most casual death sentence in the history of the world.

"Do you know what's wrong?" Count Hamnet asked as Marcovefa sent her forefinger another black look.

"They are warded. They must be warded." By the way she said it, she might have accused the Rulers of gambling with loaded dice. Still scowling at her finger, she went on, "I did not think the Rulers would figure out what I did so fast."

"Some of them must have got away after you killed that one mammoth," Hamnet said, and she nodded bleakly. He asked, "If you can't kill this lot, what can we do to them?"

"Fight them. They are still flesh." But Marcovefa

couldn't help adding, "They are a whole great glacier of flesh."

Count Hamnet would have called them a mountain of flesh, but it amounted to the same thing either way. Trouble. Deadly trouble.

"Why aren't the miserable things dying?" Trasamund demanded.

That was a good question. If the mammoths didn't start dying, the Bizogots and Raumsdalians would. "Technical difficulties," Count Hamnet answered, that being easier than admitting Marcovefa wasn't up to murdering mammoths at the moment.

Trasamund might have been a barbarian from the frozen steppe, but he wasn't a stupid barbarian. He understood what Hamnet meant when Hamnet didn't say it. "She can't do 'em in, eh?"

"Not right now. Doesn't seem that way, anyhow," Hamnet replied.

"So what do we do about them, then?" the jarl inquired.

"Fight them. What else can we do?" Another answer did suggest itself to Hamnet Thyssen. But if he screamed *Run away!*—even more to the point, if he matched action to word—he wouldn't win Trasamund's respect. In fact, he'd throw away as much of it as he already had.

"Fight them. Right," the Bizogot said tightly. His folk had tried that against the Rulers time after time, up on their home terrain. They'd lost time after time, too. Trasamund's Three Tusk clan was a shattered wreck, although he'd been coming back from the Empire when the invaders swept down through the Gap and beat its warriors.

"Oh, come on." Ulric Skakki sounded absurdly cheerful. "It'll be as simple as a Bizogot in a dice game."

"You'll answer for that, Skakki," Trasamund said. "As soon as we've walloped these scuts, you'll answer to me."

"Looking forward to it." Ulric still sounded happier than he might have.

Count Hamnet turned to Marcovefa. "All right—you can't work the spell you would have wanted to. Can you do anything else to keep the mammoths from trampling all of us?" Again, he didn't say, *By God, you'd better be able to!* He didn't say it, no, but he thought it very loudly.

He must have thought it loudly enough for Marcovefa to pick it up. Or maybe his face gave him away. She smiled and said, "Everything will be all right." But even she didn't sound sure of that, for she went on, "They have better warding than usual for them—beasts and men."

"Wonderful," Hamnet said. Better-warded mammoths than usual, and more mammoths than usual, too. Put them together and you had—what? *A disaster* was the first thing that occurred to him.

One of the Raumsdalians who'd joined his band must have come to the same conclusion. With a wail of despair, the man wheeled his horse and fled long before the Rulers drew close enough to harm him. "Somebody ought to slaughter the worthless coward," Trasamund growled.

"He's not worth wasting an arrow on," Ulric replied.

Trasamund looked disgusted. "You only say that because he's one of your folk."

No sooner were the words out of his mouth than a Bizogot galloped away just as fast as the Raumsdalian had a moment earlier. "*He's* not worth wasting an arrow on, either," Ulric Skakki observed.

"I thank God he is no man of my clan. Bad enough he is any kind of Bizogot." Trasamund still looked—and sounded—revolted.

Hamnet Thyssen wondered why. If Marcovefa couldn't stop the Rulers' mammoths, what would keep the invaders from rolling over this makeshift army and then going on with their war against Sigvat and whatever was left of the Raumsdalian Empire here in the south? Nothing Hamnet could see.

Ulric had to be thinking along the same lines, for he said, "Maybe we should all run away. Our chances here don't look so good, do they?"

"We can beat the Rulers. Why did we come back down into Raumsdalia if we didn't think we could beat the Rulers?" Trasamund said angrily. "I am not going to run from them any more. I have done too much running, more than any self-regarding Bizogot should ever do."

"Did you really plan on fighting all the war mammoths in the world at the same time?" Ulric exaggerated, but by less than Hamnet wished he did. Trasamund set his massive jaw and nodded. Ulric sighed. The Bizogot jarl wasn't going to listen to anything or anybody right now. Ulric said, "If you insist on getting killed yourself, do you have to insist on killing all your friends, too?"

"I insist on nothing." Trasamund pointed off toward the north. "There is plenty of open space. You can save your skin, if you love it so much. Go ahead and run. See if I care."

The adventurer bowed in the saddle. "As always, Your Ferocity, I thank you for the encouragement."

"You aren't funny, either," Trasamund added. "Always saying one thing when you mean the other—it gets old, Skakki. It gets old."

"Literary criticism and generalship, both from the same man. Who could have imagined it?" Ulric was so ostentatiously calm, he made Hamnet Thyssen think Trasamund had struck a nerve. The adventurer went on, "I will run when you do, Your Ferocity. Have you ever known me to run when you didn't?"

Trasamund wanted to say yes to that. When he opened his mouth, Hamnet could all but see the word on the tip of his tongue. But he didn't let it out. Hamnet knew why he didn't, too: he couldn't. Since he was a truthful man, he answered, "Well, no," as grudgingly as he could.

"There you are, then," Ulric Skakki said. "Here you are, then. Here we all are, then. Here we all are, then, in the same place. Here we all are, then, in the same boat. If you have any good ideas about how we all get out of it together—except running away, I mean—I'd love to hear them."

As Trasamund had before, he said, "If we can't beat the war mammoths, we have to beat the Rulers."

"Finding out how you propose to go about that would be nice," Ulric observed. Hamnet thought so, too. Trasamund glared instead of answering. Regretfully, Hamnet decided the jarl had no answer. Or rather, he had the same old answer: fight like a demon, and hope you came out on top. Hamnet would have liked that one better if it hadn't already proved wrong so often. By Ulric's expression, he felt the same way. With Trasamund so notoriously hard of listening, though, why point it out?

Count Hamnet glanced toward Marcovefa again. "Where are their wizards?" he asked her. "If you can do something about them, maybe you can do something about the mammoths a little later." Not *much* later, he hoped—the massive beasts were getting closer alarmingly fast.

Marcovefa looked angry and frustrated at the same time. "Don't know where the vole pukes are," she snarled. "They pretend to be nothing but ordinary warriors." She said something that sounded incendiary in her own dialect. In irate Raumsdalian, she added, "Pretend too stinking well, too."

What did that mean? Did the Rulers' wizards know they were facing Marcovefa? Hamnet Thyssen couldn't think of anything else it was likely to mean. The Rulers had little trouble against any other wizards they'd run into on this side of the Glacier. Marcovefa, though, they respected—and, very likely, feared.

Of course, they also seemed to respect, and perhaps even fear, Hamnet himself. And if that didn't say they weren't as smart as they thought they were, Hamnet didn't know what it was likely to say.

Trasamund pointed toward the oncoming mammoths. "We should advance against them," he said. "The worst thing you can do is meet the enemy's charge standing still."

Hamnet would have thought the worst thing you could do was *not* meet the charge. Retreat and flight didn't seem to enter Trasamund's mind at all. Count Hamnet wished they didn't enter his. If you were going to fight and not run, Trasamund gave good advice. Hamnet booted his horse forward. All along the line, Raumsdalians and Bizogots were doing the same. Nobody seemed enthusiastic, but nobody hung back. Hamnet usually admired that kind of dogged courage. Today, he wondered if it wasn't harebrained, not dogged.

"*There* they are!" Marcovefa exclaimed, but by then arrows were already starting to fly. Whatever Marcovefa did to the Rulers' wizards, she would have to do on her own.

Or so Hamnet thought, till he saw a host of Raumsdalian lancers burst from an orchard off to the east. They took the Rulers in the flank, spearing men on riding deer and rushing toward the enemy's war mammoths. He wondered how she could conjure up so many men and make them seem so convincing.

Then he recognized the fellow leading the Raumsdalians: Baron Runolf Skallagrim, an old acquaintance of his, and a recent comrade-in-arms. Marcovefa knew Runolf, too. But could she have remembered him well enough to put him at the head of an imaginary army? Why would she do that when adding one more imaginary warrior was bound to be easier?

"They're real!" Hamnet exclaimed. "They've got to be real!"

Ulric Skakki looked quite humanly surprised. "You mean your lady's not just spitting phantasms at the Rulers?"

"Phantasms, my left one," Hamnet answered. "Look! Tell me that's not Runolf Skallagrim in charge of them and I'll say they're phantasms."

"Well, bugger me blind," Ulric said gravely after looking.

Baron Runolf had commanded the garrison at Kjelvik, another northern town. He'd fought the Rulers with Hamnet and Marcovefa the winter before—and fled with them when a slingstone knocked Marcovefa out of the fight and let the Rulers' terrifying wizardry prevail. And he'd let Hamnet and his friends leave Kjelvik for the Bizogot country when Sigvat wanted to haul Hamnet down to Nidaros and make him pay the price for failure.

Count Hamnet hadn't seen Runolf since coming back to Raumsdalia. He'd assumed that either the Rulers or Sigvat had done for his old friend. He'd never been gladder to find himself wrong.

The Rulers hadn't expected to get attacked from the flank as well as the front. Hamnet Thyssen had seen what surprise could do to Raumsdalians and Bizogots. The Rulers might be vicious invaders from beyond the Glacier, but they were also human beings. When everything went the way they expected it to, they were as near invincible as made no difference. When taken by surprise, they proved no less immune to panic than anybody else.

Runolf's men slammed through the Rulers on riding

deer. They would have slammed through a like number of Bizogots, too. The blonds who roamed the steppe below the Glacier didn't have lancers armored head to foot in plate and chain, or the big heavy horses they would have needed to carry those armored lancers. Some of Runolf's troopers even rode armored horses.

That didn't mean they could face mammoths on equal terms. But a charging lancer was something warriors on mammothback couldn't ignore. A couple of Raumsdalians drove sharp steel into the bellies and legs of the Rulers' immense mounts. Mammoths liked getting speared no better than any other animals—or any people—would have. They screamed and bled and were lost to the fight.

Most of the time, the Rulers' wizards would have done something horrible to Runolf Skallagrim's knights before they got close enough to threaten the riding deer, let alone the mammoths. Not here. Not today. Whatever sorcerers the Rulers had with them had frustrated Marcovefa by not showing themselves. She frustrated them by blocking not only the spells they aimed at her force but also the ones they tried to use against Runolf's men.

All that left the fight pretty much the way it would have been if there were no such things as wizards and shamans. And, if anything, it left the Rulers even more discomfited than they would have been if merely—if that was merely—struck in the flank by surprise.

Trasamund bellowed in delight when one war mammoth after another turned around and lumbered off to the south. "Run, cowards! Run!" he roared after the retreating Rulers. "Can't stand it when real men come up against you, can you? Yes, run, you scuts!"

One of the main reasons the Rulers were running was a woman, not a man. Hamnet Thyssen almost pointed that out to Trasamund. Almost, but not quite—he didn't feel like quarreling with the jarl. And he had worries of his own. Retreating southward, the Rulers only moved farther into the Raumsdalian Empire. He wanted to drive them out of it, not entrench them in it more deeply.

Mammoths also moved faster than horses. If the Rulers on mammothback intended to get away, he couldn't do anything about it. Marcovefa might have, but the enemy's wizards still left her as thwarted as she left them. That added up to a victory of sorts for the Rulers, though not one they were likely to appreciate.

Hamnet rode toward Runolf Skallagrim. "Well met, by God!" he called.

"That you, Thyssen?" Baron Runolf answered his own question: "I'll be damned if it isn't. I figured the bastards on the mammoths would have done for you by now, or else the Emperor."

"That's funny," Hamnet said, though he wasn't laughing. "Bugger me blind if it isn't. I figured either Sigvat or the Rulers would've done for you by now, too."

Runolf laughed. He was older and grayer than Hamnet, and less inclined to brood about things. (As far as Hamnet knew, Runolf had never had a woman betray him, which might or might not have meant something.) "Nah, not me," he said now. "The Rulers have become close a time or three, but I managed to talk Sigvat out of it."

"*Did* you?" Hamnet said, deeply impressed. "More luck than I ever had. How the demon did you pull that off?"

"I told his courier I'd rise against him if he tried to arrest me," Runolf answered stolidly. "Sigvat must've believed me, because he hasn't given me any guff since."

"Good for you," Ulric Skakki said. "Good for you!" He turned to Hamnet. "You see? You're too loyal for your own good. Sigvat got away with doing all kinds of things to you that he never would have dared to try if he'd been a little bit more afraid of what you'd do to him."

"Maybe," said Hamnet, in lieu of admitting that the adventurer had a point. He brought things back to the business at hand: "You popped out of those trees at just the right time, Runolf."

"Well, I wouldn't have done it if I hadn't seen the Rulers all tangled up with your people," Runolf Skallagrim said. "You mess with war mammoths when you don't have to, you're sorry you did. Everybody in Raumsdalia's found that out the hard way."

"Everybody up on the Bizogot steppe, too," Count Hamnet agreed. Trasamund gave what had to be the most reluctant nod he'd ever seen from the jarl.

"Looks like you were in the middle of a straight-up fight with the Rulers," Runolf remarked. "They didn't have a sorcerer along? You haven't got one along yourself?" He shook his head. "That's not right. I know it's not. I saw what's-her-name—Marcovefa—with you."

"Yes, she's here," Hamnet said. "She and the Rulers' wizards seemed to battle one another to a standstill."

"Better than what any Raumsdalians have been able to do—that's for sure," Runolf said.

"Yes, I know." Hamnet left it there. Ulric Skakki and Trasamund probably understood why. If Runolf didn't, Hamnet didn't feel like spelling it out for him. Up till now, Marcovefa had thrashed almost all the sorcery the Rulers aimed her way. She'd had trouble with the disease they sent against the Bizogots, but she'd won straight-up contests of sorcery—till this one.

Was she weaker than usual? Had the Rulers had an uncommonly strong wizard among the ones facing her? Hamnet Thyssen didn't know, but he was sure he needed to find out. Marcovefa was the only edge he'd had on the enemy. If he didn't have that edge, what was he supposed to do next? No—what could he possibly do next?

MARCOVEFA TOASTED A chunk of riding-deer liver over a fire. She seemed more interested in eating than in answering Hamnet's questions. While she ate, she answered most of them with shrugs.

Hamnet persisted. He always persisted, no matter how little good it did him, no matter how much it irritated people who had to deal with him. Marcovefa scowled at him. When she finished the liver, she said, "I don't know what all it was. We won. Why worry about it?"

"Would we have won if Runolf Skallagrim hadn't been there to give us a hand?" Hamnet answered his own question: "I don't think so."

"Maybe we would have. I think we would have," Marcovefa said. "One way or another, I always come up with something."

"Always?" Hamnet mimed a slingstone bouncing off the side of her head. "I don't think so."

"Nothing like that this time," she said. "A little better magic than usual, that's all. Nothing to worry about."

Given half a chance, Hamnet always worried, too. "Are they finding better wizards than they did? Are they learning to block what you do better than they did? Will they be able to beat you one of these days?" *One of these days soon*, he meant, but he managed to swallow the last word.

"They learn a little. Anyone who isn't very, very stupid will learn a little," Marcovefa answered. "But they will not beat me. You don't need to worry about that." She had her own brand of arrogance. Trasamund didn't think anybody could beat him sword in hand. Any good warrior felt that way—if he didn't, wouldn't he run from any battle-field? Maybe wizards needed that same kind of certainty to do what they did.

"All right." By the way Hamnet said it, he made it plain it wasn't.

Marcovefa shook her head. "Do I have to screw you to get you to believe me? I do that if you need it."

"I want to believe you because you're telling the truth, not because you're screwing me. They aren't the same thing," Hamnet said stubbornly.

"As long as you believe me, why doesn't matter," Marc-ovefa said.

"Why matters. I've believed too many lies before, and I've believed them for too long," Hamnet insisted.

"Believe we don't lose. It is true," Marcovefa told him.

"How can you know that?" Hamnet demanded.

"How? Because I am what I am. Because I am who I am," Marcovefa said.

"How much *can* you foresee?" he asked her. "You couldn't tell ahead of time that that slingstone was going to hit you. It could have killed you as easily as not. Then what would have happened to our fight?"

"Then I wouldn't be here prophesying to you now." Marcovefa didn't sound very interested in arguing might-have-beens. "But that doesn't change anything else."

Count Hamnet muttered to himself. "By God, why wouldn't it? How are we supposed to win without you?"

"I don't know anything about *supposed to*," she said. "I know *is*. I know *is not*. Those matter. Supposed to? Who cares?"

He kept trying to get answers out of her—yes, he was stubborn. She kept on not giving them. She'd said every-thing she intended to say, or maybe everything she knew how to say. If he didn't like it, too bad. He didn't like it, and he thought it was too bad.

Runolf Skallagrim had about as many Raumsdalians with him as Hamnet did. Hamnet offered to yield command to him. Runolf shook his head. "Keep it and welcome, your Grace," he said. "The Bizogots'll listen to you better than they would to me, and our own folk will listen just as well."

"Or just as badly," Hamnet said.

"Or just as badly," Runolf agreed without even blinking. "What have you got in mind doing next?"

"Fighting the Rulers. Keeping ourselves fed. Staying alive, if we can. What else is there?" Hamnet Thyssen answered.

"Not bloody much, not right now," the other Raumsdalian noble said. "We're on our own. We don't have to worry about orders from anybody else, anybody higher. Feels kind of funny, doesn't it?"

"Feels pretty good, if you want to know what I think," Hamnet said. "When we got orders from the Emperor, how much good did they ever do? Sigvat could always take a bad situation and make it worse."

"Well . . ." Baron Runolf sounded uncomfortable. Like Hamnet, he was a man of deep loyalty. He hadn't had his nose rubbed so deeply in the cost of giving his loyalty to someone who didn't deserve it.

That thought set Hamnet laughing. Runolf Skallagrim gave him a quizzical look. He didn't explain. Runolf wouldn't have thought it was funny. But who could have imagined that Gudrid might be training for Sigvat? They were unfaithful and cruel in different ways, but so what? The infidelity and the cruelty were all that really counted.

Climbing up onto his horse and riding south let him

stop brooding about that, at least for a little while. The trouble with following the Rulers was that they were as bad as locusts when it came to sweeping up everything in their path. Hamnet almost hoped another battle would come soon. Then his forces could feast on the riding animals that fell in the fighting.

Not much to feast on here. The crops were still growing in the fields. Too many of them were growing untended: the Rulers had either killed or run off the peasants who would have tended them. They weren't ripe yet. More than a few fields had broad swaths trampled through them where the Rulers had ridden. How much about crops did the invaders understand? Anything at all? Why should they, when nothing like that would grow on the lands they were used to roaming? The Bizogots didn't—Hamnet had seen as much.

The fields and grass would keep the horses fed till fall, anyhow. That was something. But people? The Rulers might not care about crops, but they'd made close to a clean sweep of livestock. Horses, cattle, sheep, pigs, chickens, ducks, geese, turkeys? Gone. Bones at abandoned campsites told where many of them went.

Maybe some of the farmers had taken some of their animals with them when they ran away from the Rulers. Hamnet Thyssen hoped so, both for their sake and because it would bother the invaders. No matter what had happened to the beasts, though, they weren't here now to feed his fighters.

Bizogots went on eating meat that was higher than Hamnet cared to stomach. "I've done it," Ulric Skakki said. "It's nasty, but it's better than starving."

"Unless it poisons you," Hamnet replied. "It's getting to where it smells pretty poisonous."

"I'm still here," Ulric said. "Don't know what that means. Maybe I can eat like a goat, or a teratorn."

"We're all starting to stink like goats," Hamnet said. "God knows I wouldn't want to stink like a teratorn."

"Well . . . no. Neither would I," Ulric admitted. Like smaller vultures, teratorns stuck their bare, wattled heads deep into the corpses of long-defunct beasts—and people. Sometimes you could smell them on the wing.

"It shouldn't come down to anything like that," Hamnet said.

"You're right. It shouldn't." Ulric nodded sagely. "So why do you sound like a man who's whistling to keep the ghosts away?"

"Is that how I sound?"

"That's about it."

"I don't even believe whistling keeps the ghosts away. I've never run into a ghost on the loose on its own. Have you? The only ones I know about are the ones the wizards magic up."

"Hmm." The adventurer frowned in thought. "No, come to think of it, I haven't, either. All that whistling must work better than we think."

Count Hamnet snorted. "Nice to know I'll be laughing while we starve to death."

"Glad to be of service, your Grace. If you laugh hard enough, you'll wear yourself out and starve faster. You should thank me again, for my act of mercy."

"I should do all kinds of things you'll never see from me," Hamnet replied. "You can chalk that up as one more."

"All right. I will." Ulric could be most dangerous when he seemed most accommodating. "But will you answer one more little question for me?"

"I don't know. I'll try," Hamnet said cautiously—he recognized, and flinched from, that mild tone. "What is it?"

"Are the Rulers really getting the hang of Marcovefa's

magic, and of how to use their own against her? Against us, I should say?"

"You'd do better asking her," Count Hamnet said, which wasn't an answer and wasn't intended as one.

"I will if I have to," Ulric Skakki said. "Don't much want to, though. Questions like that can hurt a wizard's confidence, and sometimes thinking they can do something is what lets them do it for real. And if anybody but Marcovefa is likely to know, you're it." He aimed a forefinger at Hamnet's broad chest as if it were the point of an arrow.

"If." Hamnet felt like a target, all right. He muttered under his breath. At last, he said, "I think they may be gaining. There are lots of them and only one of her, after all. The other thing is, she hasn't been quite the same since that slingstone got her. Close, now, but not the same. What do you think?"

"Mm, you may be right," Ulric said. "So where does that leave us? What are the odds she'll get the missing bits back? If she does, when will she do it?"

"That's more than one question," Hamnet Thyssen pointed out.

"So it is. Give me an inch, and I'll take whatever I can get." Ulric filled a pipe. He had no trouble scrounging tobacco down here in the Empire—the Rulers didn't think it was worth stealing. He lit the pipe with a twig he stuck in the fire. His cheeks hollowed as he sucked in smoke.

"I believe you," Hamnet said. "A lot of girls have likely believed you, too—and then regretted it the next day."

"Oh, no. They never regret it the next day," Ulric said smugly. But he stopped asking questions about Marcovefa, questions Hamnet couldn't answer, questions he didn't want to think about.

Once the questions got into his mind, though, they didn't want to go away. Marcovefa was the best weapon the Bizogots and Raumsdalians had against the Rulers. If she wasn't weapon enough, what were they supposed to do? Give up? Hamnet ground his teeth till one of the back ones hurt. He was damned if he'd do that.

Or maybe he was damned if he wouldn't.

Runolf Skallagrim came up to him. "What's chewing on you, Hamnet?" he asked. "You look like a dire wolf carried off your cub. We won that fight a few days ago, remember? Let your face know it, all right?"

Runolf was an earnest, decent fellow. He came out and spoke his mind. Most of the time, that made Count Hamnet like him better. Not today. "How many more will we have to win?" Hamnet wondered.

"As many as it takes. My knights can wallop the stuffing out of those savages." Runolf didn't lack for confidence, either.

"Sure they can—as long as Marcovefa's able to hold off the Rulers' magic." Hamnet wished he hadn't had to say that. It only made him worry more.

"She will. Just tell her not to stop any more stones with her head, hey?" Baron Runolf thought that was funny.

Hamnet didn't rise up and clout him, which proved he liked him. But he didn't laugh, either, and that sent Runolf away in a huff.

XII

One day, the wind started blowing cool, down from the north. The Bizogots smiled. Hamnet Thyssen sighed. "Not the Breath of God, not yet," he said, "but it's a reminder there is such a thing."

"Just what we need," Per Anders said. The courier didn't seem to have gone up to the Bizogot country till he came after Hamnet and his comrades. "Maybe it will stop blowing every winter once the Glacier finally melts."

"That would be something," Baron Runolf said. "Mild all winter long? By God, I'd love it!"

"You think so?" Ulric said. "You go far enough south, you'll find places where it's mild all winter long."

"I'd like that, too," Trasamund put in.

"Let me finish, if you please," Ulric said. "Places where it's mild all winter, you don't want to be there in the summertime. Either you broil or you boil, depending on whether it's dry or sticky. If the winter's warmer, so is the summer—that's the rule."

"Well, if that's the Rule, it must be fit for the Rulers,

right?" Runolf Skallagrim said. "What should we do with 'em? Broil 'em or boil 'em?"

"Either one. Both," Hamnet said. "Talking about it's easy, though. Doing it takes more work."

Runolf chuckled. "Ah, well. If you're going to complain about every little thing . . ." Ulric thought that was funny. Hamnet, again, didn't. This time, he made himself smile. He could occasionally get away with hypocrisy because no one suspected he would stoop to such a thing.

The Raumsdalians and Bizogots mounted and spread out and rode south, looking for the Rulers—and for food. Coming across a flock of sheep the invaders had somehow missed made everyone happy. Oh, Trasamund said, "When I have a choice, I like musk-ox meat better," but his heart wasn't in the grumbling.

"Been a couple of thousand years since musk oxen ranged this far south," Hamnet said. "In those days, the Glacier covered everything down to just north of Nidaros. No Gap then—not the smallest thought of one. Nothing but ice."

"Good times, by God," the jarl said. "Things on the far side of the Gap stayed where they belonged. They didn't come down and bother honest men." To put Hamnet in his place, he added, "Or Raumsdalians."

"Ha! Bizogots are the ones who steal," Hamnet retorted. "Even a guest-friend can't go into an encampment and come away with everything he brought."

"You don't miss it. You Raumsdalians all have too many things anyhow," Trasamund said.

"You sound like Marcovefa—only she says the same thing about ordinary Bizogots, too," Count Hamnet replied.

Trasamund grunted. "Her folk don't have enough. That is nothing but the truth, by God—not enough. I saw that with my own eyes. And you Raumsdalians have too much.

Everybody knows it's so. We Bizogots, we are just right."
He thumped his chest with his right fist.

"Why was I sure you would say something like that?"
Hamnet asked dryly.

"Because down deep, you do have some notion of the
truth," Trasamund said. Runolf Skallagrim couldn't make
Hamnet laugh, but the Bizogot did. That was the silliest
thing Hamnet had heard in weeks.

Trasamund got angry because he started laughing. The
jarl took himself seriously—he always did. But before he
could heat up his argument or start a fight, a horn warned
that somebody off to the left had spotted the enemy. When
Trasamund reached over his shoulder to grab for his
sword, Hamnet knew the Bizogot didn't intend to use it
on him.

Hamnet Thyssen made sure his sword was loose in the
scabbard, too. He saw no Rulers, not yet, so it wasn't time
to string his bow. He looked around for Marcovefa. Without her, neither sword nor bow was likely to matter much.

She waved to him. If her confidence was damaged, it
didn't show. That was all to the good. She called out, but
he couldn't catch what she said. He cupped a hand behind
his ear.

Marcovefa rode closer. "We'll fix them. You see if we
don't," she said.

"Sounds good to me," Hamnet said.

"The weather is better. I hope it will help my magic."
Marcovefa seemed to think *better* meant *colder*. Having
lived almost all her life atop the Glacier, she probably did.

When Hamnet did spot the Rulers, they were herding
along a swarm of Raumsdalian prisoners. Unlike Marcovefa's folk, they didn't eat people not of their blood—or Hamnet didn't think they did. Whether they slaughtered them for
the fun of it, unfortunately, might be a different question.

Still . . . "They're nothing but guards—not real warriors," Hamnet called. "We can beat them!"

The Raumsdalians and Bizogots cheered. Hamnet hoped he wasn't lying too much. If the Rulers had a wizard along, things might get more complicated. The same was true if they attacked their captives.

Even if they didn't, he wondered what his followers would do with that flock of Raumsdalians. How would they feed them? How would they house them? People couldn't stay out in the open forever, not with the Breath of God beginning to stir. Even this far south of Nidaros, winter would be hard. He didn't want to become a herdsman of people himself.

One thing at a time, he thought. *First, beat the Rulers. Then worry about what comes after that.*

He knew when the invaders spotted his oncoming warriors. Some of them started shooting into the crowd of captives. Others swung swords. Still others rode out to face his men. One of them, plainly, was a wizard. He held up his hand, palm out, as if ordering the attackers to stop.

Marcovefa laughed. Her left hand twisted in deft passes. Surprise seemed to radiate from the enemy wizard when he discovered his magic didn't work the way he wanted it to. Marcovefa laughed again, louder.

She reached out toward the Rulers' wizard—and then she stopped laughing, because whatever spell she aimed at him didn't work the way she wanted it to, either. He stayed on his riding deer and aimed more magic at the Raumsdalians and Bizogots.

That also failed. He and Marcovefa seemed able to stymie each other, but no more. Hamnet wondered what Marcovefa thought of that. He knew what he would have thought of it: nothing good. How anxious was she about being able to work magic? As anxious as a man who had trouble rising for his woman? That was the only comparison that occurred to the thoroughly unsorcerous Raumsdalian noble. When it did, he wished it hadn't. Worrying about rising to the occasion only made you less likely to rise the next time.

Then Marcovefa gestured again—this time, Count Hamnet judged, angrily. And the Rulers' wizard threw up both hands, as if he were shot. He clutched at his chest. A moment later, he fell over. And, a moment after that, all the Rulers' bows and arrows caught fire. Their swords suddenly seemed as limp as if they would never do their women any good again.

If his weapons failed in his hand, Hamnet knew what he would do: he'd run away. What else could you do, with no hope of fighting back? The Rulers seemed to come to the same conclusion. They rode off toward the south. A few of their captives had the wit and spirit to throw rocks after them, but Hamnet didn't see that they hit anyone.

As soon as the Rulers were out of rock range, the rescued Raumsdalians turned and welcomed the army that had saved them. The sad irony was that it hadn't saved all of them, but it had saved most. Here and there, someone wept because a spouse had died or got badly wounded at the last instant before freedom returned. Hamnet didn't know what he could do about that.

And then his head came up, suddenly and sharply. Someone in the crowd of captives was calling his name. Two someones, in fact: a man and a woman. "No," he said softly, for the voices were familiar. They called again. They waved, even more insistently than a lot of the other Raumsdalians. They were filthy and haggard and scrawny, but he recognized them anyhow. "No," he said again, and covered his eyes with the heels of his hands.

Eyvind Torfinn went on shouting and waving. So did Gudrid.

"I'LL KISS YOU, if you want me to," Gudrid said. "By God, I'll kiss you and I'll mean it, too."

"If it please you, Your Grace, *I'll* kiss you," Earl Eyvind added.

"Don't do me any favors," Hamnet said—to which of them, he wasn't quite sure. He was sure he wished he had something stronger than water in the tin canteen he wore on his left hip.

"Aren't you lucky?" Ulric Skakki murmured.

"No, curse it," Hamnet answered. "As far as I'm concerned, the Rulers were bloody well welcome to Gudrid. As for Eyvind Torfinn . . ." He shrugged. He couldn't make himself dislike the scholarly earl, even if Eyvind was married to his former wife.

"There? You see?" Ulric sounded amused. That only made Hamnet Thyssen want to hit him.

"Have you got any food?" Eyvind asked. "Anything at all? We've been empty a long time."

"Horsemeat. Venison from riding deer. Maybe a little mutton. Some mammoth meat. It's not too fresh, but it's what we have," Hamnet answered. He tried not to look at Gudrid. It wasn't easy.

Earl Eyvind bowed low. "Whatever you can spare. God knows we aren't fussy, not now." A rich noble in Nidaros, he would have had every chance and every excuse to be fussy before. His shudder now said he might have eaten worse things than stale mammoth meat. Eating nothing, for instance, was much worse than that.

Seeing the sorry state the rescued captives were in, Raumsdalians and Bizogots started feeding them. Seeing the sorry state Hamnet Thyssen was in, Ulric handed him a skin and said, "Here. Drink this."

Expecting sour ale or maybe even smetyn, Count Hamnet did. Smooth, strong wine slid down his throat. He eyed Ulric with respect. "Where did you find this?"

"Oh, somewhere along the way," the adventurer said airily.

"Do you mind if I—?" Hamnet nodded toward Eyvind Torfinn.

"Go ahead. You do know he'll give it to Gudrid next, don't you?" Ulric said.

"Yes, I know that." Hamnet's voice was rough as a rasp. He shrugged, as if to say, *What can you do?* Then he leaned down and handed Earl Eyvind the wineskin. The other noble caught the rich bouquet. A broad, astonished smile spread across his haggard face. It got broader yet after he swigged. Then, sure enough, he passed it to Gudrid.

She eyed Hamnet. "I don't *suppose* you'd slip hemlock in there and poison Eyvind just for the sake of getting me," she said, her tone declaring that she didn't really suppose any such thing.

"Don't blame me for the games you'd play yourself," Count Hamnet replied, even more harshly than before. "If you want to drink, drink. If you don't, give the skin to someone else who can use it." Plenty of sorry-looking people were eyeing it with jealous, zealous attention.

Gudrid drank. He'd been sure she would. She tried to provoke him as automatically as she breathed. After blotting the ruby wine from her lips, she handed the skin back to Eyvind Torfinn, as if to claim it for their own. Eyvind had better sense. He gave it to the haggard Raumsdalian hanging over his left shoulder.

"God bless you, friend," the haggard man said, and

drank deep. Then he passed the wineskin to a woman beside him.

Ulric Skakki, meanwhile, gave Earl Eyvind a chunk of meat and Gudrid another. They both tore into it raw. They'd traveled up in the Bizogot country and even beyond the Gap. They could live rough if they had to. They were used to better things, though.

"Where did the Rulers catch you?" Hamnet asked.

Before answering, Earl Eyvind had to gulp down an enormous mouthful of meat. Hamnet was amazed not to see his throat swell like a snake's when he did it. "South of here," Eyvind said once the way internal was clear. He took another big bite and choked it down before adding, "We never expected to see you here—not that we're sorry we did."

"We're doing what we can," Hamnet Thyssen said. "I don't know if it will be enough, but we're trying."

Gudrid was eating as greedily as Eyvind. Wine and meat seemed to distract her from Hamnet, at least for the moment. *Just as well* ran through his mind.

Per Anders asked Eyvind, "Is the Emperor still safe?"

"Who cares?" Ulric Skakki murmured, but the imperial courier plainly did.

"He was the last time we saw him," Earl Eyvind replied. "That was . . . some little while ago, though. As far as I know, he isn't in this sad herd of people."

Count Hamnet tried to imagine Sigvat II, Emperor of Raumsdalia, shambling along in the midst of so many other captives. He tried to imagine the Emperor sleeping on the ground and grubbing up roots and insects like any other unfortunate. The picture made him want to smile. Maybe he was small-spirited, to relish the idea of someone else's misfortune. If he was, he would just have to live with it.

"What are you going to do with us?" Gudrid asked after some fairly monumental swallowing of her own.

What she really meant, of course, was, *What are you going to do with* me? She thought of herself first, last, and always. But Hamnet answered the question the way she asked it: "Anyone who wants to fight the Rulers is welcome to join us. We have a few extra horses and some spare weapons."

Neither white-bearded Eyvind Torfinn nor decorative Gudrid made a likely warrior. "And the rest?" she persisted.

"I don't know," Hamnet said. "I'll have to talk with Trasamund and Ulric and Runolf and Audun and Liv and Marcovefa."

"Liv. Marcovefa." Gudrid didn't try to disguise either her disdain or her amusement.

"That's right." Hamnet did his best to ignore them both. "We have to send you toward a place where you're likely to get food. Figuring out where to find a place like that may not be easy."

"You can't send us away!" Gudrid's voice went shrill. To Hamnet's amazement, she came up with a reason he shouldn't: "Eyvind knows more about the Rulers than anybody else from this side of the Glacier."

"Well, so he does," Count Hamnet admitted, deciding he couldn't very well deny it. "But what's that got to do with *you*? We may need him, but how are *you* going to help us drive the Rulers back through the Gap? The farther away from trouble you go, the better for everybody. You'll even be safer somewhere away from the fighting. You won't need to worry so much about starving, either."

"Eyvind won't help you unless I'm with him." Gudrid turned to her current husband. "Will you?" she asked ominously.

"If ground sloths and glyptodonts rose up against the Rulers, I would gladly help them right now," Eyvind Torfinn replied.

Gudrid's jaw dropped—she wasn't expecting mutiny from that quarter. Earl Eyvind was even more pliable than Hamnet had been back in the days when he was wed to her. Hearing him tell her no almost made her former husband laugh out loud.

"I'm not going anywhere without you," Gudrid declared when she'd recovered somewhat. "You need someone to take care of you, and you know it." To Hamnet Thyssen's disappointment, that held a measure of truth.

"I expect I can manage," Earl Eyvind said. "Whether you believe it or not, I'm not entirely helpless."

"That's what you think." Gudrid hardly bothered to hide her scorn.

Marcovefa ambled over. Gudrid eyed her the way a bird might eye a snake. Marcovefa paid next to no attention to Gudrid, not at first. She pointed toward Eyvind Torfinn. "We need him."

"You have me," Eyvind said.

Hamnet waited for Marcovefa to dismiss Gudrid. He waited, as he knew, with more than a little anticipation. Gudrid had a knack for ignoring him and getting under his skin like a tick. She did not have the knack for outfacing Marcovefa. As far as Hamnet knew, nobody did.

Marcovefa pointed at Gudrid. Gudrid flinched, then made a good, game try at pretending she hadn't. "We need you, too," declared the shaman from atop the Glacier.

"What?" Gudrid sounded as if she couldn't believe her ears.

"*What?*" Hamnet Thyssen knew only too well that he couldn't believe his.

"We need her, too," Marcovefa said. Then she spoke

directly to Gudrid again: "We do need you, too." She shook her head. "Doesn't anybody listen to anything any more?"

"*Why* in God's name do we need her?" Count Hamnet demanded. "She isn't worth . . . anything."

"That's not what you used to think," Gudrid said with a smile all the more provoking because it was so sweet.

"Well, I know better now," Hamnet replied. "You taught me—the hard way."

Marcovefa ignored their sniping. "I don't know why we need her. I only know we do." She eyed Count Hamnet. "Do you want to tell me you know these things better than I do?"

Hamnet wanted nothing more. Unfortunately, he couldn't. "No, but—"

"But me no buts." Marcovefa sounded as imperious—and as imperial—as Sigvat II. "If you do not believe me, ask Audun Gilli. Ask Liv. They will tell you the same."

Asking them was the last thing Count Hamnet wanted to do. No—it was the next to last thing he wanted to do. Keeping Gudrid with them was the last thing, the very last thing. "By God, I will!" he growled, and stormed off.

He found Liv before Audun. That made things worse, but not worst. "What is it?" she asked as he approached with determined stride.

He told her exactly what it was. "Does Marcovefa know what she's talking about?" he asked. "Can she know? Can't we get rid of Gudrid?" The last question was the one that really mattered to him.

"Marcovefa . . . knows all kinds of things," Liv said slowly. "Sometimes she knows without even knowing how she knows. I could do a divination to see if she is right here."

"Would you?" Hamnet hated how eager he sounded, but couldn't help it.

"Yes." Liv gave him a crooked smile. "I suppose I should be grateful you're not asking whether we can do without me."

"You hurt me," Hamnet answered, as steadily as he could. "But you didn't hurt me because you enjoyed hurting me. There's a difference. How complicated is your divination?"

"Not very. Questions with yes or no answers usually aren't." She took from her pouch a small disk of shining white stone, pierced near the edge. "Moonstone," she said, threading a thong through the small hole.

"What is the magic?" Hamnet asked.

"I ask whether Gudrid should stay with us, then let the stone fall down over my heart," Liv answered. "If she should, it will stay close to my skin. If she should not, it will leap away."

"Seems simple enough," he said.

She nodded and began chanting in the Bizogot language. She wasn't exactly asking the question, or not in so many words. Hamnet judged that she was priming the moonstone, so to speak, so it would do the asking for her. Then she put the thong over her head and let the stone fall down between her breasts. Though she showed next to none of herself in the doing, Hamnet had to look away. He still remembered how his head had lain there. . . .

"Well?" he asked roughly.

Liv's half-smile said she knew he wanted to reach inside her tunic to find out whether the moonstone disk was clinging to her. Gudrid would have worn a half-smile, too, but hers would have been full of sardonic triumph as well. Liv's was, if anything, sympathetic.

And so was her voice when she said, "I *am* sorry, Hamnet, but the magic tells me Marcovefa was right."

"Damnation!" Hamnet Thyssen burst out. "She can't be! God knows Gudrid is nothing but trouble."

"Gudrid *is* trouble," Liv agreed gravely. "But I would have to say she is not nothing but trouble. If she were, the spell would tell me Marcovefa had made a mistake. I don't think she has."

"Damnation!" Hamnet repeated. He turned on his heel and shambled off, feeling almost as betrayed as he had when Liv left him for Audun Gilli. The idea of keeping Gudrid around tempted him to sit down on the ground somewhere and slit his wrists. The certainty that his former wife would laugh if he did was one of the things that kept him from drawing dagger or sword.

Marcovefa had no trouble reading his face when he walked up to her. "You see? We do need the stupid vole after all."

That made Gudrid splutter, which gave Hamnet a certain somber satisfaction. Ulric Skakki turned away before smiling. Trasamund laughed out loud, which won him a venomous stare from Gudrid. He'd enjoyed her charms in days gone by. She didn't like it when someone else was as faithless and heartless to her as she was to her former lovers.

Hamnet was too stubborn to give up easily. "Give me one good reason why we need Gudrid," he said.

"Because I tell you so," Marcovefa answered. "Somewhere later"—her gesture encompassed all the time from the next instant to the moment when the Glacier melted away for good—"it will be better if we have her than if she is off doing mischief somewhere else."

"What do you mean, doing mischief?" Yes, Gudrid was

irate, too. "I don't do mischief. I do what I have to do."
Count Hamnet laughed at that. So did Ulric. So did Trasamund, raucously. Gudrid looked daggers at each of them
in turn.

"I mean what I say," Marcovefa told her. "I don't waste
my time and everybody else's with a pack of lies the way
you do."

Gudrid took a deep breath, no doubt intending to deny
it. Something in Marcovefa's face made her keep her
mouth shut. If she lied about lying, Marcovefa could give
her the lie. That convoluted logic brought a smile to Hamnet's face. His smile made Gudrid steam. He'd had things
happen that he liked less.

"Well. It is decided then," Eyvind Torfinn said. Maybe
a lot of what had just gone on had flown over his head. Or
maybe he was willing to pretend it had for the sake of
peace and quiet. And maybe that wasn't the worst idea in
the world. Maybe they all needed to do more of it.

"Yes," Hamnet said, and he couldn't help sighing. "It is
decided."

ULRIC SKAKKI LOOKED at the trees. He looked at the
sky. He looked down at the scarred backs of his hands.
Then he looked over at Hamnet Thyssen, who was riding
next to him. "Ever have the feeling something's about to
go wrong, but you don't know what?"

"Now and then," Hamnet answered. "Not soon enough,
usually."

"Well, we can all say that," Ulric told him. "I've got it
now—curse me if I don't. Feels like something crawling
on the back of my neck . . . and no, it's not a stinking
louse. It's more like what I felt up by Sudertorp Lake."

"I didn't say it was a louse. But why are you telling me?
Tell Marcovefa. Maybe she can do something about it."

"There you go!" The adventurer laughed cheerily. "You see? You're not always as foolish as you seem."

Hamnet bowed in the saddle. "Be careful, or you'll turn my head, or maybe my stomach, with flattery like that."

"Maybe both at once, so you can be sick down your own back. I do believe I'd pay money to watch that." Ulric Skakki raised his voice: "Marcovefa?"

"What do you want, you noisy man?" she asked.

"That's me," Ulric agreed, not without pride. "I thought you ought to know I have the bad feeling we're running into trouble."

"Oh, you do, do you? Again?" Even though Ulric had been right before, Marcovefa didn't sound particularly impressed. She wasn't mocking, but she wasn't convinced, either. "Why do you say that?"

"Because I do, that's why," Ulric answered. "I'm not out of my mind—or I don't think so, anyhow."

"How often does a crazy man know he is crazy?" Marcovefa returned.

"More often than you'd think. Look at Hamnet here," Ulric said.

Marcovefa laughed. Hamnet didn't. "Kindly leave me out of this," he said. "It's your feeling. It's got nothing to do with me, at least not till we find out exactly how crazy *you* are."

"I thought you'd known that for a long time," the adventurer said.

"If you put it that way, I have," Hamnet Thyssen returned. "I wasn't going to come right out and tell you so, though."

"No, of course not. You'd go and talk behind my back instead. I've met people like you before, I have." Ulric might have been a dancing girl scolding a mercenary who was trying to coax her into bed rather than his usual self.

When he shook a finger under Hamnet's nose, though, the Raumsdalian noble decided he'd gone too far.

So did Marcovefa. "Enough of this foolishness!" she said. "You want me to find out whether you're right, don't you?"

"If you can." Ulric sobered as fast as he'd got silly. "I mean, I know we've been in trouble before and we'll be in trouble again. If we didn't land in trouble again, it would be because we've given up on everything we're trying now—or else because we're dead. That's not what I'm worried about. Something not very far away is going to mean trouble for us pretty soon—or I think it is. The hair at the back of my neck thinks it is."

"Well, we will see." Marcovefa took two thin, flat, nearly transparent crystals out of a rabbit-hide pouch she wore on her belt. When she held them parallel to each other in front of her face, they remained transparent. But when she turned one so it was perpendicular to the other, the square where the two of them met became dark.

"How do they do that?" Hamnet asked.

"I don't know," Marcovefa answered with a shrug that said she also didn't care much. "But when I look through the darkness, all I see is what put us into danger."

Don't look toward Gudrid, Hamnet thought. He'd already lost that fight—lost it twice, to Marcovefa and to Liv. His chances of winning it now didn't strike him as good enough to make reopening it seem worthwhile. "What do you see when you look through the . . . the . . . ?" He groped for a word to describe the crystals.

"Spars, we call them—spars from the land of ice," Marcovefa said, which struck him as an oddly nautical name to come from a mountaintop above the Glacier. "As for what I see . . ." she went on. She slowly turned in a complete circle with that curious darkness held in front of her right eye.

When she started a second revolution, Count Hamnet was sure that whatever Ulric Skakki had imagined was imaginary. When, facing southeast, she suddenly stopped, he was sure that what he'd been sure of a moment before was wrong. Few sensations were more disconcerting than that; it was as if an earthquake had shaken the country inside his head.

"Well, you are right two times now," Marcovefa told Ulric.

"What is it? Do you know? Can you tell?" he asked. Somehow, by not gloating, he sounded more smug than he would have if he'd bragged about how fine his hunches were.

Marcovefa shook her head. "Something, that's all. Maybe it won't be trouble now that we know it's there. Or maybe it will be worse." Hamnet wished she hadn't added that.

"Let's go deal with it, whatever it is," Ulric said.

"Would we do better running away?" Hamnet asked.

"I didn't looked for *you* to play the coward, Thyssen," Trasamund said.

"I'm not, by God," Count Hamnet replied. "There's trouble, and then there's trouble. Some kinds you can face; others, you'd do better to stay away from. If you run toward one of those, you'll be sorry afterward . . . if you're still around."

"He's right," Marcovefa said, which silenced Trasamund. She looked at Hamnet again. "I don't know this time. We'll just have to find out—or else run away without finding out."

"If we do that, it'll come after us, whatever it is." Ulric

Skakki spoke with mournful certainty. "I say we need to see what's what."

Hamnet didn't argue any more. He walked over to his horse and swung up onto it. So did the others. He winced when he saw Eyvind Torfinn and Gudrid on horseback. They made him wonder if he wasn't bringing trouble with him instead of riding toward it. But Marcovefa seemed willing enough to let them ride along. Some people here already thought Hamnet had spoken up once too often. He kept quiet now.

Marcovefa and Ulric leading the way, they rode out. Hamnet Thyssen kept close to Marcovefa, but let her stay in front. She smiled at him over her left shoulder every so often, as if his attentiveness amused her. It probably did. What a warrior could do to keep an accomplished shaman safe . . . *Is keep other warriors away from her*, Hamnet thought. Spells reached farther than swords, but swords could strike faster.

What they rode through seemed ordinary Raumsdalian countryside. "So many ups and downs," Trasamund grumbled. The Glacier had never lain this far south, never ground everything flat beneath its massive weight. Hills and dips persisted here, where they'd been leveled up in the lands the Bizogot was used to.

Forests lay well back from the road. Hamnet's head swiveled from left to right, from right over to left. If the trouble came from either side, he'd be ready for it. He'd see it, anyway. After a moment, he realized that might not be the same thing.

If the trouble came from straight ahead, he'd see it from even farther off. He hoped he would, anyhow. If the trouble was some gigantic pitfall . . . He shook his head. He couldn't believe Ulric would have sensed such a thing.

And it wouldn't be a danger unless they came in this direction on purpose.

Marcovefa also seemed alert. She was as bright as a songbird: head up, eyes sparkling, nostrils flaring with excitement. Hamnet wondered if he was imagining some of that, but he didn't think so.

Sure enough, a moment later she started to laugh. "So that's what this is all about," she said.

"What?" he asked.

"They thought they could set a trap for us." Marcovefa held up a hand as she reined in. Everyone else stopped, too.

"What kind of trap?" Count Hamnet asked.

"I don't know—yet," she said, pointing out toward the peaceful-looking landscape ahead. "Whatever lies beyond that."

"Beyond what?" This time, Ulric got the question out ahead of Hamnet. It seemed more than reasonable enough to the Raumsdalian nobleman.

Not, evidently, to Marcovefa. Her nostrils flared again—this time, Count Hamnet judged, in exasperation. "Some sort of sorcerous barrier lies ahead," she said, as if to a group of idiot children. "Whatever is behind it, Ulric Skakki, is the trouble you rightly felt."

In back of Hamnet, Audun Gilli spoke in a low voice: "I don't sense anything up ahead."

"Neither do I," Liv answered, also quietly. "But her wizardry is stronger than ours. She may be right."

"I know," Audun said. "That's what worries me."

"What do we do now?" Even Trasamund's big voice was unwontedly soft.

"We smash the barrier. Then we smash what lies behind it." Marcovefa sounded as eager as if she were a young girl going to her lover.

"Just like that?" Hamnet said.

"Yes. Just like that." She aimed a peremptory forefinger at the barrier only she could sense. When she spoke again, she used her own dialect of the Bizogot tongue. Ulric might have been able to follow it, but Hamnet couldn't.

He also couldn't deny it had an effect. The peaceful scene ahead wavered, as someone's reflection in a pool would waver if he dropped a pebble into the water. Then it disappeared, as a reflection would if someone dropped in a handful of pebbles. It had concealed a swarm of saber-tooths and lions and dire wolves and short-faced bears. Roaring and snarling, they sprang toward Hamnet and his comrades.

XIII

"Did we really have to ride toward this?" Hamnet Thyssen asked. Without conscious thought, his hands strung the bow and found an arrow to set on the string.

"To tell you the truth, I would have been glad enough to do without it," Ulric Skakki replied. He was readying his bow with quick competence, too.

Marcovefa started laughing again. Hamnet and Ulric looked at her as if she'd lost her mind. So did everyone else, which made Hamnet feel a little—a very little—better. In the next minute or so, unless he was luckier than he deserved to be, he was much too likely to end up torn limb from limb.

"Will you share the joke?" he asked.

"They put a mask on an illusion and think it will serve," she said.

Count Hamnet thought it would serve, too. The sabertooth heading his way was almost close enough to spring. If he didn't let fly in the next few heartbeats, it would. He had to hope he could hurt it and scare it away. If he didn't . . .

He preferred not to think about that. Even if he did frighten off the sabertooth, he would have to worry about a lion or a short-faced bear next. He preferred not to think about that, too, but feared he had little choice.

Then Marcovefa pointed once more at the oncoming beasts. Laughing still, she cast another spell—to Hamnet Thyssen's relief, a brief one. As soon as the spell struck home, Hamnet cried out in astonishment. So did the rest of the Raumsdalians and Bizogots.

Rather than a swarm of ferocious wild beasts, a ragged gaggle of naked Rulers rushed toward them. The invaders from beyond the Gap must have sensed that their covering spell had failed, for they stopped in confusion, looking quite humanly astonished. A man behind them—well out of bowshot behind them—must have been the wizard who'd set the barrier and disguised his countrymen as beasts. He seemed astonished, too: astonished and infuriated. He hadn't expected to be found out, let alone outdone.

The sabertooth-turned-Ruler would have done better to keep coming. Hamnet shot him in the belly. He said "Oof!" loud enough to let Hamnet hear him clearly. Then he shrieked a good deal louder than that. The Rulers were brave, strong, and stubborn warriors, but hardly any man from any folk could have hoped to stay silent after that kind of wound.

As if the shriek were a signal, most of the other riders let fly. More of the broad-shouldered, burly men went down. The rest turned and ran as fast as they could. The Rulers seldom fled—their stern way of making war frowned on falling back for any reason. But maybe their code of honor or whatever it was granted dispensations when they got caught with their breeches down. Hamnet seldom sympathized with their predicaments, but with that one he did.

Watching them pelt back toward him only made their

wizard angrier. *He* wasn't naked—he wore the Rulers' usual fur and leather, decorated with a shaman's fringes and crystals. Hamnet was busy speeding the departing warriors on their way with arrow after arrow, but he kept glancing at the enemy sorcerer. With the men routed, the wizard was the only danger left.

He must have felt Marcovefa was the only danger to him—and he might well have been right. Even across more than a furlong, Hamnet could see him quiver with rage. The Ruler aimed his finger with as much purpose as Marcovefa had ever shown.

Count Hamnet waited for her to swat his spell aside, the way she had with the concealment and shapeshifting sorceries. Instead, to his horrified dismay, she swayed in the saddle. She might have taken a sharp right to the chin.

She shook herself, the way someone who'd taken a sharp right to the chin might do. The snarl that followed made the efforts of all the Rulers masquerading as beasts seem half-hearted beside it. *That* made Hamnet Thyssen feel better. Even if she had a foe worthy of her, she didn't seem downhearted about it.

And the Rulers' wizard did seem astonished that she still sat her horse—or maybe that she hadn't burst into flames. Hamnet got the feeling he would be vulnerable to anything Marcovefa did to him.

Before he could find out, Trasamund yelled, "Forward! After them! Kill them all, the stinking dire-wolf turds!" By the way the Bizogots and Raumsdalians spurred ahead, they were every one of them relieved to be chasing naked men and not battling lions and sabertooths. Hamnet understood that. How could he not, when he felt the same way?

But Marcovefa swore in her own dialect. All those men and horses between her and the enemy shaman must have blocked the spell she wanted to cast. She paused and began another one. While she was doing that, the Rulers' wizard also turned and ran. Like most of his folk, he was short and stocky. He showed a fine turn of speed even so.

Marcovefa held out her hands. The enemy wizard sprang into the air, higher than a man had any business doing. When he came down, he ran even faster. Marcovefa said something that should have scorched his backside all over again. Hamnet realized she'd intended to destroy him, not just singe his breeches.

"Never mind," Hamnet said. "You broke two masks and you beat him."

She gave him a look that was anything but satisfied. "These foolish little people! I shouldn't only beat them. I should make them sorry their mothers ever let them out of the nest."

She went right on scowling at the corpses of the Rulers who'd been magicked into predators' shapes. The Bizogots and Raumsdalians also scowled at them. That Count Hamnet understood: how could you steal anything from a naked man? He needed longer to fathom Marcovefa's annoyance. But then he did—to her, the bodies lying on the ground were wasted meat.

"You want to pick out a plump one, don't you?" he said.

"We all should," she said. "They could feed us for a couple of days. You leave so much on the ground, it surprises me your carrion birds aren't too fat to fly."

"We don't eat man's flesh, not unless we're starving," Hamnet said. "Even then, we don't talk about it later."

"Up on the Glacier, we are always hungry," Marcovefa answered. Hamnet nodded; he'd seen the truth of that. She went on, "But the flesh of someone from another clan—that is not man's flesh, not to us. And these are not just from another clan. They might as well be from another world."

Hamnet felt the same way about them. But he said,

"You have narrow rules for who is a man and who is not. Ours stretch wider. A good thing, too—if they didn't, what would we do with you?"

"Knock me over the head while I'm sleeping, I expect," she answered matter-of-factly. "It might be safer for you if you did. Your wizards are even weaker than the Rulers'. That means I can be more dangerous to you than I am to them."

"Yes, you can be," Hamnet said. "Do you want to be? Do you want to tell everyone what to do all the time, like the Rulers?" If Marcovefa said yes to that, he wondered if he ought to knock her over the head.

But she shook her head. "No. I don't want people telling me what to do. Why should they want me doing the same thing?"

"If everybody thought that way, we'd all be better off," Hamnet Thyssen said.

Marcovefa looked at him as if that were the silliest thing she'd ever heard. "Don't hold your breath."

ULRIC SKAKKI WAS more serious than usual—almost painfully serious, in fact. "I want to work this out," he said, toasting some mutton—definitely not haunch of Ruler—over a fire that night. "I smelled trouble."

"So you did." Count Hamnet sounded blurry, even to himself. He had a big mouthful of mutton, too: charred on the outside, bloody on the inside. "I thought you were daft, but Marcovefa didn't. That's twice now."

"Right." Ulric started to take a bite, then pulled the smoking meat away from his face and blew on it. "Too blasted hot. Where was I? Oh, yes. Marcovefa. She could tell I wasn't just jumpy, and she could tell where the trouble was, same as she did with the sickness. She's the reason we went southeast—she knew it was there."

"Can't argue with you." Hamnet didn't want to argue, anyhow. He wanted to eat.

So did Ulric. He managed to bite the mutton without burning his mouth. But that only made *him* talk and chew at the same time: "So suppose she wasn't along. Suppose we went straight south or southwest instead of southeast. We never would have run into those Rulers, and my hunch would have been worth its weight in gold—know what I mean?"

"Hmm." Hamnet chewed both mutton and Ulric Skakki's paradox. He found them both tough. At last, he said, "My guess is, if you'd smelled trouble when Marcovefa wasn't along, or if no one had smelled trouble at all, we *would* have ridden southeast and run into it. We would have found some reason to do that, and the Rulers would have taken us by surprise."

"Mm—maybe." Ulric still didn't seem happy.

"If you don't like my answers, go ask Marcovefa yourself," Hamnet told him.

"By God, I will!" The adventurer jumped to his feet and hurried over to the fire by which Marcovefa sat chatting with Audun Gilli and Liv. Ulric stooped beside her. They spoke for a little while. Then Ulric straightened. His face bore a peculiar expression as he came back.

"What did she say?" Hamnet asked.

" 'Don't ask foolish questions.' " No doubt because he spoke her dialect, Ulric could imitate Marcovefa's accent in Raumsdalian very well. He also did a good job of mimicking the sniff she could put in her voice.

Caught by surprise, Hamnet burst out laughing. "Well, it's good advice," he said when Ulric looked miffed.

"If you don't ask a question, how are you supposed to know it's foolish?" the adventurer persisted.

Is that a foolish question? Hamnet wondered. It probably wasn't. Lately, too many questions that seemed foolish turned out to have answers of life-and-death importance. "Are you turning philosopher?" Hamnet asked. "If you are, why did we bother rounding up Earl Eyvind?"

"We didn't do it on purpose. It just . . . happened," Ulric said. "I'm sure you were thrilled when we rounded up Gudrid with him."

"Thrilled. But of course," Hamnet said tightly. Ulric Skakki gave him an impudent grin. Hamnet hastened to change the subject: "Where do we go from here? What can we do to make sure the Rulers don't wreck Raumsdalia?"

"Wait till they kill Sigvat, and then beat them," Ulric answered without the least hesitation. The cynicism in that took Count Hamnet's breath away. The look on his face must have said as much, because Ulric laughed harshly. "What? Do you think I'm joking?"

"No. I think you're not. And I think I ought to cry for Raumsdalia because you're not," Hamnet said.

"Don't waste your tears. Do you suppose Sigvat would cry for you?" Ulric Skakki answered his own question: "If you do, you're a different kind of fool from the one I've seen. Sigvat only has tears for himself."

"And what kind of fool have you seen?" Hamnet Thyssen asked, as dispassionately as he could.

"You're too stubborn for your own good. You're too innocent for your own good. And you don't know enough about women for your own good." Before Hamnet could say anything to that, Ulric added, "Well, no man knows enough about women for his own good. But you knew even less than most of us poor twits. If you don't believe me, go ask—"

"Gudrid?"

"I was going to say Marcovefa," Ulric replied. "If you want to go ask Gudrid, well, you can do that. You want to know what I think, though? If you do, it only proves you're a fool about women. Anybody who wants to have anything to do with that one . . ." He gave a theatrical shiver.

"Eyvind seems to," Hamnet said.

"By God, Eyvind's a fool about women. Even a fool about women like you should be able to see that," Ulric said. And Count Hamnet nodded, because he could. Ulric patted him on the back. "There. You see? If you can see that, maybe he's a bigger fool than you are. And they said it couldn't be done!"

Hamnet got up and walked away from the fire. Ulric's laughter pursued him.

•

THE QUESTION HAMNET Thyssen had asked Ulric kept gnawing at him. What *could* they do to beat the Rulers? They didn't have enough warriors to do it in battle. He'd banked on Marcovefa's magic to make up the difference in manpower. Now he saw that, while it could make up some of the difference, it would need strange and unusual help to make up all of it.

What that help might be, he unfortunately couldn't imagine.

Marcovefa didn't want to talk about it. "Everything will be all right," she said when he raised the subject.

"Do you *know* that?" Hamnet persisted. "Does your magic tell you so? If it does, is it bound to know what it's talking about?"

"Everything will be all right . . . as long as you don't keep bothering me." She paused. "If you do keep bothering me like this, you can find someone else to bother. I have listened to as much as I want to hear. Do you understand me?"

He couldn't very well not understand her. "Yes," he growled, and swung his horse's head away so he could ride off by himself. No matter how big a fool about women he was, he could see he was on the edge of losing this one. How much bigger a fool would that make him?

He looked around. Ulric Skakki was out of earshot. That was something, anyhow—not much, but something.

A scout from the rear guard galloped up to the van. "Rulers!" the Raumsdalian shouted. "Rulers coming down from the north!"

"Let's bag them!" Trasamund said. "They may not even know we're anywhere close by. If they're just coming down into the Empire, chances are they think it's all over down here except the mopping up."

"If they do, they're wrong," Runolf Skallagrim declared. "Yes, let's welcome them to Raumsdalia."

Swinging about and heading north again was a matter of minutes. Hamnet stayed away from Marcovefa instead of asking her what she would do. Maybe he could learn. Maybe.

Since he didn't talk to her, she rode over and talked to him. That was bound to be a lesson of one kind or another. Which kind, Hamnet wasn't sure he wanted to know. "Shall we look like them?" Marcovefa said. "Will that surprise them and make things easy for us?"

"What do I know?" Hamnet answered. "Talk to Trasamund and Ulric and Runolf. If they think it's a good idea, go ahead and do it."

Marcovefa talked to the others. "They say to go ahead," she told Hamnet. "So I go ahead. The Rulers will see the spell. Not us. We do not see anything out of the sameness."

"Out of the ordinary, you mean," Hamnet said.

"Do I? I suppose I do." Marcovefa shrugged and got busy with her magic. She didn't explain it, the way she often did. She simply went ahead with the spell. Hamnet Thyssen looked at his comrades. They didn't look like Rulers to him. She'd told him they wouldn't. He felt obscurely disappointed even so.

There were the Rulers. They were on mammoths and deer, and rode through the Empire as if they had not a care in the world. When they spied the Bizogots and Raumsdalians in front of them, they waved cheerfully. Their foes looked like friends to them, anyhow.

The two bands had got quite close to each other before one of the real Rulers called out something in their incomprehensible language. Hamnet and a few others had learned tiny fragments of that tongue. No one he led spoke it well enough to fool someone for whom it was a birth-speech. The men on his side did the best they could: they kept their mouths shut.

Frowning, the broad-shouldered, curly-bearded man repeated himself. Hamnet recognized the same syllables over again. He also caught the annoyance in the—chieftain's?—voice. Whatever the Ruler said, he expected some kind of answer, and he wasn't getting it. Which meant . . .

"Let's hit 'em!" Hamnet, Trasamund, and Runolf all shouted the same thing at almost the same time. Ulric wasted no time on chatter. He simply drew his bow and shot the man who'd called out to people he thought friends. The Ruler looked almost comically astonished when the arrow sprouted in the middle of his wide chest. He slid off his riding deer's back.

More Rulers tumbled from their mounts. Count Hamnet cut one down before his foe had even drawn his sword.

Doing something like that wasn't fair, which didn't mean it didn't work.

Only a few of the enemy warriors aboard riding deer found much chance to fight back. Bizogot and Raumsdalian archers also did everything they could to shoot the Rulers on the war mammoths, and to shoot the mammoths themselves as often as they could. If the beasts went wild with pain, they wouldn't do what their masters wanted them to.

But a mammoth plucked a Raumsdalian trooper out of the saddle with its trunk and threw him to the ground. His terrified shriek cut off abruptly when the mammoth's forefoot crushed the life from him. From everything Hamnet had seen, even large animals didn't like stepping on people. Like it or not, the mammoth did it, as other war mammoths had before. Maybe the Rulers had some training trick to get the best of their reluctance.

"The illusion is broken," Marcovefa called.

"Get back out of slingstone range!" Hamnet yelled at her. She made a face, but for once did as he asked without arguing. Almost getting her skull smashed before made her less than eager to risk it again.

Another Ruler yammered nonsense at Hamnet. It wasn't nonsense to the man from beyond the Gap, of course, but it meant not a thing to the Raumsdalian noble. "Give up!" Hamnet shouted back. The Ruler either didn't understand or didn't want to.

Their swords would have to speak for them, then. Iron rang against iron. Sun-bright sparks flew. Hamnet wondered whether two swordsmen fighting in dry grass or on dry moss had ever started a fire. Then, as he beat the Ruler's blade aside the instant before it would have ruined his face, he wondered if he would live through this.

A Bizogot's arrow caught his opponent in the ribs. The Ruler grunted and then screamed. Hamnet finished him with a stroke to the neck. Body contorting in death spasms, the invader crashed to the ground.

Hamnet looked for someone else to fight. The unfair skirmish was almost over. One of the war mammoths was still fighting even though arrows pincushioned it. A few real Rulers kept up the struggle against the ambushers, but they fell one after another.

"Surrender!" Hamnet shouted in the Rulers' language— that was a word he'd made sure he learned from the few prisoners his side had taken. Only a handful of the invaders ever did it. Most preferred death in battle to what they thought of as the worst of disgraces.

For his trouble, he got abuse showered on him now. The surviving Rulers made it plain they weren't about to give up. He couldn't understand much of what they called him, but he was sure they weren't tossing him endearments.

"If they don't want to, they don't have to," Trasamund said. He drew his bow, took careful aim, and shot one of the Rulers off the war mammoth still in the fight. The rest of the enemy warriors cheered. They saw nothing wrong with dying. Quitting was another story.

Die they did. Marcovefa tried her heart-stopping sorcery on the mammoth, but it didn't work. She shrugged. "Warded," she said. "The spell is easy to block."

"Too bad. A lot of meat there." Trasamund shrugged. "Oh, well. We'll still butcher the deer and the horses that went down."

"I wish it were easy to put the mammoths out of their misery one way or another," Hamnet Thyssen said. He imagined himself wandering around with needles and skewers jabbed into his flesh. That had to be something close to what the great beasts were feeling now—and they didn't even know why it had happened.

"Well, if you want to ride up close and try for a shot in the eye . . ." The way Trasamund's voice trailed off told what he thought Count Hamnet's chances were. After a moment, he went on, "Of course, if you miss, the mammoth'll likely stamp you into the mud."

"That did cross my mind, yes," Hamnet said. "Since it was your good idea, *you* can try it."

For a heartbeat, he feared Trasamund would. Challenging a Bizogot could be dangerous, because he might feel compelled to meet the challenge no matter how preposterous it was. But the jarl shook his head. "I've seen it tried, thanks," he said. "I've even seen it work once or twice. And I've seen what happens when it doesn't." This time, his pause had a meditative quality to it. "Not pretty."

"You sure aren't," Ulric Skakki agreed. "Or isn't that what you were talking about?" He had a knack for hearing and responding to the bits of talk that would start the most trouble.

"We were talking about putting mammoths out of their misery." Trasamund eyed Ulric. "Might be worthwhile doing the same thing to you."

"Only misery I'm in right now is from the company I keep," the adventurer said. "I can put myself out of it if I want to—all I need to do is ride away." He made as if to do just that.

"Hang on," Hamnet said.

"All right, since it's you that asks," Ulric said. "You haven't insulted me any time lately, anyhow. I don't quite know why not, but you haven't."

"Give me a chance and I'm sure I will," Hamnet replied. "Where do we go from here? What do we do next?"

Ulric struck a pose. "Do I look like an oracle? Am I the

Golden Shrine?" He looked down at himself. "If I am, the architect could have done better. My body is a temple— but not that one."

"Your body is a—" Trasamund broke off. He was bigger than Ulric Skakki, and thicker through the shoulders, but no one could accuse the adventurer of being soft. "A temple to your foul mouth," the Bizogot finished, and looked pleased with himself for coming up with something.

"While you're as pure as snow is black," Ulric said.

Trasamund started to nod, then almost hurt himself stopping when he heard the whole gibe. He sent Ulric a venomous stare. "I did not believe there really were things like snakes till I finally saw one down here, no matter what some fast-talking Raumsdalian traders said. When I got to know you, though, I understood what they meant."

"Ah, well." Ulric gave back an elaborate shrug. "For a long time, Your Ferocity, I felt the same way about vultures."

Trasamund purpled. Before they could turn insults into a brawl, Count Hamnet said, "Now, children . . ." That made them both glare at him, which was—he supposed—better than having them glare at each other. He went on, "The idea is to fight the Rulers—remember? If we fight each other, we help them? We don't do ourselves any good."

"But we can have some fun." Ulric was in no mood to be helpful.

"You want fun, go to a brothel," Trasamund growled. "This is war, curse it. We have to smash the Rulers— smash them, do you hear?"

"Think so, do you?" Ulric wasn't about to give up his sport. "And here all the time I thought the idea was to hand them flowers when they came by."

"Flowers, is it?" Trasamund told him what he could do with his flowers. It struck Hamnet as uncomfortable, especially if he used roses.

"You, too," Ulric said. "Sideways." He paused for a moment. "We didn't kill all of them, I don't think. Some will go on south and tell the rest of the Rulers where we are."

"That's part of the idea, eh?" Trasamund said. "We want them to come after us. Then we can deal with them."

"I wish the Raumsdalian armies down south would give us a little help," Hamnet Thyssen said. "They haven't yet, not so far as anybody can tell."

"Too right they haven't," Ulric agreed. "The generals are probably afraid of the Rulers, and we know too bloody well that Sigvat's afraid of them."

"We have to do it on our own, then." Trasamund spoke with a certain lonely pride. Every Bizogot jarl saw his clan as being alone against its neighbors. Trasamund was bound to see this force as alone against the world. He wasn't so far wrong, either.

"What if we can't do it on our own?" Ulric Skakki went on trying to get under his skin.

This time, it didn't work. Trasamund eyed the adventurer with something close to infinite scorn. "Then we die," he said. "Bravely, I hope." Not even Ulric found a good comeback for that. Count Hamnet didn't even try. He didn't want to die bravely. He wanted the Rulers to die bravely.

And, if such a thing were possible, he wouldn't have minded seeing Sigvat II die bravely, too.

RAUMSDALIANS AND BIZOGOTS turned and moved south again. Hamnet pushed them to move fast. He had his reasons, though he didn't speak of all of them. If the warriors moved fast enough, maybe they would leave the followers behind. He could hope he would leave Eyvind Torfinn and Gudrid behind, anyhow.

But, no matter what he hoped, it didn't happen. Gudrid had kept up as they traveled through the Gap and beyond the Glacier. And she kept up now. Every once in a while, she even grinned at him. She knew he didn't want her around. His not wanting her around had to give her one more reason to stay.

The Rulers took a while, but they proved able to learn from experience. They stopped sending big armies against the band Marcovefa backboned. Instead, they began to put raiders all around them, the way dire wolves would if they were harrying a herd of musk oxen. Now one outriding Bizogot, now two or three Raumsdalians, would go missing. Sometimes they would take enemies with them, sometimes not. But the band began to shrink.

Hamnet didn't want to push Marcovefa about it. It seemed too small a matter to fuss about, too small a matter to draw the notice of a large talent. After the fourth time a small party of outriders got picked off, he changed his mind. The force needed scouts. If he couldn't send them out without sending them out to get killed, he had a problem, and so did his little army.

"I see what I can do," Marcovefa said when he told her what was wrong. "Maybe I ride with some scouts, see if I can lure the Rulers into coming after us. They get a surprise then, yes?"

That made Hamnet wish he'd kept his mouth shut. "We can't afford to lose you. You know that," he said.

"Foolishness," Marcovefa sniffed. "Any shaman who knows anything should be able to beat these foolish Rulers." Then she sighed. "But your shamans and wizards don't know much, do they?"

"We used to think so," Hamnet said. "Now . . . You and the Rulers have taught us some lessons we'd rather not have had."

"You were like this." Marcovefa closed one eye and squinted through the other one. "You were all like this, so you didn't know it. The Rulers are like this." She opened the one eye a little wider. "You need to be like this." She opened both eyes very wide. Then she winked at Hamnet.

"You're bound to be right," he said, ignoring the wink. "But even if you are, you can't always stay away from arrows or slingstones. And we can't do without you, even if you think we should be able to."

"You have a trouble, a problem. You bring it to me. Now you don't want me to fix it," Marcovefa said. "Where is the sense in that?"

"Losing scouts is a problem," Hamnet Thyssen agreed. "Losing you is a catastrophe." Then he had to explain what a catastrophe was: "Worse than a problem. Much worse."

"But you won't lose me," Marcovefa said. "Don't think so, anyway."

"You don't think so," Hamnet echoed discontentedly. "Don't you see? That isn't good enough. Without you, we're nothing."

"You are more than you think you are," Marcovefa said. "You don't know how much you are. You have no idea."

"Do you mean me, or do you mean all of us?" Hamnet's wave encompassed the ragtag army he'd helped build.

"Yes," Marcovefa answered, making herself as annoying as if she were Ulric Skakki.

Count Hamnet fumed, but only to himself. "Which?" he asked.

"I mean you, and I mean everyone," Marcovefa said. "It is not a question with only one answer. If you were not stronger than you think, the Rulers would have won a long time ago. Don't you see that?"

"Well . . . maybe." Hamnet Thyssen wasn't sure he wanted to see it. He'd got used to looking down on himself. Why not, when everyone else did. That was how his thoughts ran, anyway. Losing first Gudrid and then Liv did nothing to make him feel better about himself, either.

"No maybe," Marcovefa said. "It is a truth. An important truth, too."

"Maybe," Hamnet said again—he didn't want anyone making him happy against his will. "All I know is, whenever we went up against the Rulers in any kind of important fight before we climbed to the top of the Glacier and found you, we lost. The only reason we climbed it was because it gave us one chance in a thousand to get away from the Rulers. If we stayed down on the Bizogot steppe, the mammoth-riders would have killed us all."

Smiling, Marcovefa shook her head. "Not so simple."

"No?" Sure enough, Count Hamnet didn't want to believe anything. "Then what were we doing up there?"

"I think the Golden Shrine sent you." Marcovefa sounded as matter-of-fact as if she'd said something like *I think the Three Tusk clan sent you.*

No matter how matter-of-fact she sounded, she made Hamnet Thyssen gape. "How do you know something like that? How can you? Did God tell you?" He didn't believe God went around doing such things. He was sure God didn't do them with him. He wished God did.

"God didn't tell me anything. I don't know this is true. But I think so. We all need the Golden Shrine now. Maybe never in all the time since it disappeared do we need it more," Marcovefa said.

How long had the Golden Shrine been lost? Hamnet didn't know if he'd ever heard a number of years. Eyvind

Torfinn would know, if anyone did. What he didn't know about the Golden Shrine, nobody knew. Hamnet Thyssen didn't feel like asking him. Dealing with Earl Eyvind was too likely to mean dealing with Gudrid. As long as Hamnet didn't have to do that, he didn't want to.

But he couldn't help wondering how many people down through the ages had been sure their time was the worst one possible. They would have been sure they had to have the Golden Shrine's help, too. No matter how much they needed it, they wouldn't have got it. Some would have gone down to ruin without it. Others, he supposed, would have got through on their own.

Clumsily, he tried to explain that to Marcovefa. It seemed very clear inside his own head—much less so when he put it into stumbling words. She heard him out, then said, "Things are worse now." As before, she sounded very matter-of-fact, very sure.

"How can you know they are?" Hamnet demanded.

"I know what I know. And time is not all strung together in little pieces like beads on a string. Time *is*. All of it. At once," Marcovefa said.

Hamnet muttered to himself. That sounded like nonsense to him . . . till he remembered how she'd led the little band of Bizogots and Raumsdalians to the edge of the Glacier, to the very spot where an avalanche would make the descent less steep, less difficult. But the avalanche hadn't happened yet when they got there. She'd seen it through time, but she hadn't quite seen it *in* time. Then the time came round, and they were able to climb down.

"Why don't you know where the Golden Shrine is, then?" Hamnet asked.

The question didn't interest Marcovefa. "It is where it is. It is where it needs to be. When it is appointed to show itself, show itself it will."

Appointed to show itself. Count Hamnet wondered what that meant, and whether it meant anything. Marcovefa must have thought so. He didn't ask her to explain—he didn't think what she said would mean anything to him. He couldn't see, couldn't conceive of, all time as a single thing. He wondered if his inability was a curse . . . or a blessing.

XIV

This time, it was the Breath of God. The wind howled down from the north, howled down off the Glacier. The ice might have retreated, but it was a long way from gone. The wind might have traveled a long way, too, but it was as cold as if it had blown but a few miles.

Hamnet Thyssen had cold-weather gear. So did every other Raumsdalian in his ragtag army. Down in the far south, beyond the Empire's reach, Ulric Skakki insisted, there were countries the Breath of God never touched. Hamnet had traveled far enough south to find that likely, even if he couldn't testify to it from personal experience. But men in these parts knew they had to stay warm through the winter or die.

So Hamnet donned furs with resignation. Most of the other Raumsdalians felt the same way. The Bizogots, by contrast, gloried in the cold weather. "Snow!" Trasamund exclaimed. "About time! Everything up in the Three Tusk country would be covered in white by now."

"God's dandruff," Ulric said. He could take as much cold as anyone—slipping through the Gap to the lands beyond the Glacier in the middle of winter proved that. But he didn't enjoy it the way the Bizogots did.

"Why, you blasphemous vole!" Trasamund blurted. A Raumsdalian would have called Ulric a toad or a snake, but creatures like that couldn't survive up on the frozen steppe. The jarl did the best he could with what he knew.

"Your servant, Your Ferocity." Ulric gave back a mocking bow.

Trasamund had put on mittens, which made it hard for him to wag a finger under the adventurer's nose. Again, he did his best. "You should not speak so," he said severely. "If you do, maybe God will not choose to show us where the Golden Shrine lies. Don't you think we should be pure of mind, pure of heart, pure of speech, to deserve to learn where the Shrine is?"

To Count Hamnet's amazement, Ulric shook his head. Hamnet hadn't thought of Trasamund's argument, and it seemed to him to carry weight. But Ulric said, "If God is waiting for people who are pure of mind and heart and speech, the Golden Shrine will stay hidden to the end of time. A good thing, too, because people who are that pure are hardly people at all."

"You turn everything upside down and inside out!" Trasamund complained.

Ulric gave him another bow. "Your servant," he repeated.

Trasamund swung at him. Hamnet could have told the Bizogot that was a mistake, even if he had been baited. But Hamnet never got the chance. Ulric Skakki turned Trasamund upside down and almost inside out: he grabbed the jarl's arm, then dipped, wheeled, and threw. Trasamund's startled shout cut off abruptly when he hit the ground. Not enough snow had stuck yet to soften his landing.

Count Hamnet helped him up. "How the demon did he do that?" Trasamund mumbled, shaking his head to try to clear it.

"He's done the same thing to me," Hamnet said, reasoning that misery loved company. And it was true. "He knows some wrestling tricks I've never seen before."

"I know a trick, too," Trasamund growled. "How about Bizogot stand-down?" He'd won that brutal game against the Rulers, as Hamnet had told Tahpenes while she was a prisoner.

"No, thanks," Ulric said. "If you want me to admit your head is harder than mine, I'll do it. You don't have to prove it on me."

"You—" But Trasamund couldn't call him a coward, not after all they'd been through together. Since the word stuck in his throat, the jarl tried a different tack: "Will you show me that flip?"

"One of these days, maybe. Not right now," Ulric answered. "Don't you think we ought to ride?"

Most of the Bizogots and Raumsdalians were already mounted. Quite a few of them had watched Trasamund's sudden, unexpected overthrow. No one had seen Hamnet fly through the air, though the thud he made on landing brought palace servants running to see what had collapsed. Neither of them had got badly hurt, but Trasamund's dignity and pride took a worse beating.

The Bizogot did some more muttering. "Another time, then," he said aloud. "In the meanwhile, I will take out on the Rulers what I think about you."

"It's all right by me," Ulric said cheerfully. "If I were the Rulers' chief, I'd start running right now." Trasamund muttered yet again.

"Don't push him too hard," Hamnet said.

"Why not? What other fun do I have these days?" Ulric

eyed him with a mild and speculative air. "Or should I start in on you instead?"

"If you want to," Hamnet answered stolidly. "I can take it better."

"But that means you don't give so much sport."

"Take what you can get," Count Hamnet advised. "We need Trasamund—without him, the Bizogots fall apart like a snowball slamming into a rock. Nobody cares whether I'm happy or not. Nobody even cares whether I'm here."

"Well, I would have said the same thing," Ulric told him—if Hamnet left himself open for a thrust, the adventurer would deliver. So Hamnet thought, anyhow, till Ulric went on, "But Marcovefa thinks you're wrong, remember? I'll argue with you any day. I think twice before I decide she's made a mistake."

Hamnet Thyssen did remember what Marcovefa had said about him. Remembering it didn't mean he believed it. It made him profoundly uneasy—he didn't want to carry so much weight in the scales of the world. What he mostly wanted was to go back to his castle down in the far southeast and be left alone. He knew he was no more likely to get that than any of his other wishes.

"Marcovefa doesn't know everything there is to know," he said after a pause he hoped wasn't too obvious—if it was, it would make a liar out of him all by itself.

Ulric Skakki's knowing smirk said it did. "She may not know everything, but she knows a demon of a lot more about this business than you do. Go on—tell me she doesn't. Make me believe it." He folded his arms and waited.

However much Count Hamnet wished he could, he didn't even try. He couldn't make Ulric believe it . . . and he couldn't make himself believe it, either. Whether he liked it or not, whether he wanted to or not, he did carry weight. He wondered if he would have any say in how it got used.

You won't if the Rulers kill you, he thought. That was as true for him as it was for Marcovefa. Her safety mattered to him. His own didn't seem to.

Try as he would, he couldn't get very excited about it. With a slow shrug, he said, "We needed to ride a while ago. We're still gabbing instead."

"Yes, Your Grace," Ulric said—mockery in the guise of respect, one of his favorite barbs. Hamnet didn't rise to it. Ulric sighed. "Sure as the demons, Trasamund gives better sport."

"Pity." Hamnet methodically checked his horse's cinches and girths. When he was satisfied, he swung up into the saddle. Ulric was only a moment behind him. The Raumsdalians and Bizogots rode in a mass compact enough to let them keep an eye on their outriders. The Rulers wouldn't have an easy time picking off a few men, anyhow.

Hamnet's eyes went this way and that, this way and that. They kept coming back to Marcovefa. She might think he was important in the fight against the Rulers. He knew she was.

FAGERSTA WAS A town of no particular importance. Hamnet Thyssen had a hard time believing even the people who lived there would have said anything else. It wasn't very big or very small. It wasn't very rich. It sat by a stream deep and wide enough for small boats, but not for ships. Because it was right in the middle of the Empire and no foreign foes had come anywhere near it for at least two hundred years, people had torn down the wall that once surrounded it and used the timber and stone for buildings.

The Rulers had gone through Fagersta some time earlier in the year. They hadn't razed it; why bother? They'd plundered some, they'd stolen livestock from the surrounding farms, they'd killed and raped enough to keep themselves both safe and amused, and then they'd gone on their way.

As soon as the locals saw the mix of Raumsdalians and Bizogots approaching from the north, they sent out a man with a flag of truce. That was about the only thing they could have done. The Breath of God swirled snow all around, so Fagersta didn't discover it had new visitors—and the visitors didn't discover there was such a place as Fagersta—till they were almost on top of it.

"Oh!" the herald exclaimed in glad surprise when he got a better look at the newcomers. "You aren't . . . those people." He didn't say what he really thought of the Rulers, perhaps in case he proved wrong about who these strangers were.

"No, we aren't," Hamnet agreed gravely.

"In fact, we want to kill those people," Trasamund added.

His accent and his long, golden beard announced that, while he wasn't a Ruler, he wasn't a Raumsdalian, either. The local herald eyed him as warily as a shepherd might eye a sabertooth. That was sensible of the man, as Trasamund was at least as deadly as one of the big cats. The local soon noticed other big blond warriors among those who might be of his own kind.

"You aren't those people," he said again. This time, he added, "But who the demon *are* you?" Under the circumstances, it was a more than reasonable question.

"I am Trasamund, jarl of the Three Tusk clan." Trasamund struck a pose on his horse. He was wasting his time; the Raumsdalian knew more of Bizogot clans and their jarls than he did about riding a war mammoth. After a moment, Trasamund saw as much. He simplified things: "I'm with you Raumsdalians. The Rulers are my enemies."

"Oh." The man from Fagersta seemed to understand that, anyhow. Whether he believed it was liable to be another question. "But you're a foreigner," he said, and waited, as if hoping Trasamund would deny it. When Trasamund didn't, the local sighed. "Didn't know much about foreigners till a couple of weeks ago. Don't much fancy what we found out, neither."

"There are different kinds of foreigners," Hamnet Thyssen said. The local only grunted. He wasn't disagreeing, but he also wasn't enthusiastic about the prospect. Hamnet asked, "What did the Rulers do to this place? And who *are* you, anyway?"

"Well, my name's Hrafn Maering," said the man from Fagersta. He let out a bleak chuckle. "What did they do to this place? Anything they pleased, pretty much. You can see Fagersta's got some chunks bit out of it." His wave took in the burned and overthrown buildings all over town. Glumly, he went on, "Me, I was lucky, if you want to call it luck. They killed one of my second cousins, and they forced my wife's sister—but only two or three of 'em, and they weren't especially trying to hurt her, just to have a good time. She'll be all right, we expect, soon as she gets over the worst of the horrors, and she isn't with child."

Count Hamnet nodded soberly. Hrafn was right: as these things went, his family *was* lucky. One death, one not too brutal rape—you could pick up the pieces and go on after something like that. There still was a family to pick up the pieces and go on. Some lines in Fagersta would be destroyed altogether. Others would have a handful of people trying to recover after much worse disasters.

"When did the Rulers ride out of here?" Ulric Skakki asked. "Which way did they go?"

Hrafn Maering eyed him doubtfully, too; his sharp features weren't those of a typical Raumsdalian. But he spoke the imperial language without accent, and he also spoke with the air of a man entitled to get answers from other people. "It was only maybe ten days ago," Hrafn said. "They went that way." He pointed somewhere between south and southeast.

"Have any idea how many of them there were?" Runolf Skallagrim inquired.

"Not for sure," Hrafn said. "They rode these funny deer, you know?" By the way he said it, the deer were harder to count than horses would have been. But then he added, "They had eight, maybe ten, war mastodons with 'em."

Chances were he'd never seen a mammoth in his life till the Rulers rode theirs down into the Empire. Mammoths were creatures of the frozen steppe, beyond the evergreen woods to the north. Mastodons, by contrast, roamed the forests of the Empire and the lands on its borders; they were common in the mixed woods near Hamnet's castle. No wonder, then, that Hrafn called the Rulers' great mounts by the wrong name.

Somebody none too familiar with sabertooths might easily call them lions by mistake. He'd be wrong, but he wouldn't be *very* wrong. You could end up dead as easily, and in most of the same ways, from a sabertooth as from a lion. And the Rulers would have been just as much trouble riding mastodons as they were on mammothback.

Hamnet wondered what the invaders thought of mastodons. They would surely have found some by now. He also wondered whether the Rulers could turn mastodons into riding animals. They would have a new supply of mounts if they did.

When he asked the first question out loud, Ulric said, "They probably think mastodons are delicious."

And Hamnet couldn't even tell him he was wrong, because a mastodon, like a mammoth, was a lot of meat ambling around in one convenient package. Taming mastodons would take a long time. Killing and cooking them, on the other hand . . .

"Well, let's go after the buggers," Trasamund said.

Hrafn Maering surely spoke for all the survivors in Fagersta: "What about giving us a hand?"

"You're here. You're alive. You can put the town back together yourselves," Hamnet said. "The best thing we can do for you is kill the Rulers—if we can."

"Sigvat would do better by us," Hrafn said.

He looked very surprised when all the Raumsdalians and Bizogots within earshot started laughing fit to burst. He got mad when none of them would explain why.

"I'm going to report this to the mayor," Hrafn said. "He'll tell the chief of the diocese, and *he'll* tell the provincial governor. Then the governor will report you to the Emperor, and *then* you'll be in trouble."

Hamnet and his companions laughed harder than ever. Hrafn Maering looked bewildered. He'd come out with the most fearsome threat he knew how to make, and these people . . . took it for a joke? Count Hamnet didn't know whether to envy the local or feel sorry for him. He still lived in his secure little world, or thought he did.

The great virtue of the Raumsdalian Empire was that it had let generations of people just like Hrafn live out their lives without needing to worry about barbarians coming down over the border. Its drawback was that, when order broke down, the locals had no idea what to do.

"Good luck to you," Hamnet told him, and meant every word of it.

"God keep you," Ulric Skakki added, also in tones of great sincerity.

"You poor, sorry bastard." Even Trasamund sounded sympathetic, no matter how rough his words were.

They left Hrafn staring after them as they rode past Fagersta. "He *is* a sorry bugger," Ulric said. "He doesn't know whether to crap or go blind."

"He's already blind," Hamnet Thyssen said. "The question is whether he's better off that way. What he has to see these days isn't pretty, and he only got a glimpse of it when the Rulers went through there."

"He would have seen more if they stayed longer," Trasamund said.

"That's Hamnet's point," Ulric told him. "Yours, on the other hand, is under your hat." Trasamund needed a moment to understand what he meant. When the jarl did, he and Ulric had a fine time sniping at each other as they rode south in pursuit of the Rulers.

AFTER A WHILE, Ulric came up with something new to talk about. "All right," he said. "We've driven the Rulers away. Raumsdalia is free again."

"What about the Bizogots?" Trasamund demanded.

"Oh, the Rulers slaughtered them all. They aren't there any more," Ulric said. Trasamund bellowed irately. The adventurer held up a hand. "Fine. Fine. The Bizogots are free again, too."

"That's more like it," Trasamund said.

"But I'm still talking about Raumsdalia," Ulric Skakki

said. He turned to Hamnet. "The Rulers are gone. The Empire is free."

"Yes, you already said that," Hamnet said. "What am I supposed to do? Shout huzzah?"

"Suppose you already did," Ulric said. "What happens next? How do we make something that's broken stand on its own two feet again?"

"Sigvat won't think there's any trouble," Hamnet answered. "He'll just start giving orders and expect everybody else to follow them. And anybody who doesn't want to will end up in a dungeon."

"If Sigvat tries that now, *he'll* end up in a dungeon—if he's lucky," Ulric said. "More likely, he'll end up dead." He nodded toward Runolf Skallagrim. "Or am I wrong?"

"Depends on which orders he gives," Runolf said uncomfortably. He was as loyal as they came—if not to Sigvat, then to the idea of the Raumsdalian Empire. "If he starts throwing his weight around, he's in a lot of trouble. You aren't wrong about that, Skakki. I can hope he's too smart to try it."

Ulric and Count Hamnet both guffawed. So did Trasamund. "Tell us what's so funny," Eyvind Torfinn said, walking up. "We could all enjoy a joke like that."

Laughing still, Ulric did tell him. "Have you ever heard anything more ridiculous in all your born days?" he finished.

"One could do worse than His Majesty has done," Earl Eyvind said.

"Sure. He could have killed me outright instead of leaving me to rot in that hole under the palace," Count Hamnet said. Eyvind Torfinn turned red. Hamnet went on, "I was hoping the Rulers would chuck him into the same cell I had, but no such luck." He spread his hands. "Too bad, eh?"

"I can certainly understand how you have cause to feel resentment toward him, Your Grace," Eyvind said stiffly.

"*Resentment* isn't the word, Your Splendor," Hamnet Thyssen answered. "What I want to do is, I want to hunt him with hounds. Since I didn't get the chance to do that, I wouldn't have minded if the Rulers hunted him with mammoths. Which they did. The only trouble is, they haven't caught him yet."

More stiffly still, Eyvind said, "I fail to see why you continue to prosecute this war against the invaders, then."

"For Raumsdalia. Not for Sigvat. For Raumsdalia," Hamnet said. "There's a difference, whether you can see it or not."

"And what would Raumsdalia be without Sigvat?" Eyvind asked coldly.

"Better off, by God!" Count Hamnet said. "Better off!" Ulric Skakki whooped and clapped his hands.

Earl Eyvind looked from one of them to the other as if he'd just discovered them in his apple. "Let me rephrase that. What would the Empire of Raumsdalia be without its Emperor?"

"Oh, the Empire needs an Emperor, no doubt about it," Hamnet said. "But it needs Sigvat the way a man with a bloody flux needs a purge." He set Ulric laughing and clapping again.

Eyvind Torfinn looked pained. "He is doing the best job he can."

"That's what I'm afraid of," Hamnet said. Not only Ulric but Trasamund laughed then. Even Runolf Skallagrim smiled.

"If the times ever settle down, His Majesty will not thank you for the way you speak of him," Eyvind said.

"When he *did* thank me, I wound up in his God-cursed

dungeons," Hamnet exclaimed. "I don't want his thanks. If he leaves me alone, I'll thank him."

"Don't hold your breath, Your Grace," Ulric said. He rounded on Earl Eyvind. "And if the times ever do settle down, Your Splendor, you'll know whom to thank, won't you? Not Sigvat! He got Raumsdalia into this mess because he didn't want to listen to Count Hamnet or to me or to Trasamund or to anybody else who actually had some notion of what was going on. And I hope you recall who rescued you from the Rulers. That wasn't the Emperor, either. That was Hamnet here."

"I am not ungrateful." Eyvind's words couldn't have had sharper edges if he'd chipped them out of ice. "Nevertheless, he is not the rightful sovereign of this realm. Sigvat is."

"And if that's not a judgment on Raumsdalia, bugger me with a mammoth tusk if I know what would be," Trasamund said.

Earl Eyvind threw up his hands. "This discussion is pointless," he said, and walked away.

"He means we don't think he's right," Trasamund said. "He's not used to anybody who doesn't."

"I'll tell you something," Ulric said. "Hamnet here would bloody well make a better Emperor than Sigvat. Even a blind man can see that."

"I should hope so!" Trasamund said. "A blind man? Even a blind musk ox could see that!"

Hamnet started to laugh. Then he saw Runolf nodding, too, and realized it was no laughing matter. If Runolf could nod at the idea of replacing Sigvat, plenty of other people would do the same thing. He had to nip it in the bud if he was going to nip it at all. "I don't want to be Emperor," he said.

"But Raumsdalia needs you." Yes, that was Runolf Skallagrim.

"Raumsdalia needs somebody who isn't Sigvat. Raumsdalia needs almost anybody who isn't Sigvat. But Raumsdalia doesn't need me," Hamnet said. "I won't sit on that throne, no matter what."

"If we proclaim you, everyone will accept you," Ulric said. "Sigvat's made his name stink like a dead ground sloth."

"I will not sit on that throne," Hamnet repeated.

"You may not have a choice," Baron Runolf said. "We wouldn't do it for your sake. We'd do it for Raumsdalia."

"No." Hamnet Thyssen drew his sword. The blade had some nicks and some rust; he needed to hone it. But the point was still sharp, which was all that mattered now. "If you try to name me Emperor, I'll fall on this thing. You know me. Every one of you knows me. Am I lying? If you want to get rid of me, keep on in the direction you're already riding."

Ulric and Runolf and Trasamund eyed him. They eyed the sword. They eyed one another. Runolf Skallagrim let out a long sigh. "I think he means it."

"I know bloody well he means it." Ulric Skakki sounded disgusted. He scowled at Count Hamnet. "You're stubborn when it does you good, and you're stubborn even when it doesn't. You might as well be a mountain sheep, the way you always want to butt heads."

"Your servant, sir." Hamnet bowed, as Ulric often did. He didn't let go of the sword.

"If you were my servant, maybe you'd listen to me once in a while." Ulric flicked a finger toward the blade. "Put that silly thing away. We won't make you ventilate your liver, no matter how tempting it is."

"If he won't do it, one of you other Raumsdalians ought

to," Trasamund said. "How about you, Skakki? You're sneaky enough and to spare."

"You are joking, my dear fellow—aren't you?" Ulric said in convincing amazement. "A cabbage has as much noble blood as I do: which is to say, not a drop."

"So what? If you don't tell people, who'll know?" Trasamund said.

"Most of the time, you would be right," Ulric said. "But you'd be wrong often enough to fill Raumsdalia full of civil wars. All the real nobles would look down their noses at me."

"I wouldn't, by God," Hamnet said. "If you can do the job, you're welcome to it, far as I'm concerned. You couldn't be worse than Sigvat."

"There. You see?" Trasamund said triumphantly. "Hurrah for Ulric I!"

"Oh, shut up, you blond fool!" Ulric said. "I see Runolf here looking like grim death, is what I see. And Runolf is more your usual kind of noble than Hamnet is."

"I would want an Emperor of noble blood," Runolf Skallagrim said slowly. "What's the point to noble blood, if not to show who deserves to rule?"

"Well, then, why don't you take the crown?" Ulric said. "You're a baron, so you're fit enough. And you're not Sigvat, which gives you a leg up all by itself. You wouldn't need to worry that you're stealing the throne from me, because I don't want it any more than Thyssen does."

"Me? Emperor of Raumsdalia. *Me?*" Runolf sounded flabbergasted. Then he started to laugh. "That's the funniest thing I've heard in I don't know when. Ever, I bet!" He laughed some more.

"Maybe Eyvind Torfinn would take it on," Trasamund said.

Hamnet started to say something about that, but

swallowed it. He had nothing in particular against the idea of Emperor Eyvind. The idea of Empress Gudrid? If she were Empress, how long would he last? As long as he could outrun her henchmen, he guessed, and not a heartbeat longer.

But his comrades already knew as much. What point to beating them over the head with it? If Gudrid's word became law, Ulric was another man with a fine future behind him.

"Well . . ." Trasamund said, and then, "Maybe not."

"I do believe that's one of the smarter things you've ever come out with," Ulric said. "I wouldn't have thought you had it in you."

Trasamund said something pungent. Ulric grinned and nodded, which spoiled it for the jarl—as Ulric no doubt intended.

"Hrmph," Trasamund said. "All I want to tell you is, this Empire can't be anything much if none of you bastards wants to take charge of it."

Nobody argued with him there, either. That also seemed to disconcert him.

Snow. Sleet. Cold rain. Snow again, more and more of it. Yes, the Breath of God was blowing. Hamnet Thyssen thought longingly of Raumsdalia's far southwest, where thing like this didn't happen. Of course, the far southwest had Manche raiders and poisonous serpents and scorpions, to say nothing of earthquakes that could flatten towns in the blink of an eye.

Count Hamnet thought of serpents again when Gudrid came up to him and said, "I need to talk with you."

"So what?" He turned away. "I don't need to talk with you."

"Oh, yes, you do." She sounded very sure of herself. But then, when didn't she?

He didn't care. "I don't need to listen to you, either," he said, and walked away.

She came after him. She set a hand on his arm to slow him down. Angrily, he shook her off; the last thing he wanted to feel was her touch. "You *are* going to hear me," she said, expecting as usual to get her way.

"I should have left you for the Rulers," he said harshly. "You could try telling them what to do, and see how they like it."

"Don't be more stupid than you can help," Gudrid said with a shudder.

"I've already done that," Hamnet answered. "You cured me of it—I hope."

"Will you please listen to me?"

When was the last time she'd said *please* to him? He couldn't remember. It had been years; he was sure of that. He shook his head anyhow. "If you've got anything that needs saying, you can tell it to Ulric or Trasamund. And you can leave me the demon alone."

"Don't you care about Raumsdalia?"

"Yes, and I know you don't. All you care about is you— and sticking pins in me so you can watch me jerk and twist and bleed. Well, find somebody else, because I don't want to play any more."

"You fool! You could be Emperor!"

He stared at her. Then he laughed in her face, which made her stare at him. "Are you out of your mind? I don't want the bloody job. I wouldn't take it on a golden platter. I've been saying so to everyone who wanted to listen. I suppose that lets you out, but I mean every word of it."

"You could be *Emperor*," Gudrid repeated, as if he

hadn't spoken. "How can anybody not want to be Emperor?"

"Believe me, it's easy," Hamnet answered. "I don't want to, I won't, and nobody can make me. Not you, not Trasamund, not Ulric—nobody."

"Not Marcovefa, either?" Gudrid's voice was sly.

But Hamnet shook his head. "Not Marcovefa, either. She has the sense to believe me when I say something like that—unlike some people I could name."

She ignored his sarcasm. He might have known she would. She always did. "Think what you could do if you were Emperor," she said. "Everyone would have to do what you told them to do, or else they'd pay for it."

The look he gave her made the Breath of God seem warm by comparison. "I could send you to the dungeon. I could take your head and nail it to the north gate to warn other people not to be like you."

"Don't be silly. You wouldn't do that." She might have been talking to a foolish little boy. Before he could tell her that he would, she went on, "If you really wanted me dead, you would have killed me yourself a long time ago. You had your chances. Nobody would have said anything much, not then."

Hamnet Thyssen bit down on that like a man unexpectedly biting down on a cherrystone. Why *hadn't* he killed her when he found out she was unfaithful, not just once but again and again? "I loved you, fool that I was," he growled.

Now Gudrid laughed at him. "You just wanted somebody around who could make you feel bad. You made a mess of things with Liv the same way, and you'll do the same thing with Marcovefa. You can't be happy unless you're unhappy."

"What sort of nonsense is that?" Hamnet said. But, like

what she'd come out with a moment earlier, it sounded much less nonsensical than he wished it did.

She laughed again, knowingly this time. "You can tell it isn't nonsense. If you weren't such a fool, you would have figured it out for yourself long since."

Did she want him to hit her? Would she get perverse pleasure of her own from seeing what she could goad him into? He breathed out hard through his nose. "Say whatever you please. You will anyhow. But I can prove you're wrong."

"How?" Her chin lifted defiantly.

He took a certain sour pleasure in noting how the flesh under her jawbone had started to sag. She wasn't—quite—immune to time. "Except for being married to you again, nothing would make me unhappier than being Emperor," he said. "And I still don't want to do it. So much for your fancy talk."

"Think of all the women you could have, just with the wave of a hand," Gudrid said.

"Screwing is one thing. Caring is another—not that you know anything about that," Hamnet said.

"Not that you know anything about either one," Gudrid retorted.

Hamnet didn't hit her then, either, though his hands balled into fists. He turned and walked away once more. When she started to come after him again, he walked faster. Pretty soon, he left her behind. He stood out in the middle of a trampled field, wondering how much good that did him.

INSIDE THE EMPIRE, warfare slowed down during the winter. Food and fodder were hard to come by. That didn't always stop the Bizogots, who could get by with less than Raumsdalians could. And it didn't stop the Rulers, either.

The country they sprang from was no richer than the Bizogot steppe.

They kept striking at Count Hamnet's band, sometimes with warriors, sometimes with wizards, sometimes with both. They didn't try to wipe out all the Bizogots and Raumsdalians in arms against them—they'd learned the hard way that that didn't work, not when Marcovefa was involved. But their nuisance raids went on.

He posted a couple of Bizogots out in a temptingly open position, and put himself and Marcovefa and half a troop of Raumsdalian archers and lancers in a forest not far away. Marcovefa cast a light masking spell to try to make sure the Rulers wouldn't notice the ambush.

"What if their shaman spots the spell?" Hamnet asked her.

"I don't think he can. But if he does, those Bizogots out there"—she pointed toward the exposed men—"are lucky, because the Rulers go and bother us somewhere else."

He didn't want the invaders to do that, but held his peace. If Marcovefa didn't think an enemy sorcerer could detect her magic, she was likely right. If she turned out to be wrong, Hamnet would try something else, that was all.

He'd guessed right or baited his trap the right way. Inside of a couple of hours, a dozen or so Rulers came out of the bare-branched woods to the south. The Bizogots out in the open played dumb a little longer than they would have if they were nothing but ordinary pickets, but only a little. They weren't out there to throw their lives away, but to get the Rulers to do that instead.

When they couldn't ignore the men bearing down on them any more, they turned their horses and trotted off in Hamnet's direction. One of the Rulers pointed at them. The horses slowed, then stopped.

"Baby magic," Marcovefa said scornfully. "A pika could do this."

"You can break the spell, then?" Hamnet asked.

"Oh, yes. But not yet. No point yet," Marcovefa said. "Let them get closer."

Up came the Rulers on their riding deer. They soon could have shot the Bizogots out of the saddle, but they didn't. Chances were they wanted to have fun with them. Because of their own horror of being captured, they often amused themselves by tormenting prisoners.

The Bizogots should have dismounted and run when their horses faltered. They just sat there instead. The spell must have seized them, too. It didn't seem like baby magic to Hamnet Thyssen, but Marcovefa had different standards.

Her face wore a foxy look of intense concentration. Hamnet peered out toward the Rulers. They were in easy archery range, close enough for him to see their grins. One of them nodded toward the two Bizogots. They all laughed. The laughs sounded nasty to Hamnet. Maybe that was his imagination. Maybe not, too.

They seemed to have no idea his troop was anywhere nearby. Marcovefa's masking spell was working, anyhow.

When things happened, they happened all at once. One instant, the Rulers' wizard was laughing and joking with his friends. The next, his riding deer's antlers caught fire. Hamnet heard his startled squawk and the animal's screech of pain.

At the same time, the magic holding the Bizogots and their horses dissolved. They galloped for the cover of the woods.

"Loose!" Hamnet called. His men's bowstrings thrummed. Several ordinary Rulers tumbled off their riding deer.

The ones who didn't fall turned and raced south as fast as their mounts would go. "Charge!" Hamnet bellowed at the top of his lungs.

Horses were faster than riding deer—not much, but enough. None of the Rulers made it into the trees from which they'd emerged. Some went down fighting. Others, seeing themselves about to be captured, cut their own throats or plunged daggers into their chests.

Their wizard had somehow suppressed the flames that sprang from his riding deer's antlers. Like a short-faced bear at bay, he turned to face Marcovefa and the Raumsdalians with her. He yammered something in his unintelligible language.

Marcovefa only laughed. That seemed to infuriate him more than anything else she might have done. Instead of aiming a spell at her, he drew his sword and charged. The riding deer obeyed him as if it were unhurt. That impressed Hamnet more than he wanted to admit.

It did the wizard no good at all. Bows twanged. His magic turned a few arrows, but it couldn't turn them all—not when Marcovefa worked against him, it couldn't. He and the riding deer went down together. Their blood steamed in the snow.

"Too bad, in a way," Hamnet said. "We might have got some interesting answers if we'd been able to question him."

"He's dead. That is interesting enough," Marcovefa said. "They are all dead. Let the Rulers worry about them. Let the Rulers try to guess what happened to them. Yes, let the Rulers worry."

Count Hamnet might have liked it better had one enemy warrior got away to tell his friends exactly what had happened. Then, he could hope, they would stop trying to pick off sentries. But leaving them in the dark about their fellows' fate wasn't the worst thing in the world, either.

"Look!" A lancer pointed up into the sky. "The ravens are already circling, waiting for us to leave."

"And the vultures," Hamnet said, and then he spotted a truly enormous bird high in the air. "And a teratorn."

"Cursed scavengers," the trooper said. "Don't want them gnawing my bones when I'm gone."

"What difference does it make then?" Marcovefa asked. "Better that the scavengers eat you than that the enemy does." The lancer stared at her, no doubt thinking she was joking. She smiled back, knowing she wasn't.

XV

Even well south of Nidaros, the Breath of God pressed hard. Hamnet Thyssen had expected nothing else. The Glacier might fall back. One day, it might vanish altogether. But it still ruled the weather through most of Raumsdalia.

Life went on. So did the war against the Rulers. Raumsdalians and Bizogots knew how to handle themselves in blizzards. The invaders from beyond the Gap did, too. Bands of curly-bearded men on riding deer appeared out of the swirling snow. When they met Marcovefa, they soon regretted it. When they didn't, their warriors were a fair match for Hamnet's men and their wizards had more strength than Liv and Audun and the handful of other sorcerers who'd joined them.

Hamnet found his army getting forced north no matter what he did. He—and, more to the point, Marcovefa—could only be in one place at one time. If the Rulers struck in two or three places at once, they were bound to break through somewhere. They were bound to, and they did.

He hated going north. Not only did it mean the Rulers had retaken the initiative, it also made the weather worse. Every mile seemed to mean more snow, thicker clouds, and worse cold. And every mile farther north also seemed to mean worse foraging. He got tired of listening to his belly growl.

"Everything will turn out all right. This is still rich country," Marcovefa said.

"To you, maybe," Count Hamnet said irritably—yes, he was hungry, all right. "You're happy if you can charm mice out from under the snow."

"Why not? Meat is meat," Marcovefa said. She'd done that more than once. She ate mouse stew and toasted mouse with every sign of enjoyment. She'd eaten voles and pikas up on top of the Glacier, and mice and rabbits weren't much different. Raumsdalians and Bizogots caught rabbits, but they drew the line at mice. If they got too much hungrier, though, they might have to undraw it. Marcovefa went on, "Up on the Glacier, not so much snow to hide under. Animals here have it easy. People here have it easy, too."

"Yes, yes." Hamnet had heard that, too, often enough to get tired of it. "But what seems easy for you doesn't always seem easy to us. You don't seem to have figured that out yet."

"As long as everything will be all right, what difference does it make?" Marcovefa said.

"As long as!" Hamnet drummed his fingers on his thigh. "Things don't look all right to me, by God."

"You don't see far enough," said the shaman from atop the Glacier.

"Well, how am I supposed to?" Hamnet Thyssen waved a mittened hand through the blowing snow. "I'm lucky if I can see the nose in front of my face." As a matter of fact,

he couldn't see it right now. A woolen scarf helped—
some—to keep it from freezing.

Marcovefa (who also covered her nose and mouth)
laughed at him. "That is not what I meant. I am talking
about time."

"If I'm going to live happily ever after, God's hidden
it from me mighty well," Hamnet agreed.

She looked at him. All he could see were her eyes, and
eyes by themselves showed surprisingly little expression.
Even so, he guessed he'd disappointed her. Sure enough,
she said, "No one lives happily ever after. Living hurts.
Dying hurts. If you are lucky enough to find someone to
love, you die or the other person dies, and that hurts, too.
That hurts maybe worse than anything."

"Or you stop loving each other," Hamnet said harshly.

"Yes. Or that," Marcovefa agreed. "So why talk nonsense about happily ever after?"

"You always do know how to cheer me up," Hamnet
told her. "I think I'll go fall on my sword now."

If he was looking for sympathy—and he was—he
didn't get much. Marcovefa shook her head. "Not yet," she
said. "You still have too many things to do first. Later, if
you want to, but not yet."

"No, eh?" Nothing made Hamnet more intent on doing
something than being told he couldn't. "Who the demon
would stop me? Who the demon would care?"

I would! That was what he wanted to hear. Marcovefa
only shrugged and said, "Go ahead and try. You see then."

"Demons take me if I don't!" Hamnet was suddenly
sick of carrying the world around on his shoulders. He
tramped away, kicked at the snow till he found some
rocks, and propped his sword up in them, point uppermost. It would hurt for a little while, but not long if he fell
properly. Then the rest of the fools could bollix things up

to their blundering hearts' content. No one would be able to blame him any more. He positioned himself with great care—he didn't want this to last any longer than it had to.

Disgusted with the world, disgusted with himself, he fell forward. Instead of piercing him, the blade went with him, and he measured the length in the snow. One of the rocks that had held up the hilt caught him in the pit of the stomach.

"Oof!" he said—a most undignified noise. He spent the next couple of minutes fighting for breath. When he finally got it back, he climbed to his feet, rubbing the sore spot.

Someone less determined—someone less pigheaded—would have given up there. Hamnet Thyssen had always prided himself on his stubbornness. He brushed snow off himself, then started to laugh. Why was he bothering? Methodically, he set up the sword again. He braced it more firmly this time and threw himself down as hard as he could.

The sword snapped.

A rock—maybe the same one as last time—got him in the pit of the stomach once more. "Oof!" he repeated. This time, it really hurt. For a moment, he thought he'd killed himself even if he hadn't stabbed himself. At last, though, he managed to suck in a shuddering breath, and then another. He wouldn't perish for lack of air.

He wouldn't perish from falling on that sword, either. He picked up the nub with the hilt. He'd had no idea the blade was flawed. Maybe one of the blows he'd exchanged with the Rulers had cracked it. If he'd gone on fighting a little longer, suddenly he would have been most embarrassed.

Or maybe God just didn't intend to let him die right now.

He looked at the broken sword for a long time. Then he

muttered an obscenity and threw the hilt and nub away, as hard as he could. Snow puffed up where the fragment landed.

After another oath, he brushed more snow off himself. He started back toward camp. He was perhaps halfway there when he realized he still had his dagger, and could slash it across his throat or slit his wrist. He didn't suppose it would break in his hand. But the black moment had passed. He went on walking.

"ANYONE HAVE A spare sword?" Hamnet asked.

"I do," Ulric Skakki said. "What happened to yours?"

"Broke." Hamnet mimed snapping a stick with his hands.

"Just like that?" One of the adventurer's eyebrows rose. "What were you doing with it?"

"Trying to kill myself," Hamnet said.

Ulric laughed. "Ask a stupid question, you deserve the answer you get." He rummaged in the leather sack that held his worldly goods, then handed Hamnet a sword in a battered leather sheath. "Here you go. It'll probably suit you better than me, anyhow. A little long and clumsy for my taste, but you're bigger than I am."

"Thanks." Count Hamnet drew it. He tried a few cuts. "Kind of point-heavy," he remarked. "Better for slashing than for thrusting."

"That's what you want if you're fighting from horseback," Ulric said.

"I hope I will be," Hamnet said. Foot soldiers were at a grim disadvantage against mounted men who could strike from above—and who could leave infantry behind in a matter of minutes.

Trasamund had been trimming his nails with a clasp

knife that must have come from inside the Empire. Finishing the job, he looked up and asked, "Why did you want to kill yourself this time?"

The time before, Hamnet had warned that he wouldn't let himself live if anyone tried to make him Emperor. Now . . . Now he only shrugged. The impulse had passed, and seemed to have belonged to someone else. "It seemed like a good idea at the time."

"Kill Rulers instead," the jarl said. "When they're gone, you can do whatever you want to yourself. Till then, you have more important things to worry about."

"Thank you so much." Hamnet Thyssen bowed. "I don't know what I'd do with my life if I didn't have someone to run it for me."

"Not my job." Trasamund shook his head. "You want someone to run your life, you need a woman. Since you have a woman, she has to do it." He seemed as pleased with himself as a geometer with a new proof.

Reminded of Marcovefa, Hamnet was already reminded why and how he'd broken his sword. He didn't like to think about that. He would probably go through it again and again in his nightmares. But which would be the more terrifying dream? The one where the sword snapped, or the one where it didn't?

"What are we going to do to keep the Rulers from pushing us back farther?" Ulric asked. "If Marcovefa could lay eggs, if she hatched out twenty more like her, we'd have a pretty good chance. Or if she could be in four places at once . . ."

"She can't," Hamnet said bleakly. "We're lucky she can be one place at once, by God."

"I know what we need to do." Ulric Skakki's bright, assured tone made Hamnet certain that, whatever he proposed, it wouldn't be anything they could actually manage. And it wasn't: "We need to go back to the Glacier, climb it again, and bring back some more shamans like her."

"Go ahead," Hamnet said. "Hurry back. I'll see you here in three or four days, right?"

"But of course." Ulric grinned at him. They were both spouting nonsense, and they both knew it. The difference was, it amused Ulric and didn't come close to amusing Count Hamnet.

"Wouldn't help, anyhow," Trasamund said. "The other shamans would come from different clans. They'd likelier go after Marcovefa or one another than the Rulers. Why should they care about a bunch of people they've never seen before?"

"If you're going to complain about every little thing . . ." Ulric said. Trasamund snorted. After a moment, Ulric went on, "Well, all right. How about this? Instead of these shamans, we set all the short-faced bears moving against the Rulers. They mostly don't sleep through the winter, the way black bears do."

"That's . . ." Hamnet's voice trailed away. He'd started to say it was ridiculous, but it wasn't. What came out of his mouth was, "That's not a half-bad notion."

"It isn't, by God," Trasamund agreed. "Bears are trouble. If they'd go after the Rulers, that would give those miserable mammoth foreskins all kinds of grief."

"Have mammoths got foreskins?" Ulric sounded intrigued.

"It only matters to another mammoth," Hamnet assured him. "Now we need to see whether Marcovefa laughs at us for coming up with a foolish notion or whether she thinks she can make a magic like that."

"I meant it for a joke, you know," Ulric Skakki said.

"So what?" Count Hamnet answered. "A shipwright makes a mast to hold the sails. That doesn't mean a drowning man won't hang on to it to keep his head above water. Let's go talk to Marcovefa."

"Yes. Let's." Trasamund started away from the fire.

Not long before, Hamnet Thyssen had wished he were dead and done his best to make his wish come true. Now he was going off to find Marcovefa with a new scheme to bedevil the invaders. That was very strange—just how strange, he didn't think about till much later.

MARCOVEFA'S EYES GLINTED when she saw Hamnet. "You see?" she said. "It is not so easy after all."

"Never mind that," he answered, and she laughed out loud. He and Trasamund and Ulric Skakki took turns explaining what they had in mind. Hamnet finished with an eager question: "Can you do that?"

"It is a thought of weight. It may be a thought of merit." Marcovefa's gaze went far away as she weighed possibilities—or, for all Hamnet knew, impossibilities. After a long pause, she said, "It may be, yes. Have we here men of the bear clan? Have we men whose spirit animal is the short-faced bear?"

Raumsdalians didn't define themselves in those terms. Bizogots did. Marcovefa, whose people sprang from Bizogot stock, must have known as much. "I will ask among the folk who come from the free plains," Trasamund said. Then his blunt-featured face clouded. "The plains that once were free, I should say."

If Marcovefa noticed the amendment, she paid no attention to it. "Find one of them," she said. "Bring him to me. I will see what I can do. I promise nothing. But I will try."

Off Trasamund went. He came back half an hour later with a scarred Bizogot he introduced as Grimoald. "He is of the Bear Claws clan," he said. Sure enough, Grimoald wore a necklace of claws.

"Good," Marcovefa said. "These are the claws of the short-faced bear?" She sounded like—and was—someone making sure.

"They are," Grimoald said.

"Those are the only bears in the Bizogot country," Trasamund said. "They have others down here, and we saw still others beyond the Glacier. But if a man is of the Bear Claws clan, they are the claws of the short-faced bear."

"All right. Fine," Marcovefa said. "Shall we move these bears against our foes?"

"If you know how, shaman, I would like to do that," Grimoald said. "If I can help you do it, I will."

"You can," Marcovefa told him. "Are you allowed to take off those claws? May I hold them?"

"You may." Grimoald lifted the necklace off over his head and handed it to her. "I would not do this for any stranger, but for a foe of the Rulers I will do anything I can."

"I am a foe of the Rulers," Marcovefa said. "You may doubt many things, but you should not doubt that."

She gave the bear claws an oddly tender look as she held them in her hand. She might almost have been holding a newborn baby, not these souvenirs of one of the most dangerous beasts the world knew. Of course, a baby would grow up to be a creature that made a souvenir of short-faced bear claws. Hamnet scowled, wishing that hadn't crossed his mind.

The song Marcovefa crooned was also oddly tender. It sounded more like a lullaby than a charm. Off in the distance, though, Hamnet heard growls and snarls that didn't seem at all soothing.

"You're sure this spell is aimed at the Rulers?" Grimoald asked, so Hamnet wasn't the only one that chorus alarmed.

Marcovefa gave the man from the Bear Claws clan a bright-eyed, almost carnivorous smile. "I am almost sure," she said.

"Almost?" Now Grimoald sounded genuinely frightened. "That's not good enough. If they come after us—"

"She's having you on," Count Hamnet told him.

"Are you sure?" The Bizogot sounded anything but convinced. Then he took a long look at Marcovefa's face. Her smile, plainly, was hiding a laugh. Grimoald saw as much. He looked as sheepish as a Bizogot was ever likely to. "Well, I guess you are," he said to Hamnet.

"He is," Marcovefa agreed. She handed back the necklace. Grimoald made haste to put it on again. Marcovefa added, "What these short-faced bears can do to the Rulers, they will do."

"That's good." Grimoald clutched some of the claws. They clicked together, almost like worry beads. Hamnet Thyssen hoped the invaders would soon be the ones doing the worrying.

If they were, it didn't show right away. Skirmishing between the Rulers and the Raumsdalians and Bizogots went on every day. Sometimes Hamnet's men had the advantage, sometimes they didn't. A week after Marcovefa's magic, they were farther north than they had been when she tried the spell. Overall, then, the Rulers had advanced more than they'd retreated.

"Maybe I *should* go climb the Glacier again," Ulric Skakki said. "We could use more fancy shamans."

"Well, so we could," Hamnet said. "But we need you around here, too, you know."

"You say the sweetest things." Ulric batted his eyelashes at Hamnet. "How do I know I can believe you, though? You probably say them to everybody."

"Oh, for God's sake!" Hamnet exploded. "I'm not trying to seduce you."

"A good thing. I'm as dull and normal as you are—I like women, too," Ulric said.

"I'm sure all the women are delighted to hear it," Hamnet said.

"Well, now that you mention it, so am I." Ulric was undeniably—and annoyingly—smug.

Hamnet might have gone on harassing him, but a white-faced Bizogot came into the encampment calling his name. "I'm here," Hamnet said, standing up to let himself be seen. "What's gone wrong now?" By the fellow's tone, he was sure something had.

All the fellow said was, "You'd better come with me."

Count Hamnet had to saddle his horse before he could. That did nothing to make him any more enthusiastic, especially when the horse didn't want to exhale to let him tighten its girths. He kicked it in the ribs. That did the trick. Ulric was saddling his mount, too. "Can't let 'em play games with you," he said.

"No." Hamnet nodded. He asked the Bizogot, "Should Marcovefa see this, too, whatever it is?"

The man didn't need long to think about that. He nodded. "By God, she should."

"All right—go get her," Hamnet told him. "She can ride double with me. That way, we won't waste any more time." Nodding again, the Bizogot hurried away.

"What do you suppose it is?" Marcovefa asked as they started to ride. "He didn't want to say anything much to me. Only that it was important."

"That's more than he told me," Hamnet Thyssen answered. "I figured it out myself, though—I will say that."

They followed the Bizogot across snow-covered fields toward a stand of pines ahead. Hamnet wondered if they were riding into an ambush. He made sure his sword was loose in its scabbard. Maybe Marcovefa would scent that kind of danger ahead. He could hope so, which didn't mean he was sure of it. He checked the sword again.

Marcovefa gave no sign of sensing trouble. But that was not to say that she seemed happy. "Oh," she said, the corners of her mouth turning down.

"Do you know what this is about?" Hamnet asked.

"I have a pretty good notion, anyhow," she answered, and fell silent again. Hamnet muttered under his breath, which did him no good at all.

They rode into the woods. The Bizogot seemed to be following the trail he'd made riding back to the camp. All of a sudden, he reined in. "There," he said, and pointed between two pines.

Something lay in the snow behind them, though branches obscured the view. Whatever it was, Hamnet's horse didn't like it. The beast sidestepped and snorted, nostrils flaring.

"What is it?" Ulric asked—exactly the question in Hamnet's mind.

"See for yourselves," the Bizogot answered, his face all screwed up. When Hamnet glanced back at Marcovefa, he saw she was wearing the same expression. Yes, sure enough, she had an idea of what was going on.

He got down from his horse and tied the reins to a branch. Marcovefa slid down, too. Ulric Skakki also tethered his horse. "I always love a little excursion during the day," the adventurer said brightly. "Don't you?"

"No." Hamnet's voice might have come from a talking boulder.

He drew his sword before pushing past the pines in the way. So did Ulric. Marcovefa let them take the lead. Maybe that meant she thought she needed protection. More likely, it meant she thought they thought she needed protection. She was alarmingly good at taking care of herself.

Hamnet stopped in his tracks. Behind him, Ulric made an involuntary noise full of disgust. A short-faced bear's head lay in the snow, its blood staining the white with red. No footprints led away from it. Neither did a trail of blood drops. It might have been dropped there by magic. As soon as that thought crossed Hamnet's mind, he realized the bear's head probably had been.

"This is the Rulers' answer to your magic?" he asked Marcovefa.

She nodded. "Nothing else."

"Does it break your spells?" Ulric asked. "Or does it just say they know the spell is there and they defy you?"

She reached out with a mittened hand, as if feeling the air in front of her. When that didn't tell her what she wanted to know, she stepped past Hamnet and Ulric, stooped beside the bear's head, and laid her hand just above one ear. She recoiled, her mouth twisting. "The spell is broken," she said.

"Can you restore it?" Count Hamnet asked, and then, on second thought, "Is there any point to restoring it?"

"I think not," Marcovefa answered. "I could do it, but they would only break it again. They would have an easier time breaking it again, because they've already done it once and they know how."

The Bizogot who'd found the bear's head came up behind them. "Now you know," he said.

"Now we know," Hamnet agreed. "You could have told us back at the camp. It would have saved a lot of time."

"No." The Bizogot spat in the snow. "Some things you need to see for yourself. When Grimoald hears of this, the war against the Rulers will be to the death for him. They have desecrated his clan animal."

Hamnet Thyssen found himself nodding. The Bizogots took such things as the deadliest of insults. Ulric Skakki sometimes enjoyed being difficult for the sake of being difficult. He said, "But Grimoald wears the bear-claw necklace. Why should he care if someone else goes hunting?"

"It is not the same thing." The Bizogot seemed shocked that Ulric couldn't see as much. "Grimoald hunted with reverence. He killed with reverence. Not like . . . this." He pointed to the bear's head, which did indeed seem a sad, dejected object.

"It may have mattered to Grimoald." Yes, Ulric was determined to be difficult today. "How much did it matter to the beasts? They ended up dead either way."

"It matters." That wasn't the scandalized Bizogot but Marcovefa. "To the bear's spirit, it matters very much whether it was killed by a warrior with respect and awe or by an enemy in hate."

"And you know this because . . . ?" Ulric said.

He was bound to be teasing, but Marcovefa answered anyhow: "Because I do. Because I can feel it. Ask any shaman. They will all tell you the same."

"People tell me lots of different things," Ulric said. "Figuring out what's true is half the fun."

"This is true," Marcovefa declared. "Do you say I am lying?"

Hamnet Thyssen would not have cared to say any such thing to her. Evidently, Ulric didn't, either, which struck

Hamnet as uncommonly sensible of the adventurer. "Well, no," Ulric allowed, "but I do say you could be wrong."

"I could be," Marcovefa said, with the air of someone making a great and undeserved concession. "I could be, yes, but I am not. As I tell you, ask Liv. Ask Audun Gilli. If they tell you I am wrong, they know less of magic than I think they do."

"Never mind all this fancy talk," said the Bizogot who'd found the short-faced bear's head. "What do we do now?"

"The first thing I must do is tell the bear I am sorry for the indignity it suffered," Marcovefa answered in the Bizogot language commonly used on the steppe north of the Empire. Then she switched to her own dialect. Hamnet could follow only a word here and there. He got just enough to gather that she was doing what she'd said she would. Maybe—evidently—the apology made her feel better. Whether it did the same thing for the bear he was less sure.

Ulric Skakki's upraised eyebrow probably said he harbored some of the same doubts. If he did, though, he didn't come right out and say so. Challenging Marcovefa once was not for the faint of heart. Challenging her more than once? Very bold or very, very foolish.

At last, she seemed satisfied with what she'd done. She picked up what had to be a symbolic handful of snow and dropped it on the head. Then she returned to the usual Bizogot language to say, "We can go now. It is appeased." After a moment, she looked south, toward the Rulers' camps. "It is appeased," she repeated. "It is, but I am not."

WHEN MARCOVEFA SAID she wasn't appeased, she meant it. Marcovefa commonly meant what she said. Her cold fury puzzled Hamnet. "The bears killed Rulers. They must have," he said the next day. "Why not expect the Rulers to kill bears?"

She looked at him—looked through him, rather. "I do expect them to kill bears. Killing is part of war. Killing like that . . ." She shook her head. "No."

"What can you do about it? Anything?"

"They will pay. Oh, they will pay." Marcovefa was still looking through him. He wondered whether her eyes saw any of the real world. Then he wondered how real the world was, and whether what she saw wasn't truer, closer to the absolute heart of things, than the campfire and the snow and the smell of horses on the breeze. He didn't know; he was trapped forever in mundane reality and the orderly succession of time. Marcovefa had proved she wasn't. She went on, "Their doom hangs over them like a crag of ice."

"May it be so," Hamnet said. "How do we make it fall on them?"

"What?" Abruptly, Marcovefa seemed back in the here-and-now. Hamnet realized she had no idea what she'd just said. It shook him less than it might have; he'd seen the same thing from her before, and from others who trafficked in magic as well. He told her what she'd told him. She looked at him in surprise. "I said that?"

"I'm not making this up, you know," he answered.

"No. You are not." Marcovefa sounded more sure than an ordinary person had any business being. Well, whatever else she was, an ordinary person she wasn't. "If I said it, and I do not know that I said it, it is likely to be so."

From anyone else, something like that would have been lunacy. Coming from Marcovefa, it made an odd kind of sense. Or Hamnet thought it did, anyhow, which might have proved nothing except that his own grasp on sanity was starting to slip. "How do we make their doom fall on them?" he asked again.

"I cannot tell you that. I wish I could," she said. "It will come when the Golden Shrine is found again."

"It will?" Hamnet wondered if she would have any idea she'd come out with that.

She did. "Yes. It will. The doom of the Rulers and finding the Golden Shrine are bound together."

"How?" Hamnet asked eagerly.

Marcovefa spread her hands. They were callused and scarred: the hands of a person who'd worked hard all her life to survive. Up atop the Glacier, not even shamans had an easy time of it. "I do not know," she replied. "When it happens, you will see." Her smile pulled up only half her mouth. "And so will I. And it will surprise both of us."

"What do we do in the meantime?" Hamnet said.

"Fight the Rulers. What else can we do? If they win, if they evade their doom, prophecy melts like snow on a south-facing slope in summer."

Hamnet Thyssen scratched his head. "Then how is it prophecy?"

"If we fight them hard, they won't win. I hope they won't, anyhow," Marcovefa said.

"But you aren't sure?" Hamnet persisted.

"I am sure of what I know. But one of the things I know is that I don't know everything there is to know," Marcovefa replied.

He scratched his head again. "Does anybody know anything?" he asked.

"Of course. Just not enough." By the way Marcovefa said that, she meant it to be reassuring. To Hamnet, it was anything but. He didn't push it any further, though. If he did, he feared he would end up feeling like a dog chasing its own tail.

Compared to trying to understand what prophecy meant, riding out on patrol was a relief. He knew what he was doing there: looking for enemy warriors. He knew what he would do if he found them, too: either fight or run away, depending on how many of them there were.

He didn't mind having Marcovefa along, either, since on patrol they weren't trying to understand the whichness of what. If he came across one of the Rulers' shamans, chances were Marcovefa could beat the man.

That thought, unfortunately, brought Hamnet back to the whichness of what. Not long before, he would have taken it for granted the Marcovefa could beat the Rulers' wizards. He still thought she could, but he wasn't sure any more. That couldn't be a good sign.

Neither could the way his force of Bizogots and Raumsdalians kept falling back toward the north. If this went on, they'd retreat past Nidaros before long. When would they end up back in the great northern forests again? When would they end up on the Bizogot plains beyond the forests?

"It would not be so bad," Marcovefa said when he asked her about it.

"Not to you, maybe," Hamnet answered. "But this is better."

"No," she said. "Things are as they are meant to be. This is as it is meant to be. I do not worry about it, no matter what happens."

"You don't?" Hamnet said. "Well, I do, by God. Suppose something happens to you. What would we do then? We can't beat the Rulers without you. We've already proved that, curse it."

"You proved you did not beat them, yes," Marcovefa said. "You did not prove you could not beat them."

Hamnet saw the difference. No matter what he saw, to him it was too subtle to matter. If the Bizogots and Raumsdalians hadn't beaten the Rulers without the shaman from atop the Glacier, what were the chances they could suddenly start doing it now? *Woefully slim*, he thought.

He caught motion from the corner of his eye. It wasn't the kind of motion he was used to, the kind a man on a horse made. Riding deer had a gait with more up-and-down to it. The Rulers probably thought horses were the ones that moved oddly. That was their worry, not his.

One of the Raumsdalian troopers in the patrol also spotted the enemy riders. "There's some of the bastards!" he said, and strung his bow in one quick, practiced motion. "Let's drive 'em off!" He swung his horse toward the south.

"Sounds good to me," Count Hamnet said, also stringing his bow. "Have they got a wizard with them?" he asked Marcovefa.

"Yes, I think so." She didn't sound worried about it. But then, when did she?

The Rulers didn't need long to realize their foes had seen them. They could have pulled back into the trees, but they didn't, even though their patrol was smaller than the one Hamnet led. They didn't charge forward, either. They held their ground so they could shoot from mounts that weren't moving.

With their recurved bows, they made formidable archers. Their arrows fell among the Bizogots and Raumsdalians before Hamnet's men could hit them. Marcovefa swore in her dialect. A shaft had grazed her hand a moment before hitting the leather of her saddle. It didn't pierce the saddle and wound her horse. *Good luck* went through Hamnet's mind.

Then Marcovefa slumped over, unconscious or dead. "Poison!" Hamnet gasped—it was the first thing he thought of. He grabbed her and steadied her so she wouldn't fall down and get trampled. Her eyes had rolled up in her head; he saw nothing but white when he peeled back an eyelid.

Nothing to do but flee when their main shield was taken away. The Rulers pursued for a little while. Their harsh jeers said they had a good notion of what they'd done. But, again, horses outdistanced riding deer. Hamnet Thyssen wondered if it mattered.

XVI

Marcovefa lay in front of Hamnet, splayed over the saddle like a stag killed in the hunt, by the time the patrol got back to camp. She wasn't dead; her heart beat and her breathing stayed steady. But, try as Hamnet would, he couldn't rouse her.

He led her horse. The arrow that had grazed her still stuck up from the animal's saddle. Something was strange about the point. It seemed to be made not of iron or bronze or chipped stone or carved bone but of leaves of some sort. Leaves, of course, had no business hurting anyone unless they were poisonous. Even then, Hamnet had never heard of a venom that could strike so swiftly from such a small wound.

He'd never heard of any such thing, no. But the Rulers had.

When people in the camp saw Marcovefa all limp and pale, it as was if they'd had their hearts plucked from their chests. Some of them hung back—they didn't seem to want to know any more. Others rushed forward.

"Is she slain?" Trasamund demanded—as usual, he came straight to the point.

Hamnet Thyssen shook his head. "No. It's sorcery. Where's Liv? Where's Audun?"

They rushed through the crowd. "What happened to her?" Audun Gilli asked.

"That did." Count Hamnet pointed to the arrow. "It only scratched her, but she's been like this ever since it did."

"Get her down," Liv said. Hamnet obeyed. Liv and Audun steadied Marcovefa so he could dismount without dropping her. Then he carried her to the tent the two of them shared and laid her down on a fur robe there.

Audun uncinched the saddle from Marcovefa's horse instead of pulling the arrow out of it. He lugged the saddle after Hamnet. Was that excessive caution or common sense? Hamnet would have liked to blame the wizard for it, but found he couldn't.

Liv tied back the tent flaps to let in more light. Then she stooped by Marcovefa. As Hamnet had before her, she checked the other shaman's pulse and peeled back an eyelid. Marcovefa showed no signs of consciousness.

"I don't think she will die right away," Liv said: as much consolation as she had to offer.

"No, neither do I." If Hamnet said it, maybe it would come true. "But how could the Rulers do—this—to her?"

Liv was silent. That hardly surprised Hamnet. No wizard liked to see another wizard—especially one more powerful than she—brought down. But then, his voice even more hesitant than usual, Audun said, "I think the arrowhead is made with mistletoe."

He spoke in Raumsdalian. Even now, he wasn't fluent in the Bizogots' tongue; foreign languages weren't easy for him. Liv's Raumsdalian was also imperfect. "What is this mistletoe?" she asked.

Audun sent Hamnet a look of appeal. The only trouble was, Hamnet didn't know how to say *mistletoe* in the Bizogots' language. He did the best he could: he explained what mistletoe was. He wondered if that would mean anything to Liv. The Bizogot steppe was treeless, of course, so why would she know anything about the parasites that grew on trees?

But she did. Her eyes widened. He'd forgotten what a deep blue they were. "Levigild the hero!" she exclaimed.

Count Hamnet had heard a good many Bizogot tales or legends or whatever they were. That one was new to him, though. By Audun's blank look, it was new to him, too. "What happened to this Levigild?" Hamnet asked.

"His mother wanted to make him safe from all the danger she could," Liv answered. "She got everything in the world to promise not to harm him. But she forgot about the mistletoe—to her, it wasn't worth remembering. God didn't like what she was doing, because he was afraid Levigild would be a rival. So he had a blind man make an arrow with mistletoe for a head. He shot it, not even knowing Levigild was anywhere near him. The arrow hit Levigild in the chest, and he died."

"This arrow only grazed Marcovefa," Hamnet said. "She isn't dead—she's just . . . out. Can you bring her back?"

"I would not know where to begin against mistletoe," Liv said, which was exactly what Hamnet didn't want to hear.

Reluctantly, he turned to Audun Gilli. Use the man who'd taken one woman from him to save another? He wouldn't have, if he thought he had any other choice. If Audun did save Marcovefa, how would she show she was grateful? *However she wants to, and damn all you'll have to say about it*, Hamnet thought. "What can you do for her, Gilli?" he asked roughly.

"God," Audun said. "I don't know if I can do anything. I'm not a healer. You know that. You know what kind of wizard I am, Thyssen."

As if to remind Hamnet, a cheap burnt-clay cup grew lips and said, "He doesn't ask for much, does he? Heal her from a sorcery nobody knows anything about? Sure, that sounds easy."

Hamnet's ears heated. He *did* know what kind of wizard Audun Gilli was, worse luck. "You knew something about the wound, anyhow," he said. "You can't blame me for hoping."

"No one should be blamed for hoping," Liv said softly. "Not ever."

"Yes, you can say that, can't you?" Hamnet's voice was bleak enough to make her flinch. But his desperation drove him to speak directly to her again: "Please see what you can do to help her, Liv."

"Me? But I told you—"

"You knew about this Levigild." Hamnet Thyssen was proud of himself for coming up with the legendary Bizogot's name.

"Well, yes, but . . ." Liv struggled to put what she was thinking into words. "Hamnet, I told you—I know nothing of mistletoe except the legend! I would never have recognized it. Audun did that, remember."

"Yes, I know." The look Count Hamnet sent Audun Gilli failed to annihilate him, though not from lack of effort. It did make him turn red, which seemed a less than adequate substitute. Hamnet went on, "But since he doesn't want to try, I was hoping you might. We can't beat the Rulers without Marcovefa, you know."

"It isn't that Gilli doesn't want to try," the cup said,

puffing out ceramic cheeks it never should have owned. "It's just that he doesn't think he can do her any good."

"Crackpots everywhere," Hamnet said sadly. Liv flinched again, perhaps for a different reason this time. Even the cup winced. Count Hamnet continued, "I would ask this if Marcovefa were not my lover. I would ask this if she were a man. We need her. The fight needs her."

"I know. I understand. I believe you." Liv looked and sounded dreadfully unhappy. "But I don't know what I can do here. I don't know if I can do anything. And failing might be worse than not trying at all."

"How?" Hamnet demanded. "Is that even possible?"

"Worse is always possible." That wasn't Liv—it was Audun. "Better may not be, but worse always is. Nothing is so mucked up that you can't muck it up worse. If I've learned one thing in life, by God, that's it."

Hamnet thought it over. Reluctantly, he decided Audun had a point. All the same, he said, "If you leave her like this, she's liable to die. What happens to us if she does?" *What happens to me if she does?* But that was a different question—in most ways, he supposed, a lesser question.

"We will do what we can for her, Hamnet, and for you." Liv responded to what Hamnet had said, and to what he hadn't. Audun Gilli couldn't have looked less delighted if she'd told him he needed a tooth pulled and they were all out of poppy juice. But he didn't walk away or say no, and Count Hamnet gave him grudging respect on account of that.

"What can you do?" Hamnet asked.

"Our best," Audun answered. "How good it'll be . . ." He shrugged. "We just have to find out, that's all."

"So we do." Coming from Liv's mouth, it didn't sound like such a pronouncement of doom. She studied the inert Marcovefa as she might have studied a track on bad ground. Then she asked Audun, "What do you think? The charm with the moonstone, perhaps?"

"Perhaps," Audun said in tones of deep skepticism. In an aside to Hamnet Thyssen, he went on, "If we set a moonstone under her tongue with the proper spell, it is supposed to kindle her mind and make her wits sharp."

"That sounds like exactly what she needs!" Hamnet exclaimed. More slowly, reacting to the wizard's tone, he added, "Why aren't you happier about it?"

"Because most of the time it doesn't do what the grimoires claim it does," Audun Gilli answered. "Take any book of recipes—you'll find a few that don't turn out a dish you'd want to eat. It's the same way with sorcery. I shouldn't wonder if it's the same way with everything. And the moonstone spell is like that: it sounds better than it eats, if you know what I mean."

"I've made it work," Liv said. "Not all the time, but sometimes, anyhow."

"Then you cast it this time. If you have faith in it, it's more likely to do what you want it to," Audun said.

"I'll try it, yes." Liv hesitated before adding, "If that's all right with you, Hamnet."

"Of course. Why do you even ask?" Hamnet said.

"She can't speak for herself now. If anyone has the right to speak for her, it's you," Liv said. "So if you don't trust me to work the magic . . ."

"Ah. I see." He nodded. "As far as I know, you don't have anything against Marcovefa. That's the only thing that would make me say no. Go ahead."

Liv rummaged in one of the pouches she wore on her belt, and then in another one. At last, she nodded. "Here we are." She held a small moonstone in the palm of her hand. The stone's soft luster reminded Count Hamnet of the mother-of-pearl ornaments that sometimes came up into the Empire from the lands by the shore of the Southern Sea.

"You're going to put that under her tongue?" he asked. When Liv nodded, he went on, "What do you do if she swallows it?"

"I've never seen that happen." Liv gave the moonstone a thoughtful look. "It's small and smooth. It should pass." Hamnet eyed the stone, too. After a moment, he found himself nodding again.

When he didn't ask any more questions, Liv slid the stone into Marcovefa's mouth. Marcovefa smiled but didn't open her eyes. Liv started to chant. She used an old-fashioned dialect of the Bizogots' language, but not so old-fashioned that Hamnet couldn't follow most of it. She called on the moonstone to banish the baneful mistletoe.

Liv's hands twisted in quick, assured passes. Hamnet watched Audun Gilli watching them. Every once in a while, the Raumsdalian wizard would nod or smile in appreciation of what they were doing. One skilled stonecarver might have watched another work with mallet and chisel the same way.

"Oh, very nice!" Audun murmured at one point in the proceedings. Hamnet didn't see anything that struck him as special, but he knew he would have also missed most of the fine points of what a stonecarver was doing.

When a stonecarver finished his work, he had some carved stone he could point to. Then anyone could judge whether he'd done well or not so well. When Liv finished, she'd have . . . what? With any luck at all, she'd have Marcovefa fully restored to herself. Count Hamnet hoped for nothing less.

Liv's voice rose. "So may it be!" she said, and pointed a callused, short-nailed index finger at Marcovefa's face—or perhaps at the moonstone still in Marcovefa's mouth. Despite the winter chill, sweat soaked her hair and ran down her face. She pointed, she waited expectantly, and. . . .

Nothing happened. Marcovefa lay there. Her chest rose and fell. Her color stayed good. But her eyes didn't open. She didn't revive.

"Oh, a pestilence," Audun Gilli said softly.

Liv looked much more distressed than Marcovefa did. She was also panting from the effort she'd put forth. "It didn't work," she said, as if that were the worst thing she could think of. Right this minute, it probably was.

"It doesn't seem to have," Hamnet said. "Would trying it again do any good? Would your trying it do any good, Gilli?" Using the Raumsdalian wizard's family name instead of his individual name was less than friendly, but it was as much as Hamnet could do.

Audun Gilli didn't take offense now, as he hadn't before. "I'll try if you want," he said. "I don't know how much good it will do, but I'll try."

And he did, from the beginning. He even took the moonstone out of Marcovefa's mouth and put it back in before starting his spell. That made her smile again, but didn't revive her. His spell was different from Liv's; he used Raumsdalian in place of the Bizogots' language. Where Liv had almost ordered Marcovefa to return to herself, Audun cajoled her.

None of the differences mattered even a copper's worth. As she had before, Marcovefa still lay there. She wasn't dead. But she wasn't among those present, either.

"What are we going to do?" Hamnet Thyssen heard the despair in his own voice.

"We fought the Rulers before we ever met Marcovefa," Liv said. "We can go on fighting without her."

Neither Hamnet nor Audun Gilli said anything to that. They could go on fighting, yes. They had to, in fact. And they had fought before. The only trouble was, they hadn't fought with anything resembling success. Could they now? Hamnet had to hope so, but he couldn't see how.

"Thank you for trying," he said, half-bowing first to Audun and then to Liv.

"We need her," Liv said simply.

"Maybe Earl Eyvind will have some notion of what to try next," Audun said. "He's not a wizard, but he knows a lot."

"So he does," Hamnet said morosely. Audun might have suggested that he ask Gudrid. That would have been less appealing. Offhand, Hamnet couldn't think of anything else that would have been.

EYVIND TORFINN AND Gudrid were eating together when Count Hamnet found them. Back in Nidaros, neither of them would have dreamt of sucking the marrow out of a sheep's leg bone while sprawled out near a fire. But Hamnet had seen on the journey through the Gap that they could rough it when they had to.

He stood waiting to be noticed. Gudrid ostentatiously ignored him. He didn't mind. If anything, he preferred having nothing to do with her to having anything to do with her. Earl Eyvind took longer to see Hamnet was there than he might have, though.

At last, he did. "What can I do for you, Your Grace?" he asked.

"Well, Your Splendor, it's like this. . . ." Hamnet Thyssen told him what had happened to Marcovefa, and about the moonstone spell Liv had tried.

"I . . . see," Eyvind said slowly. "How very unfortunate."

"Hamnet never did have much luck with women, but this is ridiculous." Gudrid sounded amused.

"Your Splendor, will you please tell this . . . person I came for your advice, not for hers?" Hamnet said.

"Oh, you can talk straight to me, Hamnet, dear," Gudrid said. "It's not my fault you don't know what to do with them if you find them."

Again, Count Hamnet spoke to Earl Eyvind: "Will you please tell her I will kill her if she opens her mouth again about Marcovefa? Will you tell her I am not joking? Will you remind her we'll have a demon of a time fighting the Rulers without Marcovefa? And will you also remind her how much she enjoyed their company the last time she ran into them?"

What Earl Eyvind did say to Gudrid was, "I think you would do well not to provoke Count Hamnet, my sweet. I think you would do very well indeed, as a matter of fact."

Gudrid's eyes flashed. She didn't take kindly to anyone who tried to tell her what to do. But, for a wonder, she kept her mouth shut. Or maybe it wasn't a wonder. Maybe it was the murder writ large across Hamnet Thyssen's face.

Whatever it was, her silence kept him from grabbing his sword and keeping his promise. Instead, he asked Earl Eyvind, "What do you know about magics made with moonstones?"

"I assume Liv told you the legend of Levigild the hero?" Eyvind said. Gudrid's eyes glinted again, but she stayed quiet. One of her gifts was gauging just how far she could goad Hamnet without endangering herself. She'd pushed right to the edge—almost over it—this time, because she hadn't realized how upset he was, not only for himself but for their cause.

"She did." Count Hamnet nodded. "She used his name in her spell, I think, but it didn't do any good."

"All right," Eyvind Torfinn said. Hamnet didn't think it

was. Before he could say so, Earl Eyvind went on, "Other legends also accrue to the mistletoe, you know."

"That was the kind of thing I was hoping you could tell me about," Hamnet said. Gudrid yawned enormously. Hamnet kept pretending she wasn't there, which was the best thing that could have happened to her.

"I will tell you what I know." Eyvind paused to gather his thoughts. Hamnet pictured him riffling through an enormous codex inside his head. That probably wasn't how it worked, but the end results were about the same. Eyvind said, "You will of course have met the custom of kissing under the mistletoe on the night of the winter solstice."

"Don't bet on it," Gudrid murmured.

Hamnet went right on ignoring her. As long as she insulted him alone and not Marcovefa, he could, with effort, hold his temper. He nodded to Earl Eyvind. "Yes, of course, Your Splendor."

"Excellent!" By the way Eyvind beamed, Hamnet might have been a promising pupil.

"I don't see what that's got to do with anything here, though," Hamnet said.

"Well, neither do I," Eyvind admitted. "It was the first thing that came to mind, that's all." *It was on the top page of the codex between his ears*, Hamnet thought. Eyvind continued, "The powdered leaves, if drunk, are sovereign against the falling sickness."

"But the arrow gave her something like the falling sickness," Hamnet protested.

"I am telling you what I know of mistletoe and its uses," Earl Eyvind said stiffly. "If it does not correspond to the woman's symptoms, I am not responsible for the discrepancy."

Hamnet wanted to hit him. Even if he did, though, he realized Eyvind wouldn't understand. To the scholarly noble, this was a scholarly problem, no more and no less. Eyvind Torfinn didn't seem to grasp that, without Marcovefa to oppose them, the Rulers could do pretty much as they pleased against this ragtag force of Bizogots and Raumsdalians.

"Do you know of any charms for waking people out of a long sleep?" Count Hamnet asked.

Eyvind shook his head. "I am afraid I do not. Lacking any sorcerous capabilities myself, I never extended my investigations in that direction."

"Listening to Hamnet might put anyone into a long sleep, but I don't suppose that's magic," Gudrid said.

"No, probably not," Hamnet agreed. Gudrid looked unhappy. He'd told her before that he didn't much care if she insulted him. She evidently hadn't believed him. Too bad—he'd told the truth. She told so many lies herself, she had to expect them all the time from other people.

"Can Marcovefa eat? Can she drink? Can we sustain her until such time as we find a means to defeat this sorcery?" Earl Eyvind asked. They were all good questions—perhaps Eyvind had a better connection with reality than Hamnet had thought.

He spread his hands. "I don't know the answers to any of those. We just have to see, that's all. If we can take care of her, you're right—that buys us time. If we can't . . ." The face he made told what he thought of that prospect.

"Yes, who'd give you a tumble then?" Gudrid said.

She was lucky. Hamnet Thyssen walked away from her, not toward her. He went over to one of the cooks' kettles and dipped out a bowl of barley mush. The mush had bits and shreds of mutton in it. A baby could have got it down with no trouble. With any luck at all, an ensorcelled invalid would be able to do the same. If she couldn't, the game was up. It was about that simple.

He dipped a horn spoon into the mush and blew on it, the way he would have before feeding a baby. Then, worriedly, he slid the spoon between Marcovefa's flaccid lips.

She smiled. She ate. She swallowed. But her eyes didn't open and she showed no sign of being aware of herself. Hamnet looked at the good and ignored as much of the bad as he could. He gave her another spoonful, then another, then another. Before long, the bowl was empty. He wiped off her chin. She was no neater than a baby would have been. He didn't care. She wouldn't starve to death.

It soon became plain she had no more control over her bodily functions than a baby did. Grimly, Hamnet took care of that, too. Had Gudrid come by to mock him then . . . But she didn't. This time, her notion of how far she could push him proved good.

Liv did come by. "I will help you keep her clean, if you let me," she said. "And sooner or later—you will know when better than I do—her time of the month will come. Chances are you would sooner have me deal with it."

"Chances are you're right," Hamnet said, scrubbing his hands with snow. "I thank you for the kindness."

"She would do the same for me." Liv looked at him. "So would you, I think, even now."

"I hope so." Hamnet hesitated. Then he said, "Too bad it didn't work out."

"Yes, I think so, too." Liv gave back a nod and a smile and a shrug. "But it didn't, and we can't very well pretend it did."

That felt colder than the snow against his skin—and yet, in another way, it didn't. "I can't imagine talking with Gudrid this way," Hamnet said. "That didn't work out, either."

"Well, the difference is, you and I don't hate each other, or I hope we don't," Liv said. "You and Gudrid . . ." She shook her head and didn't go on.

Hamnet Thyssen started to deny it. No matter what Gudrid felt about him, what he felt about her couldn't be hate . . . could it? *What else would you call it, then?* he asked himself, and found no answer. "Thank you—I think," he said slowly. "You just showed me something about myself I didn't know before."

"I'm not sure I did you a favor," Liv said.

"I'm not, either. That's why I said, 'I think,'" Hamnet answered. "What are we going to do now?"

"Try to keep her fed and watered and clean," Liv said. "Try to find a magic that will lift the mistletoe spell— either that or hope it wears off on its own. A lot of spells do, you know."

"Not quite what I meant," he told her. "Pretty soon, the Rulers will realize we can't beat back their magic any more. They'll see we aren't aiming strong spells at them. Then they'll jump on us with both feet."

The shaman from the Three Tusk clan bit her lip. "You shame Audun and me."

"I didn't mean to," Hamnet said quickly. "By God, Liv, I didn't."

"You might as well have meant it if you didn't." Her voice was bleak. "It's not as if you weren't telling the truth. Marcovefa could beat the Rulers. Audun and I . . . can't. We've seen that."

"It's not your fault—not your fault in particular," Count Hamnet said. "Nobody on this side of the Glacier can beat the Rulers. We've seen that, too. So has Sigvat II, and I hope he likes it." He didn't need anyone else to tell him that he hated the Raumsdalian Emperor.

"We should be able to beat them. We'd better be able to." Liv's shiver had nothing to do with the Breath of God; it could have come at high summer. "If we can't, what's to stop them from stomping us underfoot like a mammoth stepping on a vole? Or if they don't do that, what's to keep them from driving us back through the trees and up onto the Bizogot steppe again?"

Nothing, Hamnet thought. *Not a single, solitary thing.* But he didn't want to make Liv feel worse than she did already, so he said, "Why does that worry you? It's your homeland, after all."

"But it's so much poorer than Raumsdalia. I didn't understand that before I came down here, but I do now." Liv had never been one to hide from unpleasant or inconvenient truths. "If the Rulers hold the Empire, they can come after us up on the steppe any time they choose—especially since more and more of them keep riding down through the Gap. They can squeeze us from north and south—squeeze us till there's nothing left." The shadows under her proud cheekbones might have been shadows of fear—or maybe Hamnet's imagination, usually no more energetic than it had to be, was for once running away with him.

"I hope things don't work out that way," he said.

"So do I," Liv answered. "But, however wonderful I think hope is, keeping it gets hard." She looked at him. Was she . . . hoping he would tell her she was wrong? If she was, he had to disappoint her. *Again*, he thought bitterly.

WHAT'S TO KEEP the Rulers from stomping us underfoot? What's to keep them from driving us back through the trees and out onto the Bizogot steppe? As winter went on, Count Hamnet remembered Liv's questions again and again. He also remembered the response that had formed in his mind when he heard them. *Nothing.*

Liv turned out to know which questions to ask. And Hamnet turned out to know the answer.

He counted staying alive a victory. He counted every

time his ragtag force managed to sting the Rulers another. Retreats, on the other hand . . .

Ulric Skakki joked about them: "This country looked a lot better from north to south than it does from south to north."

Hamnet didn't laugh, which seemed to irk the adventurer. Hamnet also didn't much care whether Ulric was irked or not. By then, they were north of Nidaros again. They hadn't passed right by the capital. That distressed Eyvind Torfinn and, even more loudly, Gudrid. To Hamnet, it didn't matter one way or the other.

Marcovefa drank. She ate. She sometimes smiled, though she hardly ever opened her eyes. She gave no sign of coming fully to herself. Without her, the Raumsdalians and Bizogots did what they could against the Rulers. What they could do wasn't enough, or even close.

The Rulers' confidence swelled with every new triumph, too. They regained the arrogance they'd shown before Marcovefa taught them they didn't know everything there was to know. And when you rode to a fight expecting to win, you were more likely to do just that.

When you rode to a fight expecting something to go wrong . . . Raumsdalians began slipping away from the army. Maybe they thought they could do better for themselves by giving up the fight and grubbing out a living under the Rulers. Maybe they were right, too.

"We Bizogots don't quit, by God!" Trasamund told Runolf Skallagrim one cold evening. "Your folk shouldn't, either."

"You're right. They shouldn't," Baron Runolf agreed politely. "I don't know what to do about it, though."

"Kill anybody who wants to run away." The jarl was nothing if not direct.

"If we catch them trying to sneak off, we do kill them," Runolf said. "The trouble is, we don't catch many."

"You need to try harder," Trasamund said.

"We need to do all kinds of things," Runolf Skallagrim replied. "We need to beat the Rulers again, for instance. If we do that, people will think our chances are better, so they won't want to run out on us. We can hope they won't, anyway." He eyed Count Hamnet. "How do we go about that, Thyssen?"

"I wish I knew," Hamnet answered bleakly.

"Marcovefa has to wake up," Trasamund said.

"Well, how do we make that happen?" Runolf asked.

Even more bleakly, Hamnet shrugged. "I wish I knew. Our wizards have tried. I've watched them do it. The only trouble is, they've had no luck. It's in God's hands now, I think."

"And God's done nothing but drop things since he let the Glacier melt through so these stinking Rulers could plague us." Trasamund sounded bleak himself.

Runolf sent him a measuring look, too. "The way you say that, you'll be the next one to try and run from trouble."

"No." Trasamund didn't even bother to shake his head. "I'm in this till the end. With the Rulers swarming down the way they do, I have nothing to go back to. They hold my clan's grazing grounds. The few free Three Tusk Bizogots are all here with me. We're not a big clan anymore, but we're tough."

"If you've got nothing to go back to, you may as well fight," Hamnet Thyssen said. "The ones who think they can slip away and go back to being peasants with the Rulers taxing them in place of the Empire—"

"They're all Raumsdalians," Trasamund broke in.

"That's not what I was going to say," Hamnet told him.

"Doesn't make it any less true," the Bizogot replied.

"Those are the ones we have to worry about." Count Hamnet stubbornly finished his own thought.

"But if they desert, what kind of fight can we put up?" Trasamund said.

"We came down here with an army that was mostly Bizogots," Hamnet said. "We can go on that way if we have to." *We can get driven out of the Empire that way*, he thought, but didn't speak words of ill omen aloud.

Trasamund did it for him: "We came down here with an army that had Marcovefa in it, too. Without her, we're buggered, is what we are."

"Well, in that case why do you blame the Raumsdalian soldiers for leaving the fight when they see the chance?" Runolf Skallagrim asked. "They figure they won't make any difference one way or the other, and it looks to me like they've got something."

"They may not help us lose if they desert," Hamnet said. "Sure as sure, they won't help us win."

"And I'll tell you what they've got," Trasamund added. "They've got yellow bellies, that's what."

Runolf scowled at him. The Raumsdalian veteran's hand began to slide toward the hilt of his sword. "Enough, both of you," Count Hamnet said wearily. "Too much. We're all doing the best we can. If we fight amongst ourselves, we only help the Rulers."

"If they don't fight, they help the Rulers, too." Trasamund didn't want to let it drop.

"Enough, I said." Hamnet got between the Bizogot and Baron Runolf. "Fight me first, if you have to fight somebody."

"No, that wouldn't be a good idea, either." Ulric Skakki's voice came from the gloom beyond the firelight. Turning toward it, Hamnet saw that he had a nocked arrow in his bow. "Hamnet has it straight. We're supposed to fight the enemy, not ourselves."

"But we can't fight the Rulers, either," Runolf said. "That's why men are slipping off."

"Yes, we can," Ulric said. "We can't do it right now, that's all. There's a difference. If your men have too many potatoes in the head to see it, you've got to keep banging at 'em till they do."

"You make it sound easy," Runolf Skallagrim said.

The adventurer grinned at him, there in the gloom. "It is easy . . . to sound that way. But we aren't whipped yet . . . quite."

XVII

Hamnet Thyssen stared glumly at the snow-covered trees. Fires burned in a clearing in the woods. But for Audun Gilli's small spell to get them started, the men and the handful of women who still remained with him might have had to do without.

Chunks of meat from a short-faced bear toasted over the fires. The bear was a fierce hunter, but no match for hungry men. Hamnet liked bear meat well enough. He wished he didn't have to eat it now, though. He wished he were closer to Raumsdalia's heart, close enough to go on eating beef and mutton.

He glanced toward Marcovefa. She still hadn't come back to herself. He had no idea when—or if—she would. Audun and Liv had done everything they knew how to do. It wasn't enough. She ate and drank if you put food or water in her mouth. Sometimes she smiled or frowned in her sleep. That was as close as she came to real life. But without her, all of Hamnet's wishes were in vain.

He couldn't help thinking she would have laughed and solved the mistletoe spell in a heartbeat—had the arrow struck someone else. That reflection did him no good at all, nor her, either. She didn't seem to be getting any worse. With such small encouragements Hamnet had to console himself.

None of the short-faced bear went to waste. The Raumsdalians might not have thought to roast the chitterlings, but the Bizogots did. When the Bizogots lit on a carcass, they left nothing but bare bones behind—and they'd split those for the marrow inside. Up on the frozen steppe, everything had a use. It had to have one, because the steppe held so little.

That also held true for the forest, as Count Hamnet knew too well. Towns in these parts had survived because they got grain from farther south. With the Rulers loose in the Empire, the towns wouldn't get any this winter. How many people would starve before spring?

One worry led to another. Hamnet walked over to Ulric Skakki, who was doing his own rough cooking. "How long can we last in the woods?" Hamnet asked without preamble.

"Why, till we starve, of course," Ulric answered lightly. He took his gobbet out of the flames and blew on it. When he tried to take a bite, he grimaced. "Still too cursed hot. Well, it won't be for long, God knows, not in this weather."

"Can we keep going here till spring?" Hamnet persisted. "Or would we do better to head back up onto the steppe?"

Ulric didn't answer right away; the meat had cooled enough to let him eat it. After a heroic bite and swallow, he said, "We'd have plenty up there in the springtime—that's for sure. All those waterfowl coming to nest . . ."

"Yes." Hamnet Thyssen nodded. That endless profusion of ducks and geese and swans . . . "The question is, how do we keep from starving in the meantime?"

Ulric took another bite. In due course, he said, "Eating something is a pretty good plan."

"You're being annoying on purpose," Hamnet said.

"You noticed!" The adventurer made as if to kiss him.

"Enough foolishness. Too much foolishness," Hamnet growled. Ulric Skakki looked at him as if he'd just said something very foolish. Ignoring that, Hamnet stubbornly pushed ahead: "The foraging isn't good here. You know it as well as I do, maybe better."

"It isn't good anywhere during the winter," Ulric pointed out, which was nothing less than the truth. "This is the hard time of year. Lots of people go hungry before the snow melts."

"Do you think the Rulers are hungry?" Hamnet asked.

"I hope so," Ulric said, which was something less than a yes.

"What are we going to do?" Hamnet asked: a question better aimed at God, perhaps, than at Ulric Skakki.

"Fight. Give up. Do whatever you please. Me, I'm going to make sure I don't go hungry, at least for a while." The adventurer took another large bite of bear meat. Thus encouraged, Hamnet Thyssen went away.

Runolf Skallagrim crouched in the snow in front of another fire, talking with Eyvind Torfinn. Hamnet supposed he was glad Eyvind had stuck with them; the earl knew a lot that might prove useful. The only drawback to having him along was having Gudrid along with him.

She was also eating a chunk of bear. Grease ran down her chin. Count Hamnet turned away before their eyes could meet. If he talked to her, they would only have another row. He didn't feel like it right this minute. He didn't feel like much of anything, except maybe lying down in a snowdrift and not getting up again.

Trasamund methodically stropped his sword blade. The

jarl looked like a man who expected more fighting and aimed to do the best he could with it. He nodded to Hamnet Thyssen. Crouching beside him, Hamnet nodded back. He might quarrel with Trasamund, but it wouldn't be the soul-scarring kind of slanging match he'd have with Gudrid.

"Did you think, when we met in the Emperor's palace, it would come to this?" he asked the Bizogot.

"Not me, by God!" Trasamund hardly looked up from his careful stropping. "I never dreamt there were folk who could beat the Bizogots." Fog spurted from his nostrils as he snorted. "Shows what I know, eh?"

"Shows what we all knew," Hamnet answered. "Do you still think we can win?"

"If Marcovefa comes back to herself, we've got a good chance—a decent chance, anyway. Otherwise . . ." Trasamund shrugged. "Well, who knows?" He left off stropping, tested the edge with his thumb, and grunted in satisfaction. Then he glanced over to Hamnet. "Have you tried horning her awake?"

"No." Hamnet's mouth twisted in distaste. "It would be like lying with a corpse."

"You wouldn't be doing it for fun," Trasamund said deliberately. "You'd be doing it because it might work."

"If I thought it would, that'd be different," Hamnet said. "But I haven't got any reason to think so—and neither do you."

"*Something's* got to," the jarl said.

"If magic doesn't, screwing's not likely to." Hamnet almost wished he'd picked a fight with Gudrid. "And magic cursed well doesn't—our magic, anyway."

"I know. That's why I think we should try something else," Trasamund said.

"She wouldn't even know it was going on." Hamnet

scowled at the Bizogot. "I've never been one to enjoy lay-ing women who were too drunk even to know I was there."

"It wouldn't be sport," Trasamund insisted.

Hamnet Thyssen got to his feet. "Too right it wouldn't." He strode away before Trasamund could say anything more.

MAYBE TRASAMUND WOULD have taken up the argu-ment again the next morning. He never got the chance, though, because the Rulers struck at the Raumsdalians and Bizogots at first light, riding out of a snowstorm and send-ing clouds of arrows ahead of them as they came. One sen-try came out of the swirling snow a couple of minutes before the invaders from beyond the Gap struck the main encampment. How he escaped ambush—or perhaps the Rulers' sorcery—Hamnet never found out. He never would, either, because the man died in the fighting that followed. But if the sentry hadn't brought at least a little warning, the Rulers would have stormed in by surprise, and that would have ended that.

As things were, a countervolley greeted the attackers. It tumbled several of them off their riding deer and slowed the charge from the rest. That let some of the men Hamnet led jump on their horses and storm forward. And it bought enough time for the rest to retreat.

Instead of getting caught in their clearing, the Bizogots and Raumsdalians could shoot from the cover of the trees. More Rulers and riding deer went down. For a while, Ham-net hoped the enemy had bitten off more than they could chew.

But then more Rulers struck the defenders from the east. Hamnet realized that they'd planned a two-pronged assault, but the prongs hadn't come together at quite the right moment. Struck from the front and the flank now, he found himself in a poor position to criticize the foe for faulty generalship.

"What are we going to do?" Runolf Skallagrim howled.

"Fight as much as we have to, then try to get away," Hamnet answered. "If you've got a better notion, I'd love to hear it."

"I was hoping you did," Runolf said.

Had the attack gone the way the Rulers doubtless drew it up before they launched it, it would have finished things even without surprise. Again, something must have gone wrong somewhere. Hardly anything in war ever worked just the way you planned it. Hamnet had learned that the hard way many years earlier. Now he reaped the benefits of it, such as they were.

Survival. Considering the alternative, he wasn't sorry to take it, even if he would have wanted more. "Why weren't you ready for this?" Gudrid screamed at him. "They might kill me!"

"Wouldn't that be a shame?" Hamnet nocked an arrow and shot at a shape he saw dimly through blowing snow. Harsh, guttural curses said he'd hit someone. They also said he hadn't killed his man. He wished he would have.

"Why weren't you ready?" Gudrid asked again.

"If you're so unhappy, go back to where we rescued you from the Rulers," Hamnet said. "I'm sure they'd take you again."

"Oh!" She spat at him, but it fell short in the snow. "You are the most hateful man in the world!"

"Now maybe you understand why I always thought we were so well matched," Count Hamnet returned. Gudrid said something that should have steamed all the snow for miles around. Hamnet bowed, which only made her come back with something hotter yet.

He paid less attention to her than she no doubt wanted

him to. Another Ruler on a riding deer came out of the swirling snow. Hamnet's arrow caught the deer in the neck. Blood fountained, all the redder for being displayed against the white. The deer went down. So did the warrior atop it.

Hamnet Thyssen urged his horse forward, drawing his sword. The Ruler was still scrambling to his feet when Hamnet's cut caught him just below and in front of the left ear. He let out a bubbling shriek and clutched at the spouting wound. Hamnet slashed again. The Ruler fell, scrabbling in the snow. He tried to push himself upright once more, but crumpled instead.

Satisfied he was out of the fight, Count Hamnet rode back and nocked another arrow. He was glad the bow hadn't fallen in the snow in his charge.

Runolf Skallagrim was bleeding from a nicked ear. Like scalp wounds, ears bled so much that anything that happened to them seemed much worse than it really was. Runolf might not even have noticed how much blood spattered his mailshirt. "We've got to pull back, Thyssen!" he said. "We're for it if we stand and fight much longer!"

"Now tell me something I didn't know," Hamnet answered bitterly. "Do you have any notion how much I hate running away from those whoresons again, though? Any notion at all?"

"I probably don't," Runolf admitted. "But how do you feel about them murdering the lot of us?"

"I'm against it," Hamnet said, which jerked a laugh from Baron Runolf. "I didn't say I wouldn't run—just that I didn't like it. And I cursed well don't."

"Well, neither do I," Runolf said. "But I'm with you—I like getting murdered even less. And that's what'll happen to us if we stick around much longer."

"I know." Hamnet Thyssen hated admitting that, which

didn't mean he had any choice. He asked the most important question he could find: "Is Marcovefa still safe?"

"She is," Runolf assured him, adding, "Skakki's got her up onto a horse."

He didn't mean mounted; he meant tied aboard a pack horse like a sack of dried peas. All the same, Count Hamnet nodded. "Ulric will know how to take care of it, all right." An arrow from nowhere hissed through the air between them. Hamnet nodded again, in spite of himself. "Yes, we'd better get moving."

"About time," Runolf Skallagrim said, nothing but relief in his voice. "I only hope it isn't past time."

It turned out not to be. The Rulers had had as much of the fight as they wanted, at least for the moment. If their pincer claws had worked better . . . It was, Hamnet supposed, ever so slightly reassuring to find they could make mistakes like anyone else.

They didn't pursue very hard. The forest wasn't their favorite ground, any more than it was the Bizogots'. At another time, Hamnet would have tried to turn that against them. As things were, he had to content himself with taking advantage of it.

Liv and Audun Gilli and a Raumsdalian soldier who'd been a doctor's helper did what they could for the injured. They extracted arrows from wounds, bandaged and sutured, and used both leechcraft and sorcery to stop bleeding. Against pain they could offer very little. "Has anyone got any poppy juice?" called the soldier, whose name, Hamnet thought, was Narfi.

No one said anything. After a small silence, Narfi swore. So did the man whose hurts he was tending.

Hamnet Thyssen was too worn and weary and gloomy to swear. He kept looking north. How long before they were out on the Bizogot steppe again? What could they hope to do if the Rulers pushed them out of Raumsdalia altogether? *Not much*, he thought. *Not bloody much*. But they'd already spilled too much blood to be able to give up now.

And chances were the Rulers wouldn't let him give up anyway. For whatever reason, they were convinced he was somehow especially dangerous to them. So was Marcovefa. Hamnet only wished he could see why.

Marcovefa was dangerous to them. He knew that. And they'd found a way to silence her. Only luck no stray arrows in the last fight pierced her. She couldn't do anything to defend herself against them, not now.

Nobody seemed able to do much against the Rulers. Maybe they would end up holding everything from the Gap down to Raumsdalia. If they ended up knocking Sigvat II over the head, that might almost be worth it.

Hamnet sighed. *Almost* was one of the cruelest words in the language.

HE'D HOPED THE Rulers would be satisfied with trouncing their foes once and would leave them alone for a while afterward. But he'd also seen how wide the gap between what you hoped for and what you got could yawn.

He kept scouts as far south in the forest as he could, to give warning in case he didn't get what he hoped for. And he didn't, as he discovered sooner than he wanted to.

The scouts were all Raumsdalians. The Bizogots, by the nature of things, knew little of woodscraft. One of Runolf Skallagrim's men rode back to the camp calling, "They're coming. God help us, they're all coming!"

"What do you mean, all?" Hamnet asked, hoping the scout meant anything but what it sounded like he meant.

No such luck. "Every Ruler in the world," the excited

man gasped. "War mammoths! Everything! I just saw the front end of it, but there's got to be a demon of a lot of it I didn't stick around to see!"

"Have they gone mad?" Trasamund rumbled. "They don't need all that to squash us. It's like dropping a musk ox on a mosquito."

"Maybe the Emperor is dead," Eyvind Torfinn said. "With Sigvat gone, they'd have nothing to fear in the south, and could concentrate all their power against us. We may be the last force in the field against them."

Hamnet refused to believe it. "They had nothing to fear in the south with Sigvat alive," he said. "They proved it, too, again and again. They might need to worry if they did knock the sorry scut over the head. Then they'd run the risk that somebody who knows what he's doing would take over and start fighting back."

Earl Eyvind looked sorrowful. Hamnet didn't care. As far as he knew, Sigvat had never thrown Eyvind into a dungeon for the horrendous crime of being right. Hamnet feared he himself had to plead guilty to that one.

Gudrid, by contrast, lapped up his words with vampire avidity. He knew exactly what that meant. If by some accident the Rulers didn't slaughter everyone here, and if by some bigger accident Sigvat triumphed in the south, she would tell the Emperor everything Hamnet had said. Then Hamnet would go back to the dungeon, or maybe to the chopping block, and she would have her reward.

At some other time, Hamnet would have hated her for that. He couldn't afford to indulge himself now. "There's no chance we can fight them?" he asked the Raumsdalian.

The man shook his head. His eyes were wide and frightened. "I didn't know there were that many of the buggers around," he replied.

Clutching at straws, Count Hamnet turned to Liv and

Audun Gilli. "Any hope it's a fancy bluff, with magic blowing up their numbers the way you blow up a pig's bladder before you put it on a stick?"

Bizogot shaman and Raumsdalian wizard both turned south in the same motion. They made a more natural pair than Hamnet ever had with Liv. He could see as much, however little he relished what he saw. The two of them tasted the frigid air like hunting hounds seeking a scent. Liv's lips moved as she murmured a spell. Audun's hands twisted in quick, abbreviated passes.

They both stiffened at the same time. Audun flinched as if someone had slapped him. Liv went nearly as pale as the snow that lay all around. "It's no bluff," she said softly. "They really are that strong. They want us to be able to feel how strong they are."

"God help us," Audun added.

"What do we do, then?" Hamnet asked.

"Run!" they said together. Liv went on, "If Marcovefa were awake, she might be able to slow them down. Since she isn't . . ." She shook her head. Even her lips had gone colorless.

"If we run, we'll likely have to leave the woods—leave Raumsdalia," Hamnet said.

"Wouldn't break *my* heart," Trasamund said.

"I know. But you aren't a Raumsdalian," Count Hamnet said.

"And thank God for that!" the Bizogot exclaimed.

"We do, almost every day." Ulric Skakki was rarely shy about dipping his oar in the water.

Trasamund glared at him. "Should I be so glad you're no clansman of mine?" He answered his own question: "You'd best believe I should. You'd make nothing but trouble in among the mammoth-hide tents."

"I can't help it if your women like my looks," the

adventurer said blandly, which won him another glare from Trasamund.

"Enough, both of you," Hamnet said. "Do you think we can fight the Rulers and hope to win?"

Ulric and the jarl looked at each other. Ulric shook his head without the least hesitation. Trasamund's response was slower and more reluctant, but in the end the same.

Hamnet didn't think they could fight the invaders, either. He thought they'd have to be suicidal to try. But the others might have disagreed with him. Since they didn't, he said, "Then let's get away while we still can."

"That's the smartest thing I've heard from you for a long time," Ulric told him.

"I love you, too—but not right now," Hamnet said. Ulric Skakki's laugh seemed equal parts scorn and appreciation. He ambled off to see to his horse.

They got moving before the Rulers came down on them. Count Hamnet stayed behind to command the rear guard. "You shouldn't," Liv told him. "If anything happens to you, our cause is ruined. Marcovefa said so, and I think she's right."

He shrugged. "You can't go on asking other people to put their lives on the line for you unless you put yours on the line with them every so often. They won't follow your orders if you don't, and demons take me if I see why they ought to."

"Some things are more important than a little fight like this," Liv insisted. Hamnet shrugged again. The glare she gave him put to shame the ones Trasamund had aimed at Ulric Skakki. Blue, blue eyes blazing, she went on, "All right, then. If you *must* stay behind, I will, too, and I will keep you alive if I can. You dunderhead."

"And I'll stay," Audun Gilli added.

"No. You go on. The rest will need magic, too, and

you've got more than any of the others with them," Liv said.

Audun looked mutinous, which was putting it mildly. He was no hero, but he didn't want his woman in more danger than he was—and who could blame him for that? No doubt he also didn't want Liv staying behind with her former lover—and who could blame him for that, either?

But when he tried to protest, she said, "Go. Just go." She looked as if she would draw her dagger if he said another word. Sometimes all the argument in the world wouldn't do you a corroded copper's worth of good. Audun Gilli had the sense to recognize that this was one of those times. He mooched off, kicking at the snow because he could find no better vent for his feelings.

"You don't have to do this," Hamnet said to Liv. "Not for my sake."

"Don't talk about what you don't understand," she answered, a response that almost precluded conversation.

As he waited for the Rulers, he eyed the troop of Bizogots and Raumsdalians who waited with him. They seemed steady enough. If they were impressed that he'd chosen to stay behind, too, they hid it very well. Liv's glance said, *I told you so.* She wasn't his lover any more, though, so he could ignore her without suffering for it later. Audun wasn't so lucky.

Mastodons roamed the woods by Hamnet's castle in southeastern Raumsdalia. They ate acorns and chestnuts and other nuts along with leaves and roots. There wasn't enough to support them, or the mammoths of the northern steppe, in these northern forests. That made the sight of eight or ten war mammoths coming through the firs and spruces toward him all the more jolting. *They don't belong here!* his mind shouted. The Rulers on the mammoths' backs didn't care what he thought.

The invaders shouted to one another in their harsh, braying language. First one, then another, pointed straight at him. How they could pick him out from anybody else in the rear guard he didn't know, but they could.

"You see?" Liv said quietly. She got *I told you so* into half as many words—not a bad trick.

Hamnet didn't answer. What could he say? When the Rulers started shooting, all the arrows seemed to head straight for him. Every soldier on every battlefield since the beginning of time had to feel the same way, but Hamnet feared it was literally true this time.

He threw up his shield just in time to deflect one that would have got him in the face. The arrow skipped off the bronze facing and over his head. He breathed a sigh of relief. Then he wondered why he bothered. No matter what Marcovefa thought, whether he lived or died mattered little to him.

But he was too obstinate not to make the best fight he could. He shot a Ruler off a riding deer, then—more by luck than by design—hit a war mammoth in the trunk with another arrow. The woolly mammoth wore armor of leather dipped in boiling wax, as did a lot of the Rulers. It was almost as good as chain mail, and much lighter. But the mammoth's masters hadn't tried to armor that sinuous, flexible trunk (Hamnet wouldn't have wanted to try, either).

And the trunk was as sensitive as a man's nose, or perhaps as sensitive as his hands. The war mammoth trumpeted in pain and indignation. One of the men on its back patted it—roughly, through the boiled leather. Count Hamnet thought the Ruler meant to show sympathy: more than they were in the habit of doing for any men not of their own kind.

No good deed went unpunished. The mammoth could still use its wounded member. It plucked up the Ruler and threw him down in the snow in front of it. His terrified shriek cut off abruptly as the mammoth's right foot crushed the life out of him. The great beast left one red footprint out of four for some little while after that. The other warriors who rode on it sat very quietly, trying their best not to remind it they were there.

"Well done!" Liv said warmly.

"It won't matter much in the long run. We've got to pull back any which way," Hamnet answered. He didn't want her praising him. It reminded him of what they'd been not so long before. He hadn't lain with a woman since Marcovefa went down. Wasn't life complicated enough without fresh temptations?

An arrow zipped past his head, venomously close. He realized what a bad position he was in to be worrying about any kind of temptations, fresh, salted, or pickled.

Then one of the Raumsdalians in the rear guard pointed and exclaimed, "What the demon's that?"

For a moment, Hamnet Thyssen thought it was nothing but blowing snow. Then he realized that, while it *was* blowing snow, it wasn't nothing but blowing snow. It was blowing snow and sorcery. The sorcery packed it together tighter than blowing snow had any right to get, and gave it a shape distinct from the randomly blowing snow all around it. That shape was much too much like a man's. But it was bigger than a man had any business being, and it had much larger arms.

It also had an awareness to it, an awareness that Hamnet immediately thought of as wolfish. Why, he couldn't have said, not consciously. The feeling welled up from the place that made his balls want to crawl up into his belly and his hair stand straight on the back of his neck.

Not only that, its awareness centered on him, or perhaps aimed at him. Those long, snowy arms outstretched, it strode purposefully in his direction. It left no footprints, red or otherwise. He might have known all along that it sought his life in particular. Part of him *had* known all along: the part that made his balls crawl up and his hackles rise.

He nocked an arrow and let fly. It was a shot he could have been proud of—straight through the heart, if a snow devil had a heart. Evidently not, for it didn't fall.

It did laugh at him. Its laughter was winter wind congealed: all the cold and emptiness in the world, boiled down to a pint. Count Hamnet had pierced its heart without harming it. The snow devil's laughter pierced his heart, too, pierced it and almost froze it shut.

Don't be foolish, he thought. *You did that to yourself years ago.*

Before he could even wonder what he meant, Liv started a spell. It was in a dialect of the Bizogot language so old-fashioned, he could hardly follow it. He would rather have tried to gallop away, though he had no guarantee his horse could outrun a thing half made of gale.

Then Liv switched to urgent Raumsdalian: "Quick! Shoot it again!"

"What good will that do? What good will anything do?" Yes, the snow devil had done its best to freeze Hamnet's heart, and its best was better than he'd dreamt possible.

"Shoot it!" Liv slapped his face.

His shocked bellow wasn't so loud or so shrill as the war mammoth's had been when he shot it, but was no less startled, no less outraged. He almost shot Liv. But instead he drove another arrow through the snow devil—easy now, when it was so close.

As chunks of ice broke to start an avalanche, did they scream? If they did, they surely let out a cry like the one that ripped from the snow devil when Hamnet's second arrow struck. This shaft, unlike the one that had gone before it, wounded the sorcerous apparition. No—it slew.

Wind had made the snow devil coalesce. And wind tore it to pieces in the blink of an eye. One heartbeat, it was about to lay hold of Count Hamnet. What would have happened then, he didn't know: only that it would have been nothing good. But the snow devil was gone the next heartbeat, gone as if it never existed.

"Well shot!" Liv yelled.

"Well spelled!" Hamnet yelled back.

Somewhere among the Rulers, a shriek almost as full of torment as the snow devil's burst from a man's throat. Maybe the snow devil's throat was meant for such sounds; a man's assuredly wasn't. How much of himself had the enemy wizard poured into his sorcerous creation? Enough to ruin him—worse than ruin him—when it was all lost at once.

But for that shriek, Hamnet might have kissed Liv, or she him. With it still echoing inside them, they both fought shy of that. The torment it held put out passion the same way a brass candle-snuffer dampened flame.

A nod sufficed Hamnet, then. "You did what you needed to do," he told her. She nodded, her face half proud, half horrified at what she'd unwittingly inflicted on the Rulers' sorcerer.

"I wouldn't want to do that to anyone—not even one of those people," Liv said with shudder.

Count Hamnet grunted. "He wouldn't waste any grief on you."

"Even so," Liv insisted. Remembering what the other wizard sounded like after the snow devil perished, Hamnet decided she had a point.

Another arrow snarled through the air between him and Liv. Maybe the archer who loosed it couldn't decide which of them he would sooner have killed. Maybe the next bowman wouldn't have any trouble making up his mind. Or maybe he'd just turn out to be a better shot. "Do you think we've given the main force enough time to get away?" Hamnet Thyssen asked.

"Yes. And I think *you* had better get away," Liv answered. "That snow fiend or whatever you want to call it only makes things plainer—the Rulers want you dead, and they don't care what they do to get you that way."

Hamnet grunted again. He didn't think he was important in the grand scheme of things, and resented that anyone should think so when he didn't. Ordering the Raumsdalians and Bizogots with him to fall back meant he didn't have to dwell on what anybody else thought.

The Rulers came after the rear guard, but less enthusiastically than they'd attacked at first. A wounded war mammoth and a wizard dreadfully disabled if not dead gave them pause. They were men like any others, no matter how they tried to disguise it with ferocity. Getting reminded of that reassured Hamnet . . . a little.

"They're going to let us get away." One of the Raumsdalians sounded even more relieved—and even more surprised—than Hamnet was.

Somewhere ahead of him, the main force would be heading . . . where? Up onto the Bizogot plains? Where else were they likely to go? And not nearly far enough behind him, the Rulers were getting ready to pursue them. Somehow or other, his friends would have to take along the still-unconscious Marcovefa.

That brought something else to the top of Hamnet Thyssen's mind. "Ask you a question?" he said to Liv.

"It's hard to ask anything else," she replied, as if she were Ulric Skakki. Then she nodded. "Go ahead."

He gave her Trasamund's suggestion, finishing, "Has

that got any chance of working, or is it as disgusting as it sounds to me?"

He expected it would disgust her even more, not least because she was a woman. To be taken unawares, so to speak . . . But she gave it her usual careful consideration. At last, she said, "Well, I don't see how it could hurt. What's the worst thing that could happen? You get her with child. You might do that when she's awake, too."

"But— But—" Hamnet had to work to make himself quit sputtering. "But do you think it would do any good?"

"I don't know. It might connect her to this world again—or, of course, it might not," Liv answered. "Maybe it's worth a try. Who can say? If she knew why you were doing it, I think she'd forgive you, if that makes you feel any better." It didn't, or not much. Hamnet rode on, wishing he'd kept his mouth shut.

XVIII

The Bizogot steppe. Again. Hamnet Thyssen could imagine no gloomier words, no gloomier setting. But his being here had nothing to do with his imagination. For better or worse—as things seemed, mostly for worse— here he was in truth.

He could see a long way. Except for the south, where the woods that marked Raumsdalia's frontier still lingered on the horizon, he might have been able to see forever. He knew he couldn't, but the illusion was very strong.

It felt all the stronger because he'd come out from among the trees so recently. They didn't simply cut down how far you could see. They also made the eye focus more clearly than it had to here on the plain.

Hamnet didn't see any war mammoths coming after the battered remnant of the force that still resisted the Rulers. He didn't see any of the invaders on their riding deer. He didn't miss them, either. If he never saw them again, he wouldn't have shed a tear.

When he said as much to Ulric Skakki, the adventurer shrugged an elaborate shrug. "Well, neither would I,"

Ulric said. "But that doesn't mean I don't expect to see them before long."

"I know." Hamnet bared his teeth in something that wished it were a smile. "They'll be along sooner than we wish they would. I never thought the rear guard would be able to do as much to them as we did."

"Good for you, by God," Ulric said.

"Good for Liv," Count Hamnet said. "She deserves the credit. If not for her, that snow devil would have slaughtered the lot of us—starting with me." He shuddered at the memory. Had those frozen arms closed on him . . . He didn't know what would have happened. The only thing he knew was, it would have been about as bad as anything could be.

Ulric raised an amused eyebrow. "If you listen to her tell it, Your Grace, you're the hero."

"Me?" Hamnet snorted. "That's ridiculous! All I did was stay alive, and I didn't think I'd manage that."

"Ridiculous, eh?" Ulric's eyebrow climbed higher yet; Hamnet hadn't thought it could. "Audun Gilli doesn't think so. The way he's moping around, he thinks Liv's going back to you any minute now."

"He may think so. I don't," Hamnet said.

"Yes. I know." Ulric Skakki. "But then, you've always been blind to what women are really thinking, haven't you?"

Hamnet opened his mouth to deny that indignantly. Then he closed it without saying anything. When he opened it again after some thought, what came out was, "I wouldn't be surprised."

"No, no. You're always surprised—that's what I'm trying to tell you," Ulric said. Count Hamnet made as if to hit him. Laughing, Ulric ducked.

"You know what I meant. You're being difficult on purpose," Hamnet Thyssen said. Ulric doffed his fur cap, as if at a compliment. Hamnet might have know he would, but continued anyhow: "Besides, not only is Liv not my woman any more, I've got another one."

"Well, so you do," Ulric allowed. "But does it still count when she's gone into hibernation?"

"I . . . don't know," Hamnet said slowly. Then he told the adventurer what Trasamund had suggested.

Ulric never wasted time making up his mind. "You ought to try it," he said at once. "Even if it doesn't work, how are you worse off? How are any of us worse off, eh?"

"The idea's disgusting," Hamnet said.

"I don't see how," Ulric Skakki answered. "No more than bedding a woman after she's had too much to drink. If you tell me you've never done that, I'll call you a liar to your face. And if she cares for you to begin with, she won't mind—not as long as you don't make a habit of it, anyhow."

"Mmpf," Hamnet said. Ulric could be much more persuasive than Trasamund was. "I still don't think it'd do us any good."

"How are you worse off if it doesn't?" Ulric repeated. "It won't hurt you to try. I've heard some people even enjoy it." Hamnet made as if to hit him again. Ulric had to duck faster this time. As he did, he added, "It won't hurt Marcovefa, either, not unless you're even clumsier than I think you— Ow!" Hamnet did hit him that time.

"You deserved it," Hamnet said.

"That's what you think," Ulric said. "Did you ask Liv about this? What did she tell you?"

"She told me I should," Hamnet answered reluctantly.

"Well, then, you ought to listen to her," Ulric Skakki said.

Count Hamnet scowled. "It's like forcing a woman. By God, it *is* forcing a woman. That's never been my notion of a good time. Besides, any man who forces a woman who's also a wizard will probably end up a eunuch. Or if he doesn't, he'll wish he did, because something worse will happen to him."

"I could point out that you're a stiff-necked idiot," Ulric said.

"You don't need to. I already know that," Hamnet told him.

"I'm so glad. But that isn't what I was going to say." Ulric looked and sounded exasperated. "I was going to say that you force a woman you don't know, or maybe a woman you hate. You and Gudrid, now . . ."

"Leave Gudrid out of this," Hamnet said in a voice that might have blown straight off the Glacier. It wasn't that he hadn't thought of forcing her and then cutting her throat, or maybe his own. He had. One of the things that held him back was the conviction she'd be laughing at him while one of them or the other gurgled toward death.

Ulric made placating motions. "I was, I was. Here's what I was trying to tell you. You don't hate Marcovefa, right?"

"You know I don't. You'd better know I don't," Hamnet said.

"Yes, yes. Fine. Wonderful," the adventurer said. "If you love her, if you do this with love—or with something as close to love as your wizened little soul has in it—you won't be forcing her. If it works, if she wakes up, she'll thank you."

"And I thank you for your sweet and generous compliment," Hamnet Thyssen said.

Ulric doffed his cap again. "I am your servant, Your Grace."

"You're the south end of a northbound horse, is what you are," Hamnet said.

The cap came off once more. "You say the kindest

things. But kindly let me finish. If it doesn't work, if you don't rouse her, the Rulers will kill all of us—you, her, me, everybody—pretty soon anyhow. It won't matter. So either you'll do some good or you won't, but I don't see you hurting anything much."

That made much more sense than Hamnet wished it did. It made so much sense, he couldn't think of a thing to say in reply. Instead of saying anything, he turned his back and walked away from Ulric Skakki. The adventurer called his name. Count Hamnet kept walking. If Ulric had laughed, Hamnet might have turned back . . . with murder in his heart. But Ulric, for a wonder, had the sense to keep his mouth shut.

Tramping along staring down at his own feet, his head full of unhappy thoughts, Hamnet almost bumped into someone. That made him look up—and wish he hadn't. "You might say, 'Excuse me,'" Gudrid told him.

She was the last person he wanted to have anything to do with then, which only proved God didn't pay attention to what he wanted. *As if I didn't know*, he thought sourly. Aloud, he said, "I might do all kinds of things. None of them has anything to do with you."

"Oh, I know that. You might screw the blond savage, for instance, when she isn't awake to tell you what a miserable—"

Count Hamnet knocked her down. It wasn't quite a punch, but she landed in the snow suddenly enough to startle a squawk out of her. Breathing hard, Hamnet said, "I've listened to everyone else about that. I don't have to listen to you—and I don't intend to, either."

Gudrid got to her feet. She was ready to say something more: Hamnet could read it in her eyes. But whatever she read in his eyes made her shut her mouth with a snap. After a cautious pause, all she did say was, "Well, if you're going to be that way about it . . ."

"You'd best believe I am," Hamnet growled. He strode away from her as he had from Ulric Skakki. Like Ulric, Gudrid realized her usual mockery wouldn't be a good idea now.

This time, Hamnet tramped along with his head up. If he kept an eye out for trouble, maybe he could steer clear of it. He walked away from Runolf Skallagrim. Runolf hadn't given him advice about Marcovefa, but that didn't mean the other Raumsdalian wouldn't.

And he walked away from Trasamund. The jarl had already told him what he thought. That wouldn't stop Trasamund from doing it again. Trasamund liked to hear himself talk, and he was stubbornly convinced he was right all the time. A whole great swarm of mistakes he'd made weren't enough to convince him otherwise.

But was he making a mistake this time?

"Whatever I do, it will be wrong. Everybody will blame me for it, whatever it turns out to be," Hamnet muttered. But that wasn't the worst. He knew what the worst was. "Whatever it turns out to be, I'll blame myself for it."

Did he want to blame himself for doing nothing or for doing something? Either one might be wrong. If he did nothing, things wouldn't change. That seemed obvious. If he did something . . . his suspicion was that things wouldn't change anyway. Then he would have done something he would much rather not have, and would have done it for no reason.

His mittened hands folded into fists. "It will be wrong," he said again.

Marcovefa would have laughed at his dithering. He could hear her inside his mind. She never seemed to have doubts. *Yes, and look what not having them got her*, Hamnet thought.

Stamping along by himself didn't do him any good. He went back to the camp. Liv was feeding Marcovefa bits of broiled hare and giving her sips of water melted from snow. If Marcovefa couldn't chew and swallow, she would have starved by now. As things were, she'd lost flesh; her skin stretched tight across her cheekbones. They'd all done the best they could to give her enough, but feeding her as much as she would have eaten on her own wasn't easy.

"Any change?" Hamnet asked.

Liv shook her head. "None I can find." She might have said more—Hamnet could see that. She might have, but she sensibly didn't. She understood Hamnet well enough to know that trying to push him toward something was more likely to make him go away from it.

Trasamund and Ulric Skakki had never figured that out. Actually, Hamnet wasn't so sure about Ulric. Say what you would about the adventurer, but he was a clever fellow. Chances were he knew how Hamnet worked. Sometimes, though, he used what he knew for his own amusement, not for what others might think of as the general good.

Count Hamnet brought himself back to what lay before him. "Is she wet?" he asked.

"Let me see." Liv reached under the waistband of Marcovefa's trousers, as she might have with a toddler. She shook her head again. "No, she's still dry. I changed her not long ago." She paused. "She's eaten about as much as it looks like she's going to, too."

"All right. I'll take her to my tent for the night." Hamnet bent and lifted Marcovefa. Yes, she'd lost weight since the mistletoe arrowhead struck her down. Her lips shaped a smile as Hamnet straightened with her in his arms. Her eyelids fluttered, but her eyes didn't open. Not for the first time, Hamnet wondered how much went on inside her head. And, not for the first time, he owned himself baffled—he had no way to know.

Keeping Marcovefa from freezing while the Breath of God blew was hardly easier than keeping her fed. They swaddled her in furs and blankets and hoped for the best. So far, the best had been good enough. She hadn't even got frostbitten fingers or toes. Raumsdalians knew a lot about fighting cold. Bizogots knew even more.

Hamnet's tent had thick mammoth-hide walls, with the long, dark hair still on the outside. It was crowded for two, but that was all right; it let their body heat warm the air inside faster.

No one but he would know what went on inside the tent. Well, Marcovefa might, but he didn't really believe she would. That was what had held him back ever since Trasamund suggested . . . what he suggested. The idea reminded Hamnet too much of lying with a corpse.

But if he tried it once, after it failed he could tell Trasamund . . . and Ulric Skakki . . . and Liv . . . and Gudrid . . . and Runolf Skallagrim . . . and anyone else who asked him that it *had* failed. Then maybe people would leave him alone. He could hope so, anyhow. Of course, the odds were that after it failed the Rulers would overrun them pretty soon. In that case, he would be too dead to need to justify himself to anybody.

He looked at Marcovefa, there in the gloom barely pushed back by one sputtering, fat-stinking lamp. She might have lain peacefully asleep—but he knew too well she didn't.

If it does some good, she'll forgive you. If it doesn't, she'll never know, he thought. The same thing had occurred to him many times before. What had always stopped him was that, if it did no good, *he* would know.

Maybe it was worth one try, for the sake of the fight against the Rulers. He knew he wouldn't be doing it for his own pleasure. And, a moment later, he knew he was talking himself into doing what he'd intended not to do.

And so he did. No one would be able to say any more that he hadn't done everything he and anybody else could think of. He still had trouble believing it would make a difference when nothing else had. *But there is—I suppose there is—the chance I'm wrong. As if I've never been wrong before!*

He made love to her as if she really were there with him, as if she could enjoy it, too. If he was going to rouse her, didn't he need to rouse her in a different way first? Or did he? Was the connection between this and waking her entirely mystical?

Was it entirely imaginary? Even as he moved, that struck him as much more likely.

He finished. Then he pulled up his trousers and put Marcovefa's back onto her. Even with the tent flap closed, even with the two of them in that small space, it wasn't warm in there.

Then he waited. And he waited. And he waited a little longer. And, when nothing happened, he went on waiting till the lamp ran out of fat and went dark, plunging the inside of the tent into something that would do for darkness absolute till he met the genuine article.

And then, weary and despairing, he lay down beside Marcovefa. He didn't intend to fall asleep. No matter what he intended, he did.

"WHAT HAPPENED IN that fight? How did I get back here? Why don't I remember? Did I get drunk last night? I don't feel hung over."

Hamnet Thyssen opened his eyes. That did him some

good—daylight leaked in through the tent flap, and a bit more under the bottom of the tent. Marcovefa was sitting up beside him. For a moment, he simply accepted that. Then, more slowly than he might have, he took in what it meant. "By God," he whispered. "It worked. It really did."

"What did?" she asked. Before he could answer, she repeated, "I don't feel hung over," and went on, "But why am I so—so tired? It's like I haven't done anything for a long time, so even sitting up like this wears me out."

"Yes." Hamnet nodded dizzily. "It's just like that, as a matter of fact."

"What are you talking about?" Marcovefa, by contrast, sounded irritable. Her stomach rumbled. "I'm hungry," she declared, as if daring him to doubt it. "It's like I haven't had enough to eat for weeks."

"It's just like that, too," Hamnet told her.

"Will you please make sense?" She'd gone beyond irritable—she sounded as if she'd hit him if he didn't do what she told him in a hurry.

"I don't know if I can, but I'll try." Hamnet Thyssen told the story as quickly as he could.

Marcovefa heard him out. She stayed quiet for some time afterward. Then she said, "We are on the steppe again? Not in the forest? If you are making some kind of joke with me . . ."

"Why would I do that?" Hamnet said. "All you have to do is stick your head out of the tent. You'll find out whether I'm telling the truth about that."

"Yes," Marcovefa admitted. Another silence followed. Then she asked, "What is this mistletoe? I never heard of it. We don't have it up on top of the Glacier."

"I'm not surprised," Hamnet said. "It's a small plant. It grows on trees. I don't even know whether the Rulers knew about it before they came down into the Empire.

Maybe they learned about it from a Raumsdalian wizard, or maybe they found out about it by themselves. I don't suppose we'll ever find out. Any which way, they used it on you, and for a long time all the magic we could think of to use didn't do a thing against it."

"And you ended up . . . screwing me awake?" Marcovefa laughed. "Why didn't you think of that sooner?"

"I couldn't believe it would work." Hamnet heard the dull embarrassment in his own voice. "Well, I owe Trasamund an apology. I won't be sorry to give it to him, either." He muttered something under his breath.

"What is that?" she asked.

"I said, it didn't seem right to take you when you weren't there to know what I was doing. Almost like taking an animal."

That made her laugh again, this time in surprise. "All these big animals you have down here—you could do something like that. I never thought of it before. But this worked, so I don't mind. And if it didn't work, I wouldn't mind then, either, because I wouldn't know."

"I finally figured that out for myself," Hamnet answered. "It was about the last thing we had left to try."

"Can I get something to eat now?" Marcovefa asked. "With my belly full, I will figure out how to pay the Rulers back."

"If you can get up, they should have something over at the fires," Hamnet said. "If you can't get up, I'll bring you something. You need to get your strength back—it's been a while."

She tried. She plainly didn't have an easy time of it, but she managed. "*How* long has it been?" she asked, wobbling. Hamnet told her. She shook her head in disbelief. "And I don't remember anything after I got hit, not anything at all. I wondered how I came to the tent, not how half a season passed away. But my body tells me half a season did."

"Well, come on," Hamnet said. "You're here again, and a good thing, too. Not having you told us how much we need you, by God." He hesitated, then added, "And I've missed you."

"I would have missed you," Marcovefa said. "I didn't miss anything."

Hamnet made do with that. He left the tent first, then held out his hand to help Marcovefa. She blinked against the light when she emerged, and swayed like a sapling with the Breath of God blowing. But she stubbornly stayed on her feet.

They'd slaughtered a musk ox the night before. Chunks of the carcass lay in the snow. No worry about keeping meat at this time of year, only about keeping scavengers away from it. Pretty soon, when the sun turned, the weather would warm up—but the scavengers wouldn't go away.

Ulric Skakki was worrying a couple of ribs off a larger slab of meat. Alert as a lion, he looked up the instant he registered motion out of the corner of his eye. But, while motion didn't surprise him, one of the people making the motion did. "What have we here?" he said, jumping to his feet and giving Marcovefa a courtier's bow. "The face is familiar, but the name. . . . It'll come to me, I'm sure." Then he raised an eyebrow in Hamnet's direction. "And?"

One word was plenty. "And Trasamund turned out to be right," Hamnet said. "Who would have imagined it?"

"Everyone but you thought he might be," Ulric answered. "You see? You have a magic wand after all."

That made Marcovefa laugh till she almost fell over. It made Hamnet's ears feel as if they were on fire. "How much more meat is left on that slab?" he asked gruffly. "Enough for her and me?"

"Oh, I expect so." Ulric ambled over to toast the ribs he'd taken.

Hamnet cut off two for Marcovefa and then two more for himself. "I could eat these raw," Marcovefa said. "We would do that every so often, up on the Glacier. Not always enough dried dung for a fire. Raw meat isn't bad."

"I've done it, too," Hamnet said. "Go ahead, if you care to. I like them better cooked, though."

"Well, so do I." Marcovefa made her way over toward the fire. She still swayed, but she managed. Hamnet followed. He was ready to grab her if she faltered, but she didn't. He judged she was running more on determination than strength. Well, determination would serve, at least for a little while.

She didn't cook her meat for very long, but tore at it with strong white teeth. Hamnet let his char a bit more on the outside. He wasn't so desperately empty as she was. He and Liv had done their best to feed her while she was beyond herself, but he knew they hadn't done well enough.

"Ha!" Trasamund shouted the moment he saw Marcovefa. The jarl pointed a beefy forefinger at Hamnet Thyssen. "I told you so. Took you long enough to listen, didn't it?"

"You tell me all kinds of things," Hamnet said. "I suppose you're bound to be right every once in a while." So much for an apology.

Trasamund's answer was brief, definite, and highly obscene. Had he said it in a different way, Hamnet would have tried to kill him. As things were, he only grinned. Marcovefa giggled. She could do that at the same time as she ate. Anything noisier might have made her slow down.

That shout from the Bizogot made other people stick their heads out of their tents to find out what was going on. "They might be so many marmots when a fox yips,"

Marcovefa said. She had an excuse to pause: she'd stripped one rib of meat and was about to start on the other. "I'll want more after this," she told Hamnet.

"Nobody will stop you," he said.

But he wasn't quite right. Trasamund came over and gave Marcovefa a big, smacking kiss. After he broke away from her, musk-ox grease gleamed on his lips. Liv embraced her. So did Runolf Skallagrim and Audun Gilli. Everybody wanted to make much of her. She wanted to eat, and she did.

Ulric Skakki nudged Hamnet. "Nice to have hope again, isn't it?" the adventurer said in a low voice.

"Hope." Count Hamnet tasted the word. In some surprise, he nodded: it seemed even richer and more mouth-filling than musk-ox marrow. "Hope." He said it again, savoring the taste. "Yes, by God. It is!"

"We've been a sad, raggedy lot lately—plague take me if we haven't. Only the stubborn buggers stuck at all," Trasamund said. "Well, things will look better soon. You can boil me for an egg if they don't."

"You can boil all of us if they don't," Hamnet said. The Bizogot jarl didn't try to tell him he was wrong.

The fuss over Marcovefa finally brought Eyvind Torfinn and Gudrid out of their tent. "Well, well!" the scholarly earl said. "What do we have here? Hale again, are you? What splendid news!"

If Gudrid thought the news splendid, she hid it very well. She glanced over to Hamnet. "Dead in bed, just like you," she said.

"Not dead—just asleep. And better that than a foe in bed," Hamnet retorted. They eyed each other with complete mutual loathing. Not for the first time, Hamnet wondered why she didn't back the Rulers since he opposed them. The only answer he'd ever found was that they likely didn't want anything to do with her . . . even in bed. She couldn't care for that. Well, too bad.

"I am hale, yes. I have Hamnet to thank that I am hale," Marcovefa said to Earl Eyvind. She eyed Gudrid, who suddenly lost her bluster. This side of murder, Hamnet was unlikely to do much to her. Magic offered Marcovefa so many unpleasant possibilities.

Gudrid started cutting up meat for breakfast. Marcovefa went over and got herself some more from a different chunk of the musk-ox carcass. Gudrid watched her warily. Count Hamnet wondered whether Marcovefa could work any magic at all, weak as she still was.

When Gudrid brought her meat to the fire, it exploded into brilliant white flame. Gudrid let out a startled shriek. She thrust her hand into the snow, so the sudden burst of heat must have burned her.

Eyvind Torfinn hurried over to her. "How bad is it?" he asked anxiously.

"Not—too." Gudrid looked at her hand. "No, not too. But only luck it isn't. That horrible bitch—" She sent Marcovefa a glare full of daggers.

"If you would leave off quarreling with her and with Count Hamnet, you would give her no excuse for harassing you." Eyvind Torfinn sounded earnest and sensible.

That, of course, did him no good with Gudrid. "How am I supposed to eat?" she shrilled. "There's nothing left of that piece of meat."

"Try another one, then." Yes, Earl Eyvind was sensible. "I'm sure everything will be all right this time."

"*I'm* not." But Gudrid's only other choice was going hungry. She worried another gobbet off the carcass. Marcovefa, whose new rib had cooked in the most ordinary way imaginable, sat there smiling and watching her do it. Gudrid muttered to herself. Hamnet thought she wanted to tell Marcovefa to look away but didn't have the nerve. He doubted whether he would have had the nerve himself.

More than a little apprehensively, Gudrid took the new piece of meat over to the closest fire. It didn't burst into white flame. It burst into searing green flame instead. Gudrid squalled and soothed her hand with snow—although, again, the real damage seemed small.

"How am I supposed to eat?" she asked again, plaintively this time. Marcovefa . . . smiled.

MARCOVEFA SEEMED TO gain strength far faster than finally getting enough to eat again could account for. By the end of her first day awake, she wasn't far from where she had been before the Rulers wounded and enchanted her. So it seemed to Hamnet Thyssen, anyhow. "Did you enjoy making Gudrid squawk?" he asked her.

"Yes," she said matter-of-factly. "Did you enjoy it, too?"

"Some." Hamnet felt uncomfortable admitting it, but he would have felt more uncomfortable lying.

"Good. She should leave you alone. If she has not got the sense to do that, she will find out other people will not leave her alone. Me, for instance." Marcovefa hesitated, something she rarely did. "But maybe I should have just slapped her instead of using a spell, even one that is not so big."

"What? Why?" Hamnet asked.

"Because the Rulers, curse them, they felt it. I could tell. They know I am awake again," Marcovefa said.

"Oh." The small word carried a lot of freight. "They'll . . . try to do something about that, won't they?"

"Yes." Marcovefa's brief answer was freighted, too. "I am dangerous to them—and so are you."

"Me? Everybody says so, but I wish I could believe it," Hamnet said.

"Who woke me? You did!" Marcovefa said. "Could anyone else have done that? I do not think so! Do we have a better chance with me or without me? With me, I think. And you put me back in the fight."

"That doesn't make me dangerous. It makes you dangerous," Count Hamnet insisted. "And you are. You know it, and the Rulers know it."

"And they know about you, too, and they fear you," Marcovefa told him.

"The Rulers don't fear much of anything." Hamnet despised them, which didn't mean he didn't—reluctantly—respect them. Say what you would of them, they made formidable foes.

"They fear us. Not just me. Us." Marcovefa sounded so certain, she challenged Hamnet Thyssen not to believe her. And then she did something altogether different: she changed the subject. "You know how you got me to wake up?"

"Yes. I finally listened to Trasamund," Hamnet answered. "That isn't something you want to do every day, not if you have any sense."

"This is not what I meant. You should know it is not," Marcovefa said severely. "You know what you did to make me wake up?"

"Of course I know what I did," Hamnet said. "If it had been anything else, I would have tried it sooner."

"I was not awake then. I did not wake up till the morning. I am awake now." Marcovefa waited with what Hamnet took to be quickly shrinking patience.

A heartbeat or two more slowly than he should have, Hamnet realized why her patience might be shrinking. "Well, then," he said after the light dawned, "let's see what we can do about that."

What they did was what they'd done the night before.

As Hamnet had known it would be, it was a great deal better with both of them awake to take pleasure in it. Afterward, Marcovefa stroked his cheek. "We do all right together."

That was less than enormous praise, but enough to make Hamnet nod. "How much more can you hope for?" he said. Even managing to keep that much would be better than he'd done with Gudrid or Liv.

As if picking the thought from his mind, Marcovefa said, "I am surprised you did not kill that mouthy woman while I lay asleep. She is like a flea—she bites and jumps away and then bites again."

"I came close a couple of times," Count Hamnet admitted. "But people talk if you kill a woman."

"Let them. She is gone after that, and no one has to listen to her any more," Marcovefa said ruthlessly.

Hamnet didn't care to think about that. Thinking about it was too likely to tempt him to do it. He changed the subject instead: "The Rulers' wizards can sense you're yourself again?"

Marcovefa nodded. "I said so. I was not spinning fables."

"They'll come after you, then. They'll come after all of us." Hamnet Thyssen wanted those to be questions. They came out as flat statements.

She nodded again. "It is as we said this morning—I am sure they will. They are not fools. They would not be so much trouble if they were. If I were fighting us, I would come after us once I got such news. Would you not?"

"Too right I would," Hamnet said regretfully.

"There you are, then." Marcovefa might have been a schoolmistress going through a proof in geometry. Back in his school days, Hamnet had never imagined lying naked on a mammoth hide with a schoolmistress. Most teachers in Raumsdalia were men. Most of the ones who weren't were neither young nor attractive. He supposed that rule was bound to have exceptions, but he'd never met one.

Again, he hauled his thoughts back to the business at hand: "How can we beat them?" But that wasn't the question he really needed to ask. He asked the one that was: "*Can* we beat them?"

"They would not worry so much about us if they did not think we could," Marcovefa answered.

"How?" Hamnet asked bluntly.

"I don't know. We will have to find that way." Marcovefa asked a question of her own: "Do you think you can find the way again?"

Most of the time, Hamnet would have said no—it was too soon, and he not young enough. But he found he could after all, so he did. As he'd seen before, having a shaman for a lover wasn't the worst thing in the world. No, indeed.

XIX

Sudertorp Lake was thawing. Spring was in the air. So were countless thousands—millions, more likely—of waterfowl, all bound for the marshes around the lake to breed.

In years gone by, the Leaping Lynxes would have settled in their stone huts to live off the fat of the land as long as it lasted. No more: the Rulers had smashed that Bizogot clan. And Marcovefa didn't want to go back toward the eastern edge of the lake, where the Leaping Lynxes' village stood.

"Why not?" Hamnet asked her. So did Trasamund. So did Liv. So did Audun Gilli. So did Ulric Skakki. So did Runolf Skallagrim and everyone else who knew her.

"It is not lucky," she answered. When people tried to argue with her—and a lot of them did—she added, "Are you the shaman, or am I?"

Liv and Audun had magical talents of their own. Neither claimed talents to match hers, though. Earl Eyvind tried to use logic against her. Logic he had in plenty, though no more sorcerous talents than one of the ducks that dabbled in the chilly lake.

Marcovefa heard him out. She respected logic and knowledge. Having heard him out, she smiled and repeated, "It is not lucky." After a moment, she continued, "You may go there, if you think you must. If you have no joy of it, do not blame me."

Eyvind Torfinn spluttered. "That makes no sense!" he complained.

"Then go—you and your wife," Marcovefa said. "See what happens to you."

"You sound as if you'd be glad to get rid of us," Eyvind told her.

"You said it, not me," Marcovefa replied. Hamnet Thyssen wasn't sure how much Eyvind knew about Gudrid's feuds with practically everyone else. More than the scholarly earl let on, odds were. He was sure Eyvind stopped arguing with Marcovefa. He was also sure neither Eyvind nor Gudrid left the band of Bizogots and Raumsdalians still in the field against the Rulers.

And he was sure the Rulers were moving against that band, though cautiously. Scouts reported squadrons of the invaders, along with their riding deer and war mammoths, both to the north and to the south. For the time being, though, the Rulers didn't try to close with their enemies. They seemed content to gather strength for the fight once it did begin.

"They won't fool around when they come after us this time, will they?" Trasamund said grimly.

"Think of it as respect from the enemy," Count Hamnet told him.

"I've been thinking of it that way all along," Ulric Skakki said. "Even so, I could do without the honor. If you can't . . . well, in that case you're foolish in ways I never gave you credit for."

"Which ways *did* you give him credit for?" Now Trasamund sounded intrigued.

Ulric answered without the least hesitation: "Well, he's foolish about women, of course. And he trusts people too bloody much. And there's his confounded stubborn sense of duty." He watched the jarl nod eagerly, then continued with a certain relish his voice hadn't held before: "But for sheer blockheaded stupidity, give me a Bizogot every time."

Trasamund swore at him. Ulric's grin was raw impudence. Hamnet Thyssen considered the adventurer's charges. "You son of a whore," he said. "I can't even tell you you're wrong."

"I am your servant, Your Grace," Ulric Skakki replied. "Did I mention your deplorable habit of speaking the truth when a lie would serve you better? No, I don't believe I did. Well, no matter. Emperor Sigvat would have more to say on that score."

Hamnet expressed a detailed opinion on what His Majesty could do about it. Sigvat II would have had to be improbably limber to accomplish even a quarter of it. Trasamund guffawed. Ulric grinned again. Hearing Hamnet's suggestions, Runolf Skallagrim asked, "Who's that you're telling off?"

"Nobody important," Hamnet said. "Only the Emperor."

Runolf looked troubled. "You really shouldn't joke like that, Thyssen. Haven't you seen what happens when you do?"

"Too right I have," Hamnet said. "But who's joking?"

"He's right, you know," Ulric said. By Baron Runolf's scowl, he knew nothing of the sort. Sighing, Ulric spelled it out for him: "If Sigvat were important, the Rulers would go after him as hard as they could, right? Are they doing that? Are they doing anything close to that? Not likely! What *are* they doing? They're pulling their warriors and mammoths out of Raumsdalia so they can come after us. How important does that make Sigvat?"

Runolf Skallagrim grunted. "Well, all right. If you're going to put it that way . . . But you still shouldn't say rude things about the Emperor."

"I'd say them to his face if he were here," Count Hamnet told him. "He deserves a lot of the blame for what's gone wrong. If he hadn't decided the Rulers weren't dangerous, the Empire would be better off. I don't know if we could have beaten the Rulers, but we would have given them a better fight. I'd bet on that."

Since Runolf didn't answer, Hamnet hoped he'd made his point. Up in the sky, an arrowhead of geese flew toward Sudertorp Lake, and another, and another. There were also ducks and swans and snipes and coots and every other sort of bird that lived on water or by it. They knew what season of the year it was, or would be soon. Hamnet Thyssen didn't know how they knew, but they did.

Trasamund eyed the waterbirds and shorebirds, too. "Mosquito season any day now," he said dolefully. The bugs knew when to hatch. Hamnet didn't know how they knew, either. He only wished they didn't.

WHEN SPRING CAME to the Bizogot steppe, it came in a rush. One day, the snow lay thick and drifted on the ground. The next, it was gone, and everything was green and growing, with flowers splashing the plains with color. It couldn't really have happened so fast . . . could it? Looking back, Count Hamnet supposed that was impossible, but it didn't seem so at the time.

Sudertorp Lake had already thawed. The new year's growth around the lakeshore sheltered the incoming birds. Ulric Skakki baited a hook with bits of offal and pulled several fat trout out of the lake. Fishing fascinated the Bizogots. Most streams up here held nothing to catch because they froze top to bottom during the winter. As it so often was, Sudertorp Lake was different.

Ulric's catch fascinated Hamnet for another reason. "How did you happen to have a fish hook?" he asked the adventurer.

"I have all kinds of things," Ulric replied with dignity. "Never can tell when one of them will come in handy."

"Where did you get the hook?" Hamnet persisted.

"Down in Raumsdalia." Ulric could be maddeningly opaque when he told the truth. As if to explain himself further, he went on, "The Bizogots don't make 'em, you know. Even if they did, they'd carve 'em out of bone. They wouldn't use bronze."

Hamnet gave up. All right, so Ulric found a way to take advantage of something where nobody else could. What was so surprising about that?

The Rulers skirmished with the scouts the Bizogots and Raumsdalians set out. They didn't seem eager to close with them, though. Hamnet wondered at that. Actually, he wondered less than he marveled. "They're afraid of you," he said to Marcovefa. "That's the only thing holding them back."

"If they were smart, they would strike soon," she answered. "But they are the Rulers. They are not smart—not as smart as they think they are. Not as strong as they think they are, either."

He looked at her. "How long did you lie there with your spirit disconnected from your body?"

Marcovefa shrugged, as if to say that was of no account.

"If I had stayed all together, we would not have come up here onto the steppe," she said. "We need to be up here."

"Why?" Count Hamnet asked bluntly.

She only shrugged again. "I do not know yet. When the time comes, I will know. I think I will, anyhow."

"What happens if you don't?" Hamnet inquired.

"Then maybe the song does not have the ending the singer first intended to give it," Marcovefa said. "But I do not think it will turn out like that. When I need to know something, I know it. Till then . . . Till then, I only think I need to know it."

She could be almost as maddening as Ulric. The one thing she lacked was his smiling insolence. But if she only thought she needed to know something now, Hamnet couldn't be too angry at her for not actually knowing it. He didn't suppose he could, anyhow.

More and more Rulers came down from the direction of the Gap and up from Raumsdalia. As far as fighting strength went, they could have crushed their foes in a couple of hours, if not sooner. But more than fighting strength went into the balance. So did sorcerous strength. There, thanks to Marcovefa, the Rulers felt less confident.

When Bizogots encamped, their mammoth- and musk-ox-hide tents scattered all over the landscape, each one pitched wherever its owner happened to want it. Raumsdalian army encampments weren't much neater. No one in the Empire had seen much point to imposing order on something likely to get torn down the next day.

As they were in so many ways, the Rulers were different. Hamnet Thyssen had seen that the moment he first set eyes on one of their camps out beyond the Gap. They pitched tents in rows and in squares. No matter where they were, each of their camps always looked like all the others.

And when a troop encamped in different places night

after night, each man's tent always sat in the same place in the grid. Their warriors always knew where to find a friend or a superior or a shaman. Their beasts were always tethered in the same positions.

That had its advantages, especially in emergencies. It was one more reason they beat the Bizogots and the Raumsdalians far more often than they lost to them.

Count Hamnet watched from the natural dam of rocks and dirt and underground ice that contained Sudertorp Lake as more and more of those dark squares filled the low-lying lands to the west. War mammoths and riding deer went back and forth among the encampments. Count Hamnet supposed men on foot did, too, but most of them were too far away for him to see.

He turned to Ulric Skakki. "I didn't know they had so many men," he remarked, and quickly went on, "If you say, 'Life is full of surprises,' I'll bash you over the head with a boulder."

"In that case, I'd have to be bolder than I am to say it." The adventurer's eyes twinkled. "As a matter of fact, they've got more men than I figured, too."

"What are we going to do about it?" Hamnet asked heavily.

"Good question," Ulric said. "What *are* we going to do about it?" If he couldn't be difficult one way, he would be another.

"I was hoping you might have an answer," Hamnet said.

"You should always hope. That way, when things don't work out, you'll be properly disappointed." As usual, Ulric was most outrageous when he sounded most reasonable.

"Sooner or later—probably sooner—the Rulers will decide they've got enough mammoths and men and magicians to smash us flat," Hamnet said. "Then they'll set out to do it. How do you propose to stop them?"

"I expect I'll fight," Ulric answered. "If fighting looks hopeless, I expect I'll run. Not many more choices, are there?"

"Well, there's always dying," Hamnet said.

"I'll do that. So will you. But you can bugger me with a pine cone if I'll do it by choice," Ulric said.

Marcovefa walked over to them. Eating greasy goose and duck agreed with her. She wasn't hollow-eyed any more, and her cheekbones no longer showed as sharp prom-ontories under tight-wrapped skin. "What are you two go-ing on about?" she asked.

"Dying." Only Ulric could make the word sound so cheery.

Marcovefa looked back at Sudertorp Lake, at the marsh plants springing up all around it, and at the waterfowl whose wingbeats sometimes made speech difficult because of their astounding abundance. She turned and looked at the Rulers' encampments to the west. Then she looked down at the mossy boulder she was standing on, and at the ice that still survived in the shadowed crevice between it and the dirt around it.

And then she started to laugh. Whatever was going on in her mind, it was so funny that she had trouble stopping. Laughing still, she kissed Ulric. Before Hamnet's jeal-ousy could flare, she kissed him, too. As he held her, her shoulders shook with mirth.

"What's so funny?" he asked.

"Dying," she said. "Oh, there will be a great dying, all right." That might have been the best joke in the world. She laughed so much, she got the hiccups. Hiccuping and giggling and shaking her head, she ambled back toward the forlorn encampment the Bizogots and Raumsdalians had set up just south of the earthen dam.

"I knew I was a funny fellow," Ulric Skakki remarked, "but I didn't think I was *that* funny."

"Neither did I," Hamnet assured him. "Now we need to find out one more thing." Ulric made a questioning noise. Hamnet explained: "Whether you really are."

WHEN THE RULERS finally decided they were ready to move forward against the ragtag band of Bizogots and Raumsdalians still opposing them, they took their time forming a battle line. Maybe they wanted their foes to see everything they had and to despair. If so, they knew how to get what they wanted.

Hamnet Thyssen had never seen—had never dreamt of—so many war mammoths drawn up side by side. He'd never imagined so many riding deer all in the same place. More than a few Rulers were on horseback, too; the invaders had quickly learned to make the most of what this new land offered them.

They couldn't keep that large a force fed for long. Soon, the mammoths and deer and horses would strip every growing thing from the ground around their encampments. Even sooner, Hamnet thought, the enemy warriors would eat everything bigger than a mosquito.

Of course, the Rulers didn't have to hold their army together long. As soon as they'd disposed of their foes, they could disperse across the broad Bizogot steppe.

Trasamund shaded his eyes with the palm of his hand. "I wonder how many of them I can kill before they finally drag me down," he said.

"I wonder if we'd have a better chance fighting somewhere else." Hamnet didn't want to talk about running, not with Trasamund. Unlike Ulric, the jarl would take it the wrong way. Seeing what the Rulers were about to hurl at them made him cast about for ways to do it, though.

"Some of us can get away. Maybe most of us can." Ulric himself came closer to directness. But he added, "I don't know how much of a fight we'll ever put up afterward if we do ride out."

"How much of a fight can we put up here and now?" Runolf Skallagrim asked: a painfully cogent question.

"We need to stay here," Marcovefa said. "This is where we make our stand."

Fear and doubt filled everyone else. She seemed serene. "What do you know that we don't?" Hamnet asked her.

"Why, what I know, of course." She sounded surprised he needed to ask.

"And that is?" he persisted.

"It certainly is," Marcovefa agreed. For a moment, he was furious. Then, slowly, he realized it was one of those things she might know but had no words for. He'd seen that before, with her and with other shamans and wizards. Sometimes it all came together at the proper moment.

Sometimes, of course, it didn't. If it didn't this time, he couldn't imagine their getting another chance.

Several men on riding deer moved out in front of the Rulers' war mammoths. "Their wizards," Marcovefa said. "They think that, if they can kill me first, everything else is easy."

"Are they right?" Hamnet blurted.

"Yes. This time, yes." She nodded with as little fuss as if he'd asked her whether the sun was shining.

"Can they do it?" Trasamund found a more urgent question still.

"I don't know," Marcovefa answered, still calmly. With what seemed like irrelevance to Count Hamnet, she added, "The Glacier is melting." Then she said, "If they do not kill me, I will kill them." Hamnet liked the sound of that much better.

But the Rulers were going to have their try first. Marcovefa gestured to the men around her, as if to say they would be none too safe if they stayed close to her. Neither Hamnet nor any of the others moved more than a pace or two.

The enemy wizards put their heads together. They might have been talking about some game. And so they were, but to the victors here went life. The wizards separated again. One of them pointed not at Marcovefa but at the sky above her head.

Lightning crashed down, though the day was bright and sunny and clear. But it didn't strike Marcovefa. Instead, it smote the earthen dam a couple of bowshots north of where she stood. Steam rose from the riven ground. Another bolt of lightning struck. Again, Marcovefa deflected it. More steam spurted from the dam enclosing Sudertorp Lake.

And Marcovefa laughed—not a mirth-filled laugh, but one that made Hamnet's hackles rise. God might have laughed that way, thinking of a particularly nasty joke. Marcovefa pointed down toward the Rulers' wizards. "Fools!" she shouted in her own dialect. "You dig your own graves, fools!"

They couldn't have heard her—they were too far away. Even if they had heard her, they wouldn't have understood her. Hamnet Thyssen barely did. Ulric Skakki saw the same thing. "What is she going to do?" he whispered.

"I don't know," Hamnet whispered back. "I'm not sure she knows herself. But whatever it is, I wouldn't want it aimed at me."

The Rulers' wizards must have felt the same way. The one who'd pointed at the sky extended his hand again, not above Marcovefa this time but straight toward her. Fire spurted from his outstretched finger, fire that Hamnet somehow realized was powered by all the enemy magicians together.

That spear of flame took only a couple of heartbeats to fly from the Ruler to Marcovefa. She gestured with her right hand. Instead of cremating her, the fire also smashed against the earthen dam. The sound of that impact was like red-hot iron dropped into a bucket of water, but magnified a hundredfold.

When the fiery gout also went wide, the Rulers' wizards seemed to slump on their riding deer. They'd tried two strong weapons and failed with both. Now, their manner said, it was Marcovefa's turn.

She looked toward the dam of earth and rock and ice, the dam toward which she'd deflected their spells. When she did, the Rulers' lead wizard let out an anguished howl Count Hamnet heard clearly no matter how far away the man was. The wizard knew what would happen next, even if Hamnet didn't.

Marcovefa chanted in her own dialect. Hamnet understood a word here and there—no more. Ulric knew more of the speech of the folk who lived atop the Glacier. He lost his usual air of studied calm. "She can't do that!" he yelped. ". . . Can she?"

"Do what?" Hamnet asked.

Then Marcovefa did it. She swept both hands upward, then theatrically brought them down. "Now!" she cried— Hamnet understood that with no trouble at all.

And the earthen dam erupted. All the ice within it either melted or turned to steam. Boulders flew high into the air. One of them came down just a few yards in front of the Rulers' wizards. Only frantic passes from Marcovefa kept the stones from squashing her and her companions.

Hamnet Thyssen noticed all that, but only peripherally.

Once, a couple of thousand years before, Nidaros, the imperial capital, had stood by the eastern edge of Hevring Lake. Then the Glacier retreated and the weather warmed. The dam of earth and ice that held in Hevring Lake melted and collapsed—and the lake poured out. What had been its bottom was some of the most fertile farmland in the Empire . . . and the lands to the west, for mile after mile after mile, were scabby, wrecked badlands—all that remained after a flood bigger than human imagination could grasp poured through.

Count Hamnet didn't have to imagine a flood like that. He watched one with his own eyes. As Marcovefa's magic melted the dam that had restrained Sudertorp Lake for so long, it burst free. The roar of those rushing waters dwarfed anything Hamnet had ever heard from the throat of lion or bear.

How high was that frothy, muddy, stone-filled wall of water? As tall as ten men? Twenty? More? He didn't know, not exactly. He knew it was tall enough and to spare.

Somehow—sorcerously?—he heard the Rulers' wizards scream even through that immense roaring. Their leader tried to do something to deflect the doom thundering down on them. Marcovefa clapped her hands once in what had to be admiration for the effort.

The lead wizard wasn't strong enough, even with all his friends behind him. Even if he would have had the strength, he didn't have the time he needed to shape the kind of spell that might have done some good. The wall of water struck him, struck the rest of the wizards, and swept them away.

In less than the blink of an eye, it smashed into the war mammoths behind the wizards. A few minutes earlier, Hamnet had thought that the line of great beasts was one of the most fearsome things he'd ever seen. Now he had to change his opinion. He got a few brief glimpses of mammoths tossed like bathtub toys on the flood. Other than those, the heart of the Rulers' armed might vanished without a trace.

So did all the warriors on riding deer and horses. So did the neat squares of tents that were the Rulers' encampments. So did . . . well, everything in the path of what had been Sudertorp Lake.

"God!" Trasamund said—the most reverent Hamnet Thyssen had ever heard him sound.

Even Marcovefa was impressed. "I didn't think it would do *that*," she murmured.

"What *did* you think it would do?" Ulric Skakki inquired.

"Drown them. That, yes," Marcovefa said. "But all this? This is more than I bargained for."

Hamnet suspected it was more than anyone would have bargained for. There off to his right, less than a bowshot away, Sudertorp Lake was emptying like a pot with a hole in its side. All of them still had to shout to make themselves heard over the roar of the water.

"God!" Trasamund said again, this time on a different note.

"What is it?" Count Hamnet asked.

"The lake will run dry, yes?" the Bizogot said. "No more water here. No more marsh around the edge. What will the waterfowl do when they come here to breed?"

It was a good question, and one Hamnet hadn't thought of. After a moment, he said, "Back in the day, the birds must have come to Hevring Lake the same way. Hevring Lake went away, but we still have waterfowl. I suppose we still will once Sudertorp Lake dries out, too."

"Mm, you're likely right," Trasamund replied. He turned to Marcovefa. "If the Rulers hadn't broken the

Leaping Lynx clan, the Lynxes would all want to kill you for ruining their hunting grounds."

"If the Rulers hadn't broken the Leaping Lynxes and done everything else they did, Marcovefa wouldn't have needed to break the dam," Hamnet said. "Sooner or later, it would have melted through by itself, though. They couldn't have kept their easy springs and summers forever."

They'd had them. He thought fondly of all the duck and goose fat he'd eaten near Sudertorp Lake. But Trasamund was right. This hunting ground would never be the same. Even now, waterfowl and shorebirds were flying up in alarm as the meltwater lake drained.

Ulric pointed off to the west. "A mammoth just washed ashore over there. Must be a mammoth—I couldn't see anything smaller that far away."

"Is it moving?" Hamnet asked. He couldn't spot it. Maybe he didn't know where to look.

"No," Ulric said, and then, "I don't know about the water birds, but the teratorns and the vultures and the ravens will feast like never before."

"Let them eat the Rulers. Let them eat the war mammoths. Let them raise their chicks on the riding deer," Trasamund said. "I rejoice that they enjoy this bounty from the invaders."

Eyvind Torfinn and Gudrid came up to stare at the spectacle Marcovefa had unleashed. "My, my," the earl said. "What an amazingly opportune coincidence . . . Excuse me. Did I say something funny?"

No one answered him for some little while. Hamnet and Marcovefa and the others were too busy laughing. "Don't you pay attention to *anything*?" Ulric asked at last. "Didn't you see the thunderbolts coming down out of the sky? Didn't you hear them? Or are you blind *and* deaf?"

"Neither, I hope," Eyvind replied with dignity. "But surely those thunderbolts could not have caused—this."

"They didn't." Hamnet pointed to Marcovefa. "She did."

"Probably luck, with her taking the credit for it," Gudrid muttered.

"What do you say?" Marcovefa needed only four words to suggest that, if she didn't like the answer, Gudrid would go into Sudertorp Lake and come out the way Ulric's distant war mammoth had.

Gudrid did own a first-class sense of self-preservation. "Uh, nothing," she said quickly. "Nothing at all. Just—clearing my throat." She nodded. "Yes, that's all I was doing."

Nobody called her on it. Marcovefa had to know she was lying. But putting her in fear must have been almost as good as pitching her into what was left of Sudertorp Lake.

Hamnet Thyssen looked back at the lake. Was he imagining things, or was the water level already a good deal lower? "I wonder how long it'll take to empty out altogether," he said.

"If we knew the volume and the rate of flow, it would be easy to calculate," Earl Eyvind replied.

"And if a teratorn knew how to play the trumpet, he might end up Emperor Sigvat's bandmaster," Ulric said. Eyvind Torfinn sent him a reproachful look. The adventurer took no notice of it.

Trasamund bowed low to Marcovefa. "This is vengeance. I thank you for it. All the Bizogots thank you for it."

"This is better than vengeance," Marcovefa said.

"You are a wise woman. No one doubts it." As if to emphasize that, the jarl bowed again. "But tell me, if you will, what can be better than vengeance?"

"Victory is better," Marcovefa answered. "In getting vengeance, you can throw yourself away to no purpose but killing. Here you have vengeance, and you have not thrown yourself away."

Trasamund weighed her words. "It is so," he said at last, wonder in his voice. "By God, it *is* so!" He bowed even lower this time.

Count Hamnet looked out to the west again. All he could see where the Rulers' army had been were raging waters. How many miles did the flood already stretch? How many more would it reach? Wandering Bizogots and beasts and perhaps even the odd Ruler who hadn't joined in this attack would get swept away without ever knowing how or why the dam at the west end of Sudertorp Lake had broken down.

That would matter to them—for a very little while. In the larger scheme of things, it hardly counted. "The Rulers are ruined. They're wrecked," Hamnet said. He liked the sound of that so much, he repeated it.

Liv and Audun Gilli shyly approached Marcovefa. "Forgive us for not offering help, but—" Liv began.

"We thought you could take care of it for yourself," Audun broke in.

"And we were right," Liv said.

"By God, were we ever!" Audun stared in awe at the rampaging lake. He whistled in admiration. "We didn't know what you were going to do. Whatever it might be, we didn't expect *this*." His wave encompassed the torrent.

"How could anyone expect—*this*?" Liv said. Turning back to Marcovefa, she asked, "Did you?"

The shaman from atop the Glacier shook her head. "I knew we could beat the Rulers. I knew we *would* beat the Rulers. How? They showed me themselves, when they threw thunderbolts and fire toward me and I sent them into the dam. That showed me the way. I told them they were digging their own graves, and I was right."

As Trasamund had before her, Liv bowed to Marcovefa. "I am glad it showed you the way." Then, to Hamnet's surprise, she also bowed to him. "If you hadn't helped keep her safe, and if you hadn't brought her back to herself, we wouldn't have won. This is why the Rulers feared you—and had reason to."

"It would have been all right without me," Hamnet said.

"Yes, I think so, too." If anyone was less ready to give Hamnet Thyssen credit than he was himself, it had to be Gudrid.

"I do not." That was Marcovefa, and not even Gudrid thought arguing with her was a good idea. Sometimes Marcovefa sounded like anyone else. Others . . . Hamnet wondered whether God spoke through her. She wouldn't have said so. She would have laughed at him. But how else could she seem so knowing, so authoritative? She awed and alarmed even other wizards.

She'd awed and alarmed the Rulers, and with reason. They'd tried their best to kill her, only their best turned out not to be good enough. When she finally turned the tables, they found out how good her best could be. *That* lesson wouldn't need repeating.

As if thinking along with him, Trasamund said, "With luck, we can deal with the ones who trickle through the Gap now. I think most of the Rulers who were going to come already got here."

"And most of the ones who'd already got here got swept away," Hamnet added.

"Yes." The jarl nodded. He smiled. "Amazing how happy one word can make you, isn't it?"

"If you have to pick one word, that one's more likely to

than most," Hamnet answered. Smiling still, Trasamund nodded.

While everyone else kept looking west and watching the floodwaters rampage across the Bizogot steppe, Eyvind Torfinn chose to look east. He suddenly stiffened, as if transfixed by an arrow. Only his right arm moved, to point out into what had been the middle of Sudertorp Lake.

Hamnet Thyssen's gaze followed Earl Eyvind's outthrust forefinger. Hamnet suddenly found himself transfixed, too. How long had those graceful gilded domes, those delicate columns, lain under the water? Had anyone imagined they were there? Had they been there when the Glacier rolled down from the north, too? How long had they been there before *that*?

"Is it—?" Hamnet asked.

"Yes." This once, Eyvind Torfinn's nod was as authoritative as anything Marcovefa could manage. "That is the Golden Shrine."

XX

And so it was. Count Hamnet realized he'd seen those domes before, in miniature. He needed a moment to remember where. Then he did: in the jewel hidden in Earl Eyvind's bedpost. How old was that jewel, anyhow?

A moment later, he realized it had to be Eyvind's, not Gudrid's, for she said, "It can't be. Everybody knows the Golden Shrine is only a tale for children—and foolish children at that."

"That *is* the Golden Shrine," Trasamund said. "It must have hidden under the lake all this time—and under the Glacier before that, because once upon a time the Glacier stretched down farther than this."

"True. Once the Glacier stretched down almost as far as Nidaros. I was thinking about that not long ago," Hamnet Thyssen said. "Hevring Lake melted through and made the badlands off to the west. Thanks to Marcovefa, Sudertorp Lake's gone and done the same thing."

"It's nonsense." Gudrid's laugh had a brittle edge. "It's impossible! Even a fool should be able to see that."

"Only a fool would say that," Marcovefa replied. Awe

lit her face as she pointed out toward the structure in the emptying lake. "That is assuredly the Golden Shrine."

"It can't be," Gudrid repeated. "How do you know it is?"

"It's a shrine. It's golden. It just appeared out of nothing like a miracle." Ulric Skakki ticked off points on his fingers as he made them. "What more do you want? Egg in your beer?"

"You're making fun of me!" Gudrid said shrilly.

"When you say silly things, you can expect other people to make fun of you," Ulric observed. Gudrid glared at him. Hamnet saw that, but he didn't think the adventurer did; Ulric's eyes were fixed firmly on the Golden Shrine. "Up till now, going through the Gap and beyond the Glacier was the most marvelous thing I ever did. I imagined it always would be. Now I see I was wrong."

Hamnet nodded. He hadn't dreamt he could do anything more amazing than to pass through the Gap and see what lay on the far side of the Glacier, either. He hadn't even thought the Glacier *had* a far side; he'd believed it went on forever. Like Ulric, he'd been wrong.

When Gudrid went on protesting that the buildings the emptying lake revealed couldn't possibly be the Golden Shrine, Hamnet cut her off with a sharp chopping gesture. "Most of us are going over there no matter what you think it is. You can come with us or stay behind—whichever you please."

"You can't talk to me that way," she said.

"No?" He looked at her. "I just did." He turned away. She went on complaining, but he ignored her after that.

The Bizogots and Raumsdalians who'd come this far had mounted for a last desperate battle against the Rulers. They greeted Marcovefa with thunderous cheers—much of their joy, no doubt, was transformed relief that they wouldn't die in the next few hours. She blushed like a girl as she waved to them, which only made their cheers redouble.

And they took up a chant: "The Shrine! The Shrine! The Golden Shrine!" It could have sounded better, since some spoke Raumsdalian and others the Bizogots' tongue. No one seemed inclined to criticize.

Before long, Marcovefa and the ragtag army's other leaders were also on horseback. The rest of the warriors behind them, they rode east along what had been the southern shore of Sudertorp Lake. It was a shoreline no more, as Sudertorp Lake was a lake no more. Waterfowl flew in wild confusion. Hamnet hoped they would find new nesting grounds.

Even if the Golden Shrine was visible now, he wasn't sure how anyone could reach it. Sudertorp Lake might be vanishing, but wouldn't its bottom prove impenetrable ooze that glued men and horses in place and might suck them down never to be seen again?

Earl Eyvind had another thought: "After so very long, how much could have survived in there? I'm astonished the buildings themselves have."

"Now that you mention it, so am I," Hamnet Thyssen said. "We'll see, that's all. We're here. It's here, however it got here. We can't do anything else but find out, can we?" Eyvind shook his head.

"It is the Golden Shrine," Marcovefa said. "It is as it is meant to be. We will see what we are meant to see, learn what we are meant to learn."

"What will that be?" Hamnet asked.

She gave him a dazzling smile. "If I already knew, I wouldn't learn anything, would I?"

Even as they rode toward the Golden Shrine, more and

more of it emerged from the lake. The outgoing flood should have wrecked it, but seemed to have left it unharmed. Of course, if it truly had lain under the Glacier for centuries uncounted, that should have ground it to powder. Obviously, no such thing had happened.

When Hamnet Thyssen wondered why not out loud, Earl Eyvind said, "It is the Golden Shrine. If the ordinary laws of nature applied to it, it would be something else altogether. It is the Golden Shrine *because* those laws do not apply. That is not the only reason, but it is a compelling one."

"The old man is right," Trasamund rumbled. That made Eyvind Torfinn look imperfectly delighted at the agreement. Marcovefa nodded without any opinions about his age. He seemed happier then.

"It's the Golden Shrine," Hamnet said. "Whatever's wrong with us, whatever's wrong with the world, now the Shrine can fix it."

"An ancient verse says we take no more away from the Shrine than we bring to it," Earl Eyvind remarked.

Marcovefa nodded again. This time, so did Ulric Skakki. Frowning, Trasamund asked, "What the demon does that mean?" Hamnet would have said more or less the same thing if the jarl hadn't beaten him to it.

Eyvind Torfinn only shrugged. "The text may be corrupt, and it is certainly obscure. We shall be able to do what the author could not—we shall discover for ourselves what he meant."

"Seems plain enough to me," Ulric said. But then he waved his hand. "I may be wrong, God knows. The truth may be hiding under what looks plain, the same way the Golden Shrine hid under Sudertorp Lake. I wonder why nobody out in the lake ever looked down and saw it."

"It did not wish to be seen," Marcovefa replied. Talking about a building in that way should have been nonsense. Hamnet had the feeling it wasn't.

"I suppose it didn't want to get crushed when the Glacier rolled down from the north, either," Ulric said, which had already occurred to Hamnet.

"It must not have. Had it wanted that, be sure that would have happened," she said. Ulric started to answer, then seemed to think better of it. Count Hamnet didn't blame him. He wouldn't have known how to answer that, either.

A goose flew up from its nest, wings thundering. Audun Gilli pointed at what looked like a paving stone half covered by lakeside plants. "Isn't that the start of a road out to the Shrine?" he said.

Hamnet was on the point of saying he thought that was ridiculous. Before he could, Marcovefa nodded briskly. "Yes, I do believe it is," she replied. At that, Hamnet swung down from his horse and walked over to the nest the goose had abandoned. He picked up and hefted an egg. "What are you doing?" Marcovefa asked.

"What with everything else that's gone on, I wondered if we'd found the nest of the goose that lays the golden eggs," he answered. "Doesn't seem that way, though. Too bad." Replacing the egg he'd taken, he mounted again.

Marcovefa scratched her head. Maybe her folk didn't tell that story. But she didn't ask any questions. Audun was right. That road did lead out toward the Golden Shrine. And, next to the Shrine, even golden eggs weren't important enough to worry about.

HOW LONG HAD it been since men last visited the Golden Shrine? How long had it been since the Glacier rolled down from the north and . . . covered it? Hamnet Thyssen asked Earl Eyvind. The scholar only shook his head and spread his hands. "Thousands of years—that's all I can say. If you ask me how many thousands, well, for this your guess is as good as mine."

" 'Thousands of years' seems close enough," Ulric Skakki said. Count Hamnet wasn't inclined to argue with him.

To look at it, though, the Golden Shrine might have vanished from human ken day before yesterday. Or, for that matter, it might never have vanished at all. The tiles that decorated the outer walls were decorated with what looked like an elaborate, sinuous script. But if it was writing, it wasn't writing of a kind Hamnet had ever seen before.

He glanced toward the widely traveled Ulric Skakki. When he caught the adventurer's eyes, Ulric only shrugged. He couldn't read those sparkling tiles, either. He and Hamnet both looked at Eyvind Torfinn. Eyvind wasn't so widely traveled. But he was widely—and deeply—read. That might count for more.

Then again, it might not. "If you are wondering, gentlemen, I must confess that I have never seen the like," he said.

"Oh." Hamnet couldn't hide his disappointment.

Ulric was looking around. "Most of the lake bottom's just mud and gravel, the way you'd expect," he said. "But not this road, and not the ground right in front of the Golden Shrine."

"You're right." Hamnet wondered why he hadn't noticed that himself. Maybe because the road leading toward the Golden Shrine seemed so ordinary. No mud or gravel fouled the flagstones. They weren't even wet. They should have been, but they weren't. Which meant they weren't ordinary, either, even if they seemed to be.

Neither was the grass growing in front of the Golden

Shrine. It *was* grass, not some underwater weed. It grew there as if the Shrine had been standing in the sun for all these years. Hamnet knew better, but the illusion remained convincing.

Trasamund chuckled nervously. "Next thing you know, that door will open and a priest or shaman or whatever you want to call him will come out and bid us good day."

"Don't be more ridiculous than you can help," Gudrid snapped.

Eyvind Torfinn coughed. "My dear, in our present state of knowledge—or rather, of ignorance—calling anything ridiculous would be, well, ridiculous.

Hamnet reached out and tapped Trasamund on the arm. "Once upon a time, you said we'd fight it out in front of the Golden Shrine's door. If you still want to try it, Your Ferocity, I'm ready."

The jarl started to reach over his back for his great sword. Then he stopped and laughed and shook his head. "Let it go, Thyssen—let it go. With this in front of me, I can do without the sport. Unless you think your honor's touched, of course. If you do, I'll gladly oblige you."

"Right now, letting go is better," Hamnet said, glad Trasamund didn't want to hold him to their promise. He nodded to Marcovefa. "You must have expected all this."

"Not me," she said. "I always thought beating the Rulers would have to happen up here on the Bizogot plain. I didn't understand why that was so till just before the end. And the Golden Shrine . . . Who could expect the Golden Shrine? You hope. You imagine. You never expect."

A goose alighted in a puddle on what had been the bottom of Sudertorp Lake. The bird seemed bewildered at the changes that had turned its world all topsy-turvy. Hamnet Thyssen understood how it felt.

The road ran straight to the Golden Shrine. Had it really lain there under the waters of the lake? Had it really lain under the Glacier even longer? Like the Shrine, the road showed no signs of any such mishap. Had they been somewhere else—perhaps not even on or in or of this world at all—and suddenly appeared here when the Rulers were swept away?

However tempting that was, Count Hamnet couldn't believe it. Both the roadway and the Golden Shrine gave the impression of belonging where they were. He couldn't have said why or how they did, but it was so.

He slid off his horse and walked toward the doorway. A polished brass knocker was fixed to the door just below eye level. *Why isn't it green with patina?* he wondered. When the Golden Shrine wasn't dripping—when it wasn't ground to dust—he had no idea why that detail puzzled him, but it did.

Gudrid laughed harshly when he reached for the knocker instead of the latch. "Do you truly think someone will open it?" she jeered.

"I don't know what to think right now," Hamnet answered. "And if you think you do know, you're wrong."

The knocker swung smoothly in his hand. He rapped with it once, twice, three times. The clear, sharp sound echoed out over what had been Sudertorp Lake. The goose in the puddle took off. Hamnet paused, then knocked three more times.

"Oh, well. So much for that," Ulric Skakki said. "Now try the latch."

Hamnet was reaching for it when the door into the Golden Shrine swung open on silent hinges. *Magic*, he thought, *or maybe the power of God. Is there any difference?*

A woman in a golden robe looked out at him and his companions. "Good day," she said. That was what he heard, anyhow, although it didn't match the motion of her lips.

Trasamund laughed raucously. "Ha!" he told Gudrid. "D'you see? Do you?" She pointed her nose to the sky, pretending not to hear.

"Welcome," the woman went on. "We haven't had visitors in . . . oh, quite a long time." She wasn't very large. Her hair was light brown, her eyes somewhere between green and hazel. By that and by her cast of features, she might have been either Raumsdalian or Bizogot—or both, or neither.

"She speaks my dialect," Marcovefa said, and then, "Oh. It must be a translation spell. If the Rulers sometimes use them, why should we be surprised the folk of the Golden Shrine do, too?"

"It is a translation spell," the woman in the golden robe agreed.

In a way, Marcovefa's words made good sense to Hamnet. In another . . . "How *are* there folk of the Golden Shrine?" he asked. "This place has, mm, been through a lot, hasn't it?"

"Yes—and no. That is the only answer I can give." Smiling, the woman stood aside. "Come in. You will see for yourselves."

There was only one problem with that: no one wanted to stay behind and hold the horses. After some argument, Hamnet said, "We'll just tether them, then. I don't think anyone will steal them, not on the grounds of the Golden Shrine." He glanced toward the priestess in some embarrassment.

Her smile didn't falter. All she said was, "I think you are right. They are also unlikely to stray." One by one, the Raumsdalians and Bizogots dismounted. They queued up behind Count Hamnet. The horses hardly needed tethering. They seemed content to crop the grass growing outside the wall.

"You'll be the first one in," Ulric told Hamnet. "Someday, somebody'll write your name in a history book."

"Now tell me something that matters," Hamnet said. Ulric chuckled. Hamnet walked through the door and into the Golden Shrine.

It was warm in there, not warm as if summer were here, but warm as if the Glacier had never rolled south, warm as if the Breath of God never blew. Some of the plants that grew in the courtyard lived far, far to the south, in lands where the Breath of God didn't reach. Others Hamnet Thyssen had never seen before, on this side of the Glacier or the other.

He pointed to one of them. "Have those grown here since before the ice began to swell?" he asked.

"You might say so," the priestess answered. "Or you might not."

"Why do you talk in riddles?" Marcovefa demanded. "This is the Golden Shrine. This is the place where there should be answers, not more questions."

"The answers are here," the priestess assured her. "Whether you can understand them all . . . That, I fear, is one more question." She smiled to show she wasn't mocking Marcovefa.

More priestesses and priests came out to greet the awestruck newcomers. Like the first one, they might have been Raumsdalians or Bizogots . . . or they might not have. The one thing Hamnet was sure of was that they weren't close kin to the Rulers.

As Hamnet had, Eyvind Torfinn pointed to some unfamiliar flowers. "Where do these come from?" he asked.

"Why, they grow here," the priestess said.

"I see that, yes." Earl Eyvind nodded. "But where did they come from before they grew here?"

"They grew out in the world before the Glacier came down," the priestess replied. Her eyes twinkled as she waved to include her colleagues. "So did we. Things outside the Shrine have changed more than they have here."

"How much more?" Eyvind asked. "Have you yourself been here since before the Glacier advanced?"

Put that way, the question sounded innocuous. What if he'd asked, *Are you thousands and thousands of years old?* That would have meant the same thing, but it wouldn't have sounded the same. Oh, no—not even close.

"You had to call us forth," the priestess said. "If you hadn't, we would have gone on in near-nothingness till someone else did. A day? A month? A year? A century? Where we were, none of them mattered very much. We noticed—about the way you would notice an itch. After we scratched, it was gone. And once it was gone, it was forgotten."

"Could the Rulers have, uh, called you forth?" Hamnet Thyssen used her term for it, having no better one of his own.

The priestess frowned. "I do not like to say anything is impossible—the fullness of time often makes a mockery of the word. But I will say, knowing what I know of the Rulers, that the idea strikes me as most unlikely."

"What *do* you know of the Rulers?" Trasamund asked. "If you're so mighty, why didn't you do something about them?"

"Those are two separate questions," a priest remarked, coming up beside the priestess who'd done all the talking till now. He had a handsome face and a light, pleasant voice. He didn't seem dangerous. Hamnet wondered how much that proved. Very little, unless he missed his guess. The man went on, "Which would you rather we answer?"

"Either," Trasamund said. "Both."

"No." Ulric Skakki shook his head. "Tell us why you didn't do something about the Rulers."

"How do you know we didn't?" the priest said, smiling. "They were stronger than you in almost every way. Yet you prevailed. How?"

"Because I found a spell that poured Sudertorp Lake out onto them," Marcovefa answered proudly.

The priest didn't lose his smile. "And how do you think that spell came to you?" he asked. "What did you know of lakes, living up atop the Glacier all your life?"

How did he know that? Marcovefa hadn't said anything about it, not in his hearing. Did he recognize her dialect? That was the only thing that occurred to Hamnet, but it also struck him as unlikely. The Golden Shrine had lain under Sudertorp Lake all the time Marcovefa's folk lived up there . . . hadn't it?

Or maybe these priests and priestesses were simply wizards who put not only the rulers but also Marcovefa to shame. Marcovefa might have thought the same thing. "If you can give me that spell without my knowing it, why don't you rule the world instead of staying under a lake?" she asked.

"Because we have enough sense not to want to rule it," the priest answered. The priestess beside him nodded.

Hamnet Thyssen hoped the man in the golden robe spoke the truth. If the fellow didn't . . . *Well, what can you do about it?* Hamnet asked himself. He didn't see any- thing. What could a butterfly do about a mammoth? Try not to be there when its feet came down, that was all.

Ulric Skakki still held a small, tight smile on his face—the smile, perhaps, of a man fighting hard not to be impressed, or not to show how impressed he was. "Now you're in trouble," he told the priest. "Now you don't have ice or water covering you up any more. Now all the cursed fools in the world will make tracks for this place, expecting you to show them how to be wise." His grin grew even tighter and more self-mocking as he added, "We're here, after all."

"They will be disappointed," the priest said.

"Fools often are," the priestess agreed. "But not all of you here are fools. If you were, you would not have done what you did."

Not all of us? Hamnet wondered. He also wondered—and knew he would wonder for the rest of his life—how much they'd really done themselves. He couldn't know for certain, and he couldn't blindly accept whatever answers he got here. He knew he was a fool, but he hoped he wasn't that kind of fool.

"Here is one thing more for you to think about," the priest said. "No one takes away from the Golden Shrine even a barleycorn more than he brought to it."

"I knew a verse to that effect," Eyvind Torfinn exclaimed proudly.

Ulric bowed to the man in the golden robe. One of his eyebrows quirked as he straightened. "You can say that. I may even believe you when you do. But do you think it will do you any good? Do you think fools will pay any attention? If they did, by God, they wouldn't be fools."

"Well, we will worry about that when the time comes." The priest's voice stayed mild. "It has not come yet."

Eyvind Torfinn had gone over to another priest and was doing his best to talk the man's ears off. Hamnet had never seen him so excited. Well, here he had his heart's desire. With some men, that was one particular woman. With others, it was gold and jewels piled high. All Earl Eyvind had wanted was to find the Golden Shrine. He'd never dreamt he would, but now he had.

Gudrid could also see that women weren't the first thing on Eyvind's mind. More particularly, she could see *she* wasn't the first thing on his mind, or on anyone else's. Hamnet could tell she didn't fancy that. If she wasn't the center of attention, she had trouble believing she was real.

Liv and Audun Gilli were talking with a priestess. The woman in the gold robe nodded and gestured. Liv looked entranced, Audun astonished. Maybe they wouldn't take a barleycorn away with them, but Count Hamnet would have bet they were gaining something.

Hamnet laughed, not altogether pleasantly. To the priest and priestess before him, he said, "Good thing you're up here on the Bizogot steppe and not in Raumsdalia. Emperor Sigvat would try to tax you or make you tell him whatever you know or try to close you down."

To his surprise, they looked amused. "Some things never change," the priestess said. "I don't suppose we expected this to be different from the way it was in the old days."

"In the old days . . ." Hamnet echoed. What did that mean to these people? "Are those the days before the Glacier moved south this last time?"

"Yes," she said.

"What *were* things like then? Do you know what things were like before the Glacier came forward time before last?" Hamnet wasn't Eyvind Torfinn, but if you weren't curious about ancient days in a place like this, you probably had no pulse.

"There were empires and kingdoms and wandering tribes. People were people," the priestess said. "And when the Glacier moved, a lot of them died."

"So we're the descendants of the ones who lived," Hamnet said.

"You would be unlikely to derive from anyone else." The priestess' smile didn't keep Hamnet from blushing.

"Do you remember those days yourself? Were you here for them?" he persisted. "How did this place survive when the Glacier came down on top of it?"

"I was here for some of those days: the worst time, when people saw they couldn't stop the Glacier and despaired," she answered. "But, as I said, I have not been here for all the days since, not in the usual sense of the word. Those days went around me, not through me—that is the best way I can put it."

"But the Glacier didn't go around the Golden Shrine. The Glacier went over it. Then Sudertorp Lake covered it," Hamnet said.

"That is so," the priestess agreed.

"Then how—?" He'd already asked once. Would asking twice do any good?

Marcovefa touched his arm. "Let it go," she said. "I know more shamanry than your folk do. These folk know more than that much more than I do. They will not be able to explain it. Could you explain taming a horse to a baby making messes in its drawers?"

"I am not a baby," Hamnet Thyssen said stubbornly.

"Your friend may have said that. I did not," the priestess assured him. "I—" She broke off. Suddenly, she didn't look mild or amused. Her eyes flashed. That wasn't aimed at Hamnet. He would no more have wanted it to be than he would have wanted a longbow aimed at his bare chest from five paces. "Where is the woman who came in with you?" the priestess demanded.

Marcovefa stood beside Hamnet. Liv and Audun were

still talking with that other priestess. A sinking feeling filled Hamnet. "Gudrid?" he asked.

"If that is her name." The priestess sounded impatient—and angry. "Where is she? She has gone where she is not welcome."

The garden courtyard had several entrances. One, of course, opened onto the outside world. Who could guess where the others led? The priests and priestesses here already knew. If they didn't want strangers around, who could blame them? Hamnet Thyssen wouldn't have left the courtyard without getting someone's leave first. But Gudrid always assumed she was welcome anywhere.

"I'm sure she meant no harm," Hamnet said, though he wasn't sure of any such thing. He wondered why he defended his former wife, even knowing she wouldn't have done the same for him. The only answer he found was that the two of them belonged to the same time. He might have put in a good word for a Ruler who'd wandered away from the crowd.

"You may be sure of that. I am not." The priestess turned away from him and spoke to her colleagues. All of a sudden, Hamnet stopped being able to understand her. He looked over at Marcovefa. She shrugged—she couldn't follow what the priestess was saying, either.

An irate squawk came echoing out of one of the dark entranceways. Hamnet sighed quietly—yes, that was Gudrid. "Take your hands off me!" she said. "I didn't do anything!"

Two priests steered her back out into the courtyard. One had hold of each elbow. She tried to kick one of them, but his leg wasn't there when her foot swung through. Hamnet couldn't seen how she missed him, only that she did. He could also see that he wouldn't have tried antagonizing

those men. Their faces warned—warned him, anyway—
they had no patience for foolishness.

The priestess gestured. The two priests let go. Gudrid
came forward all the same. Plainly, she didn't want to. As
plainly, she had no choice. "I didn't do anything!" she
repeated, louder this time.

"Why did you go off where you had no business going?" the priestess asked in a voice like beaten bronze.

Gudrid looked innocent. She did it very well—certainly
well enough to have fooled Hamnet before. That made
him distrust it now. "I didn't know I wasn't supposed to,"
she said, wide-eyed. "I was just looking around."

"Is that so?" the priestess said.

"By God, it is!" Gudrid's eyes got wider and more
innocent-seeming than ever.

Beside Hamnet, Marcovefa stirred. He thought he knew
why. He wouldn't have used God's name in this place, not
if there was the slightest chance he might be forsworn.
With Gudrid, as heartache had taught him, there was always that chance.

Gudrid's right hand went to one of the pouches on her
belt. Her expression changed from innocent to horrified—
she didn't want that hand doing any such thing. It opened
the pouch even so. What her hand took from it was a jewel
on a chain. The chain was of some silvery metal, but Hamnet didn't think it was silver. The jewel might have been an
opal, but was more brilliant and shed more coruscating
rainbows of light than any opal he'd ever imagined. He
could see why Gudrid would have admired it. That she'd
been rash enough to take it appalled him.

"Did you bring this into the Golden Shrine?" the priestess asked, surely knowing the answer already.

Gudrid made a ghastly attempt to smile as she shook

her head. "N-No," she said; not even she, with all her gall, could keep her voice from wobbling.

"How did it end up in your belt pouch, then?"

"I . . ." Gudrid paused. *I just grabbed it because I liked the way it looked* wouldn't do. She did manage to put a better face on it than that: "I wanted a little something to remember the Golden Shrine by."

"A little something?" The priestess raised an eyebrow. "Do you have any idea what you stole?" She gestured. The jewel in Gudrid's hand flared bright as the sun. Gudrid squawked. Hamnet wondered if it burned her. Evidently not. She showed no pain. "Do you?" the priestess repeated.

Hamnet noticed the woman didn't say what it was or how important it was. In a place like this, even such a marvel might be no more than a toy. He wondered whether Gudrid was too flustered to see that.

He suspected she might be. "I—I meant no harm," she quavered. He would have pitied her. Even knowing what he knew, he would have. He disliked himself because that was true, which didn't mean he could help it.

The look the priestess gave her made the Glacier seem warm. "Do you recall what you heard when you came in here?" the gold-robed woman asked.

"Nobody told me not to go looking at things." Even now, Gudrid tried to rally. She said something obviously true, something which also pulled attention away from the sorry truth that she hadn't just looked.

It didn't work. Hamnet hadn't thought it would. Maybe Gudrid hadn't, either, but she'd tried. The priestess' voice, though, remained implacable: "No. That is not what I meant. No one leaves the Golden Shrine with more than he—or she—brings to it. Did you hear that?"

"I didn't think you were talking about *things*." Gudrid tossed her head. "I thought you people meant spiritual silliness."

"Spiritual? Material? Under the One Stone, what is the difference?" the priestess said. Count Hamnet had never heard that name for God before. The priestess went on, "We meant what we said. We commonly do. And so you will take no more away than you brought."

A priest strode up to Gudrid. She handed him the jewel and the chain. He made them disappear; Hamnet couldn't quite see how.

The priestess pointed her forefinger at Gudrid. She murmured something in a tongue Hamnet didn't understand. Gudrid's eyes went blank. A look of idiocy spread across her face. Eyvind Torfinn cried out in anguish. In his own way, he had to love her.

"She will never remember anything of her time here," the priestess said. "Never. Nor may she ever return. That is her punishment." Face softening slightly, she spoke to Earl Eyvind: "She will regain her wits, such as they are, when she leaves this place. Be thankful the Golden Shrine knows mercy, even for those who may not deserve it."

Eyvind bowed—creakily, as an old man would. "I am thankful, priestess. Gudrid would be, too . . . if she knew."

"She will not." The woman in gold sounded altogether sure. Eyvind Torfinn sighed and bowed again.

Taking his courage in both hands, Hamnet Thyssen said, "May I ask you something, priestess?"

"Not about that woman. I know you were also connected to her once. The judgment is made, and will only grow harsher if you push me."

"I was wed to her once, yes, but I will not say anything about that," Hamnet replied. "I want to know what to tell

Emperor Sigvat about the Golden Shrine—and every-thing else that's happened."

Slightly but unmistakably, the priestess' lip curled. "Oh. Him. Tell him this." She spoke four words in another language Hamnet didn't know. He repeated them after her till she nodded, satisfied. "They are truly ancient: from the time before the time before the Glacier last advanced," she said.

Hamnet repeated them once more. "But what do they mean?" he asked.

"When this Emperor Sigvat hears them, he will know," the priestess promised. "And so will you." With that, Count Hamnet had to be content.

XXI

Not everyone who'd gone into the Golden Shrine wanted to leave so soon. Liv and Audun Gilli seemed to be learning things. So did Marcovefa. Trasamund and Runolf Skallagrim looked as if they were enjoying a safety they hadn't known for too long. Ulric Skakki might have been a sponge; he was soaking up as much as he could. He might not be able to take away more than he'd brought, but he seemed ready to try.

Eyvind Torfinn, though, kept twisting like a man in pain. And Hamnet noted that the priests and priestesses seemed steadily less welcoming. The men and women in gold steered the strangers toward the doorway by which they'd come in. Gudrid came along with everyone else. She could walk, but not much more. Her eyes stayed blank. A thin, shiny line of spittle ran from the corner of her mouth down to her chin.

"May God keep you safe," said the priestess who'd ensorcelled her.

"What *is* God?" Yes, Ulric was still doing his best to come away with something.

The priestess smiled at him as she opened the door. "Why, exactly what you think he is."

That might have been true, but it wasn't helpful. "Thank you so much," Ulric said with a bow. His grin was wry.

"Happy to help," the priestess answered sweetly. The adventurer laughed and spread his hands, owning himself beaten.

As soon as Gudrid walked outside, her face cleared. She looked around behind her. "Oh! The Golden Shrine!" she said. Then she went on toward her horse. Her interest in the place seemed to end right there. Hamnet Thyssen decided that the priestess had been merciful after all.

"Where do we go now?" Trasamund asked.

"Wherever we please. The Rulers are beaten," Marcovefa said.

That was true . . . now. Would it stay true? How many more invaders would come through the Gap? What would happen when they did? Hamnet decided to worry about that when it happened . . . if it did.

For now, he had other things to worry about. "The priestess gave me a message to take to Sigvat. I don't understand it, but she said he would. And so I need to go south. Anyone who wants to come with me is welcome— I'd be glad of the company. But I'll go alone if I have to."

"I'll come," Ulric said. "I want to see him get this message from the Golden Shrine. I don't know how these people can be so sure he'll understand it. He doesn't understand much."

"I will come with you, too," Marcovefa said. "I have my reasons." She didn't explain what they were.

Hamnet didn't press her about them. Instead, he asked, "Did you understand what the priestess told me?"

"No." She shook her head. "From not just before the last time the Glaciers moved, but from the time before that?" Her eyes went wide with awe. "I had never dreamt of so deep a time."

"Who would have? Who could have?" Hamnet said. "Only the folk here. I wonder if these are the same ones who saw that distant day."

"Nothing about this place would surprise me anymore. Nothing," Marcovefa said. Count Hamnet nodded. He felt the same way.

His horse seemed happy enough to ride away from the Golden Shrine. It had no trouble staying on the narrow road that led from the Shrine to the former shore. The mud to either side of the road seemed as thick and wet and un-inviting as it had when Hamnet rode out onto the lake bed toward the building from days gone by.

Trasamund looked over his shoulder. Hamnet under-stood the gesture—he not only understood it, in fact, but imitated it. In a low voice, Trasamund asked, "Do you think we'll ever come back here?"

"Come back?" Hamnet started to laugh. "I never thought—I never dreamt—we'd come here once. I'll worry about doing it again some other time."

"Well, when you put it that way . . ." Trasamund also chuckled sheepishly. "I was looking at that wall of war mammoths. I was looking at the Rulers' shamans out ahead of them. Meaning no disrespect to Marcovefa, but I thought I was a dead man. I thought we were all dead. I was angry, because I hadn't got as much of my revenge as I wanted."

"How far has that wall of water gone now?" Hamnet murmured. "How much has it carved up?"

"Probably just kept going till it smashed up against the mountains." Trasamund pointed far off to the west. "Maybe there's a new lake over there now. The clans that roam that part of the plain must be mighty surprised. Where'd all this water come from?" He mimed a surprised Bizogot very well.

"Are you riding south with me, or will you head back up toward the Gap?" Hamnet asked him.

"I'm with you for now," Trasamund answered unhappily. "My clan is broken. One of these days, I may go back. With luck, we can keep more Rulers from coming down into our land. But that's for another day, not this one. The Bizogots aren't ready to try anything so grand." He sighed. "My folk are not really ready for anything."

"And the Empire is?" Count Hamnet suspected there would be endless uprisings and revolts and attempted breakaways. All he wanted to do was stay clear of them. Whether he'd get what he wanted . . . he would just have to see.

A few of the Bizogots who'd stuck with the band rode off across the steppe on their own. With the Rulers crushed, they'd try to find a clan to which they could adhere. Or they might try to live on their own. Hamnet wouldn't have wanted to try that, but the Bizogots knew this country more intimately than he ever could.

Off in the distance, a man on a riding deer saw strangers on horseback approaching and rode away from them as fast as his mount would take him. Not all the Rulers were dead, then. Well, that would have been too much to hope for. Most if not all of their wizards were. That mattered more than anything. The surviving warriors might make brigands, but brigands were a nuisance. They wouldn't overrun the Bizogot steppe or overthrow Raumsdalia.

"I do wonder what those words mean," Marcovefa said.

Hamnet wasn't sorry to think about something besides the fall of empires. "So do I," he answered.

HAD HAMNET BEEN coming north, the scraggly fields of oats and rye ahead wouldn't have been worth noticing,

much less talking about. Since he was riding south, out of
the great dark forests that marked the Raumsdalian Empire's northern border, those sad little fields took on more
meaning.

"We're back in the country where crops can grow," he
said, pointing toward the weedy green.

Ulric Skakki nodded. So did Runolf Skallagrim and
Eyvind Torfinn and Audun Gilli. Raumsdalians themselves, they understood what that meant. North of these
fields, people either brought grain up from where it would
grow or did without, living by hunting and gathering like
Bizogots.

"Back in civilization," Earl Eyvind said, perhaps incau-
tiously.

"Huh!" Trasamund said: a scornful sniff. "I didn't see
the Golden Shrine showing up in Raumsdalia." Eyvind
Torfinn opened his mouth, then closed it again. That
might have been the wisest thing he could have done.

If it was civilization, it was no more than the ragged
edge. The local farmers didn't want to hang around and
talk things over with men on horseback who carried weapons. They ran their livestock off into the woods. Pines and
firs and spruces didn't stop growing south of the forest
line. It was only that other plants could claw out a foothold
there along with them.

"They ought to know we aren't Rulers. We don't ride
deer—or war mammoths, either," Runolf said.

"Even if they know, it's not obvious they'd care," Ulric
pointed out.

"What's that supposed to mean?" Baron Runolf had
served the Empire his whole life, and took its inherent
goodness for granted.

Ulric Skakki had also served it for many years. As far
as Hamnet could see, Ulric took nothing for granted. "I'll

tell you what," he said now. "It means they think Raumsdalians would be just as happy to plunder them as the Rulers would. And you know what else, Your Excellency? I'd bet they're right."

Runolf Skallagrim spluttered. "We are His Majesty's soldiers, by God!"

"All the more reason to run, wouldn't you say?" Ulric replied. Runolf spluttered some more. He looked to Hamnet for support. Hamnet had none to give him: he sided with Ulric here. Seeing as much, Baron Runolf eyed him as if he were in the habit of accosting young girls.

Hamnet sighed. Runolf was a decent sort. Men like him had been Raumsdalia's backbone for generations. They had their limits, but within them were solid as iron. He'd been a man like that himself, till too much to do with Sigvat turned him into another kind of man altogether. Well, that was nobody's fault but the Emperor's. If Sigvat didn't care for the kind of man Hamnet was now, he had only himself to blame.

Riding up alongside him, Ulric spoke in a low voice: "What do you suppose dear Sigvat will do after you give him the message from the Golden Shrine?"

"Depends on what it means," Hamnet answered. "I feel like a seed that hasn't sprouted, but I don't know if I'm a lily or a stinkweed."

"Well, Your Grace, I've got news for you," Ulric said. "If those folks in the fancy gold robes have anything good to say about Sigvat—or to him—they're dumber than I think they are."

"Or maybe we're dumber than they think we are, because we can't see how wonderful Sigvat really is." Hamnet Thyssen considered that. Then he shook his head. "No. I'm sorry, but no. I've been stupid all kinds of ways, but if I were *that* stupid I would've died a long time ago."

"I feel the same way," Ulric said. "Of course, we could be wrong."

"Yes. We could. I used to think the Glacier stretched north forever, so the Gap couldn't melt all the way through." Count Hamnet sighed. "Shows what I knew, didn't it? But if Sigvat's a good Emperor, if he's done even a lead slug's worth of good against the Rulers, I think I'll go ride off and find a land somewhere that isn't so wonderfully ruled."

"Come up to the plains," Trasamund boomed. "Even if you're dark, you'd make a pretty fair Bizogot. I'm not trying to butter you up, either—I've said the same thing before."

"So you have," Hamnet agreed. "And maybe I will. Or maybe I'll go way down into the south so I don't have to think about the Glacier at all any more. Ulric here has seen more of that part of the world than I have."

"Too hot's as bad as too cold," Ulric said. "Worse, maybe. When it's too cold, you can put on more clothes or make a fire. When it's too hot, what can you do? Sweat— that's about it. And too hot will kill you just as easy as the Breath of God will."

"Not too hot right now. Not too cold, either," Hamnet said. "Let's ride down toward Nidaros while the weather stays good."

ON THEIR WAY to the capital, they skirted the badlands Hevring Lake had gouged out after its earthen dam broke. They rode across the rich cropland that had been lake bottom when the edge of the Glacier lay not far north.

"One of these days," Eyvind Torfinn said, "wheat and barley may grow on the bed of Sudertorp Lake, around the Golden Temple."

"That's Bizogot country, by God," Trasamund declared.

"It is now, yes," Earl Eyvind said. "When the weather

was colder, nomads roamed near Nidaros, too. Two thousand years ago, Nidaros was a hunting camp beside a meltwater lake. No one can say what the weather will be like two thousand years from now."

Trasamund muttered discontentedly. Ulric Skakki said, "No one, eh? What about the folk in the Golden Temple?"

Eyvind inclined his head. "You have something there—they may be able to do that. But even if they can, I don't believe they will. Do you?"

After brief consideration, Ulric answered, "Well, Your Splendor, when you're right, you're right."

Gudrid looked from one of them to the other as they talked about the Golden Shrine. Hamnet watched her. She heard them. She understood them. She knew there was such a thing as the Golden Shrine. She seemed to have some idea that they'd gone there. But she hadn't the faintest notion that she'd been inside the Shrine herself. Hamnet didn't think she ever would. The priestess there knew what she was doing, all right.

He snorted quietly. As if that were in doubt!

Because the land east of what had been Hevring Lake rose, and because Nidaros' towers rose even higher, the capital was visible from a long way off. Less smoke rose above it than had been true before the Rulers sacked it. "I wonder if any enemy warriors are still skulking in the ruins," Hamnet said. "If one of them puts an arrow through dear Sigvat, what the priestess told me back at the Shrine won't matter."

"She said you were to give those words to the Emperor," Marcovefa said. "I think that means you *will* give them to him. I think it means he will not die before you do it. I think it means you will not, either."

"In that case, I ought to ride away from Nidaros, not toward it," Hamnet said.

"If you do, chances are you will find that Sigvat is not in Nidaros," Marcovefa answered. "And where he is, chances are you will be there, too. You cannot flee your fate. It will find you no matter what you do."

Hamnet sighed. She was likely right. "Oh, I'll go on," he said. "Whatever this word I'm carrying is, I do want to let him have it."

Ulric grinned wickedly. "How d'you mean that?"

"Just the way I said it," Hamnet replied. Ulric's grin got wider.

Raumsdalian guards manned the gates of Nidaros once more. They started to laugh when Hamnet told them Sudertorp Lake was gone and the Golden Shrine had reappeared at last. "You blockheads! Where the demon do you think all the Rulers went?" Runolf Skallagrim demanded angrily.

"Why, we ran 'em out, of course," said the sergeant, or whatever he was, in charge of the gate crew.

That only got him more abuse from the travelers. He might have used his petty authority to try to keep them out of the capital, in which case he might also have ended up dead in short order. But Marcovefa gestured, and the gate crew and her companions all saw Sudertorp Lake flood free and destroy the Rulers' host, and then saw the Golden Shrine gleaming on the lakebed.

"What do you think now?" Hamnet Thyssen asked the underofficer, an ominous rumble in his voice.

"Pass in, folks. Pass in," that worthy replied, and added a sweeping arm gesture to the invitation. "I don't know whether you're lying or not, but I don't intend to mess with people who can work wizardry like that."

"Congratulations," Ulric Skakki told him. "Maybe you're not as stupid as you look." The underofficer scowled, but he didn't do anything more than scowl. That might have proved Ulric's point. The Raumsdalians and Bizogots rode into Nidaros.

COUNT HAMNET HAD traveled through Nidaros' streets after Sigvat fled and the Rulers plundered the city. Nidaros was better off now than it had been then. If he hadn't seen it then, he would have given up on it in despair now.

Soldiers seemed to stand on every street corner, swords and spears shining in the sun. Nobody did anything much where the armed men could see. But too many houses and shops were still obviously empty. People could prowl alleyways and break into places like that without much trouble. Maybe some of them were locals returning after they escaped the sack of the city. Maybe others were squatters who'd make good neighbors once they settled in. But Hamnet would have bet most were looters and thieves.

A body hung from a makeshift gibbet. A placard around its neck said I STOLE GRAIN. The corpse was fragrant and bloated enough to have hung there for some time. It might make other ambitious gentlemen thoughtful. Or, on the other hand, it might not.

"I wonder what the palace is like," Ulric remarked.

"What will you bet it looks better than anything else in the city?" Hamnet said. "If Sigvat has any money left in the vaults, he'll spend it on himself first and everybody else afterward."

"I didn't get to be as rich as I am by taking foolish bets," Ulric told him.

"How rich are you?" Trasamund asked. Ulric peered inside a belt pouch, sighed, shrugged, and didn't answer.

Even the gesture was enough to make beggars clamor for coins. The soldiers on guard duty did nothing to hold them back. Begging had never been illegal in Nidaros. If more people were begging now than ever before, times were harder than they'd ever been. And, if the soldiers hadn't served Sigvat, most of them would have been begging, too.

Hamnet remembered that no banners had flown above the imperial palace when he went through Nidaros after Sigvat fled. Those banners were back now. He nodded to himself when he noticed them. Sure enough, Sigvat looked out for Sigvat, first, last, and always.

Some of the guards in front of the palace had seen Hamnet and Ulric before. "You!" one of them exclaimed.

"Yes, us, by God," Hamnet answered. "So you ran away with the Emperor and then came back, did you?"

The guardsman turned red. "You can't talk to me that way!"

"I just did," Hamnet said. "And I'll kill you if you annoy me much more. My conscience won't ache—I've killed plenty of men better than you'll ever be in your wildest dreams."

That he meant it—and that he could do it—must have been only too plain to the unhappy guard. "What are you doing here, anyway?" the man demanded.

"I'm bringing His Majesty a message from the Golden Shrine." Hamnet gave back the exact literal truth.

All the guards laughed. "Now tell me another one— one I'll believe," the mouthy trooper said.

"He is telling you what you should believe, for it is so," Eyvind Torfinn said.

"Who are you, granddad, and what the demon do you know about it?" the guardsman snarled.

"I am Earl Eyvind Torfinn, and I know about this because I was inside the Golden Shrine with Count Hamnet here."

"I am Baron Runolf Skallagrim, and so was I," Runolf said.

The guards put their heads together. Two authentic noblemen, neither one known to be in bad odor with the Emperor, had vouched for Count Hamnet. Ulric Skakki and Hamnet exchanged small, tight smiles. Which of them Sigvat liked less was an interesting question. Ulric hadn't spoken up for Hamnet, nor did Hamnet blame him. His word might have done more harm than good.

There was a classic solution to this kind of problem, and the palace guard who'd done the talking found it. "I can't decide on my own," he said. "I'll send one of my men in to see what His Majesty wants."

"To see what some fancier flunky wants, you mean." Hamnet Thyssen enjoyed saying what was on his mind. He'd got in trouble for it before. He might again. He enjoyed it anyhow.

Although the guardsman reddened again, he almost shoved one of his troopers toward the doorway they protected. "Go find out His Majesty's pleasure."

Sigvat's pleasure was bound to be something young and pretty and sweetly rounded. A sour nobleman like Hamnet didn't come close. The ironic glint in Ulric's eye said he was thinking along those lines, too. This time, neither of them said anything.

After a few minutes, the guard who'd been sent in to enquire came back with astonishment all over his face. "His Majesty wants to see him!" he exclaimed in obvious disbelief.

"He *does*?" The talky palace guard seemed even more amazed. "Well, fry me in dung and call me a Bizogot's dinner!"

"What was that?" Trasamund rumbled ominously.

Maybe the guard hadn't noticed him or Liv till then. If he hadn't, he wasn't doing his job as well as he might have. He offered a rather sickly smile. "No offense intended, I'm sure."

"I'm not," Trasamund said. "If I thought you were worth killing, I'd argue with Count Hamnet for the privilege. But my guess is you'll choke to death on your own foot one day before too long."

Another guardsman snickered at that. The mouthy one gave him a look composed of three parts vitriol and one part flaming pitch. The unlucky guardsman tried to pull into his mailshirt like a turtle pulling into its shell. Hamnet interrupted that little drama, saying, "So—we can go in?"

"I guess you can," the guard replied.

"Then we will," Hamnet said, dismounting. And he did, his companions right behind him.

THE INSIDE OF the palace was more like the rest of Nidaros than Hamnet had expected—which only meant the Rulers had plundered it more thoroughly than he'd thought. Even carpets and wall hangings had disappeared. They'd probably been cut up to help keep the invaders' tents warm. For all Hamnet knew, the flood from Sudertorp Lake had swept some of them away.

A workman stood on a ladder scrubbing at something on a wall. Most of the big graffito was gone now, but Hamnet could still make out one of the striped beasts of prey the Rulers called tigers. The Rulers might no longer be a menace here below the Gap. Like riding deer and big-horned bison, tigers seemed likely to stay around.

Runolf Skallagrim also eyed the graffito. "I wonder what that tiger was hunting," he remarked.

"Probably Sigvat," Hamnet answered.

The servitor leading him and his comrades to the throne stopped in horror. "How dare you say such things?" he squawked. "How *dare* you?"

"Oh, it's easy," Hamnet assured him. "I just open my mouth, and out they come."

"Yes, and look how much fun you've had because of it," Ulric said.

Eyeing them as if they'd suddenly sprouted fur and stripes and fangs and claws, the servitor said, "His Majesty will not be pleased."

"That's all right, son," Hamnet said cheerfully—Sigvat's man was much younger than he was. "After the Rulers, after climbing the Glacier, after the Golden Shrine, I'm not going to worry about the Emperor of Raumsdalia."

"After . . . the Golden Shrine?" the servitor echoed. "But that's nothing but talk—isn't it?"

"Sure—the same as the Gap melting through is nothing but talk," Count Hamnet said.

"It's as real as roasted armadillo," Ulric added. Not knowing what to make of that, the servitor fell silent, but his eyes were as nervous as a restive horse's.

Just outside the throne room, more guards relieved Hamnet and his companions of their weapons—of most of them, anyhow. Hamnet still had a holdout knife in his boot top. By Ulric's quirked eyebrow, the guards had also searched him less perfectly than they might have. No wizard checked to see if Sigvat's men had missed anything, as one had when Hamnet and Ulric first met Trasamund here. Not everything around the Emperor was back to normal yet.

Walking into the throne room underscored that. Sigvat's throne had been of gold and ivory and glittering jewels. Now a stout wooden chair probably taken from a palace dining room replaced it. All the rest of the rich ornamentation in the throne room was gone, too. Maybe the gold had helped weigh down the Rulers as the unleashed waters of Sudertorp Lake washed over them. But Hamnet Thyssen doubted whether lighter pockets and belt pouches would have made much difference.

The Emperor's surviving ministers looked leaner and poorer than they had the last time Hamnet saw them. So did Sigvat II. The robe he wore might have suited a tolerably prosperous trader. Before the Rulers chased him out of Nidaros, he wouldn't have been caught dead in it.

Hamnet grudged a bow. "Your Majesty," he said gruffly. Ulric Skakki followed his lead. So did Trasamund. And so did Audun Gilli, the man of least account among those who'd begun this adventure.

Sigvat scowled. He was still as sensitive to slights as he'd always been. "What's this nonsense about Sudertorp Lake and the Golden Shrine?" he snapped.

"Your Majesty, it isn't nonsense," Count Hamnet said. Everyone with him nodded except Gudrid. She would never testify about the Golden Shrine. As quickly as he could, Hamnet told the Emperor what had happened.

Sigvat looked down his nose at him. "You expect me to believe this nonsense?"

"You had better believe it—it is true." That wasn't Hamnet: the Emperor wouldn't have believed him. It was Marcovefa. She stared straight into Sigvat's watery brown eyes. "Believe it—it is true," she repeated.

Sigvat obviously didn't want to. Just as obviously, he found himself compelled to. He looked angry and frightened at the same time. Marcovefa might be sure her sorcery didn't measure up to that of the Golden Shrine, but it outdid anything Raumsdalians could match.

"All right, then. *All right*," Sigvat said furiously. "So you *did* go inside the Golden Shrine. Well, what kind of message did those people in there have for me?" In spite of everything, he preened a little. "It must be important—I must be important—for them to know about me."

I must be important. Yes, that usually lay at the heart of Sigvat's thoughts. "I carry the message, Your Majesty,"

Count Hamnet answered. "They told me it was very ancient—not from before this last time the Glacier ground south, but from the time before that."

"Yes, yes." The Emperor sounded impatient. "Give it to me, then."

Whatever kind of seed Hamnet was, he would sprout now. "As you say, Your Majesty, so shall it be." He took a deep breath, then spoke the first strange word the golden-robed priestess had imparted to him: "*Mene.*"

Suddenly, he no longer seemed to see Sigvat II's throne room, but another one, one he'd never imagined before, much less seen. And somehow everybody else in this throne room saw that one with him, and saw the fierce, swarthy, curly-bearded man (plainly not a Ruler, even if he had something of their aspect) in the strange robe staring at the writing on the mud-brick wall to the left of the throne on which he sat. Hamnet had never seen those characters before, either, but he knew they said *Mene.*

As he'd been bidden to do, he said it again: "*Mene.*"

In his vision—if it was but a vision, if he wasn't really there—he saw the glowing word appear once more. He saw the curly-bearded king or emperor (for surely the man could hold no lower rank) gasp and turn pale under his dark skin.

"*Tekel,*" Hamnet Thyssen said, slowly beginning to grasp the words he carried.

Tekel sprang into being on the wall to the swarthy king's left. He gasped and clapped a horrified hand to his forehead. He was beginning to understand, too.

Was Sigvat? Hamnet couldn't tell. He dwelt more in that other world, that lost and ancient world, than this one. And, he realized, whether Sigvat followed now hardly mattered. The Raumsdalian Emperor would in a moment. Count Hamnet intoned the priestess' last word: "*Upharsin.*"

What had to be that last word appeared on that wall in fiery letters. Suddenly, Hamnet Thyssen—and, he was sure, everyone else in the throne room—saw that wall and that ancient chamber no more. An enormous set of scales presented itself. In one pan lay a heavy stone weight. In the other stood that curly-bearded king in his odd royal robes.

The scales were free to swing. The one with the weight sank down. The one with the king from those unimaginably distant days rose: he could not measure up to that which tested him.

And then, without warning, the figure on the scale's rising pan changed. It was no longer the nameless, forgotten king from a bygone age. Instead, it wore Sigvat II's face . . . and his robe.

Hamnet didn't doubt what he saw, or what it meant. No one who saw that could misunderstand it. *You don't measure up, either, Your Majesty,* he thought. *No. Your former Majesty.*

As abruptly as it had engulfed him, the vision faded. He was back inside the Raumsdalian Emperor's throne room with all his senses once more. Along with everyone else in there, he stared at the Emperor.

Under that terrible, merciless scrutiny, Sigvat II went red and then white. A ghastly attempt at a smile played across his face; it flickered and went out like a guttering flame. He opened his mouth to say . . . something. But what *could* a man say after . . . that? Count Hamnet had never imagined a condemnation straight from God, but that came closer to describing what he'd just witnessed than anything else he could conceive. Sigvat's mouth stayed open, likely for no better reason than that he'd forgotten to close it.

Without a word, one of the imperial ministers turned away, and then another and another and another. Sigvat did make a sound then, a small one: the sound a wounded man might make when he was trying to hide his pain.

Trasamund walked up to him. With rough sympathy, the jarl set a hand on Sigvat's arm. "You'd better go now, while you still can," he said, not unkindly. "You hang around here, somebody's going to stick a knife in you, and quick."

"What did I do to deserve—*that*?" Sigvat's wave took in everything everyone had just seen.

Maybe he thought nobody would give him an answer, but Count Hamnet did: "You didn't do anything to stop the Rulers, but after other people took care of that for you, you came back and tried to pick up the reins you'd dropped. Lots of people would have thought you had no right, but the folk from the Golden Shrine did more than think. They went and showed you."

"They went and showed everybody else, too," Ulric Skakki added. Did he sound amused? Hamnet thought so.

Sigvat also must have, because he started to reply. Trasamund forestalled him, saying, "If you hustle, you've still got a chance to get out of the palace alive. Leave your robe for whoever needs it next, go somewhere a long way off, change your name, and try and pretend you never heard of Nidaros."

That struck Hamnet Thyssen as good advice: better than he would have given Sigvat. It must have struck the suddenly ex–Raumsdalian Emperor the same way. He slid down off the poor makeshift throne and made his way toward the entrance to the throne room. By the time he got there, he was trotting.

Eyvind Torfinn bowed to Hamnet. "What is your will, Your Majesty?" he asked.

"No!" Hamnet said sharply. "No, by God! You can't make me wear the crown, and neither can anybody else. If you try, I'll go up to the tallest tower and throw myself out on my head—or else I'll just fall on my sword." He'd tried that before, and failed. He didn't think he would if he tried again. "I'd rather die than be Emperor of Raumsdalia, and I mean it. If you want the job, Your Splendor, you can have it."

Hamnet remembered that would make Gudrid Raumsdalian Empress. He couldn't think of a better reason to go see what the hot countries in the distant south were like.

But Earl Eyvind shook his head, even if Gudrid looked furious when he did. "Thank you, but no," the scholarly noble replied. "The Emperor should be—in times like these, had better be—a stronger man than I."

"Maybe we can dice for the crown," Ulric suggested. "Loser gets it."

"We should care more about the Empire than that." Earl Eyvind's voice was starchy with disapproval, but he said no more. How could he, when he'd just turned it down himself?

"Somebody'll grab it before too long," Ulric said. Hamnet nodded, but he was thinking, *As long as it isn't me!*

XXII

Hamnet Thyssen didn't linger long in the imperial palace. True, he'd brought bad news for Sigvat II straight from the Golden Shrine. But he *had* brought bad news for the Raumsdalian Emperor. The aura of glamour surrounding the first was enough to let him get out of the palace unscathed. He didn't think he would have lasted more than a few hours at the outside had he tried to hang around.

He didn't see Sigvat alive or dead. Maybe the Emperor really had got away and was busy memorizing his new name. Stranger things had happened. Before Hamnet first met Trasamund, he would have irately denied the possibility. Since then, he'd gone beyond the Gap. He'd climbed to the top of the Glacier and met the folk who lived up there. He'd gone inside the Golden Shrine. All of those were at least a little stranger than the chance that Sigvat might act like a sensible human being.

Ulric Skakki didn't overstay his welcome, either. He waited impatiently with Hamnet for grooms to lead their horses out of the stables. "Well, Your Grace, what now?" he asked.

"I'm going home," Hamnet said simply. "Anybody who tries to drag me out again will have to lay siege to the place . . . if it's still standing, anyhow."

"What if it's not?" The adventurer was as full of annoying questions as ever. His twisted grin said he knew as much.

"God knows, in that case." Hamnet shrugged. "Maybe I'll keep on going south, the way I've talked about. Or maybe I'll turn around and go up onto the steppe and see what kind of Bizogot I make."

He was about to ask what Ulric intended to do, but Ulric beat him to the punch again: "And what about Marcovefa?"

"What about me?" Marcovefa asked from behind them. They both jumped. She went on, "Why do you ask somebody else? Do you think I cannot take care of myself? Are you so foolish?"

"Mm—I hope not." For once in his life, Ulric sounded faintly embarrassed.

"He asked me what I wanted to do, and I told him I was going home," Count Hamnet said. "Then he asked about you, and you answered before I could. I didn't know what you were going to say, anyhow."

"I will come with you. I will see your home. After all, you have seen mine," Marcovefa said. "Whether I will stay after that"—she smiled— "we can both find out."

Ulric nudged Hamnet. "Take her up on it," he stage-whispered. "You won't get a better bargain."

"Do you think I'm too stupid to figure that out for myself?" Hamnet said.

"By your track record, yes," Ulric answered. The worst of it was, Hamnet could hardly tell him he was wrong.

Marcovefa glared at the palace guards and grooms. "Where is my horse?" she demanded. "Do I have to start turning people into voles to get the rest of you to do what you should be doing anyhow?" The servitors all but stumbled over one another in their haste to do what she wanted.

"This is how it ends," Ulric said, not sadly but in a matter-of-fact way. "We did what we set out to do—enough of it, anyway—and now we go back to taking care of things for ourselves." He sketched a salute. "Luck, Thyssen. Maybe we'll run into each other again one of these years."

"Maybe we will. Nothing would surprise me any more." Hamnet clasped the adventurer's hand while grooms led out their horses—and Marcovefa's.

"Me, I'm heading south myself. I've had enough of ice to last me a long time," Ulric said. He'd made noises like that before. Maybe he meant them. Or maybe he aimed to throw any possible pursuers off his trail.

He did ride south, which soon separated him from Hamnet and Marcovefa, who made for the east gate. Hamnet could have gone out the south gate just as well; his keep and the lands surrounding it lay far to the southeast. But Ulric Skakki had it right: breaking apart was how things ended.

Or so Hamnet thought, till somebody let out a deep bass yell behind him. He looked back over his shoulder. Here came Trasamund, bulling his horse through traffic so the locals glared at him. "You won't get away from me like that," the jarl boomed. "I guested you as long as I could up on the plains. About time you pay me back, the way a guest-friend should by rights."

Hamnet laughed and sketched a salute. "At your service, Your Ferocity."

Trasamund bowed in the saddle and started to laugh himself, but abruptly choked it off. "You may as well forget the title. Without a clan to rule, I don't deserve it any more. The world's a miserable place."

"You've seen the Golden Shrine—you've gone into it—and you say that? Shame on you," Marcovefa told him.

"It is," Trasamund insisted. "We never would have seen the Golden Shrine if the Rulers hadn't wrecked the Bizogots, and they started with my clan."

"More to the world than your clan," Hamnet said. "More to the world than Raumsdalia, too."

"Oh? Then why aren't you riding off to God knows where with Ulric Skakki?" Trasamund said. "You're going back to the one little piece of ground that belongs to you. I'd go back to the tents of the Three Tusk clan, except they aren't there any more." He wiped away a tear, whether real or rhetorical Count Hamnet wasn't sure.

"You're welcome to come along with us if you care to," Hamnet said, as a guest-friend should. "My home is yours for as long as you care to stay there."

The jarl bowed in the saddle again. "Well, I do thank you for that. And, like I said, I'll take you up on it—for now, anyway. If I wander off one of these days, it won't be on account of anything you've done. I don't expect it will, I mean. But I don't know if I can stay in one place the rest of my days."

"Neither do I," Marcovefa said.

"Well, neither do I," Hamnet Thyssen said. "We'll all find out. As long as I stay away from Nidaros—and as long as Nidaros' troubles stay away from me—I suppose I'll get along wherever I am." He reached out and set a hand on Marcovefa's arm. "The company is pretty good."

"Are you trying to sweet-talk me?" she asked.

"Not right this moment," Hamnet said. "When we stop to rest tonight, we'll see how I do then." By the way she laughed, he had a good chance of doing well.

But her laugh cut off as shouts and screams and the clash of blade against blade rang out behind them, from the direction of the palace. "Oh, God!" Trasamund said. "It's starting already, isn't it? Cursed fools didn't waste any time."

"What happens in a Bizogot clan when the jarl dies and nobody's set to succeed him?" Hamnet asked. Trasamund grunted: as much of a concession as Hamnet was likely to get.

"What do we do now?" Marcovefa asked. The martial racket was getting louder and coming closer.

"We get out of here, quick as we can." Hamnet urged his horse up into a trot. "The only thing worse than getting stuck in the middle of a war is getting stuck in the middle of a civil war."

"That makes more sense than I wish it did," Trasamund said. He and Marcovefa booted their horses forward, too.

To Hamnet's relief, nobody at the eastern gate recognized him. "What's going on back there?" a guard asked, pointing in the direction from which he and his companions had come. "Sounds like the whole world's going crazy."

"It does, doesn't it?" Hamnet looked as blank and innocent as he could. "All we want to do is get on our way before whatever it is catches up with us."

"Smart," the guard said solemnly.

One of the other soldiers at the gate said, "Somebody who went through a few minutes ago said the Emperor was leaving town again. That doesn't seem right, does it? I mean, those stupid Rulers or whatever the demon they are haven't given us so much trouble lately. Why would His Majesty want to leave now, then?"

Count Hamnet, Marcovefa, and Trasamund looked at one another. As if animated by the same puppeteer, they shrugged at the same time. Hamnet Thyssen lied straight-faced: "I don't know anything about that, either."

"We'll all find out, I guess." The guard eyed his colleagues, who nodded. He waved to Hamnet. "Pass on through."

"Thanks." This time, Hamnet was altogether sincere. Probably no one since the Golden Shrine had done him a bigger favor than this gate guard who waved him out of Nidaros. What was liable to happen in the capital over the next few days wouldn't be pretty.

He and Marcovefa and Trasamund hadn't got more than eight or ten yards out of the gate before one of the guards howled in dismay. Looking back over his shoulder, Hamnet saw the man had clapped a hand to his forehead: a theatrical gesture, but plainly heartfelt. "Those idiots! Those God-cursed idiots!" the guard cried. "They've started a fire!"

That only made Hamnet ride harder. He neither knew who *they* were nor wanted to find out. Whoever *they* were, he agreed with the guard: anybody who started a fire inside a city was an idiot.

"At least the Breath of God isn't blowing," Trasamund said.

If it were, whatever the Rulers hadn't ruined in Nidaros might go up in flames. And . . . "I don't think the maniac with a torch cared," Hamnet said.

"Somebody ought to cut him in half and leave the pieces where people can see them," Trasamund said. "That's what we'd do up on the steppe. Anybody else who gets ideas can see what they'd cost him."

"I hope somebody does," Count Hamnet said. "But it isn't my worry, thank God. Raumsdalia can sort it out without me." He sat straighter on his horse, as if a heavy weight had lifted from his shoulders. "Have you got any idea how good it feels to be able to say that?"

"You can stay in your castle place for a while," Marcovefa said shrewdly. "Sooner or later, though, the world will come looking for you again."

Hamnet Thyssen didn't argue with her; she was much too likely to be right. He just said, "Later, I hope." He and Marcovefa and Trasamund rode away from Nidaros, and from the new plume of black smoke climbing above it.

SWEAT RAN DOWN Marcovefa's face. "Does it get this hot every summer down here?" she asked.

"Most summers, anyhow," Hamnet said. He didn't find the weather especially hot. But then, he hadn't spent most of his life atop the Glacier.

"How do you stand it?" Marcovefa asked.

"It's pretty warm, all right," Trasamund added.

"All what you're used to." Hamnet left it there. "People who grow up south of here wouldn't be able to stand the winters in the Bizogot country." He didn't say anything about the winters in Marcovefa's homeland. He wasn't sure he'd be able to stand those himself.

"More and more of these broad-leaved trees. I think they look funny." Suddenly, Marcovefa turned into a connoisseur of forests, although she'd never so much as imagined a tree, broad-leaved or otherwise, till she descended from the Glacier. "What good are they?"

"There's always the wood," Hamnet said. He took that for granted, but Marcovefa wouldn't; even Trasamund might not. "And some of them have nuts that are good to eat. And in the autumn, before the leaves fall off, they turn red and orange and gold. For a little while, the forest looks as if it's on fire—not in a bad way, you understand. It's beautiful, but it never lasts."

"I've seen a little of that," Trasamund said, and

Marcovefa nodded. The jarl went on, "I've never understood *why* the leaves change colors before they die."

"I can't tell you. I don't think anyone else can, either," Hamnet said. "My best guess is, it just happens, the way a man's hair goes gray when he gets older."

"Maybe." Trasamund lost interest in the question. He pointed toward something at the edge of the woods. "Good God! What's that?"

"A mastodon," Hamnet answered. "Haven't you seen them before, coming down into Raumsdalia?"

"I've had glimpses, but that's all." The Bizogot stared and stared. "It looks like a woolly mammoth, if you can imagine a woolly mammoth made by somebody who's heard about them but never seen one. Its back is too flat—it ought to slope down like this." He gestured.

"*I've* seen woolly mammoths," Hamnet pointed out.

He might as well have saved his breath. Trasamund went on as if he hadn't spoken: "Its ears are the wrong shape. They're too big, too. And look at the funny way its tusks curl. And mammoths are supposed to be almost black, not that . . . that tree-bark brown, I guess you'd call it."

"They can be pests," Hamnet said. "They raid orchards and they trample down grain fields."

"You don't bother to tame them, do you?" Trasamund asked.

"I've heard that lumbermen sometimes do. Mastodons are big enough and strong enough to shove tree trunks around better than just about any other beasts. But apart from that, no," Hamnet replied. "We hunt them, though. We use the meat and the hides and the ivory and the hair."

"Woolly mammoth hair is better," Trasamund said. "It's longer and thicker. I like the color better, too."

"Which is all very well, I'm sure, only we haven't got

any woolly mammoths in Raumsdalia. Plenty of mastodons in the forests near my castle. They're nuisances there. That's the other reason we hunt them: to keep them from tearing up the crops."

"How much farther to your castle?" Marcovefa asked. To her, mastodons were only a little stranger than mammoths; she'd come to know both beasts since descending from the Glacier.

"Maybe a week's travel: a little less if we were in a tearing hurry," Hamnet answered.

"How long do you aim to stay?" Marcovefa asked, and then, "How long will we stay?"

"I don't know how long I'll stay. A while, anyhow. Till things settle down a bit—if they ever do," Hamnet said. "And I can't really say how long you'll stay, can I?"

"You have something to do with it. If I decide you make me angry and don't make me happy, I go," Marcovefa said. But she added, "So far you haven't—quite."

Trasamund guffawed. "High praise, Thyssen!"

"Better than I've done with women up till now," Hamnet said, as calmly as he could. "Maybe I've learned something. Maybe Marcovefa just puts up with more than Gudrid or Liv did." He glanced over at her. "What do you think?"

"Me? I think you know me better than to think I put up with much," Marcovefa replied. "So far you are not *too* bad, in bed or out."

Trasamund started laughing again. Hamnet's ears felt as if they'd caught fire. He made the most of it he could, saying, "Thank you—I think."

"You're welcome—I suppose," Marcovefa told him. But she was smiling when she said it. Now Trasamund laughed at both of them. They took no notice of him;

lacking encouragement, he eventually ran down. They all rode on in what was—Hamnet hoped—a companionable silence.

SOMEHOW, NEWS OF Sigvat's fall spread faster than Hamnet had imagined it could. He thought he and Marcovefa and Trasamund would be the outermost ripple of news from the pebble that had dropped in the palace at Nidaros. But they weren't. Whenever they stopped in a village or a town, people had heard that the Emperor was Emperor no more. Some of them had even heard that he'd fled because the Golden Shrine judged him unworthy to rule.

"I heard that, all right," said the tapman at a serai about halfway to Hamnet's keep. "Don't know that I believe it, but I heard it. Till all this talk started, I don't know that I believed there was any such thing as the Golden Shrine. People talk about it, sure, but people talk about all kinds of things that aren't real. But I've never heard 'em talk about it the way they do nowadays, so maybe there's something to it after all."

"It's true," Hamnet said solemnly. Marcovefa and Trasamund nodded. Hamnet went on, "I wouldn't mind another mug of ale. It's tasty."

"I thank you for that—I brew it myself," the tapman said, not without pride. As he dipped up another mug for Hamnet, he continued, "You folks sound like you know what you're talking about." Hamnet had listened to a lot of tapmen in his time. He knew this fellow wasn't necessarily saying he believed them.

"We do," Trasamund said. "We were there."

"Where? At the Golden Shrine or in the palace?" No, the tapman didn't believe they'd set eyes on either place.

"Both," Marcovefa told him. He didn't call her a liar—

you had to be very bold or very stupid to do that—but disbelief still stuck out all over him. She nudged Hamnet. "Say the words again—the words you got from the Golden Shrine."

"*Mene. Mene. Tekel. Upharsin.*" He felt sure he was pronouncing them badly. But chances were no one else born into this age of the world could have done any better. These words were extinct—except, thanks to the priests and priestesses of the Golden Shrine, they weren't.

Marcovefa murmured a spell. Suddenly, Hamnet saw himself saying those unimaginably ancient words to Sigvat II. By the way the tapman's jaw dropped, so did he. Hamnet also saw those words on the wall, saw the long-forgotten king's awe and fear, and Sigvat's as well, and saw the balance in which they were both weighed and found wanting.

The vision faded fast, which was nothing but a relief. "Well?" Trasamund asked the tapman. "Were we there, or not?"

"You were," the man whispered. "I don't know how, but you were. How did you come to be at the heart of—well, everything?"

"Maybe it just worked out that way," Hamnet said. "Maybe the Golden Shrine or God—if there's a difference—meant it all along. I don't know. I don't expect I ever will. I'm beginning to think the how doesn't even matter. However it happened, we were there, that's all."

"You didn't even say anything yet about Sudertorp Lake breaking free and drowning all the Rulers and their shamans," Trasamund observed.

If the tapman's ears could have pricked erect like a dire wolf's, they would have. "I didn't think I should," Hamnet said. "Marcovefa worked the magic. I only watched it."

"And keep me alive. And bring me back to myself," Marcovefa said. The tapman's eyes got bigger and bigger.

"Anyhow, not quite all of them drowned," Hamnet said. "But I don't think they'll kick up much trouble for a while."

"By God, you're not making any of this up, are you?" the tapman said hoarsely. "You really saw those things. You really did those things, too."

"We saw them," Hamnet agreed. "We did them."

"Then what are you doing *here*?" the tapman said. "Nothing ever happens here. No one who doesn't live in Gufua knows it's here or knows its name. Nobody cares to, either."

"That sounds plenty good to me, at least in a place where we'll stop for the night," Count Hamnet said. Marcovefa and Trasamund both nodded. Hamnet went on, "Sometimes, what you want most is not to need to worry. If, uh, Gufua can give us that, we're glad to take it." Till the tapman named the hamlet, he hadn't known what to call it. His companions nodded again.

"If you'll tell your stories and work your spells for the folk here, you needn't pay for food and lodging," the tapman said.

Hamnet looked at Marcovefa and Trasamund. Then he set silver on the bar. "I mean no disrespect, but paying's the better bargain." He got more nods from them.

"Have it as you please." The tapman didn't seem sorry to scoop up the coins. "It was only a thought. The bedchambers are upstairs."

After filling his belly with roast pork and barley bread, Hamnet went up to one of those bedchambers. He made sleepy, lazy love with Marcovefa. Then he slept. Nothing bothered him till morning. If he hadn't had somewhere else to go, he might have been tempted to stay in quiet, forgotten Gufua.

*   *   *

As the road came out from behind a stand of trees, Trasamund pointed. "Somebody up ahead of us."

"Well, so there is," Hamnet said. "What about it? Are you worried about one man? Let him worry about us."

"I'm not worried about him," the jarl replied with dignity. "A bit surprised to see him, is all. Not many people on the road these days, or so it seems."

"Would you go traveling if you thought the Rulers would kill you or ordinary bandits would knock you over the head?" Hamnet said.

"If I had to," Trasamund said stubbornly.

"This fellow has to." Marcovefa sounded as certain as only she could.

"Who is he? You sound as though you know," Hamnet said.

"A traveler." Maybe Marcovefa was being annoying on purpose. Or maybe whatever told her what she knew about that man also told her to keep it to herself. Hamnet shrugged. If they caught up with the stranger, he'd find out then. And if they didn't, the fellow didn't matter.

They were gaining. Hamnet needed a bit to be sure, but eventually had no doubt. Neither did the lone man. He tried to get more out of his horse, but it seemed to have nothing left to give. Either it was a horrible screw to begin with or he'd already ridden it into the ground. By the way it carried itself, Hamnet guessed the latter.

"Bugger me with a thornbush," Trasamund said after a little while. "I know who that is."

"So do I." Hamnet Thyssen clicked his tongue between his teeth. "I didn't want to say anything. I kept hoping I was wrong. Well, no such luck."

Marcovefa raised an eyebrow. "After everything that happened, you still believe in luck?" Hamnet had no answer for her.

"We ought to—" But Trasamund broke off, shaking his big, fair head. "Who the demon knows what we ought to do?"

A little more time went by. The man in front of them turned in the saddle and shook his fist. "Weren't you satisfied in Nidaros?" he shouted furiously. "Do you have to follow me and gloat, too?"

"We didn't," Hamnet said. "Only a . . . chance meeting, Sigvat." He wouldn't look at Marcovefa. He'd talked about chance to the tapman in Gufua, too. But it was as dead a word as luck. And he'd never imagined calling the Emperor—the former Emperor, now—by his bare, unadorned name.

"Likely tale," Sigvat jeered. "Well, if you want to kill me, I suppose you can, but I'll make the best fight I'm able to." He started to draw his sword.

How many times had Hamnet wanted to kill him? He'd thought he had plenty of reason to do it, too. Sigvat was right—it wouldn't be hard. But what was the point now? "Go your way," Hamnet said. "If I never see you again, that will suit me well enough. You might want to take the south fork, not the one that runs southeast. I'm bound for my castle, and I don't promise you a warm welcome if you turn up there."

In a low voice, Sigvat said, "I heard Skakki was heading straight south."

"Too bad," Trasamund said. "And you made more enemies than just our lot, you know."

Sigvat's mouth twisted. "I did what I could."

"To make more enemies? I believe that," Hamnet Thyssen said.

"You wouldn't have dared talk to me that way when I was on the throne," Sigvat said, flushing angrily.

"The demon I wouldn't," Hamnet retorted. "I tried to

tell you the Rulers were more trouble than you thought, and I was cursed well right. But you didn't want to listen, and finally you flung me in your dungeon so you wouldn't have to. That didn't make me wrong, though. You found out. Too bad you managed to run from Nidaros after the Rulers beat your armies. I was hoping they'd pitch you in there so you could see what it was like."

"We'd never had an invasion like that. I thought you were exaggerating things to make yourself seem more important," Sigvat said.

"You would have done that," Marcovefa said. "So you judged Hamnet from yourself."

By the way Sigvat scowled at her, that shot struck too close to the center of the target. "I turned out to be wrong," he said. "But I thought the chances were good that I was right."

"And so you almost pissed the Empire straight into the chamber pot," Hamnet said. "If not for Marcovefa, you would have. No wonder the Golden Shrine didn't think you measured up."

"I wouldn't have believed that, either, if I had any choice," Sigvat said.

"You have none. None at all," Trasamund said. "That is not a judgment from man. It is a judgment from God. Everyone who was in your throne room knows it."

Sigvat wanted to call the jarl a liar. The urge was written all over his face. Only one thing stopped him, Hamnet judged: Trasamund was obviously telling the truth. Instead, Sigvat said, "Go ahead and mock. I hope it makes you happy." As obviously, he hoped anything but.

To Hamnet, Trasamund said, "We ought to knock him over the head. He's too stupid to learn anything from all the mistakes he made."

"If the Golden Shrine had wanted him dead soon, it

would have taken care of things," Hamnet said. "This is worse. He was the Emperor of Raumsdalia. Now no one will hearken to him for the rest of his life, however long he lasts. If he doesn't learn that much, he won't live long. But I won't stain my hands with his blood. As far as I'm concerned, he's not worth killing."

Sigvat went from red to white. "Curse you, Thyssen," he whispered.

"You can't," Hamnet said matter-of-factly. "You've already cursed yourself. Nothing you throw at me will bite." He gestured to his companions. "We may as well ride on."

"What if this—thing—tries to shoot us in the back?" Trasamund said. "He's got a bow."

"He won't. He can't." Marcovefa sounded sure, as only she could. Hamnet believed her. Sigvat's grimace of impotent fury said he did, too.

They rode past Sigvat. Hamnet didn't look back. No arrows came hissing after him. He never saw Sigvat, once the second Emperor of Raumsdalia of that name, again. He never heard that anyone else did, either.

A STONE KEEP warded by a wooden palisade. Fields and orchards around it. Woods of oak and elm and ash and hickory and chestnut off to the east, where Raumsdalia's border petered out. Hamnet pointed toward the keep. "Hasn't changed much since I went away," he said.

"Did you expect it to?" Trasamund asked.

"You never can tell," Hamnet answered. "If we've seen anything the past few years, we've seen that."

Farmers weeding in the fields looked up as the travelers rode by. Not many folk came this way, as Hamnet had reason to know. One of the peasants called, "That you, Count?"

"I think so," Hamnet said, which made the fellow grin.

"You take care of whatever you needed to do out in the world?" another farmer asked.

"Most of it. For a while," Hamnet replied.

The man nodded. "About what you can hope for." He went back to weeding.

Marcovefa eyed Hamnet. "Yes, this is your country. These are your people."

"I never tried to tell you anything different," he said.

A shout rolled out from the palisade: "Who comes?"

"Hamnet Thyssen, with friends," Hamnet answered. "Is everything well, Gris?"

"You'll see for yourself soon enough," his seneschal said, and then, not to Hamnet, "Open the gates, by God!"

They creaked open. They'd creaked before Hamnet rode away, too. His retainers stared at his companions. "Are those what they call Bizogots?" a man asked doubtfully. He might have been talking about glyptodonts or other beasts he didn't look to see in this part of the world.

"We're Bizogots, sure enough," Trasamund rumbled. Marcovefa stirred, but she didn't argue. Her folk sprang from the Bizogots, even if they didn't think of themselves as belonging to them anymore. Mischief in his pale eyes, Trasamund went on, "I wouldn't be surprised if you were a Raumsdalian."

"That's right," the man said automatically. His friends realized Trasamund was joking half a heartbeat before he did. They laughed at him. He went red.

Hamnet looked around. Everything looked pretty much the way it had before he rode off to answer Sigvat's summons. He hadn't thought he'd stay away so long or do so much while he was gone. As he dismounted, all the time between then and now might have fallen away.

Or it might not have. "How much trouble did you have this past year?" he asked.

"Well, there was some," Gris admitted. "We heard some new barbarians got loose up in the north. Don't think we saw any ourselves, but plenty of people running from them came by. They going to cause more trouble?"

"No, I don't think so," Hamnet answered.

"Thanks to you," Marcovefa said, and slipped an arm around his waist. The men and women in the courtyard murmured—more at the gesture, Hamnet judged, than at the news. They wanted him wed, or at least attached. They wanted an heir, so things would stay smooth after he was gone.

He put his arm around Marcovefa's shoulder. "Thanks more to you," he said. She nodded. She wasn't shy about taking praise. The locals murmured on a different note. Hamnet went on, "Sigvat's off the throne."

That brought surprised exclamations—the news hadn't got here, anyhow. "Did you cast him off it?" Gris asked.

"No, not really," Hamnet replied, and the last couple of words brought fresh muttering. Ignoring it, he continued, "The Golden Shrine had more to do with it."

Outcry this time. He'd known there would be. He told the story, and spoke the words in the forgotten language he'd delivered to Sigvat II. Marcovefa worked her magic again, so his retainers could get some sense of the power those words had. Gris said, "Who's Emperor, then, if Sigvat isn't?"

"How come you're not?" another man asked Hamnet before he could say anything.

"Because I don't want the throne. Because I'd rather come home," he answered. Several of the locals nodded. They understood that urge to return to the familiar. It wasn't always a good urge—Hamnet thought of the trouble he could have missed if Gudrid hadn't drawn him like a lodestone for so long—but it was strong. He turned back to Gris. "When we left Nidaros, nobody was on the throne. They'll likely fight it out to see which greedy fool gets to set his fundament there. But we're so far from the center of things, I don't think any civil war will touch us here. Hope not, anyhow."

The seneschal considered. "Odds are decent," he said at last. "So what will you do now that you're back?"

"About what I was doing before," Hamnet replied. "I liked it well enough, except when . . . things got in the way." Things. Gudrid. Sigvat's summons. The Gap, melted through. The Rulers. The invasion. The war. The dungeon. Sudertorp Lake, pouring out as if God were pushing it— and maybe God was. The Golden Shrine. *Mene. Mene. Tekel. Upharsin.*

Things.

"What about you people?" Gris asked Trasamund and Marcovefa. By the way he used the last word, he was giving them the benefit of the doubt.

Trasamund spoke first: "I'll stay here a while, anyway. I've got nothing to go back to up on the plains—the Rulers made sure of that."

Marcovefa eyed Hamnet as she answered, "I will stay as long as I am happy. If I am not, it will be time to go."

He nodded. "That'll do. I hope you stay a long time. I'll try not to make you unhappy—but you never can tell. If I've learned anything since I went away, that's it. You never can tell."

"And I will try not to make you too unhappy with me," Marcovefa said. Hamnet nodded again. That was as close to a promise as he'd ever got from her, and more than he'd come to expect. She looked around. "This is not much like the top of the Glacier, but it is not a bad place."

"Most of the time, it isn't," Hamnet agreed. What more could you say of any place? Not much, not as far as he could see.

"Good to have you back, lord," Gris said. Heads bobbed up and down in the courtyard. As long as people thought it was good, they would help make it so. Hamnet didn't know how long he could stay here peacefully—no, you never could tell—but he aimed to make the most of it, however long it turned out to be.